Praise for
THE SPIRIT PHONE

"*The Spirit Phone* is a surreal time-warp of a story involving historical personages like Nikola Tesla, Thomas A. Edison, and Aleister Crowley in an imaginative debut novel by Arthur Shattuck O'Keefe, who marionettes his dramatis personae of famous characters with page-turning ease. Startlingly original and strangely engrossing, I kept thinking this is E.L. Doctorow's *Ragtime* on psychedelics. We are no doubt witness to a new talent in the speculative fiction genre, a writer who has a deep understanding of historical figures and events and knows the true meaning of creative fiction."

Rex Pickett, author of *Sideways*

"This is a strong first novel and gripping read, with a neatly crafted plot that seamlessly blends weird technology and supernatural events. It's well set up for both further adventures and a potential film adaptation. Watch this space!"

Matthew Allen, screenwriter for the producers of such films as
Terminator 2: Judgement Day, *The Boondock Saints*, and *The Equalizer*

"In this novel you will encounter mystery, suspense, adventure, whimsy, science, occultism, and teleportation through time and space, all in a very entertaining mix. I highly recommend *The Spirit Phone* for anyone who seeks a lively and intelligent read."

Bruce Boston, four-time Bram Stoker award-winning author of
Dark Matters and *The Guardener's Tale*

"For fans of alternative historical fiction, *The Spirit Phone* delivers. What a wild, entertaining romp, following Tesla, Edison, and Crowley through space and time. This tale unfolds with demonic glee."

Richard Thomas, author of *Spontaneous Human Combustion* and Bram Stoker /
Shirley Jackson nominee

"*The Spirit Phone* succeeds page by page, especially in the compelling interactions of two Victorian era geniuses, one of science and one of the occult. With relentlessly engaging dialogue and fantastic, gripping scenes, this book is a multifarious pleasure not to be missed."

Ryan Blacketter, author of *Down in the River*

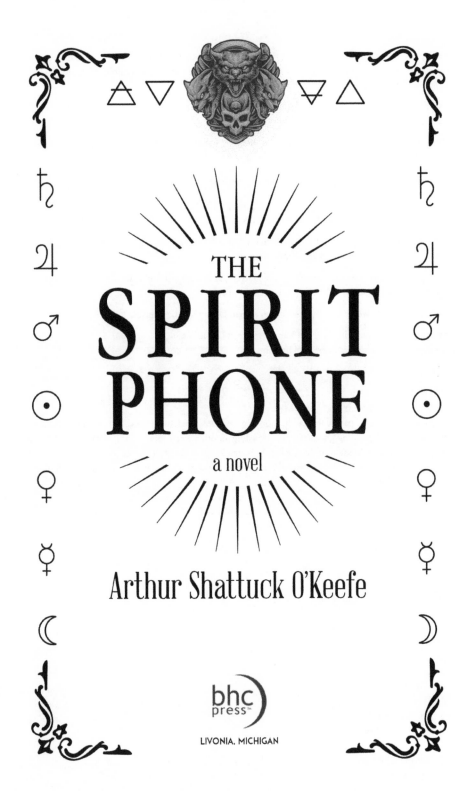

THE
SPIRIT
PHONE

a novel

Arthur Shattuck O'Keefe

bhc
press™

LIVONIA, MICHIGAN

THE SPIRIT PHONE

Published by BHC Press

Library of Congress Control Number: 2021944528

ISBN: 978-1-64397-322-7 (Hardcover)
ISBN: 978-1-64397-323-4 (Softcover)
ISBN: 978-1-64397-324-1 (Ebook)

For information, write:
BHC Press
885 Penniman #5505
Plymouth, MI 48170

Visit the publisher:
www.bhcpress.com

A dedication shared, and not divided.
This book is dedicated to

Eileen Mary O'Keefe (née Shattuck)

Erika Shannon O'Keefe
and
Shiho Nishinouchi

If we do persist upon the other side of the grave, then my apparatus, with its extraordinary delicacy, should one day give us proof of that persistence, and so of our own eternal life.

—Thomas Alva Edison—

The Diary and Sundry Observations of Thomas Alva Edison
Published posthumously, 1948

Chapter VIII: "The Realms Beyond"
(Redacted from subsequent editions.)

THE SPIRIT PHONE

1

August 26th, 1899

"**I**f you fall, you're dead."

"Shut up."

"You don't even know if this will work. It's—"

With an act of will, the internal dialogue is quashed, is nothing, has never existed. The young man peers into the blackness toward the unseen wall of rock.

He moves up its face with care and precision, existing in the moment. The wind, the snow, the ache of muscle and bone, the expanse of mountain above and below: all yield to his focused will.

He knows an event of importance is imminent, but has so far failed to learn its nature. This does not bother him. Certain insights take time and effort, and he realizes—grudgingly—that despite his talents, he still has much to learn.

What concerns him most is a perception, clear and unmistakable: that the event in question carries a physical danger, a malignance.

At twenty-three, he is in impressive health. Yet this may be a warning of terminal illness, his perplexity a subconscious blocking of its source. The idea of such a hidden fear gives him impetus. As much to prove his unflinching stance in the face of mere physical death as to discover what will transpire, he is doing what no mountaineer in his right mind would attempt: scaling part of a Himalayan peak, alone and at night. He estimates that he is at one thousand feet above his starting point.

The physical solitude, the extreme bodily effort, the physiological effects of altitude, all these and more act as catalysts for the conditions needed. Soon he will have an unobstructed channel to the source of the warning. Demon? Angel? Spirit? God? A thing not sentient? Whatever it is, he is about to attain contact. The method employed is one he has never attempted. He cannot allow himself to believe he is not ready.

He realizes he has stopped climbing. The weather has cleared. The rock wall is visible, illuminated by the half moon and the infinite, faraway stars. The time and place are right. He intensifies the focus of his will. The wind, the sky, the mountain he clings to, the ache of his limbs: all recede into a black void in which there is only the self. Still in-physical, yet at the astral level of consciousness, he directs his focus, awaiting perception.

He senses something wrong. He sees nothing, hears nothing, yet feels surrounded, then enveloped, by a presence of undiluted evil. He is immobilized.

Then a savage merging of oblivion and agony, as if buried alive in a boundless expanse of living, malignant soil invading the self, violating him, becoming him. Every fiber, every atom, strains with the effort to expel it, to escape.

Then a deep male voice: "You vain little fool. You thought this was all about you."

He snaps back into the astral-yet-physical state. For a second, he feels he is floating. He turns his head to see the wall of rock moving upward in a rapid blur.

2

August 27th, 1899

Someone is dead in there.

The thought, almost involuntary, occurred to Walter Stern as the yacht came into view, framed within the narrow window of the horse-drawn Black Maria. He knew this was a murder, not a simple assault. He could tell that Donnelly, sitting across from him, realized it as well. That useful and unpleasant instinct, born of long experience.

Neither arc nor incandescent lamps had been installed in this part of Manhattan, and the few gas lamps cast the pier in a blend of yellowish light and shadow. Bull's-eye lanterns shone through the yacht's cabin windows, illuminating the officers within.

The crime reporters who kept constant watch on Headquarters from across the street were conspicuous in their absence, and both men knew why: they had left the scene after getting word that Stern was on the way. This was a code of sorts. They knew Stern, who was not required to appear personally at crime scenes, would fill them in later with key details in exchange for curbing their enthusiasm in certain cases. This was one such case.

Though not obligated to do so, Stern included graveyard shifts in his routine. He and Donnelly had responded from Headquarters to an anonymous telephone report of screams from a yacht parked at the pier near South Street and Gouverneur Lane on the East River. Local jurisdiction fell to the First Precinct, but Stern was the inspector with overall homicide case oversight, and on a hunch had decided this might be a crime of particular interest.

The policeman driving the Black Maria brought the horses to a halt near another police wagon just short of the pier. Stern and Donnelly stepped onto the street, its stone paving still wet from a recent rain. The lingering smell of ozone hung in the air. The thunder had been shattering, and Stern was glad they hadn't had to come out in the storm. He would in theory have preferred a motorized truck, but they were notoriously delicate things, prone to breakdown. At least the models publicly available.

The driver disembarked to stretch his legs as the officer in charge of the First Precinct detachment exited the yacht and walked toward Stern and Donnelly. Stern was glad to see it was Howard Taylor, a competent and methodical detective.

"Inspector, Sergeant. Thank you for coming," said Taylor.

"Good evening, Detective," said Stern. "There's a victim?"

"There is. But the condition of the cadaver is unusual. I think you'd better see for yourself." They walked toward the yacht.

They entered the cabin, greeted by the mingled odors of lamp oil and blood. The corpse lay revealed in the beams of the bull's-eye lanterns held by two uniformed officers. Another was writing in a notebook illuminated by the lantern of a colleague. Donnelly crossed himself.

"Unusual indeed," said Stern. "Any other victims? Anyone hiding on board?"

"Still undetermined," said Taylor. "I have four men searching below."

"Photographs?"

"Taken. Fortunately, without setting the boat on fire." Night photography required the use of magnesium flash lamps, notorious for massive sparking. Stern turned his attention back to the corpse.

The conditioned reflex of descriptive categories went through Stern's mind: white male, pale complexion, about thirty years of age, clean-shaven, conventionally dressed in a brown suit, dark hair, medium build, repeatedly stabbed, lying on his back. Copious blood loss, covering much of the deck. He estimated the number of wounds at forty to fifty. Nothing truly out of the ordinary, except that the man's right hand had been severed at the wrist and was missing.

Stern borrowed a lantern from one of the officers. Crouching, he shone it upon the blood surrounding the corpse.

"Fingerprints in the blood," he remarked, then focused the beam onto the stump where the hand had been.

"Murder weapon? Any blades?" he asked.

"Nothing yet," said Taylor.

"Have you found the hand?"

"No."

Just then, a uniformed officer put his head through the door. "Detective Taylor. No one else on board, sir, living or dead."

"All right. Start checking for any prints we may have missed." Though fingerprint detection in police work was not universally adopted, Stern had made it mandatory in all homicide cases, along with keeping fingerprint records on all criminal suspects.

Stern took in the scene for a few more seconds. Then he said, "All right, Taylor. Donnelly and I will get out of your way. I'll await your preliminary report. We'll be on the pier. Let us know if you need any assistance."

Shortly, the two men stood by the East River, a contrast in physique and dress. Stern was well into his forties, tall and athletic in his gray suit with matching homburg. Donnelly was a decade younger, shorter and stouter if also fit in his blue uniform, its brass buttons reflecting the gaslight in twin vertical rows. In contrast to this contrast, they both sported mustaches with linked muttonchops, dark and neatly trimmed, framing ruddy complexions.

They took a moment to admire the moonlit view of the East River and the glimmer of gaslights on the Brooklyn shore. Then Donnelly said, "It's bizarre. Where the hell did the hand go?"

"Possibly taken as a souvenir," said Stern. "But it may turn up in the search of the boat."

Donnelly removed his blue cloth helmet, ran a hand through his hair, and yawned. "I hope this doesn't take too long."

The yawn was contagious. "I heartily concur, Sergeant. But it'll take as long as it takes. In the meantime, let's enjoy this lovely evening on the waterfront."

Gazing at the black water flowing toward the Atlantic, Stern pondered what he had just seen. He was certain the stabbing of the victim and the removal of the hand had been done by two different blades.

The murder weapon was certainly an ordinary knife of some kind. The stab wounds were punctures and slashes, the rough and jagged product of a dull blade. The missing hand was another matter.

Whatever had been used to sever the hand had a razor-sharp edge. He doubted even one of the famed katana of Japan could make such a smooth, perfect cut. Every bone, blood vessel, and sinew at the wrist stood out in sharp relief, like an anatomy illustration.

But why use two different weapons? Anyone with the tool and the expertise to cleanly slice off a hand with one stroke could easily have decapitated his victim—or used the sharper blade to prolong the victim's agony, if desired—rather than go through the trouble of stabbing him repeatedly with a much duller blade. Unless the killer and the hand-amputator were two different people who had arrived at different times? But that still left unanswered the question of motive in stealing a human hand.

Stern's thoughts were interrupted by Donnelly, who had pulled out his watch to emit a grunt of dissatisfaction. "I hope those fellows finish soon. It's getting close to three."

"Inspector Stern," came the voice of Detective Taylor, who had exited the yacht and was walking toward Stern and Donnelly.

"Still no sign of the hand," he said upon reaching the two men. "But I believe we've found the murder weapon. And something else of interest."

Stern and Donnelly exchanged a glance. "Well done, Taylor. Any clues as to the victim's identity?"

"Nothing. No registry papers or any other documents on board."

"No surprise there. All right, Sergeant. Let's have a look."

They boarded the yacht. Careful to avoid stepping in the congealing pool of blood, Taylor led them to a bulkhead near the front of the cabin. A large panel had been removed and placed to one side.

"A hidden room," said Donnelly.

"More like a closet, Sergeant," said Taylor. "But wait till you see what's inside."

Two officers moved aside to allow Stern and Donnelly a view of the interior.

"Well, now," said Stern.

The space was about four feet square. An electrical wire protruded from a hole in the middle of the forward bulkhead and lay in a loose coil upon the deck. The end of the wire had been stripped of insulation, exposing a few inches of its copper interior. Next to it lay a fruit knife, its blade covered in blood. The walls were painted white, highlighting in gruesome contrast the many specks of blood spattered upon it. Just above the hole from which the wire ran out was a large symbol, painted in black.

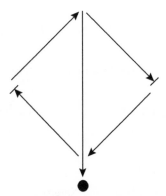

Placed against the forward bulkhead, directly in line with the symbol, was a small wooden table. Its top was charred and blackened, splintered pieces broken off and scattered upon the deck. Cut into the center of the table's top was a hole about three inches wide. Unnoticed by Taylor, Stern pocketed one of the splinters.

"Human sacrifice?" asked Taylor. "Some kind of devil-worshippers?"

"I can't claim expertise on the details of devil worship," said Stern, "but I don't imagine it would involve sacrifices with kitchen utensils. Still, this room seems intended for some kind of ceremonial purpose. Taylor, has the entire boat been searched for prints?"

"Yes. We've found them in abundance. I'll have them analyzed tomorrow."

"All right. Get the boat impounded and into a city warehouse, under guard, right away. We'll also need to check its registry, if there is one."

Stern knelt to examine the coil of wire. "Whatever was done in here involved electricity. Do you know where this wire leads?"

"That's another strange thing," said Taylor. "We'll have to tear into the bulkheads to be absolutely certain, but it looks like that wire leads up to the yacht's lightning rod."

"The lightning rod?"

"Yes. Seafarers call it an air terminal, I think. It seems the man was attempting to electrocute himself. The wire from the rod is supposed to lead down to the bottom of the hull, on the outside, so that lightning strikes are grounded. Even if he were doing some kind of maintenance, there would be no reason to have the wire come in here."

"That would explain the state of this table," said Stern. "Yet the body shows no sign of having been struck by lightning." A lightning strike typically caused obvious physical trauma, especially scarring in the shape of fernlike branches. "And what, I wonder, was the purpose of cutting an opening into the top of this thing?"

"To hold something?" answered Taylor. "A bowl, maybe?"

"Maybe."

As Stern stood up, a uniformed officer approached him and Taylor. He was a sergeant with gray muttonchops and a reddish nose, easily the oldest man on the yacht by a decade.

"Inspector, Detective," he said.

Stern regarded him and said, "Yes, Sergeant...?"

"Flanagan, sir. Been with the department since '66." He spoke with an Irish accent undiminished by several decades in New York.

"What is it, Flanagan?" asked Taylor.

"Sir, it's been nagging at me since we found this fellow, and now I'm sure. I know him. Picked him up for picking pockets in Five Points. Summer of 1885. June, I believe."

"You're sure about this?" asked Stern.

"Yes, Inspector. I don't recall his name, and he was just a pup then, but it's the same face. I might not have remembered, but we'd been trailing him for a while. And he was an odd lad. Dreamy, like his head was somewhere else. Not what you'd expect in a cutpurse."

"1885," said Stern. "You wouldn't have taken fingerprints." The fingerprint records system was less than three years old, and mostly confined to the Homicide Division.

"No, sir," said Flanagan. "But we made a record and took his photograph."

"Sergeant Flanagan," said Stern, "your first task tomorrow will be to arrive at my office at Police Headquarters at 9:00 a.m. sharp. I will ensure you have full access to all arrest records. I suggest you start at June 1st, 1885."

"Yes, sir."

Stern turned his attention to the rest of the officers.

"Gentlemen! As you are aware, a culprit may give himself away by displaying knowledge of a crime, especially details not made public. This case, as I'm sure you have noticed, is especially distinctive. We also need to avoid copycat crimes, a public panic, or sensationalism in the press. From this moment, you are all under strict orders to discuss the details of this case with no one. Is that understood?"

Stern was answered with a chorus of "Yes, sir!" and "Yes, Inspector!"

"All right. Let's get the evidence collection finished and pack it up."

Stern turned to Taylor. "One more thing. Did you find any other bladed instrument? One that could have severed the hand?"

"I know what you mean. I've never seen such a clean cut. But every blade on board is just a kitchen or utility knife, all duller than the class dunce."

"All right. Do another search once the boat's impounded, just in case. Good work."

Taylor began supervising the remaining evidence collection. Once he was out of earshot, Donnelly spoke barely above a whisper. "Inspector, I think we may have more to worry about here than just public panic and yellow journalism."

Stern stared at the symbol painted on the bulkhead. "Indeed, Sergeant," he answered. "I think you'd better switch to plain clothes for a while."

3

There is a mountaineer lying on the floor of my parlor.

It was an unexpected thought to have, especially at three o'clock in the morning. At first, its reality did not quite strike home as Nikola Tesla, in a rare moment of profanity, muttered, "What the hell?" in his native Serbo-Croatian, the entirety of his tall and slender frame the very picture of incredulity and annoyance as he stood clad in his pajamas. As perhaps the greatest inventor of his generation, he considered planning and preparedness crucial to his success, so he didn't like surprises. Yet here was a surprise lying on his floor. A mountaineer.

At least he was dressed like one, in a camel-colored outfit complete with parka and climbing boots. He was young, perhaps twenty years younger than Tesla, with an even paler face and a generous stubble of beard. Despite the bizarre nature of the situation, this detail mildly offended Tesla, who shaved daily and kept a neatly trimmed mustache.

"Sir! What is the meaning of this?" he exclaimed in an English both heavily accented and fluent. "What are you doing in my home?"

He glanced at the locked door. "How did you get in here?" The young man, eyes closed, made no reply. Tesla could see he was breathing, either unconscious or feigning unconsciousness. Intoxicated, perhaps.

He thought of calling the hotel staff to have the intruder ejected, then hesitated. His was the mind of an investigator, and the mystery of the situation intrigued him. He wanted to figure this out on his own before getting anyone else involved.

How had this man gotten in? Even if he somehow possessed a key, the door was both chained and locked. Through a window? Perhaps he had scaled the building. That would explain his clothing, in a sense. But there had been a heavy thunderstorm, and a wet, slippery building exterior would have impeded any such attempt. Besides, Tesla was sure he would have been woken up by the sound of a window opening rather than the thump he had heard, presumably the sound of the man's body hitting the floor.

Tesla was famous. However this young fellow had gotten in, perhaps he was some sort of deranged devotee intent upon invading his home in the middle of the night instead of attending one of his public lectures.

The man's body began jerking in violent spasms. Alarmed, Tesla turned to telephone the front desk for medical aid when a faint, raspy voice said, "Wait."

Turning from the phone, Tesla saw the young mountaineer, still on the floor, eyes wide open.

"Please don't. I'm all right. Aftereffects."

"Of what? Opium?"

"Teleportation. Could I possibly lie on your sofa?"

4

The young man now seemed less pale. He lay half-reclined, back against an armrest of Tesla's sofa, smoking a pipe he had stashed along with a packet of tobacco. He seemed fatigued, yet possessed of considerable mental energy.

He was dark-haired, of middling height and build, face a contrast of fine, boyish features and beard stubble. He carried himself with a rakish, cocksure air, his accent marking him as upper-class English, or at least the pretension of it. The sort of people who tended to eccentricity, in Tesla's view. Perhaps it was his weekly custom to arrive at people's homes at three in the morning dressed as a mountaineer, claiming to have teleported in.

"Not that I've never used opium," he said. "But in my experience, the after-effects never involve convulsions."

"I wouldn't know," said Tesla. He had put on a robe over his pajamas and was standing near the window, arms crossed, gazing with suspicion at the young visitor, who gazed back with a cryptic, appraising look as he puffed at his pipe, the smoke's pungent, fruity aroma pervading the parlor.

"By the way," the stranger said after a moment, "please forgive my rudeness." He indicated his pipe. "It's Perique, from Louisiana. I smoke mine soaked in rum. Would you care to try some?"

"I don't smoke," said Tesla, marveling that this fellow saw not sharing tobacco as a greater offense than invading someone's home in the middle of the night.

"Ah, yes. From what I've read, you take meticulous care of your health. It's a commendable way of living."

In the young man's tone and smile, Tesla detected the faintest hint of mockery. He was no longer in an investigative mood.

"Thank you. And since you seem to have recovered from…whatever it was you did, I must insist you exit my domicile."

"I'm afraid I can't do that, Mr. Tesla."

"Sir," said Tesla, "it is half past three in the morning, and I would like to go back to sleep."

"A perfectly understandable desire, sir. I ask only that you grant me five more minutes of your time to explain my presence here. If, after that, you still wish me to exit your domicile, I shall do so without protest."

Tesla leveled his gaze at the young man and glanced at the grandfather clock near the door, then back at his visitor. "The clock is ticking, Mister…"

"Crowley. Aleister Crowley."

"Proceed."

"I am a mage, sir, of considerable powers."

"You picked a strange time and place to perform a magic show."

"Please, Mr. Tesla, if you'll allow me."

Tesla sighed. "Go on."

"I am not a stage magician who does sleight of hand." The cocky smile was gone. "I am a practitioner of—allow me to spell it—*m-a-g-i-c-k*. *Magick.* Occult knowledge and powers. Gained by way of tapping into the very wellspring of the universe."

Tesla looked at him blankly for a moment, then burst into laughter. "I see! So that's what you meant by having teleported here."

"Yes." If Crowley was offended by this response, he didn't show it. He puffed at his pipe, his expression matter-of-fact.

"And so, Mr. Magick-with-a-*k*, what prompted you to visit—I'm sorry, *teleport* into my home?"

"The teleportation itself was to save myself from certain death. Unfortunately, the psychic resources I depleted to do so were such that no teleporting is possible for at least several months. Even over short distances."

"An assertion which conveniently pardons you from having to demonstrate evidence of your claims." He motioned toward the door. "Sir, I am—"

"Please, Mr. Tesla. My five minutes are not used up, I believe. As to why I teleported *here*, I must confess ignorance, as this was not my intended location. I'd never considered covering such a distance to be possible."

"The distance from where?"

"Tibet."

"I'm sorry I asked."

"I there encountered a malignant entity which I am convinced threatens humanity itself, in a way I am not precisely sure of. It attempted to destroy me by some form of psychic attack while I was scaling a mountain rock face. In my struggle to ward it off, I fell. I was about a thousand feet up, so I attempted to teleport to my base camp, but somehow ended up here."

"Even if I were to believe your story, what does this have to do with me?"

Crowley considered the question for a moment. He had only a vague understanding of how and why he had come here, yet he also knew it was crucial. He tried to think of the most convincing way to convey this to his famous, unwilling host. But he felt exhausted and decided to simply state what he knew as clearly as he could.

"I need your help and you need mine," answered Crowley. "We must combine our skills to combat that which threatens the very fabric of humanity. Based upon my studies, I have a vague intimation as to its nature, which we can discuss later. That is all I can gather at the moment."

That which threatens the fabric of humanity? He's insane, thought Tesla. Yet he didn't appear to be a danger to anyone, so it seemed best to humor him for the moment. Hoping to convince the young man that he had teleported into the wrong place, he said, "My skills? I'm an inventor, not an occultist."

"It may well be your inventive skills which come into play. Besides, you do take an interest in the metaphysical, do you not, Mr. Tesla? Please try to have an open mind about what I am telling you."

Tesla eyed him narrowly and glanced at the clock. "One minute remaining."

"What if I could prove to you that everything I've said is true? At least that I am a mage in the literal sense. More to the point, if you can give me a physical explanation for how I got in here, I'll leave now."

Tesla went to the door and examined the chain. It was securely in its slot, where he was positive he had placed it before retiring. There was no sign it had been tampered with. He went to the nearest window and opened it, bringing forth its characteristic squeak and rattle. He was a light sleeper. Even if Crowley had somehow scaled the building from outside to the thirteenth floor and let himself in through the window, the noise would have woken him up.

He turned to Crowley. "All right," he said. "Prove it."

Pulling a brass tamper from his pocket, Crowley extinguished the pipe and placed it on the side table. He stood up. The cocksure smile had returned. "We'll need to use your bedroom."

"The bedroom? Why?"

"We need to lie down on your bed together."

"Now see here, sir!"

"Mr. Tesla, I promise that what I have planned is not of a sexual nature. Besides, you're a little too old for me."

Tesla winced. "I require no such information about your…personal life, Mr. Crowley. Whatever you have planned, let us proceed."

They entered the bedroom. Tesla's bed was easily large enough to accommodate both men. Crowley closed the bedroom door, walked over to the slightly opened window and closed it. "It works better in a warm room."

"What does?"

"You'll see. Please lie down."

I can't believe I'm doing this, thought Tesla as he complied.

"I'm going to induce within us both the astral state of consciousness."

"The astral what? So this is just going to be a mesmerizing trick?"

"Hardly, sir." He pulled the blankets over Tesla. "There, nice and snug. After what I've been through, I really have no business doing this. But I can call upon certain resources to supplement my strength, and time, I believe, is of the essence. I'm going to induce the prerequisite state first in you, then myself. Then we will take a little trip."

"A trip? What are you talking about?"

"Please close your eyes and relax."

The last thing Tesla felt like doing was relaxing, but he closed his eyes. "Breathe deeply, please," came Crowley's voice. Tesla took a deep breath and exhaled.

To his mild surprise, he began to relax, his body growing gradually heavier until he could not move a muscle. His body felt asleep, while his mind remained awake. He was overcome by a deep and peculiar tranquility, alien yet almost familiar.

He heard, or rather perceived in his mind, Crowley's voice. "That should do it. I'll get myself set up and then we're off." *Off to where?* thought Tesla. To his surprise, Crowley answered, "You'll see."

"All right, then," said Crowley in Tesla's mind. "Don't try to move your body, but *visualize* getting out of bed."

What?

"Please indulge me, Mr. Tesla."

Tesla found himself sitting up and looking at Crowley, who was standing by the door.

"I seem to have actually gotten up instead of just—"

"You're doing fine. Come over here, please."

Tesla complied. "So, an interesting hypnotic trick. It proves nothing."

Crowley nodded toward the bed. "Look." Annoyed, Tesla turned around.

He saw two men lying in the bed, asleep. They were himself and Crowley.

With a shock of realization, in a split instant Tesla was drawn to the bed like a stretched rubber band that had been released. He stopped an inch from his body, staring at his own face with its eyes closed, mouth half-open.

"Let me in!" he shrieked, in a state of near panic. He then realized he was floating horizontally above his body, around which he felt something invisible, like an envelope of solid air. "Why can't I get in? Something is…am I…?"

"Relax, Tesla, you're not dead," said Crowley, stepping over to the bed and passing a hand before him, palm outward. Tesla felt an unseen, gentle grasp as he was returned to a standing position.

"What is this? What is happening?"

"I've erected a low-grade energy barrier to prevent what you're now attempting. It's a common first-time response, but I need you to stay in this state long enough for me to show you something."

"That's me—you—we're…"

"Outside the physical, yes. Simply put, our present state is in fact 'us,' and these…" He motioned toward the bed "…are temporary appendages of physical space-time. But since we're so used to them, our astral forms tend to mimic them."

"My God, this is incredible!"

"Yes, well, I don't do it very often. I've employed more practical magick in the past twenty-four hours than I normally do in a month. It's mostly bookwork, and a fair amount of ceremonial operations. But this is a unique situation."

"So now what?"

"I'll do the driving. Just mentally focus on staying with me. Off we go."

Tesla felt drawn once again as if by a rubber band, and a grayish, indistinct blur rushed past him. He couldn't see Crowley, yet somehow felt his presence just ahead of him. This was beyond belief. But it was happening. Then suddenly everything stopped.

5

The first thing Tesla saw was Crowley's smiling face right in front of him. "We've arrived. Recognize this place?"

Tesla looked around. They were standing on a street corner, the night illuminated by the yellow glow of gaslights. The buildings were decrepit and bleak, the residents more so. He immediately recognized the Tenderloin district, a wretched bastion of vagabonds, street gangs, prostitutes, and morphine addicts. The street signs at the corner indicated Seventh Avenue and Thirty-Second Street. In a nearby alley entrance sat an unkempt bearded man with a vacant expression.

"How did we get here?" Tesla asked Crowley, who looked no longer pale and tired, but of a healthy color.

"The same way we got from your bed to your bedroom doorway—astral projection. Though to get here, we moved through a conduit of the astral plane."

"But the distance…"

"Physical distance is irrelevant. But this sort of place—physical space-time—is not the astral form's natural environment. It takes extra concentration for me to keep us here, but we'll only need to stay long enough for me to show you what I need to."

Tesla looked down at himself, raised his palms, and turned them over. "I feel normal. I feel like I am in my physical body, standing on the street."

"That is to be expected. Now please allow me to direct your attention to the brothel yonder." He indicated a four-story building across the street.

Three women stood outside, two at the base of the front steps and one at the top, attempting to catch the attention of passing men.

Tesla felt a wave of mild revulsion, but Crowley seemed unfazed, even amused. "Charming," he remarked.

Tesla grew impatient. "Are we here to view prostitutes on a street corner?" Then a thought occurred to him. "Can they see us?"

"No to both questions," said Crowley. "We're not here to view these enchanting ladies, per se, but rather to witness a phenomenon of the astral state which, in this instance, relates to them. Ah, here we are. See that fellow coming up the street? Now watch this."

A tall young man in a threadbare sack suit and bowler walked up to the base of the steps and began speaking to one of the women. He seemed shy and furtive, but his intentions were obvious.

"Perhaps it's his first time to visit such an establishment," said Crowley.

"What—" began Tesla.

"Just watch."

The woman turned to her colleague and said something. The two began laughing. The man looked annoyed and continued speaking. After a moment, he walked up the steps and spoke to the third woman, who stared into space and said nothing.

"They can't see him!" Tesla exclaimed.

"Precisely," said Crowley.

"The man is a ghost."

"Well, in a manner of speaking, so are you and I at the moment. But in his case, he is physically dead and doesn't know it. Hence his vain attempt to solicit the services of those ladies."

"How did you know he was going to come here?"

"I didn't know *he* was going to come here, but I knew someone would. Now look behind you."

Tesla turned and saw the bearded man from the alley. He was standing now, wielding a club, bloodshot eyes filled with rage.

"Bastards!" he screamed. "Bastards! You did this to me! I'll kill you all!" No one on the street reacted.

Tesla staggered back, alarmed. "Relax," said Crowley. "He can neither perceive nor harm us."

The man began flailing his club at passersby, screaming with each swing, the weapon passing through each oblivious would-be victim. The only exception was a teenaged boy who shuddered, looking confused and uneasy as the phantom club went through him.

"He's the sensitive type," remarked Crowley.

Soon the man seemed to grow tired and despondent, his attacks diminishing until he sank back down onto the floor of the alley, his club fading into nothingness.

"He can't see us?" asked Tesla.

"These types perceive only in-physical humans. And sometimes spirits on the same corrupted level as themselves."

"Corrupted how?"

"As I mentioned, they're dead—physically dead—yet oblivious to it. Crudely put, the essence of human life is the soul. Or spirit, if you like. When you die physically, your soul—*you*, actually, the physical body being a temporary vessel—goes somewhere else."

"Where? We're on Thirty-Second Street."

"Yes, but one usually goes to one of the multifold aspects of nonphysical reality. These include everything one may attribute to Heaven and Hell, yet that is only a small part of it. It's poorly understood, even by me. But those two men are trapped here, on the physical plane, because they don't realize—or don't want to realize—they are dead. That fellow with the club isn't going anywhere until he decides to get over his now futile desire to murder people."

"Well. Other spiritual realms. Ghosts who don't know they're dead. This is all quite fascinating, but…"

"You're wondering why I'm showing you this and what it has to do with what we discussed in your parlor."

"Yes."

"All will soon be clear. For now, will you agree that all this"—he indicated their surroundings—"is not some mesmerist's trick? That it's real?"

Tesla look around briefly. "Yes. I cannot consider otherwise."

"Good," replied Crowley in a tone of deep relief. He then paused, looking puzzled.

"What's wrong?" asked Tesla.

"Nothing, really. It's just that this place seems familiar somehow. Familiar yet different. But I'm sure I haven't been here before, either astrally or physically."

"Then how did you choose it?"

Crowley shrugged. "I just picked a Tenderloin address at random."

"Could you have come here astrally and then forgotten?"

"Unlikely. In any case, let us return to the physical. Please focus upon staying with me, as before."

The rushing gray blur and rubber band sensation were repeated. Tesla could feel rather than see that they were moving in the opposite direction.

He opened his eyes and found himself back in his bed.

"Fun, wasn't it?" asked Crowley, lying next to him.

6

Tesla sat up, ran his hands over his chest and head for a moment, and looked around. "Amazing," he said.

"I can teach you to do it on your own, if you like. But right now, we've other fish to fry."

"Wait a moment," said Tesla. "The clock reads 3:41 a.m. It was 3:40 when we…departed. How is that possible?"

"Time is not the same in the astral state, Mr. Tesla. That's the best explanation I can give you for now. Let's return to the parlor, shall we? Though I must say, I hesitate to leave this very comfortable bed." Tesla noticed that Crowley's pale, fatigued countenance had returned, though his mental energy seemed undiminished.

They sat down, Crowley on the sofa, Tesla in an easy chair. Crowley relit his pipe.

"The thing that tried to kill you in Tibet," said Tesla. "Are we not vulnerable to it? Why didn't it attack us on Thirty-Second Street? What if it comes here?"

Crowley shook his head. "No sign of it. It seems to be exploiting a situation of opportunity over which it has no control and which is now closed to it. We're safe at the moment."

"I hope you're right."

"I am. Now, let me explain this as well as I can." Crowley began to describe the relevant points of his background.

Having studied the occult arts since the age of twelve, he had devoted his life to "magick"—as distinct from "magic," or what he regarded as sham mysticism. His goal was illumination, to understand what he could of the origin and meaning of existence, and the ultimate potential of man's knowledge and power. To that end, he had traveled the globe, seeking out esoteric tomes and spiritual teachers. Many were fakes, while others were adepts with true insights from whom he had learned what he could.

"To make a long story short," he said, "I am probably the most powerful mage on the planet, and an expert alpinist to boot. And I'm only twenty-three. Not bad." He flashed the cocky smile, and Tesla felt a sharp contrast between his long-held perception of the self-effacing spiritual adept and the total lack of humility this young man presented.

"Most recently," Crowley went on, "I've spent time in Tibet, for purposes of both arcane studies and mountaineering. It was there I began receiving intimations of an impending calamity. I at first assumed it was personal, a warning of a physical illness."

"You can psychically detect a physical illness?"

"That's not the half of it. There's a fellow here in America—in Kentucky, I believe—who specializes in it. Anyway, I could access neither the source of the warning nor its nature. So I decided to climb a mountain."

Crowley explained how he had attained the astral-yet-physical state, and spoke again of the entity that had attempted to destroy him and of the unintentional—and so far inexplicable—teleportation into Tesla's home.

"Was this thing a ghost, like we encountered tonight?" asked Tesla.

"No. Well, perhaps. I don't know yet. But it felt like something much more powerful. It tried to destroy me, both physically and psychically."

"Why?"

"That's the question, isn't it? My best guess is that I am considered a threat to its plans, whatever they are. But there is another puzzling element. The time difference between here and Tibet."

"What do you mean?"

"It was about three o'clock in the morning on August 26th, local time, when I was scaling the rock face."

"You did it at night? That's—wait a minute."

"Yes. New York is eleven hours behind Tibet. Teleportation is essentially instantaneous, so it should have been four in the afternoon on August 25th when I got here. Instead, I somehow arrived nearly thirty-six hours later. I decided not to mention this, as it would have been harder to convince you."

"Well, after what you've shown me, I believe you. But how is this time discrepancy possible?"

"Unknown. But it's got to be important, and something that thing doesn't want me to know. Yet I also sense that any active attempt at recollection would be counterproductive."

"All right. But what does this entity have to do with what you showed me tonight? You said the spirits we encountered in Tenderloin were weak by comparison."

"Yes. Elevation from such a state can be achieved only through a long, gradual learning process. The thing in Tibet, on the other hand, is a highly powerful version of those two."

"How so?"

"Unlike them, it knows exactly what it is, and likes it. It is a paradox. Spiritually devolved, yet immensely powerful. High astral intelligence, yet morally corrupt. And obsessed with the infliction of suffering for its own sake."

"You mean it is some kind of demon?" asked Tesla.

"No. Demons can be willful and arrogant, but they do not tend toward gratuitous violence. They're even useful if you know how to command their allegiance."

"What about angels, then? Do they exist as well? Can you seek their aid? What about God?"

"I shall…make inquiries, as it were. However, based on previous experience, I believe those entities one may term angelic will not intervene, for obscure reasons of their own. As for God, well, there's a topic which raises more questions than answers. I've made my prayers, for whatever it's worth."

"But whatever this thing is, and whatever its intentions toward you, what does it have to do with me? I'm an inventor, not a mystic."

Crowley regarded Tesla for a moment, thoughts flashing through his mind in an instant. *I'm here because I need you and you need me. That much I know. And I know I can trust you. But can I rely on you? Can you face what needs to be faced? Will we survive, or even exist, when this is all over?* This brought a fear to Crowley he knew he must master. He placed it deep within an armored storage box of his psyche for later purging, and answered Tesla.

"You keep saying that. Yet I think you're a bit more of a mystic than you let on. But as I mentioned, the problem is not so much what they have planned for me as what they have planned for humanity."

"They? I thought there was only one of them."

"I've met one so far. There must be others."

"Why? One sounds bad enough."

"An impression I gathered from the encounter. When it grabbed me, it tried to prevent any attempt at thought perception and nonverbal communication."

"Telepathy?"

"To put it crudely, yes. But it couldn't block me completely. I managed to perceive several items of importance which correlate with certain researches of mine ."

Crowley spoke of stories he had encountered over the course of his studies, of which almost nothing existed in extant records: tales of lofty, cruel tyrants of the ancient world intent upon summoning powerful spirits whom they believed could provide them with unlimited power and wealth, even godhood, in exchange for being brought into the physical world. Only three such attempts were successful, but then brought ruin and death to the summoner. The first two dated back to earliest antiquity, probably Sumer, with all details essentially lost. The third, reputedly, had been by Caligula, cruelest of the Caesars, who had declared himself a living god and was eventually assassinated.

"Did the Roman record include a name for these things?" asked Tesla.

"There's no record as such. But those closest to the emperor called them *ferox phasma.*"

"'Fierce phantom.'"

"Or 'wild phantom,' or 'wild ghost.' It's unclear whether the summoning process involves outright possession or simply an irresistible influence."

"And the rarity of these occurrences indicates it's difficult to summon them."

"Yes. It requires a special substance, though knowledge of its identity has been lost. It is reputedly both time-consuming and difficult to acquire, thus only wealthy, powerful despots could hope to accomplish contact. It is also said to involve the use of lightning strikes, which could explain the low success rate."

"So we're safe from these things for now, you say?"

"Yes, for now. It feels like they're in a hurry to somehow access earth directly. And then all hell will break loose. Literally." Crowley's eyes began to droop. "But for the time being," he said, yawning, "I don't suppose you have a guest room?"

"Yes. But there's something I don't quite understand. These things. *Ferox phasma.* From what you've said and shown me, I gather they mean humanity the gravest harm, suffering and death."

"Yes."

"Why?"

"To put it simply," said Crowley, "it's their idea of fun."

Tesla, his countenance a shade paler than usual, showed Crowley to the guest room.

7

The restaurant of the Waldorf-Astoria Hotel was quiet this late Sunday morning. Crowley and Tesla sat at Tesla's favorite table. Crowley drank coffee, absorbed in a copy of the *New York World*. The waiter had brought Tesla a glass of milk without being asked.

Crowley was now bathed, clean-shaven, and dressed in a dark-blue suit obtained from a clothier he knew in the city. Despite it being Sunday, he had appeared at the door of the man's home, located above the shop, and insisted upon his immediate need for garments. Now well-supplied with several suits, bowlers, and homburgs, he had enjoyed the stares of amazement while hailing a hansom cab in his mountaineer's garb, minus the parka, given the balmy late August weather.

Tesla wasn't sure where the young man's money came from but assumed he was independently wealthy and left it at that. Though Crowley could obviously afford to occupy his own lodgings, on an unspoken agreement the two men had decided to share quarters, with Tesla as the impromptu host.

Tesla, for his part, was also living well, partly through patent royalties. It was all such a change from the quiet village in a quiet corner of the Austro-Hungarian Empire he had left so long ago. Still, he realized he was beginning to live beyond his means. Residing in the large hotel suite he considered his "apartment" was rather an extravagance, but it was a lifestyle he'd grown accustomed to.

It occurred to him, not for the first time, that even to live with all the conveniences of modern technology was a fortunate thing. While public electric lighting was now common, less than one tenth of American households had electrical service. It was just too expensive for most people. Tesla hoped to change all that.

Crowley took a sip of coffee and looked up from his newspaper. "Don't you read the paper in the morning?" he asked Tesla.

"Not during breakfast. It's unsanitary."

"Hmm." Crowley glanced at the front page and frowned. "This is yesterday's edition. Though I suppose it's good to catch up on old news after a month in Tibet." He asked the waiter to bring him one of today's papers when they arrived.

Crowley took another sip of coffee, then looked at his cup with a quizzical expression.

"What's wrong?" asked Tesla.

"Nothing," replied Crowley. "Waiter! A cup of cocoa, please." He placed the coffee aside. "I'm not usually one to have a sweet tooth. By the way, why do you have a stack of eighteen napkins?"

"It is a strange affectation, I suppose. I am somewhat preoccupied with the number three and numbers divisible by it."

Tesla began to polish the silver with his napkins. Crowley was nonplussed but made no comment. He turned his attention to the scene outside the window.

Men in suits and bowlers, women in their more elaborate hats, ankle-length skirts, and shirtwaists. Carriages, wagons, motorcars, and bicycles traversing the street beneath the green trestle of the elevated train. And beneath the trodden stone blocks lay the endless streams of copper carrying forth a power unheard of in all the bygone ages. What we are pleased to call modern civilization, now imperiled in a way Crowley could not quite define.

A newsboy walked into view across the street and dropped his burden of newspapers, which began to sell quickly. Three men huddled together to read the front page of a single copy. With some animation they seemed to be discussing its content.

"Some big news, apparently," said Crowley. Tesla paused in his polishing of the silver to steal a sidelong glance out the window, then resumed the work. Crowley continued observing, and within a couple of minutes, the papers were sold out. The newsboy looked happy.

"So," said Tesla. "These things. The Ferox."

"*Ferox phasma*, yes. Nasty pieces of work, by all accounts. Such as they are."

"And they tried to kill you because they saw you as a threat to their intentions."

The waiter brought the cocoa, and Crowley took a long sip.

"Ah, that's good. Right. As I said last night, they're immensely powerful yet spiritually corrupt, obsessed with carnal experiences and unimaginable cruelty." There was a slight annoyance in Crowley's tone, as of a teacher repeating the same essential fact to a slow pupil. They sat in uncomfortable silence for a few minutes before the waiter arrived with their breakfast. Crowley tucked into his bacon and poached eggs with relish. Tesla took a bite of his plain buttered toast.

"At the risk of being redundant, I again submit to you that I am an electrical engineer. An inventor. A scientist. I don't see how I can be of any help in this."

The waiter came by and handed Crowley a copy of the day's *New York World*. "Here you are, sir. Quite an amazing item on page one."

"Thank you," replied Crowley, handing the waiter the old paper and beginning to read.

"Apparently you can be of help, or I wouldn't be here. There is an alarming possibility in all this."

"An alarming possibility? Which one would that be?"

Crowley held up the paper, showing Tesla the front-page headline.

Edison's New Invention: A Means to Communicate With the Dead!

Famous inventor calls his device "the Spirit Phone," claims it will revolutionize human consciousness and civilization.

"Oh my," said Tesla.

"Yes. I doubt this is a coincidence. They apparently plan to break in with technology. Edison was the logical person to do it. Other than you, perhaps."

"Henry! Bring me a copy of today's paper!"

"Which one, Mr. Tesla?"

"It doesn't matter. *The New York Times*."

"Isn't that unsanitary?" asked Crowley. Tesla scowled at him, then began to read.

Edison's Spirit Phone: Inventor Claims Communication With the Dead, Has Applied for Patent for New Device

West Orange, NJ, Aug. 26—Thomas Edison, prolific inventor of many devices of our modern age, claims to have developed an apparatus for communication with the spirits of the dead. The Spirit Phone, as he calls it, was developed in Mr. Edison's laboratory in West Orange, New Jersey under conditions of extreme secrecy, presumably to prevent information on its design from being revealed to competitors. Details of its exact construction have, as of this writing, not been publicly released. While the device is not yet available in stores, Mr. Edison's company, Edison Manufacturing, is taking delivery orders. The announcement has been greeted with alarm and condemnation from prominent members of the clergy...

Searching the pages, Tesla came upon an advertisement.

WONDER OF THE AGE!!!
THE EDISON SPIRIT PHONE

Dispense with the rappings, crystal balls, and Ouija boards of séances and spiritualists. By means of modern science and engineering, you may contact your departed loved ones beyond the veil.

$200

Not available in stores. Orders may be placed by correspondence with:

The Edison Manufacturing Company
65 Fifth Avenue
New York, New York

Thomas A. Edison

"And people say I am eccentric," said Tesla. "Either this thing really is the wonder of the age, or Edison has lost his mind. Are you saying he has been possessed by one of those things, and they made him make this instrument?"

"Not necessarily. It could be something he was already working on, and which the Ferox wish to take advantage of. In any case, for want of other information, we have to assume they intend to use this device—if it functions as advertised—to break into our space-time."

"Before you went to sleep, you mentioned something about the process for summoning the Ferox requiring a special, hard-to-obtain substance. What is it? How is it used?"

"My information is sketchy. There is an alloy referred to as the Essential Composite that is used to summon them. It is composed of the Seven Planetary Metals: gold, silver, tin, copper, iron, mercury, and lead. Plus two additional substances."

"Which are?"

"I don't know precisely. One is called the Essential Element. There is no known record of its composition. Despite the name, it may be a chemical compound. What I do know is that it's rare and difficult to find. Those who sought contact typically spent years gathering enough to initiate a summoning."

"Where did they obtain it?"

"Again, the record is vague. It is said to occur naturally in trace amounts where it can be found. Once enough is obtained, it is combined with the other elements, the proportions of which are also secret, to make a bowl or similar vessel used in a ceremony to attain contact."

"And what is the other substance?"

"It is known as the Secret Element, and is supposedly very easy to obtain."

"So what is it?"

Crowley shrugged. "I don't know. That's why it's called the Secret Element."

"So this spirit phone—assuming it works—is a latter-day version of a Ferox summoning? Edison never struck me as the type to try conjuring evil spirits."

"Edison's intentions may well be innocent and his device based upon a purely technical inquiry. But we have to assume the Ferox intend for it to serve as an access method, even if people can also use it to contact the spirits of their dearly departed. To confirm this, we need to get one of these things. You can assess its composition, and I can determine its ultimate function."

"It is not as simple as that," said Tesla. "Privately arranged preorders for those who have some kind of connection with Edison will surely be filled immediately. But for most people, even orders for phonograph models already in production require a long wait. I don't think I can get my hands on one of these things so easily, even through a third party. Edison and I are not on the best of terms."

"So I've heard," said Crowley. "Then there's only one thing to do. We have to steal a spirit phone."

8

August 28th, 1899

Tesla sat near the front row of the packed lecture hall, waiting for the first public demonstration of the spirit phone to begin. There were mostly men in the audience but a few women as well, their hats colorful islands in a sea of bare male heads. Members of the press sat in the front row to the right. He looked at his watch and wondered if Crowley would be able to show up as he had promised.

"No. No stealing of spirit phones, Mr. Crowley," Tesla had said in response to the young man's rash suggestion. "Especially as my laboratory is located around the corner from the New York City Police Department." Noting the demonstration at Columbia College announced in the paper, he had insisted they attend it instead of committing a felony. As one of the most famous members of the American Institute of Electrical Engineers, Tesla could get in with no difficulty.

They needed unfettered access to a working model. Tesla was confident he could build one as long as he could hear Edison's explanation and see the device, but for one snag: he could not determine the spirit phone's precise metallic composition simply by sight. If it was as important as Crowley thought, Edison would refuse to disclose it, at least until his patent was approved.

"Leave that to me," Crowley had said.

Tesla had lectured here several times himself, the first such event having secured his public reputation a few years after his falling out with Edison. He assumed Edison had chosen this venue deliberately.

A lectern stood on the right side of the podium. In the middle was a table, and upon it an object covered by a black silk cloth. This, presumably, was the invention everyone had come here to see. It made for an irregular, tent-like shape, and its presence yet invisibility added to the sense of anticipation pervading the room. As one who often utilized a touch of the dramatic to showcase his own inventions, Tesla could only approve.

A man walked to the lectern and began to address the audience.

"Ladies and gentlemen, thank you for your attendance this evening. We are honored tonight to have as our guest a man who truly needs no introduction, though I shall have to introduce him regardless." Brief laughter erupted from the assemblage. "Here to demonstrate the functioning of his latest invention, which he describes as a spirit communicator, or spirit phone: ladies and gentlemen, please welcome Mr. Thomas Alva Edison!"

Amidst the thunderous applause, a smiling Thomas Edison walked toward the lectern. Though well into middle age, his brown hair noticeably graying, he radiated a youthful and confident energy. His eyes met Tesla's for a moment, and they nodded to one another in recognition, Edison's expression betraying his surprise for only an instant.

Tesla, Edison had assumed, would disdain attending such a demonstration and then publicly express skepticism as to his invention's authenticity. His appearance here was an unexpected development, but he had no time to consider it now. Arriving at the lectern, he began to speak.

"Ladies and gentlemen, thank you very much for attending this evening's demonstration. In all of man's investigations into nature, long has he pondered the ultimate question: what is our fate upon release from this mortal coil? Do we exist beyond the grave?

"For untold ages, humanity has had to be content with answers from the authorities of religion and metaphysics which, while perhaps persuasive, lack definitive scientific evidence. Even the new field of psychical research has resulted in little more than the exposure of many so-called mediums as tricksters and frauds.

"But now, ladies and gentlemen, that time is over. The dawn of a new era for mankind has arrived. It is now possible to communicate directly with the spirits of those departed from this world, and perhaps even spiritual entities of other natures as well. Not by means of the mysticism of séances or Ouija boards or crystal balls, but by technology."

Edison glanced to his right and nodded. An assistant came onto the podium and stood next to the black-shrouded object.

"Ladies and gentlemen, I give you…the spirit phone!" The black silk cloth was whipped off with a flourish. The hall erupted in applause, followed by murmurs. Tesla was immediately puzzled. *This can't be a communications device,* he thought.

Its most prominent feature was a slender cone, dark-gray and metallic, suggesting the horn of a phonograph. This was inserted upright, narrow end down, into a wooden base upon which it shared space with other components. Next to the horn sat an electromagnet: a cylindrical iron core wrapped with electrical wire. It lay on its side, attached by wires to a battery composed of two electrical dry cells, one-and-a-half volts each. A switch to activate the current was set next to the cells.

This is it? Tesla thought. *A phonograph horn, an electromagnet, and a couple of dry cells? He's cracked.*

"I realize many of you are now wondering how this apparatus can be a means of communication to anywhere, let alone the spirit realm," said Edison. He explained that while the precise physical processes of the device were yet to be understood, it was the metallurgical properties of the horn which primarily caused it to function, with its geometric proportions also playing a role. The electromagnet placed next to it, he indicated, was also essential, but not in itself remarkable. Despite its weak magnetic field, objects of ferromagnetic metal were best kept away to prevent interference with the spirit phone's function.

At a gesture from Edison, all the electric lights in the hall but a few were turned off. He walked over to the spirit phone and switched on the electromagnet. A low hum emanated from the horn, and a light-blue glow began to surround the device.

"The blue aura you see is a side effect, its exact cause currently unknown. We assume its manifestation results from the same metallurgic content which, upon exposure to the electromagnetic field, causes the spirit phone to function.

"And as to that function: I wish I could say to you that we may call upon any and all deceased personages with whom we wish to speak, and that I might summon Julius Caesar or George Washington to have a chat with us this evening. While this may not be impossible, what we have observed thus far is that the spirits of those who were known to the operator in life are most easily summoned by specific concentration upon the personality of that person in combination with calling out his or her name.

"Other than that, what we may refer to as 'random spirits' may also be contacted, with whom conversation on various subjects is possible. As it would be unfair to favor only one or two of our assemblage tonight with the chance to speak with their dearly departed, it is a so-called random spirit with whom I shall attempt contact."

Edison turned to face the spirit phone, his profile to the audience. With an expression of deep concentration, he intoned, "I seek communication with a willing entity." He repeated the phrase twice.

"Hello," came a male voice from the horn. There were gasps among the audience, then silence as Edison held up his hand.

"Hello," said Edison, lowering his arm. "Thank you very much for joining us this evening."

"You're very welcome." The voice carried a slight metallic distortion, but Tesla immediately recognized it as Crowley's. "And please allow me to take this opportunity to congratulate you, Mr. Edison, upon the success of your invention."

"Thank you. But you have me at a disadvantage, sir. May we have your name?"

"My name is Yessar-Smik. I am, in your terms, a being of a higher plane of spiritual evolution. For the benefit of the members of your press, I shall spell my name." The reporters wrote into their notepads as the letters were spoken. "And please don't forget the hyphen. Now then, I have an important message for all of humanity I would like to share this evening. But first, I have a question for Mr. Edison."

"Yes?"

"Would you be so kind, sir, as to explain the precise metallurgical composition of the horn through which I now speak?"

There was a long moment of silence. Then Edison said, "I'm sorry, but that information is, for the moment, confidential."

"Oh, pretty please." The audience erupted into laughter.

"Mister...Yessar-Smik, you place me in a rather awkward position."

"Perhaps Mr. Edison's assistant would like to tell us."

The assistant looked dazed for a moment, then began to speak in a rapid, mechanical voice. "Precisely equal parts of carborundum and of seven metals: gold, silver—"

"Shut up!" shouted Edison, silencing the assistant, who now wore a confused and mortified expression. Edison looked abashed, but soon composed himself.

Tesla was barely able to keep his face from betraying his thoughts as he spied Edison stealing a glance at him. *Is that what it is? Incredible.*

"Very well," said the voice from the horn. "Please forgive my imposition. And to show there are no hard feelings, I shall deliver my vital message to the human race: please get plenty of fresh air and exercise, and indulge in spirits only in moderation."

In the midst of more laughter, the voice said, "I bid you all a good evening."

Edison switched off the spirit phone, and the lights were restored.

"Are there any questions?" he asked. Dozens of hands shot up amidst the cacophony of voices drowning one another out.

Within a couple of minutes, Tesla somehow managed to escape the throng of reporters surrounding him for comments. After stating that he had found Edison's demonstration interesting, but would for now reserve judgment on the spirit phone's functionality, he excused himself and hailed a cab.

Entering his apartment, he exclaimed, "Crowley! That was brilliant! But I think Edison is going to fire that poor assistant. Crowley?"

Tesla walked into the guest room to find him on the bed, eyes closed. Blood covered much of his face.

"Crowley!" Tesla cried as he went to the bed.

Crowley opened his eyes and whispered, "What's carborundum?" before fainting.

9

Tesla was no doctor, but Crowley's life seemed in no imminent danger. The bleeding from his eyes, nose, and ears had soon stopped. His breathing and pulse were regular. Tesla grabbed a cloth, soaked it in hot water in the bathroom sink, and returned to the guest room.

Crowley came to as Tesla was wiping the blood from his face. "Ugh…my God, this is…rather unpleasant."

"How do you feel? Can you see and hear me?" asked Tesla after cleaning off the last of the blood.

"Yes. It's like the worst hangover ever, multiplied tenfold." He grimaced and put his fingers to his temples. "That thing had an energy barrier impeding my access. I could tell something was wrong with my physical body, but managed."

"Do you need a doctor?"

"No. A good night's sleep will do. And perhaps a bit of whiskey?"

Tesla left the room and soon returned with a bottle of bourbon and a shot glass, which he set on the nightstand. He poured a shot and handed it to Crowley, who immediately drained it.

"Thank you, sir. Another, please?"

After the second shot, he said, "That should do it, I think. Just a couple of things before I retire. That spirit phone. It works, in its way, but there's no way the Ferox can use it to attain communication with in-physical humans."

"What do you mean? You used it to communicate."

"Yes, but barely. And it was more than simply communication. I had to travel there astrally and get inside the thing. Into the horn."

"Inside? You could fit inside it?"

"Yes. I doubt more than half a dozen living adepts could have done it. That thing prevents access by anything beyond a certain level of intelligence. All you'll get are semi-sentient entities who soon start mimicking or paraphrasing you. I call them parrots."

"Parrots?"

"Yes. Initially, it will seem like the person you seek, and speak with a degree of sophistication. Then later it starts to sound like an idiot. Sort of like a sprinter trying to run a marathon: impressive, but only at first. That thing Edison demonstrated is basically an electrical Ouija board."

"But you said the Ferox were corrupted, like those two in Tenderloin. Devolved."

"Yes, but they possess advanced astral *intelligence* plus spiritual corruption. A Ferox can't get through without a tremendous effort, and neither will anyone's dead granny."

"So Edison is faking it?" asked Tesla.

"No. It's hard to perceive these things even under optimal conditions, but I think Edison is unaware of this. He believes he's devised a genuine spirit phone, by whatever definition. It seems like they didn't test the thing well enough."

To Tesla, this was not a complete surprise. In the race to achieve priority, an inventor might well exaggerate his actual progress. Edison's perfection of the filament for his incandescent lamp had come several months after the awarding of his patent in 1880. Yet Tesla knew firsthand that Edison was also a driven, inexhaustible tester of everything he developed. Was he worried someone else might be attempting to invent a spirit phone?

"All right," said Tesla. "But if these Ferox are trying to access Earth, and Edison's spirit phone can't be used for that, how are they going to attempt entry? And Edison interrupted his assistant. The seven metals he began speaking about—"

"Are almost certainly the Seven Planetary Metals. Once I compelled him to begin speaking, I was able to focus upon his thoughts sufficiently. But what is carborundum?"

"A silicon-carbon compound. Also called silicon carbide." Tesla related to Crowley the story of carborundum, one of the most significant yet little known developments of the new industrial age.

As the nineteenth century progressed, more and more tools, equipment, and machines made of metal came to be designed and manufactured on an ever-greater scale. Industrial mass production in turn caused an increasing demand for abrasive materials for use in grinding, shaping, and polishing the metals such items were composed of. As the abrasive material needed to be harder than metal, one obvious choice was diamond. Natural diamond, however, was rare and expensive, and an efficient, economical way to artificially create a suitable substitute proved elusive. Then, in 1890, a chemist from Pennsylvania named Edward Goodrich Acheson, while attempting to synthesize artificial diamond, instead stumbled upon a process for cheaply producing a compound of silicon and carbon by heating a graphite core surrounded by sand, salt, and carbon. The result was carborundum. While not as hard as diamond, it had proven highly useful as an abrasive, with one million pounds per year produced since 1896.

"Does it exist in nature?" asked Crowley.

"Rarely. In meteorites, mostly. I think we're both coming to the same conclusion, Mr. Crowley."

"Yes. A substance rarely found in nature, combined with the Seven Planetary Metals to summon a *ferox phasma*. Carborundum is the Essential Element, now cheaply produced in massive quantities. And now with convenient, plentiful electricity, there's no need to use lightning strikes."

"Speaking of which," said Tesla, "lightning has tremendous electrical pressure, ten million volts or more, with a massive energy discharge. Edison's spirit phone has a three-volt battery. Are you sure lightning was employed by the ancient summoners of the Ferox?"

Crowley shrugged. "Perhaps no fixed voltage is needed beyond a certain level. Besides, how else could they have accessed electricity?"

"Hmm. Let's defer that. In any case, the instrument demonstrated tonight cannot be used to contact them," said Tesla. "And what about the Secret Element? The ninth item?"

"No perception of it. But there's something I did perceive, barely, from Edison's thoughts. With a spirit phone, he has made some kind of contact far beyond what is possible with the device at Columbia. I think it's the prototype. There is some crucial difference between it and the models he intends to sell, yet he is somehow unaware of this."

"Then this difference may be the Secret Element. But how is he not aware of it?"

"I don't know, but I think I can guess who he's speaking to. We'd best sleep on it."

"Yes. You're sure you don't need a doctor?"

"Quite sure. A good night's sleep and breakfast should fix me up. Thank you for your hospitality, Mr. Tesla." He closed his eyes.

"You're welcome," whispered Tesla as he turned to leave the room.

"Oh, Tesla," called Crowley.

Tesla turned to see the pale, smiling countenance.

"I think we may need to steal a spirit phone after all."

Tesla thought it best not to argue the point. He sighed. "Good night, Mr. Crowley."

"Good night, Mr. Tesla."

10

Thomas Alva Edison sat at the rolltop desk in his office, situated on the second floor of his so-called invention factory. It was nearly midnight. He was alone in the building, and the only illumination in the room was that of the green-shaded electric lamp set upon his desk. Next to the lamp was a bottle of Vin Mariani, his favorite tonic. He poured himself a glass and drained it. Refilling the glass, he reflected briefly upon the night's events.

Things did not go quite as he had hoped. That carborundum, gold, and silver were essential to the spirit phone would be in all the papers tomorrow. But there was no way to change what had happened, so he did not dwell upon it. In any case, it was of little importance. He had silenced his assistant before he could reveal the other elements of the horn. As to why the man had suddenly begun to blurt out the information, he seemed at a loss to explain, and apologized abjectly. Edison let him off with a stern warning, assuming that the spirit calling himself Yessar-Smik had somehow mesmerized him.

It was a clear night, and through the open window behind the desk, the cool evening breeze and the chirping of crickets drifted in. Switching off his desk lamp, Edison turned his swivel chair around to view the countless stars of the Milky Way. He wondered whether, on a planet circling one of those stars, there might be life, or perhaps even civilization. He recalled Tesla having spoken of attempting contact with the hypothetical denizens of Mars.

Tesla. Edison could see the flash of surprise in his eyes at the assistant's mention of carborundum. Not a use for the stuff anyone had anticipated. But then, no one had predicted that bamboo could be used as an electric light filament. Would Tesla now be able to build his own version of the spirit phone, like the gas-filled phosphor-coated globes he claimed had made the incandescent lamp obsolete?

He turned his chair back around to face the desk and switched the lamp on. Fishing a key ring from his pocket, he unlocked the top right drawer of his desk and removed from it a folded sheet of paper. It was strange, he thought, that he still felt compelled to read this. He could speak with her directly now, so why bother? But some instinct he could not quite place urged him to read the letter again and again. He had memorized its contents, yet never tired of seeing it. Unfolding it, he began to read.

My Darling Mary,

It is I, your Thomas.

I wonder, can you somehow perceive the words I write here? I dearly hope so. It is now 1885, and the year since your passing has been the hardest I have ever had to bear. After you were gone, to attempt invention seemed futile and meaningless. I could think of little else but my desire to see you again, or at least to hear your voice.

And yet the drive to invent, to create that which has never existed, never truly left me. It has rather lain dormant with the grief I have endured in your absence. But now, the desire to reach you and to invent have become as one, inspiring me to conceive mankind's ultimate invention: The Spirit Phone.

With all I have accomplished, can I not use my inventive skills to somehow speak with you again?

Here, then, is my plan...

Finishing the letter, he folded it up again and placed it back in the drawer, which he locked. Selecting another key from the ring, he unlocked the bottom left drawer, then hesitated.

He was afraid of the conversation he was about to have, yet he badly wanted to have it. It was like this each time. His hands trembled ever so slightly as he reached into the drawer.

He removed a plain-looking pinewood box. Placing it on the desk in front of him, he opened its hinged top. Inside was a metallic cone inserted into a wooden base, set next to an electromagnet and two dry cells. To all appearances, it was identical to the device he had demonstrated at Columbia.

He switched it on. Then came the low-pitched hum, and the faint blue aura.

"Andreas," said Edison.

"Hello, Al," replied a voice from the horn. "It's good to speak with you again." It was a deep male voice with a cheerful, energetic air and a strange accent Edison couldn't quite identify. It was slightly distorted, like someone speaking into the rotating blades of an electric fan. Despite Edison's partial deafness, he always heard this voice clearly.

"It's good to speak with you too. Regarding my public demonstration tonight…"

"Yes, there was a slight problem. Someone playing a bit of mischief. It is of little importance. I shall ensure it does not happen again."

"I see. Thank you."

"You're quite welcome. We are happy to see your priority of invention established. Your work is very important for the advancement of spiritual knowledge on the physical plane. There is much for you to do, and much for us to reveal to you." His voice was comforting. A voice you could trust instinctively.

"Yes…but are you sure it wouldn't be better for someone besides me to convey the metaphysical aspects of this whole thing? When I came up with the idea for the spirit phone, I just wanted to determine whether we lived on after death and whether communication with the dead was possible."

"Questions you have managed to answer admirably."

"But now you're telling me I need to usher in a new and higher level of consciousness for the human race. I'm not qualified to do that. Why not let Temple handle it? He seems to know about such things. And this thing was partly his idea anyway."

It was a point Edison had raised before, and the answer was always the same. Each time, Andreas's response made him feel reassured, but as time went on, he eventually became uneasy again, prompting Edison to bring up the subject once more.

"We have other plans for Temple. Besides, Al, there is no one qualified. Yet. But there will be. You. Allow me to elucidate. I think it's safe to say you could get hired as an electrical engineer at any company in the world, were you to apply for the job."

Edison chuckled. "Yeah, probably."

"Where did you go to school to learn all that? I'll tell you. You didn't. You learned on the job, starting as an itinerant telegraph operator, learning everything there was to learn and more, before there was even a recognized field of electrical engineering."

It was how every electricity specialist learned back then, but Edison knew there was truth in Andreas's words. With virtually no formal schooling, as a teenaged telegrapher he had devised a timer to automatically transmit a signal every half hour so his boss wouldn't know he was napping on the job. By his twenties, he had perfected the means for telegraphs to receive and transmit four messages on the same wire. And that was only the beginning.

"By the same token," Andreas continued, "there is no school for obtaining the knowledge that will illuminate humanity, nor for how to improve the spirit phone to put that knowledge to use. For both of those, I'll teach you everything you need to know. Your genius and tenacity will do the rest."

"Yes," said Edison. "When?"

"Patience, Al. I will let you know when the time is right. In the meantime, I believe there is once again someone here who would like to speak to you. I'll leave you two alone." Edison felt the familiar anticipation, the racing of his heart.

"Darling," came the voice, sweet and familiar even through the tinny distortion of the spirit phone.

Edison closed his eyes and took a deep breath, composing himself. Each time was just as moving as the last.

"Mary," said Edison. "You came."

11

August 29th, 1899

Crowley sat in one of several private phone booths set in a row at the side of the hotel lobby, holding the cuplike receiver against his ear. He checked his watch. Ten minutes since requesting the overseas connection. Despite his fatigue from the experience at Columbia, he had made himself get up to perform this task, being careful not to wake Tesla. It was just before three o'clock in the morning.

"Good morning, Continental Travel. May I help you?" It was the young, cheerful voice of an Englishwoman.

"Yes, thank you. My name is Pierce. I have a tour reservation I would like to confirm."

"Certainly, sir. Your reservation number, please?"

"Zed-zed-three-one-two-seven. The tour of New York City."

"Yes. Mr. Pierce. Your reservation is confirmed. Your tour conductor will be Mr. Parr."

"Thank you."

Crowley hung up the phone, paid the charges at the reception desk, and walked out the main entrance of the Waldorf-Astoria.

He was soon able to catch an electric hansom cab, one of many introduced to the city two years before. Like its noisier gasoline-engine counterpart, it was in appearance a horse-drawn cab minus the horses, with the driver seated above and behind the covered passenger seat. Crowley got in and opened a sliding panel on the roof to address the driver.

"The Museum of Natural History, please."

"The museum is closed, sir."

"I know. Just take me there." He shut the panel.

The hum of the electric motor began as the car accelerated.

The cab stopped at the museum's main entrance on West Seventy-Seventh Street in the center of a long stretch of Neo-Romanesque architecture in brownstone taking up hundreds of feet of the street. Crowley paid the fare and got out. The cab pulled away.

Crowley stood in front of the entrance, and before long a tall man in a dark suit and bowler walked up to him. He was young, about Crowley's age, and wore a businesslike smile.

"Good evening," the man said. "I'm Parr. Continental Tours." He spoke in that precise inflection of the Queen's English honed by public schools and career ambitions.

"Good evening," Crowley said. "I'm Pierce. I believe my reservation is confirmed."

"Word was you were in Tibet."

"I was. I unexpectedly needed to come to New York."

"For what?"

"It's a long story. Something extraordinary and dangerous is materializing. I need help."

"That has been anticipated."

"How?"

"That's another long story, and I don't have all the details, but…" He looked aside for a moment, then back at Crowley. "Everyone in the organization has standing orders not to render you any assistance."

"What?"

"Nor to hinder you. But the orders were very clear."

"Why?"

"Officially, that's all I can tell you. But there's word on the grapevine. Unconfirmed."

"Tell me."

"I heard that the order came down to us in a memorandum. A very old one."

"What are you talking about?"

"It had been sitting in the archives for 290 years, sealed with orders not to open it until 1898. Its existence was unknown to everyone except a few at the top. And somehow, it mentions you by name. I don't know who wrote it, but it supposedly says that any attempt to aid you would result in disaster. Of what kind, I don't know."

"How do I know this is true?"

"You don't, though I've no reason to lie. This is another of those situations with no rational explanation where they chuck it aside and let people like you handle it."

"What the hell do they expect me to do?"

"Whatever you think best." He clapped Crowley on the shoulder. "Terribly sorry, old boy. Wish I could help. Good luck."

He turned and walked away into the night.

"Shit," said Crowley. After a minute, he began to search for a cab to get back to the hotel.

12

"I must say, the meals at this hotel are quite satisfactory." Crowley smiled as he sliced into his large cut of medium-rare sirloin, next to which sat three eggs over easy. This morning's *New York Times* lay beside the plate. He paused, raised his eyebrows, and said, "I think it's going to be an eventful morning."

"I don't like the way you say that," said Tesla. "Hopefully it will not be as eventful as last night. You have quite the appetite, considering what happened."

"Yes. A strong expenditure of magickal energy always makes me hungry afterward. Mmm." He closed his eyes in an ecstatic expression as he chewed the steak. "Divine. So you're certain we don't need to remove the spirit phone from Edison's laboratory? Physically accessing it will be sufficient?"

"Yes. I only need to reconfirm its exact dimensions and scrape a sample off the horn for later analysis. Then we can see if your theory holds true. But it will be dangerous. If caught, we of course face the prospect of prison. Edison would spare no expense in prosecuting me."

"I'm confident we can manage not to get caught. But what is it between you two? I recall occasionally reading vague references in the press. It seems like more than a professional rivalry."

"I used to work for Edison. We had different ideas about the direction electrical advancement should take, the most famous example being our disagreement over alternating versus direct current." It was well-known that while Edison had championed direct current, or DC, as a safer and more effective way of delivering electricity, Tesla had insisted that alternating current, or AC, was the wave of the future, and had proven it with his famous AC polyphase system, installed in the Niagara Falls hydroelectric power system in 1896. It had been done through an alliance between Tesla and engineering entrepreneur George Westinghouse, who, if anything, was an even fiercer rival to Edison than Tesla.

Crowley knew of a dispute over whether it was Tesla or the Italian engineer Galileo Ferraris who had first devised a viable AC motor design, but saw this as a topic best avoided. Instead, he said, "Yes, and it seems that history will vindicate you. Yet you seem bitter about something personal. I don't mean to pry, but if it could affect the course of our investigations…"

"I will tell you the story, then," said Tesla.

In 1884, after having spent two years as a junior engineer with the Continental Edison Company in Paris, Tesla had been transferred to work directly for Edison's machine works in Manhattan. He soon gained a reputation for being as tireless and energetic as Edison, and was well-regarded in the company. Though Edison had rejected Tesla's proposal of a project to design and market an alternating current power system, he accepted the young Serb's idea to redesign and improve Edison's existing direct current dynamos. Tesla worked tirelessly for nearly a year, not only improving the efficiency of the dynamos significantly but installing a new type of automatic control system.

"The manager at Edison's machine works had promised me a fifty-thousand-dollar bonus if I could do as I had promised with the dynamos. Then he reneged, claiming he had offered it as a joke. Edison declined to intervene. I was convinced such a promise could not have been made without his approval. I immediately resigned."

While Tesla's story was not widely publicized, Crowley was aware of it, and also of the rumor that Tesla had merely offered to sell his AC patents to Edison for fifty thousand dollars, which Edison declined. Or had the manager perhaps really made the offer in jest? Not knowing or caring which version was true, Crowley decided not to comment upon it.

"Your feelings are understandable. But we must focus upon stopping the Ferox. Discrediting Edison's spirit phone for its own sake cannot be a consideration. There is too much at stake."

"I understand. So you are still convinced the Ferox intend to use the spirit phone to…invade our space-time, as you put it. Through possession?"

"Perhaps. But possession by a spirit, however powerful, cannot be maintained indefinitely. I think they intend something different, unprecedented. There must be another, secret type of spirit phone, of which I believe Edison's prototype is one. The thing he demonstrated last night is a decoy. Yet Edison seems unaware of it, so the question is: a decoy set by whom?"

"It is a perplexing question. But perhaps the simplest solution would be to publicly state what we have learned, then let the competent authorities take over. I could easily gather reporters from all the major New York newspapers for a surprise announcement."

"Do you think they'd believe us?"

Tesla considered the question for a moment. "No. They would think I was simply jealous of Edison's invention. Or that I had gone insane. I already have a reputation as an eccentric, so talk of evil spirits and possession to the press would only cement it."

Crowley glanced, smiling at the pile of eighteen napkins. "I can't imagine why."

Tesla shrugged. "Still, we could consider it as a last resort. Though I am at a loss as to how we are going to stop these monsters, unless a closer look at a spirit phone will indeed solve our dilemma."

"We have to try. Almost all I know was gained from that one interaction in Tibet, but I'm convinced that if they get through under the right conditions, they'll turn this planet into a monstrous playground of agony and despair. If possession is involved, for all we know they might be invulnerable to physical attack, or have psychical abilities we can't even imagine."

Crowley sipped his coffee, then stared at the cup in his hand with a puzzled expression.

"What's wrong?" asked Tesla.

"Nothing's wrong, exactly. It's just that my chocolate craving is back."

"George! Cocoa for Mr. Crowley, please."

"Right away, sir."

"Thank you. I'm always hungry after an intense use of magick, but this is new."

Crowley's cocoa arrived. Sipping it, he felt a vague memory on the edge of his consciousness, just outside recollection. Something important. A place.

He took another sip. The memory came closer.

"What is it?" asked Tesla. Crowley silenced him with an upraised hand, then drained the cup.

"Wait," he said, closing his eyes. The sound of diners speaking, of cutlery against plates, of the clop-clop of hooves outside—all faded into silence as the restaurant's mingled aromas of bacon, toast, and freshly brewed coffee diminished into the scent of nothing.

◆ ◆ ◆

It is a deep recess of consciousness, an antechamber of the mind. Crowley stands in an empty expanse of white, and before him is a cat, black and sleek with green eyes. Then the instant perception: She is what you need to remember. If you want to hold her, don't chase her. Let her come to you.

In this waking dream, he crouches, then holds out a hand toward the cat. Slowly, she walks over to him. She rubs her face against his hand, then against his shins, purring. She allows Crowley to pick her up. Holding her, he stands up, scratching under her chin as she continues to purr, eyes closed. She begins to change shape, expanding into a place which surrounds Crowley, putting him into its presence and immediacy.

He is here. But what is here? He cannot perceive it properly. It is a large place, and bright. He is confused, annoyed, then angry. Flashes of perception come, then vanish: bright and ugly...get in line...fornication...Fine, I'm leaving...incompetent, lazy swine...Sir, I will call the police...Come on, you daft cow! Sing the line!

Then it is gone, and he stands again in the white expanse, holding the black cat. She fades to nothingness and his arms are empty, and with a pang of loneliness, he misses her.

◆ ◆ ◆

Crowley opened his eyes, the sights and sounds and smells of the dining room rushing back into his perception.

"Are you all right?" asked Tesla.

"Yes. I've remembered something. It's about the teleportation. The time gap. The cocoa is acting as a mnemonic. But it's still very unclear."

Tesla turned in his chair. "George! More cocoa for Mr. Crowley, please!"

The extra cocoa had no discernable effect. The recollection, such as it was, had passed. Crowley related what he could to Tesla.

"I experienced a vague yet intense recollection of a strange, brightly lit place. I had the impression of waiting in a very long line."

"A place you visited but now cannot remember? And you think this relates to the teleportation time gap you mentioned?"

"For now, we have to assume so. But attempting to force the memory will be futile. We'll have to—"

"Crowley, look out!" shouted Tesla as he stood up.

A young man in a cook's uniform had walked to the table, pulled a revolver from his pocket, and pointed it at Crowley's head. His face was contorted in rage. People began running out of the restaurant. Crowley turned around in his seat. "Good morning. I was wondering when you were going to show up."

The cook's trigger finger worked back and forth. He looked down at the gun, the rage in his face mingled with confusion.

"I see you are having difficulty firing that weapon, sir," said Crowley. "I assure you, you will not be able to."

"Someone call the police!" shouted Tesla.

"It is so rude of you to interrupt our breakfast."

"You can't keep this up forever," said the cook. "You're straining, getting weaker."

"We'll see. Do you think killing me would accomplish anything?"

"Yes, actually. You interfering, nasty little maggot."

"Since we're here, perhaps you could enlighten us as to what you and your associates have planned." He closed his eyes and held up his right hand, palm-out in front of him.

The cook laughed. "That's not going to work, maggot, even if you can stop me from snuffing out your worthless life. You only delay the inevitable. We will prevail. Justice will prevail."

"Justice?" asked Crowley. "Could you elucidate?"

The cook ignored the question. Though the restaurant was nearly empty, he looked around and said to no one in particular, "Do you hear that? We're going to get you. We're going to *make—you—suffer*." He uttered the last three words in a low sensuous whisper. "It's going to be fun. It's what you deserve." He turned his head to look out the window. Three policemen were scrambling toward the restaurant, pistols in hand. The cook turned back to Crowley, smiling. "You cannot stop the tide of history. It is inevitable." He grinned as he placed the revolver to the side of his head.

"No!" shouted Tesla. The report sounded throughout the room as the man crumpled to the floor, dead. Next to his head a pool of blood began to form, rapidly expanding outward as the officers rushed in.

Crowley slumped in his chair, and a thin line of blood trickled from his nose. "See? An eventful morning," he said as he wiped it with his napkin.

13

Dust motes traversed the afternoon sunbeams, the light lending a mellow yet cheerful aspect to the police station's fourth-floor meeting room, mitigating its spartan plainness. At the table sat Crowley and Tesla, side by side. Across from them were the two plainclothes officers in their sober charcoal-gray suits: the middle-aged, tough-looking inspector and the sergeant, a somewhat younger man who also appeared formidable, if stocky. Before them sat a document folder, fountain pen, and notepad. The inspector was rearranging the order of some papers from the folder.

Inspector Stern considered for a moment how he was going to approach the questioning. It was an especially unusual situation now that the famous Mr. Tesla was involved. He disliked the deception, which sometimes went with the job, and was sure he could trust Tesla. In the end, he decided to follow the established protocol, bending the rules at whatever point his instincts and common sense told him would warrant it. With a nod to Donnelly, who then picked up the pen, Stern began the session.

"I am Inspector Stern and this is Sergeant Donnelly. Thank you for agreeing to answer questions regarding today's incident. I promise to make this as brief as possible. Sergeant Donnelly will take notes. First, may I ask how you gentlemen became acquainted?"

"I stopped by the Waldorf-Astoria restaurant the other day," Crowley said, "shortly after arriving in New York. I encountered Mr. Tesla and couldn't resist inquiring as to why he had a stack of eighteen napkins on his table." Tesla gave Crowley a dark look but said nothing.

"We got to talking, and it turned out we both had an interest in the arcane and esoteric, despite our somewhat different backgrounds. We've become fast friends, I should say."

"I see," said Stern. "You reside at the Waldorf-Astoria, Mr. Tesla, and the assailant was employed there. Were you acquainted with him?"

"No. He was a cook. I am naturally more familiar with the waiters, maître d', and so on."

"Of course. He was in any case a new employee, hired under the name Owen Howell, which we are now certain was false. Efforts to determine his true identity are underway, though I suspect they will not yield much. Mr. Crowley, you appear to have been the primary target. Had you ever met the assailant before today?"

"No. Perhaps he mistook me for someone who had wronged him in another lifetime."

"An interesting way of putting it, sir. You mentioned an interest in the arcane." Stern produced a small folded sheet of paper from his vest pocket. "I'd like to ask whether you recognize this." He unfolded it and placed it on the table between them.

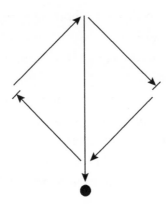

Crowley looked at the paper, his brows knitted in concentration.

"I don't immediately recognize it, though it appears intended as an occult symbol. And yet..."

He picked up the paper and studied it more intently. Then he saw that beyond it, on the window sill behind Stern and Donnelly, was the black cat. Tesla seemed not to have noticed her, which made sense, as Crowley realized she was a manifestation of his own subconscious, an aid to accessing what was hidden. She was translucent, the window just visible through her. She stared at Crowley. A memory drifted into the edge of perception, flashing through his mind in an instant.

◆ ◆ ◆

Staring into the emerald-green eyes of the cat, he sees something within and beyond them: a pair of plump female hands, cupped with the palms upward. Floating between the hands is a small white point of light. He understands that within this light is the secret of the symbol on the paper, and other secrets he must learn. Vital secrets, all of which must be learned by rote.

◆ ◆ ◆

In nearly the same instant it had appeared, the memory vanished, and the cat was gone, and he felt again the craving for chocolate. *Learn the secrets by rote? What the hell does that mean? Never mind that now.* "There is something familiar about this mark," said Crowley. "I feel I have seen it before."

Tesla spoke. "Inspector Stern, why have you shown us this? Is it connected to the incident today?"

Stern and Donnelly exchanged a brief, meaningful look. Stern nodded, then turned to Crowley and Tesla.

"Mr. Tesla, there is something I must tell you, and I request that you keep it in the strictest confidence."

"You mean that you and Sergeant Donnelly are already acquainted with Mr. Crowley. Yes, I have surmised that much."

Crowley laughed. "How?" asked Stern.

"Instinct, perhaps? You do not interact with one another as strangers. I also assume your connection is professional in some way. But why didn't you mention it before?"

"My apologies, Mr. Tesla. It isn't that we don't trust you, and it is obvious that Mr. Crowley vouches for you."

"I do," said Crowley. "And it's nice to finally see where you work, Walter." He looked around the room, his features betraying an expression of mild distaste. "Though it's a bit…unaesthetic."

"It's a police station, Aleister." He addressed Tesla. "Sergeant Donnelly and I have had, as you surmise, certain professional dealings with Mr. Crowley in the past. The only people in this building now aware of that are we four. In circumstances such as these, it is standard procedure to maintain the pretense, at least initially, that Mr. Crowley is a new acquaintance. For reasons of security."

"No offense taken, sir. Please allow me further speculation. You state a professional association with Mr. Crowley, who does not at all strike me as the police officer type. You and he are citizens of different nations. I therefore infer that you and Sergeant Donnelly are intelligence agents of some kind, concurrent with your occupation as police officers. Mr. Crowley acts in an analogous capacity for his own government." He turned to look at his companion. "You are a spy, Mr. Crowley."

Crowley grinned. "Tesla, you are amazing. As for being a spy, well, I'm a bit of a freelancer. Stern and Donnelly are the career men."

Donnelly turned to Stern. "I knew he'd figure it out."

"Mr. Tesla," said Stern, "your reputation for deductive logic and keen instinct is well-deserved. In truth, we mostly conduct regular police work, though occasionally our investigations are of special interest to our federal contacts, in which case we employ somewhat unconventional methods."

Crowley broke in. "Well, back to this symbol. You found it on the cook's body, Stern?"

"Literally. It was tattooed on him."

"Where?"

"The left buttock."

Crowley burst out laughing. "You're joking."

"No. He apparently wished to keep it secret."

"Do you know where it was made?"

"No. We have people inquiring."

"All right," said Crowley. "Also, contrary to my initial assumptions, that fellow was not possessed by a Ferox or anything else. But he was manically insane."

"Ferox?" asked Stern.

Crowley summarized all that he and Tesla had experienced and learned thus far, starting with the teleportation from Tibet. Stern and Donnelly showed no sign of skepticism. *Past professional dealings indeed,* thought Tesla.

"One thing I find puzzling," said Crowley, "is the cook's mention of 'justice' and 'the tide of history.' He sounded like a revolutionary. So far as I know, political ideals play no role among those who seek the *ferox phasma.*"

"I see," said Stern. "So you think today's incident is also linked with Edison's invention. By the way, when reading about the spirit phone demonstration, I noticed that 'Yessar-Smik' is an anagram for 'Kiss my arse.'"

"A more appropriate pseudonym than I'd realized," said Crowley.

Tesla interjected. "We need access to Edison's prototype to confirm its composition. I also need to reconfirm its dimensions and components, such as they are."

It must have been plain to Stern that this would involve a break-in, though he seemed unfazed. "When do you plan to do this?" he asked.

"Tonight," answered Crowley. "After midnight. The Edison laboratory in West Orange."

"I see. Mr. Tesla, you offered a somewhat equivocal appraisal of the device to the press. May I request a more candid assessment?"

"As to its technological facets, I am at a loss to explain how it functions at all. It is a metallic cone next to an electromagnet. There is no reason, based on any scientific principle I know of, why such a thing should allow one to communicate with a next-door neighbor, let alone a spirit in another realm. But somehow it works."

"Yet the effect is less than one might desire."

"Yes," said Crowley. "We think there's another model, one that can connect with the Ferox. That's why we're breaking into Edison's laboratory."

"I see. Before we proceed further: Mr. Tesla, I acknowledge your right to remove yourself from this situation. However, should you choose to remain and investigate matters with us, it is within my power to deputize you."

"I will remain involved, Inspector." He indicated Crowley. "Someone needs to look after this young man. He overexerts himself."

"Very well. Sergeant, if you would brief these gentlemen on the yacht incident."

Donnelly detailed what had been found two nights before on the yacht on the East River, including several subsequent developments. The painted symbol in the yacht's hidden space was identical to that tattooed on the left buttock of both Crowley's would-be assassin and the yacht victim. As for the latter, the place where his hand was severed had inexplicably healed over with no visible scar tissue. Even more puzzling, the fingerprints found on the murder weapon, with which the victim had been stabbed forty-seven times, were identified as those of the man's own missing right hand. No fingerprints other than his were found anywhere on the vessel.

"There was a thunderstorm," said Tesla. "He was trying to use the wire to channel lightning into the room."

"And succeeded, apparently," said Crowley. "Was there any indication he had been struck by lightning?"

"None," answered Donnelly. "The coroner's assessment is that he bled to death."

Crowley set his elbows on the table, chin resting on interlocked hands, and knitted his brows. "Much of this is not conventionally possible. Even if one allows for the rapid postmortem healing of the wound, it seems unlikely a man could stab himself forty-seven times, then with geometrical precision cut off his hand before he dies."

"Yes," answered Donnelly. "Especially as the stab wounds include nine in the back."

Tesla leaned back in his chair, arms crossed. "Might the murderer have wrapped the hand around the knife before departing the scene, taking the hand with him?"

"Analysis of the prints indicates the hand strongly gripped the knife," said Stern.

"In that case, I think the man's right hand was the culprit," said Crowley.

"You're saying the man was murdered by a disembodied hand?" asked Tesla.

"Yes," said Crowley. "Stern, you identified the fingerprints of the missing hand as those of the victim. I assume he had a criminal record. Who was he?"

Stern opened the file and referred to the documents therein. The victim on the yacht was identified as one Marcus Reinecker. Police records made reference to his adoption at age twelve by a German couple who had immigrated in 1881, settling in Little Germany on the Lower East Side. That same year, both stepparents were found dead in their beds, cause of death unknown. Marcus was taken in by the Sisters of Charity orphanage, but ran away at sixteen and joined the Five Points Gang. Though questioned several times on suspicion of burglary and pickpocketing, there were no convictions. He fell out of view in 1890. After his body was found on the yacht and identified, it was determined that since January of 1899 he had been living in modest but comfortable circumstances, again in Little Germany, occupation unknown.

"On the yacht where his body was found, one of our officers recognized his face and recalled an arrest fourteen years ago," said Stern. "We found the arrest record, including his photographs but of course no fingerprints. Once we had a name, we managed to find his current address and dusted for prints."

"Which matched those of the corpse?" asked Crowley.

"Yes. Only one person's fingerprints were found in Reinecker's apartment, so we must assume they're Reinecker's. The left-hand prints we found match those of the corpse's left hand, and the right-hand prints match those found on the knife used to stab him to death."

"Was anything else of interest found in the apartment?" asked Crowley.

"No," said Stern. "Clothing, knickknacks, magazines, a bit of disarray. Just what you'd expect to find in a bachelor's digs."

"You said he'd been adopted," said Tesla. "Who were his real parents?"

"Unknown," said Stern. "We have no information on events before his adoption, including his birthplace and birthdate. No relatives have ever been identified."

"Besides the identical tattoo, is there any evidence that Howell and Reinecker were acquainted?" asked Tesla.

"None that we have found thus far," said Stern.

"That table you described," said Crowley. "With the hole in the top. It seems to have been intended to hold a ceremonial vessel. Was any such thing found? Something metallic?"

"No," said Stern. "However, I have at my disposal certain equipment lacking in the police department. On a splinter from the table, I detected microscopic traces of a silicon-carbon compound, presumably carborundum. And all seven of the metallic elements you've mentioned."

"Could you determine the exact proportions of the chemicals?" asked Tesla.

"Unfortunately, no."

"The same composition as the horn of Edison's spirit phone. Are you going to question him?"

"However sure we are of that, Edison's assistant named only carborundum, gold, and silver before Edison silenced him," said Stern. "It's too tenuous a parallel to question him and thereby jeopardize the secrecy of our investigation. So I will be interested to hear what you find in his laboratory."

"Of course," said Tesla. He turned to Crowley. "Are hands supposed to get severed during *ferox phasma* summonings? Assuming that's what it was."

"My best guess is no. It strikes me as unique to this case."

"And the boat?" Tesla asked Stern. "Was it his?"

"Yes. He had a mooring spot at the Peter Stuyvesant Yacht Club on City Island. But when we attempted to cross-check the boat registry he had presented when applying for membership, we found it was a forgery."

"Could I possibly have a look at Reinecker's body?" asked Crowley. "And that of my would-be assassin?"

"Yes. We can visit the morgue presently. Mr. Tesla, because of your rather prominent public profile, I suggest with all due respect that you not accompany us."

"Agreed, Inspector. I'll wait for you and Crowley in my laboratory. It's just around the corner from here, at 46-48 East Houston Street. The fourth floor."

"We shouldn't be too long," said Crowley. "Stern, might we possibly buy some chocolate on the way?"

14

Crowley ate chocolates from a paper bag as he walked in a slow circle around the corpses, naked and laid out upon their gurneys: Reinecker with the missing hand and dozens of gaping stab wounds, Howell with the bullet hole in the side of his head. Stern stood against the wall nearby. Edward Fitzpatrick, the Chief Coroner, observed at a distance with his two assistants. All three eyed Crowley with undisguised curiosity.

"Viewing cadavers doesn't seem to diminish your appetite, Mr. Crowley," said Fitzpatrick.

Crowley bent to inspect the end of Reinecker's right arm. It was perfectly flat, covered by skin with no scar tissue. Eyes fixed upon it, he spoke. "Doctor, if I may confirm what has been related to me regarding Mr. Reinecker: there was once a hand attached to this arm, and an obvious amputation wound which healed within twenty-four hours after the body was discovered. Is that correct?"

"Yes. And I do hope you'll keep this information strictly confidential, Mr. Crowley."

"Absolutely," he said, not taking his eyes from the body.

"Thank you. Inspector Stern has informed me that you are an expert on arcane belief systems and…occult matters. I must admit, the circumstances of this case are perplexing."

"Might I ask that the cadavers be turned over, Doctor?" At a motion from the coroner, the assistants did as Crowley asked. The nine stab wounds Donnelly had referred to were visible on Reinecker's back. On the left buttock of both corpses was the same symbol Stern had earlier shown to Crowley and Tesla.

"The seat of the problem," said Crowley. "Precisely the same tattoo, but for one difference. I note that while the lines of Mr. Howell's tattoo are sharp and distinct, those of Mr. Reinecker are somewhat thicker and apparently faded."

"Yes," said Stern. "The condition of Reinecker's tattoo indicates he received it before he was fully grown, the tattoo slightly distorting with bodily growth. Assuming his recorded age of thirty is accurate, it was about fifteen years ago at the latest. Howell's reported age on his employment application was twenty-one, which seems about right, so his tattoo was done more recently."

"I see." Crowley requested a short interval of silence, during which he stood, eyes closed and right hand outstretched, before each cadaver in turn. The assistants exchanged a brief expression of incredulity. After a minute, Crowley opened his eyes and declared his examination complete.

Fitzpatrick then ordered the assistants to return the bodies to the vault, noting that it was important to keep the remains as cool as possible, and that these would need to go to Potter's Field soon. They wheeled the gurneys into an adjacent room. Soon returning, they were dismissed.

"Potter's Field. Then no one has claimed them as relatives," said Crowley.

"That's correct." Fitzpatrick glanced over his shoulder to make sure the assistants had gone. "And there is something else."

Stern and Crowley exchanged a glance. "Which is?" asked Stern.

"You'll think I've gone mad, Walter, but…you may recall an incident from about three years ago. I was called in by the police to question an armed robbery culprit who was on the verge of death from gunshot wounds."

"Yes. It was just before I took over Homicide. I wasn't on the case, but I remember. The Bank of New Amsterdam. In a struggle for his gun, the robber shot the bank president, then shot himself."

"Yes. I went to the hospital to question him. He said he had a wife and child and that poverty had compelled him to attempt the robbery. But he refused to give any information about his identity except that he had been born in the West. He was obviously near death, but when I asked if he required the services of a priest or minister, he answered, 'I have a religion, but it is a peculiar one; not many persons would believe in it. I am sure no priest or minister would.'"

"Did this man have the same tattoo on his backside?" asked Stern.

"It's more than that. Yes, he had the tattoo, and in the same place. But Walter…it was the same man."

"What are you saying?"

"The man who shot the bank president and himself and then died of his wounds in 1896. The man you found dead on that boat. Reinecker. It's the same man. Or his twin brother, at any rate."

"The latter would seem more likely, Doctor," said Crowley. "I know of no way a dead body can be resurrected. At least none that would make the person appear normal. Nor eliminate the scars of a gunshot wound."

"Nor eliminate the scar of an amputated hand?" asked Fitzpatrick.

"We have positively identified the victim as Marcus Reinecker," said Stern. "There is no record that he ever had siblings, including an identical twin brother. Are you sure about this, Ed?"

"Positive, Walt. I remember him. And a twin, or even a close relative, would be the more logical explanation. And yet…I know it seems irrational, but somehow it *feels* to me like he's the same man."

Stern shook his hand. "All right, Ed. Thanks. We'll look into it. And I promise, mum's the word. Just one more thing." He pulled a small leather case from his valise. "Could I possibly get a blood sample from each cadaver? Strictly off the record."

15

It was about half an hour on foot to Tesla's laboratory, and Crowley was tired after the expenditure of magickal energy in the morgue. Despite this, he wanted to walk as a way to clarify his thoughts, and Stern agreed.

Crowley took a chocolate out of his bag every so often and ate. Vague and fragmentary images of the ugly, brightly lit place and the small floating point of light played at the edges of his recollection. Along the streets, the ubiquitous horse-drawn wagons and hansom cabs vied for space with bicycles and the occasional automobile.

"Why take the blood?" asked Crowley. "No blood analyses at the morgue?"

"I dislike the policy, but they often don't," said Stern as they turned from Mulberry onto East Houston Street in the late summer twilight. "It's often viewed as a wasted effort if the cause of death seems obvious. But I have a hunch, and there is a particular test I want to perform. It includes dissolving the sample in a strong acid, then inserting a copper strip, followed by a spectral analysis using X-rays."

Crowley knew little of X-rays except that they had been discovered by a German scientist a few years before and you could use them to see through things. "I'll take your word for it. But why not just ask Fitzpatrick to do it?"

"He seems a bit overwhelmed. And I would prefer to do it myself, just to be sure. So, what do you think so far?"

"We're in over our heads, Walter. Something big and nasty is materializing."

"Do you find Fitzpatrick's story plausible?"

"Marcus Reinecker coming back from the dead? A twin brother seems more likely. Still, the removal of the hand was done by powerful magick.

I'll explain in more detail once we meet Tesla. I'm rather curious to see his laboratory."

"So am I. By the way, how are your people treating you?"

"Negligently, at the moment. And yours?"

"Some unsettling changes. Recently, replies to my communiqués take longer, even urgent ones. And I now have counterparts around the country. They want us numerous and localized. 'Compartmentalization,' they call it."

"That sounds positively annoying."

They arrived at the seven-story brick building which housed Tesla's laboratory. A ghostly luminescence shone through the fourth-floor windows. Entering, they climbed the stairs. Crowley was slightly out of breath by the time they got to Tesla's door. "Come in," came Tesla's voice at Stern's knock.

The high-ceilinged room was lit by large, globular lights. Stern immediately recognized these as Tesla's gas-filled, phosphor-coated electric lamps, which operated with no wires or filaments. He could also identify many of the various items arrayed about the space, such as the several models of Tesla's famous alternating current motor, as well as the wire-wrapped poles topped with metallic spheres, designed to transmit power wirelessly. But to Stern there was mystery here as well, odd-looking devices the functions of which even he, with his technical expertise, could only guess at. As someone well-versed in the application of technology rather than its creation, he felt a bit out of his depth. Crowley simply looked around with a smile and said, "Remarkable."

"Hello," said Tesla. "Welcome. Have a seat." He motioned to a table and chairs set up before a strange-looking coil of wire about ten feet in diameter, set within a large square frame. His manner was cordial yet imperious, like that of a man holding court.

Crowley thanked him, settling himself into one of the chairs. Stern followed suit.

"No lab assistants?" asked Stern.

"I have a couple," said Tesla as he sat down to join them, "but I assumed we would need privacy, so I gave them the rest of the day off. So, what did you learn at the morgue?"

Crowley explained what he and Stern had seen and what Dr. Fitzpatrick had told them.

"Born in the West. A peculiar religion. Hmm," mused Tesla.

"But no information was obtained beyond those statements, despite a thorough investigation," said Stern. "No family of his were ever identified. I suppose if these Ferox are worshipped, that could qualify as a kind of religion."

"They are worshipped, in a sense, by some," said Crowley.

"And your appraisal of the two bodies? Of Reinecker's missing hand and lack of scar tissue?" asked Tesla.

"As for Howell," said Crowley, "I could ascertain nothing beyond the obvious fact that he is dead. Reinecker is another matter. His hand was not cut off by a blade. It was removed by magickal means. I detected a totality of separation."

"What do you mean?" asked Stern. "Of course the hand was completely separated."

"That's not what I mean," answered Crowley. "Yes, there was a complete physical separation of the hand from the body. But beyond that, the hand has become a separate entity, capable of independent action."

"You've mentioned this before. You think there is a living, disembodied hand moving around out there somewhere?" asked Tesla, horrified distaste on his features.

"Yes. And I'm now even more convinced that the hand is what killed Reinecker once it was separated. A previously integral part of the body, separated from the whole, capable of independent and destructive action with no consequence to itself. This is the key. Imagine your hand is capable of thought and decides to kill you. If it has any sense of self-preservation, it will hesitate, as murdering the rest of the physical body will also result in its own death."

"You mean that Reinecker somehow arranged a transfer of consciousness into his hand?"

"Yes, most likely his own consciousness," said Crowley. "Yet this ritual—the summoning of a *ferox phasma*—and this apparent effect do not seem to match up."

"Reinecker has become a living hand," said Tesla with a shudder.

Crowley smiled at him. "You're looking a tad green, Tesla."

"Aleister," said Stern, "you said this totality of separation is the key. The key to what?"

"To the Ferox's plan. One thing I have learned is that every soul is ultimately connected, all elements of a single universal mind. Thus there are consequences to committing evil which could be called a kind of justice, what the Hindus call karma. To hate another is to hate oneself. To rob, cheat, rape, torture, or murder is ultimately to do so to oneself. It all comes back to you. This is how we learn. It's a slow process. But what if you could *cancel* it? What if you could find a way to permanently and totally separate yourself from the collective soul? Just as Reinecker, his consciousness transferred to his hand, could destroy his own body with impunity."

"You think the Ferox plan to separate themselves from this...collective soul," said Tesla.

"Yes. If they can accomplish this, they can then do whatever they wish with no consequences to themselves, ever. And 'whatever they wish' is decidedly unpleasant."

Tesla, who had turned a shade paler, said, "Then we must do whatever we can. Whatever is necessary."

"Yes," said Crowley. He ate another piece of chocolate from the paper bag, then said, "And we need to delay getting into Edison's lab."

"Yes," said Tesla. "You are much too exhausted to do any such thing, let us—"

"No," said Crowley. "Edison's lab will have to wait, but we still need to go out. I'm getting closer to discovering what happened in the time gap while teleporting from Tibet to your apartment. My chocolate craving is a mnemonic. It's allowed me to remember something important. The place. I think it's here in Manhattan."

"Where?" asked Tesla.

"The place we made our astral journey to. That corner in Tenderloin with the brothel. I need to visit it."

"Astrally?" asked Stern.

"Physically."

"Not to patronize the brothel, I assume."

"No," he said in exasperation. "Tesla, we need to go. Now. It's important. I don't yet know why, but it's vital."

"All right," said Tesla. "We will go there. But not now. First, let us get something to eat. Then you need to sleep, and we will go there in the morning."

"Tesla—"

"Aleister. I am not a physician, but it is plain that you are on the point of collapse. I know time is of the essence, but it is also true that without some rest and nourishment you will be worse than useless in our enterprise. I insist."

"He's right, Aleister."

Crowley knew they were right. Ever since the attack in Tibet, he had been experiencing waves of fatigue, the use of magick requiring a gradually greater effort. He wanted to go to the spot in Tenderloin as soon as possible, but his weariness overcame him.

"All right, fellows," Crowley said. He then crossed his arms on the table, set his head upon them, and was immediately fast asleep.

16

August 30th, 1899

It felt strange for Tesla to be physically standing in a place he had previously visited as a "ghost," and his first impression was of warm, humid air rank with the odors of stale beer and horse manure, the latter visible in various places on the street.

He and Crowley stood in the same spot as during their astral journey, though instead of the wee hours of the morning, it was just after 10:00 a.m. The gaslights stood unlit. Horse-drawn carriages and the occasional motorcar traversed the street. Pedestrians, some women but mostly men in work clothes and flatcaps, walked the sidewalks. Among these were the native-born, both black and white, though it was a largely Irish area with the occasional Italian, Greek, or Pole. The proverbial melting pot of immigrants and the children of immigrants.

A small group of boys, clothing frayed and dirty, went by, pulling a large cart filled with rags. Tesla recalled the newsboys' strike that had ended in a compromise on pay just four weeks previously. The boys and girls who sold papers for a pittance were largely from immigrant families, including many Eastern Europeans, like Tesla himself. While he could not help taking pride in his accomplishments, at that moment he also reflected that he was in many ways fortunate.

Crowley was refreshed from ten hours of sleep on a cot Tesla and Stern had carried him to, then a hearty breakfast of ham and three eggs over easy at the Waldorf-Astoria. He seemed in good spirits. It was Wednesday morning, and

Stern had routine police duties to attend to, though he had asked the two men to keep him appraised of developments.

"A lovely morning! You were right, Tesla. It's amazing what a bit of rest and a proper meal can do." Crowley was willing to go alone, but Tesla was curious to see the result of this vaguely defined mission. Now he was beginning to regret his decision.

"I just realized," said Tesla, "that when we traveled here in the astral state, I couldn't smell anything."

"You could have, but it takes some training."

"I see. Well, I don't wish to inconvenience you, but may we make this as brief as possible? I am somewhat hypersensitive to odors, and this part of town is unpleasant. In an olfactory sort of way. They don't seem to clear the manure here so often."

"Yes. One moment, please." Crowley closed his eyes.

After a minute, he opened his eyes and looked at Tesla with a slightly confused expression. "There's supposed to be a train station here."

"What are you talking about?"

"With an entrance leading underground, there." He pointed across the street. "I was waiting in line, annoyed at some kind of delay. It happened during the teleportation from Tibet to your apartment."

"You're not making sense. There has never been a train station here, even assuming you could be at one during a teleportation."

"You will recall that the apparent passage of time when we arrived here astrally was longer than its in-physical passage. Past, present, and future are all conterminous, and ultimately nonexistent."

"Your reasoning seems confused. We didn't physically teleport here the other night, did we? And even if you were somehow at a railway station, there is obviously none here. You're not thinking of Grand Central Depot?"

"No. That's north of here, on Forty-Second Street, is it not? No, it was here. Yet it wasn't." He closed his eyes again, putting his fingers to his temples.

"Have you ever read *The Time Machine* by H.G. Wells?" asked Tesla. "If all time is truly conterminous, then perhaps your experience took place in a different time."

Crowley opened his eyes and turned to his companion. "Mr. Tesla, you put me to shame. It should have been obvious to me."

Tesla shrugged. "Just a hypothesis. And your faculties have been under strain recently."

"You are too kind, sir. But yes, they have been. The madman in the restaurant was right. I am growing weaker somehow, albeit slowly. I don't know why."

"Perhaps you just need more rest," said Tesla.

"If there is time. Speaking of which, as you point out, if there has never been a railway station here, that can only mean one thing."

"That the railway station you refer to existed—or rather will exist—in the future?"

"Yes. Are there any construction plans you know of?"

"No, but the railroad barons are ruthless in their desire to expand. So you believe you traveled into the future during the teleportation process?"

Crowley looked distracted. "It's hard to say. I feel that it was an actual train station, and yet it was not."

"I am afraid you have lost me. An illusory railway station?"

"Something like that."

Tesla couldn't quite see what Crowley was driving at, but wishing to escape the unpleasant odors of this place, he decided to let the matter drop for now. "Well, let's return, shall we?" he urged. They began to walk along Thirty-Second Street, on the lookout for a cab.

"You said attempting to force the memory to return would be fruitless," said Tesla, "yet we must somehow elicit it. Perhaps you should sleep tonight instead of going spirit phone hunting. We can go to West Orange tomorrow night."

"No, it needs to be tonight. Measures to safeguard the prototype may become stricter because of the demonstration at Columbia. And to save you the trouble of building a spirit phone, I propose we conduct a test of the prototype."

"I was afraid you would say that. It means staying longer in Edison's laboratory, increasing the risk of discovery."

"Surely a man of your technical genius can ensure we proceed undetected."

"You're trying to manipulate me by appealing to my vanity."

"Yes." Crowley grinned.

17

Having taken the train into Orange, they made their way into West Orange and now walked along the town's main boulevard, their path illuminated by electric streetlights. It was just after 11:30 p.m. Tesla carried a bulky suitcase, Crowley a valise.

It was a peaceful-looking community of obvious affluence with well-maintained, handsome buildings. The four Oranges of New Jersey—South, East, West, and just plain Orange, from which the railway service commenced—served as a refuge from the crowding, crime, and grime of more urban locales. At least for those, such as Thomas Edison, who could afford to live there.

Crowley asked Tesla if there might be a saloon in town. There was. Under Tesla's subdued protests, they went. He knew the place but had never been inside, having long doubted the cleanliness of the typical drinking establishment. He also advised against having a drink in such circumstances, but Crowley insisted that having just one would do no harm, and they had in any case decided to wait until well after midnight to begin their task. And besides, he was hungry.

The saloon was large and plush, the sort of place anyone but a Temperance Unionist would deem respectable. There were few customers. A young man in shirtsleeves played ragtime on a piano. The manager invited them to sit where they pleased, adding in a lower voice that there were games of chance in the back, if they were so inclined. Before Crowley could answer, Tesla declined politely but emphatically.

They chose a table. Tesla placed the suitcase underneath it and sat facing away from the door to the gambling room.

Crowley's eyes locked on to Tesla's as he sat down. "Ah, I see now," he said.

"What?" asked Tesla in a tone of irritation.

"You've never come in here because you are drawn toward gambling but strive to resist the temptation."

"Are you reading my mind?"

"Not at all. Just a bit of basic psychology and common sense. What were you doing in this town, anyway? It's close to the city, and pleasant enough, but it seems a bit provincial for your tastes. You weren't here working for Edison, I assume."

"A few years ago, there was a fire in my laboratory. Not the one I have now, a different place. Virtually everything—my life's work—was destroyed."

"Yes. I recall reading about it."

"Yes. The depression I experienced was beyond description. But at least no one was hurt. So I needed a place to work, to conduct experiments. Edison let me use his laboratory here. He lets many experimenters use the place, but…"

"Due to your rivalry, he might have said no."

"But he didn't. I can never forgive him for the shabby way he treated me as his employee, but I can never repay him for the kindness he showed me when I needed it the most."

A young blonde woman came up with a pad and pencil. "What can I get you gentlemen?" she asked, smiling. She was quite beautiful.

Crowley placed a hand over his heart. "Eyes bluer than the Mediterranean in summer. Fortune has blessed us to encounter the most enchanting waitress in the state of New Jersey." Through her laughter he asked, "I don't suppose you have any ale?"

"I'm sorry, lager only, sir."

"Ah, the insidious Teutonic influence upon your nation."

"I beg your pardon, sir," she said in mock offense. "My grandparents came to this country from Saxony."

"And they are doubtless people of exceptional quality to have such a charming granddaughter." The girl blushed, her smile growing broader. "Lager will be fine. What's yours, Uncle Nicky?"

"A double shot of bourbon, please."

"And…" Crowley looked at the blackboard behind the bar. "…shepherd's pie, please. Uncle Nicky?"

"No food for me, thank you."

"Yes, sir. I'll get your drinks first." She walked away, her glance lingering on Crowley for a second. Crowley turned, smiling at Tesla.

"Let me guess," said Crowley. "You're worried about microbes."

"Yes. I hesitate to even drink here, but the bourbon's alcohol content should have an antiseptic effect. And must you act the rake? We're on a serious mission here."

"Just making conversation. I assumed she was German and thought I'd get a rise out of her."

"'Uncle Nicky?'"

"Well," he said, then lowered his voice. "I think 'Nikola' or 'Mr. Tesla' might be a bit imprudent under the circumstances." He looked at the bar for a moment, then back at Tesla. "Shall I ask her to bring eighteen napkins?"

Tesla scowled but said nothing. The girl came back with their drinks.

"Have you actually seen the Mediterranean in summer?" she asked Crowley.

"Indeed I have."

"I want to go someday. I'm especially interested in the Romano-Carthaginian rivalry."

"I think you're a bit late," said Crowley. "It's already been settled."

"You're quite the humorist, sir. I mean I've won a scholarship to study classical literature at Barnard College in the fall. Virgil's *Aeneid* is my favorite poem."

"Congratulations. But aren't you repelled by all the violence?"

"I've heard no such rumors about the college, sir."

"Touché! I mean the poem, of course."

She bent closer and whispered in Crowley's ear. "It's not nearly as violent as what's going to happen to you two." She straightened up and said, matter-of-fact, "I'd love to take you both into the back and fuck you and then eat you alive, like a praying mantis does when she mates."

The color had drained from Tesla's face. Crowley looked flabbergasted.

"What's wrong, Mr. Charming? Wondering why you couldn't detect me? It's because you're growing weaker as we grow stronger. You're finished."

"Why didn't you try to kill us?" asked Crowley. "You had the drop on us."

"Why bother? It doesn't matter. We've already won. I'll get your shepherd's pie."

"You're not possessed either," said Crowley as she turned away. "You're just insane. Like the chap at the Waldorf."

She turned back to him. "True illumination is condemned as insanity by the ignorant."

"I'm not convinced you're telling the truth. Perhaps you could show everyone in the room your tattoo so we can all be certain."

She grimaced. "You pig."

"Why ally yourself with ultimate evil?" asked Tesla.

"Evil? Evil is the world as it is. A new era of justice has dawned. Now that the machine is made, nothing can stop it."

Justice? Again? Crowley thought as he and Tesla exchanged a glance.

"Do you realize what you're dabbling in?" Crowley asked. "You think you'll simply start studying the classics at Barnard come autumn? The things you are calling forth will kill you. Right away, if you're lucky."

"You're lying. The world will become a paradise. It will be the end of prejudice and inequity."

"In a sense, I agree," said Crowley. "Humanity will be tormented, tortured, and murdered on a basis of full equality."

She turned away with a contemptuous look and walked toward the bar.

"She's not possessed?" asked Tesla. "You're sure?"

"Yes. She's just insane. I hope my pie hasn't gotten cold."

"How can you eat at a time like this?"

Crowley shrugged. "I'm hungry."

"If she knows our plan, she could tell the police."

"She won't. You heard what she said. And now that she has my attention, I can see it in her mind. She's been ordered not to interfere with us."

"Ordered? By whom? Why?"

"Unknown. It's hard to get anything detailed." He eyed the girl, who was standing by the bar waiting for the pie. "But, just in case…"

Crowley blew her a kiss with his right hand while the fingers of his left made a series of rapid and complicated taps on the table. The girl responded with an amused smile, looking confused for barely a second, then smiled again.

"What was that?" whispered Tesla.

"I have affected her memory. As soon as she leaves here, she will forget having encountered us. At least for a couple of days." He put his fingers to his temples and winced. "But it's getting harder to do this stuff. The difficulty comes and goes."

The girl arrived and placed the pie before Crowley. "Here you are, sir," she said as though the previous conversation had never taken place.

"Thank you. How much do we owe you?"

"Thirty cents, please."

Crowley handed her a half-dollar coin and said, "Keep the change."

"Thank you." She placed the coin in a pocket of her apron. Briefly glancing under the table, she said to Tesla, "Your stupid toys won't do you any good." Then, bending down and placing her face next to Crowley's, she whispered, "Hey, handsome, have you asked your friend why he's leery around gambling places? It's an interesting story." She stood up and said, "Good evening, gentlemen." She smiled and turned away.

Tesla looked at the girl as she walked off, then turned to Crowley. "Are you sure the pie's not—" Crowley held up a hand to silence him. The other hand was hovering about two inches above the pie.

"No. It's not poisoned." He dug in with relish. "Beef, not lamb. This is a cottage pie. Still, it's not bad."

"You amaze me, Mr. Crowley. Again."

18

August 31st, 1899

They had determined no plan as to how they would pass the time prior to entering Edison's laboratory. On an unspoken agreement, they simply stayed in the saloon, drinking coffee—which Tesla generally avoided—and talking. A prominent topic of conversation was their puzzlement over the girl's apparently utopian objective in summoning the *ferox phasma*. The cook in the Waldorf, however deranged, seemed to have had a similar motive.

She had soon finished her shift and gone home. Following her was out of the question. She could simply scream that they were mashers and they would be apprehended, and then they would have to explain why Nikola Tesla and a young Englishman were in West Orange, New Jersey stalking an innocent young girl.

After his last cup of coffee, Crowley pulled a small flask from his pocket and took a long draught.

"What was that?" asked Tesla as Crowley put away the flask.

"Vin Mariani. Just a bit of a tonic to sustain me for the work ahead."

"Just a bit of cocaine-laced wine, you mean. Fine, just as long as you are not intoxicated."

"I am not, sir. Let us depart."

It was just after one thirty in the morning as they left the saloon. They walked along the main street, their way again illuminated by the incandescent streetlights.

"I'm not surprised they've electrified the place, seeing as Edison has his lab here," said Crowley. He pulled a brown paper bag from his valise. "So, you remember how to get there?"

"Of course. Chocolates again?"

"Chocolate-covered raisins," said Crowley between mouthfuls. He offered some to Tesla, who declined.

After a short while, Tesla said, "The lab is not far ahead. Let us take a temporary detour." He led Crowley off the street into a wooded area, and soon the night became darker as a dense canopy of branches covered their way. The glow of the streetlights could still be seen between the trees.

Tesla had not explained to Crowley the details of how he would help ease their entry into the laboratory. He silently admitted that this was due not so much to time constraints as to ego. After all Crowley had shown him, he wanted to spring some surprises of his own.

Placing the suitcase on the ground, he opened it. Inside was a short metallic pole with a metal ball placed at one end and a flat panel serving as a platform on the other. It was attached by wires to a battery. Tesla stood the pole up.

"That looks familiar," said Crowley.

"Yes," said Tesla. "There are several larger versions in my laboratory. I've made a few adjustments to this one. There should be enough power for our purposes. You're sure you can get the door open?"

"Positive."

"Very well. I do not know exactly how long the effect will last, but it should be sufficient for us to complete our task." He flipped a switch on the panel and the pole began to hum.

"What's going to happen?"

"You'll see." They produced gloves from their pockets and put them on.

After about a minute, the woods were suddenly darker. Crowley looked toward the street. "The streetlights are out."

"Yes."

"What did you just do?"

"I have blown out the town's powerhouse," said Tesla as he closed the suitcase and picked it up. "And disabled Edison's alarm system and emergency generator. Let's go."

They soon arrived at the site of Edison's laboratory, a large complex of red brick buildings barely visible in the darkness, surrounded by chain-link fencing. The main gate stood between pillars of brick, with a guardhouse on the left. From the windows shone the beam of a bull's-eye lantern. No street traffic or pedestrians were in evidence.

Skirting the gate, they walked rapidly along the right side of the complex until they came to the back of the long three-story main building, its windows black like empty sockets. Crowley scaled the chain-link fence to drop down on the other side. With a small grunt, Tesla managed to throw the suitcase over to be caught by Crowley, who nearly fell over with the weight of impact. Then Tesla scaled the fence himself.

They walked to the back entrance. Crowley pulled a small leather case from his inside pocket. From within the case, he took two long, thin metal pins. Kneeling, he inserted them into the door's keyhole. Within a minute, there came from the lock a barely audible click.

Crowley turned to Tesla, nodded, and opened the door. Tesla went in first, then Crowley, who closed the door behind him.

Tesla pulled two small metal tubes from an inside pocket and handed one to Crowley. With the flip of a switch, from each came a steady beam of light, sufficient to see by. Crowley had read that the recently invented flashlight produced a weak light lasting only seconds.

"Better than the ones you can usually buy," whispered Crowley.

"Of course," replied Tesla. "Come on. Edison's office is upstairs."

Until Edison's patent was awarded and full mass production could commence elsewhere, under license, the first spirit phones for the market were almost certainly being made in another part of the complex. But for now, at least, that was of no importance. Their objective tonight was the prototype.

They had agreed it would most likely be kept locked inside a drawer of Edison's desk. To access the stairs, they walked through the high-ceilinged room past shelves and tables filled with countless pieces of technology, large and small: cables, storage batteries, incandescent lamps, phonographs in various states of disassembly, shelves filled with countless jars of chemicals, various hand tools, and more. They came to the stairs. A painted wooden sign stated:

```
┌─────────────────────────────┐
│           NOTICE            │
│      No Person Other Than   │
│      2nd Floor Employees    │
│     Are Allowed Admittance  │
│       To This Department    │
│        Except On Business   │
└─────────────────────────────┘
```

"Upstairs is where the interesting stuff happens," said Crowley.

"Yes. Let's go." The stairs creaked as they ascended, their way illuminated by the beams of the flashlights.

Crowley easily picked the lock on Edison's office door. They entered. A roll-top desk stood at the far end of the room. Crowley approached it, then closed his eyes, head down, with his left hand palm-outward.

He opened his eyes. "Found it. Bottom left." Then he began to search his pockets and said, "Damn."

"What's the matter?"

"I left my bag of chocolate raisins in my valise in the woods. Do you have any sweets on you, by any chance?"

"No! For God's sake, man, you can have chocolate later. Get on with it."

"All right. Sorry."

Crowley knelt and inserted the pins into the drawer lock. In a few seconds, he had it open. From within it he removed a rolled-up tube of paper and placed it on the desk. "Plans, apparently," he remarked. This was followed by a pine-wood box with a hinged top. The last item was a notebook with the handwritten title *Spirit Phone Model SP-1*.

"If there were only a way to copy this quickly," said Crowley.

"No need," answered Tesla. He handed his flashlight to Crowley. "Might I ask you to focus both beams on the notebook?" Tesla began turning the pages at such a pace that Crowley could barely make out any text. He soon placed the notebook on Edison's desk and briefly perused the plans, upon which were drawn top and side views of the spirit phone with various notes.

"All right," said Tesla.

"All right? You might have spent five seconds per page. You've memorized it?"

"More or less. It's more like a diary than a research record. Some interesting revelations. I can give you the details later."

"You amaze me, Mr. Tesla. Again."

Tesla smiled. "Let's open the box."

Crowley opened the top. They looked inside.

"This is it," said Tesla. "The one at Columbia wasn't housed in a box, but other than that, it appears identical."

"So we're going to try it out?"

"In a moment. Let us proceed according to plan."

Tesla reached into an inside pocket and pulled out a small paint scraper and a white handkerchief. He scraped the inside of the spirit phone's horn three times, then with the handkerchief he wiped the place he had scraped six times. Placing the scraper back in his pocket, he then folded up the handkerchief carefully. Crowley had taken out a small leather drawstring pouch and was holding it open. Tesla placed the handkerchief inside the pouch. Crowley closed it and placed it in his pocket.

Tesla opened his suitcase and extracted what appeared to be an oblong wooden box with a toggle switch and three round metal plates in a row at the top. Each plate had a single screw attached at one side. He set the device on the floor and from each of its corners pulled up thin, telescoping strands of metal. Antennae, he called them, noting that they were made of aluminum.

"Is this a battery?" asked Crowley.

"Among other things. Despite the power outage, it can draw power wirelessly from my device in the woods."

Reaching into the suitcase again, Tesla took out a flat sheet of copper mesh. This he unfolded into a cage-like cube somewhat larger than the spirit phone, its top side forming a hinged door. Placing the hollow cube on Edison's desk, he opened its top and placed the spirit phone inside.

He then removed from the suitcase a small wooden box with a single switch and two copper hooks, with a coiled up electrical cord ending in a three-pronged plug the like of which Crowley had never seen. He hooked the device onto one side of the copper cage and inserted the cord into a socket of the box on the floor, revealed by rotating one of the round plates on its screw.

"So this is the Faraday cage," said Crowley.

"Yes," said Tesla. "Invented by your countryman. Are you ready to make the call?"

"Please do the honors, sir. A non-mage might be a better test of its capabilities."

"Very well." Tesla flipped the switch on the battery, then switched on the spirit phone. The horn hummed as the blue aura began to envelop it.

"Michael Faraday, scientist of great renown," said Tesla. "I wish to speak with you."

This was the most difficult way to use the device, according to Edison, and they had decided to test its limits. Faraday had passed away thirty-two years before, and neither Crowley nor Tesla had ever met him.

From the spirit phone came no sound but its low electrical hum.

"Michael Faraday, I seek the boon of your wisdom and knowledge."

Still no voice was heard.

"Nothing is happening," said Tesla.

"Try it once more."

"Michael Faraday, I request to speak with you."

Again, nothing.

"Maybe you should try it," said Tesla.

"All right. Michael Faraday, scientist of great renown, I crave an audience."

"Who summons me?" came a voice from the horn, in English. It was male and deep, its accent British, though with the same tinny effect as that heard at Columbia. Tesla immediately shut the top of the cage, then flipped the switch on the box attached to its side.

"My name," said Crowley, "is not so important. However, I would like to confirm, if possible, whether I am actually speaking to Michael Faraday, or rather to his immortal soul."

"What have you done?" said the voice, its tinge of panic just discernible.

"We have made it a bit difficult for you to leave," said Tesla. "You are now confined within a charged copper cage, grounded to keep the electrical field inside."

"Quite an irony, is it not?" said Crowley. "Trapped within your own invention. Assuming, of course, that you really are the spirit of Michael Faraday."

"You filthy bastards! I'll kill you both!" screamed a high-pitched female voice from the spirit phone. At least it had the quality of a scream, but its volume was low. The accent was now American.

Tesla and Crowley looked at each other, then back at the spirit phone. "Well, it would seem," said Crowley, "that you are not Mr. Faraday after all."

"Wait," she said. "I recognize you. You're that mage." The last word carried unmistakable mockery. "I've been told about you and your friend. You think you're so clever, but we're going to rip you both to pieces. You just wait. Little turds."

"Madam," said Crowley. "Such unladylike language."

"It won't be ladylike when I rip your balls off either, you devious little shit!"

Crowley produced a folded-up sheet of paper from within his vest pocket, unfolded it, and placed it upon the desk. On the paper was written a series of block letters within the squares of a grid.

M	A	A	B	H	A	D
A						
A						
B						
H						
A						
D						

He then intoned, "Lirion, I seek your aid, and command you to appear before me now."

In the next instant, a young woman stood before Crowley. She was tall with fair skin and aquiline features. Her auburn hair was tied at the top, her green eyes inquisitive. She was dressed stylishly in a white shirtwaist with leg-of-mutton sleeves and a dark green skirt.

"You called me, sir?" she asked.

"Yes." He indicated the spirit phone, still glowing blue. "There is an entity currently trapped within this device. I believe she—or it—is involved in a plan which imperils the human race. I wish you to discover as much as you can about its identity and the details of its intentions."

"So you're a demon," said Tesla in undisguised wonder.

She regarded him briefly. "I am." Then she addressed Crowley again. "I am bound to obey you, as one of your familiars. However, the cage placed around this device will make it difficult for me to interrogate the entity."

"Ha!" cried the voice from the spirit phone. "Demon bitch, serving your mage. What other little favors do you do for him, sweetie?" Lirion's only response was a look of amused contempt.

Crowley said, "The cage is necessary to isolate it, and we expect it will not hold indefinitely. This is your specialty, Lirion. Just do the best you can."

"Very well," she replied. Turning to the spirit phone, she closed her eyes, head inclined, and raised her right hand, palm outward.

"Get out of me, you dirty little whore!" screeched the woman's voice. Lirion, brows knitted, slowly closed her palm into a fist. From the spirit phone came a long, agonized scream, which grew louder, then stopped, as if a needle had been lifted from a phonograph.

Lirion opened her eyes. "She has escaped," she said.

"Did you discover anything?" asked Crowley.

"Not very much, I'm afraid," she replied. "She has a…I believe the current human term is 'psychopathic personality.' Her intentions toward you and your companion are of an extremely violent nature."

"You don't say."

"She is, at least potentially, very powerful. Within the astral realm, she is limited in mobility, but her intention is to…" Lirion paused to consider her words. "…enter this realm physically. This entails what is commonly termed reincarnation. However, that is not her intention. Yet she wishes to enter this space-time physically. It is a contradiction. I do not understand."

"There is possession."

"Yes, but as you are aware, possession is both difficult and temporary. I could not tell if her intentions included such, but her desire is a permanent transformation into physical earth life."

"You mean she wants to become human?" asked Crowley.

"She is human. In terms of space-time on earth, I could not precisely determine her previous life span and locale. But I did perceive a name: Katie Bender."

"Anything else?"

"Yes. She is convinced she will become extremely powerful upon attaining physicality here, and able to wreak destruction and misery upon the human race. And she is very eager to do so. That is all."

"I see. Thank you, Lirion. You're dismissed."

With a nod, she vanished.

For a long moment, they said nothing. Then Crowley spoke.

"I wanted to believe these creatures were nonhuman entities of some kind. But no. The Ferox are people. Perhaps the logical extension of human evil. Is there any hope for us? Humanity, I mean."

Tesla regarded the spirit phone for a moment, then turned to Crowley. "I believe there is. These monsters—for that is truly what they are—represent the lowest depths to which man can sink. But because there is a depth, there is also a height. Let's show these bastards what we're made of."

Crowley had to smile at his companion's unusual lapse into the vernacular. He nodded and said, "All right."

"But first, let's put things back the way they were and get out before the power comes back on." He switched off the charge to the Faraday cage and said, "Bender. That name is familiar."

"I need some chocolate."

19

Typing quickly was not among Tesla's skills, and the going was slow as he transcribed the essentials of Edison's notebook from memory, occasionally stopping to unjam keys. As the typewriter's clacking continued, Crowley ate chocolate and browsed around the laboratory.

The horn scrapings within their pouch sat on a table amid an array of equipment Crowley found interesting, if puzzling: a kind of box with wires, dials, and a translucent screen, with a device he took to be a microscope. Tesla had said that after completing the transcription, he would use something called X-ray spectroscopy to determine the sample's metallic content. It sounded similar to Stern's description of the blood analyses.

Crowley shifted his attention to a larger version of the instrument Tesla had used in the woods of West Orange. "So, you can transmit power wirelessly with these things?" he asked. "I read somewhere that you want to use them to supply the world with free energy. Something about harnessing 'the earth currents of electricity.'"

Tesla paused in his typing. "Something like that. Sh. I have to concentrate." The clacking resumed.

It looked as though Tesla would be a while, so Crowley decided to review the information they had gotten from the newspapers on file at the Columbia College Library. He pulled a notepad from his pocket and opened it to the items he had copied from an article published in 1873.

THE BENDER FAMILY

Great Excitement Over Increased Unearthings of Crime— A Little Girl Buried Alive.

Parsons, Ks., May 12—Col. Bondinot, who has just returned from the scene of the Bender murder, reports three more graves discovered yesterday. Over three thousand people were on the ground, and a special train has just arrived, with seven cars, filled with people. There is intense excitement all over the country, and a firm determination to ferret out the parties engaged in the murders. It is understood that a large reward will be offered by the community and the State for the arrest of the assassins. Nearly all the bodies of the dead are indecently mutilated. It is considered certain that a little girl was thrown alive into the grave with her father, as no marks of violence were found on the body.

Katie Bender, along with her parents and elder brother, had settled near the Great Osage Trail in Kansas in 1870, setting up a general store and an inn. They were self-described spiritualists, and Katie, an attractive young woman claiming to be a medium, offered alleged psychic readings for a fee. From the time the Benders established their homestead, travelers in the vicinity of their inn began disappearing at an alarming rate.

An ensuing investigation revealed a hidden cellar in their house, its floor coated with dried blood. A dozen corpses were found buried on the property, all with obvious signs of brutal murder. It was the common assumption among investigators that the division of homicidal labor involved father and son bashing in the victims' heads from behind, immediately followed by the mother and daughter slashing their throats. By the time of this discovery, the Benders had fled the area. They were never apprehended.

Crowley wondered if the entire family, if physically deceased, had all evolved—or rather devolved—into *ferox phasma*. He was also still at a loss as to how exactly such a process could take place.

He pulled his watch from his vest pocket and opened it. It was two in the afternoon. They had been working more or less without pause since the strange encounter in Edison's lab, but Tesla seemed capable of operating on very little sleep. Crowley, for his part, was exhausted, and decided to take a nap on the cot.

Putting the bag of chocolates on the small night table, he lay down. He soon fell into a deep sleep and began to dream.

Never has he been in a place so brightly lit. It is a big place. A train station. It doesn't seem like a train station, yet he knows that it is one. He doesn't know how he knows this. He is puzzled, yet he doesn't care.

There are people walking around him, dressed in strange clothing: Men in close-fitting, plain-looking suits with gaudy neckties and no hats. Women dressed like the men, some with trousers, some with skirts only coming down to the knee. People of both sexes and all ages in short trousers and brightly colored undershirts with odd symbols on them. He feels it is strange. Yet he feels it is normal. The feeling that it is normal slowly grows stronger. He wanders around for what feels like forever.

There are electric lights built into the ceiling. Bright squares. The light is stark and white. There is a large board showing departures, and the words and numbers themselves are electric lights. He looks around. It is all so bright, so plain, so functional. He decides that it is an ugly place.

"Aleister, darling," says a woman's voice behind him.

He turns around. She is old, her long gray hair tied up to crown her head. She wears normal clothing. No, not normal. Not for here. It is a dress. The skirt goes almost to the floor. She wears spectacles. She smiles at him.

"Aleister, this is never going to work. There's only one way to remember. Come stop by the shop. I'll show you what to do."

Crowley opened his eyes. He sat up, grabbed the bag of chocolates, and stuffed a few into his mouth.

"Ah, you're awake," said Tesla. "I hope you feel better. I've finished transcribing the notes and analyzing the horn sample. There's—"

"Tesla," he interrupted, standing up. "There's no time for that now. I've got to get to Bleecker Street right away."

"Bleecker Street? Why?"

Crowley walked to the door, grabbed his bowler from the hat rack, and said, "Are you coming?"

20

They walked in the afternoon sunlight, east on Bleecker Street, toward the sign hung outside the door which simply said *Village Books*. The shop was housed within the first floor of a vine-covered building of red brick, five stories tall. The sign in the window said *Closed*.

"It's closed," said Tesla.

"For us it's open," said Crowley. He pushed open the door, causing the bell to tinkle.

"Ah, you're here," called a friendly female voice. "Kindly lock the door." Tesla slid the bolt lock.

As might be expected, books lined the walls from the floor almost to the ceiling, housed within cases of cherry and walnut. A wine-colored curtain behind the counter parted, and a tall, slender lady of about seventy appeared. She was the woman from Crowley's dream. "Aleister, darling," she said, smiling.

"Sadie," he answered, smiling back.

Coming from behind the counter, she went to him and they embraced. Holding his face between her hands, she looked up at him and said, "You got my message."

"Yes, I believe so," replied Crowley. "I was dreaming, but I can't recall much about it. I remember you telling me to come to the shop."

"Yes. We'll get to that presently. My, you look exhausted. Though I've given up trying to get you to look after your health."

She turned to Tesla. "Mr. Tesla. It is indeed an honor to have you in my shop." Her manner suggested that she had somehow expected him to arrive, and at this point, such a thing did not surprise Tesla.

"The honor is mine, madam." He bent to kiss her hand. "To have such a collection of books is truly a sign of intellect and taste. These volumes have not been chosen at random."

"You flatter me, sir!"

"Not in the least. I see you have Shakespeare, Chaucer, Cervantes, and so on. Works to be found in any antiquarian collection. But I also see English translations of Obradović and Radičević. Masterpieces of Serbian poetry. You certainly know your books."

"I strive to, at any rate," she said, smiling. "Well, come on in the back. Tea is ready." They followed her behind the curtain.

Soon they were seated around a large table, having tea and scones. Sadie held a folded newspaper in her lap.

Tesla noticed that, unlike the front of the shop, the bookcases in this room contained volumes with titles in various languages suggesting the arcane or, as Crowley would term it, magick. Some of the bindings had unusual symbols the nature of which Tesla could only guess at, while others were blank. All the books looked quite old.

"I assume," said Sadie, "that whatever difficulty you are having relates to this?" She set the newspaper on the table. It was that day's *New York World*. She indicated a story at the bottom of the front page.

First Among Spirit Phone Users
Relate Disturbing Experiences

Communication with something, but what? Reports exist of alleged spirit voices claiming to be departed loved ones, yet seemingly "stupid," repeating back users' sentences or making vague, nonsensical statements. The Edison Company spokesman has declined comment other than to say that a public statement will be issued in the near future.

New York, Aug. 30—The Edison Spirit Phone, dubbed the Model SP-1, was placed on the market amid great fanfare on August 27. In less than a week since the instrument's debut, the Edison Company has filled approximately 100 orders, many of which have been for residents of this city. A representative of this newspaper was able to speak with four such Edison customers, and all uniformly report that while the device seems to allow communication of some sort, whoever or whatever speaks exhibits vagueness, repetitiveness, or even stupidity. One man in his 40s stated, "I used the device as instructed in the manual it comes with, wishing to speak with my wife, who had passed away from an illness last December. There was a voice from the horn, and it resembled hers in life. At first, things seemed normal, so to speak, as we exchanged the pleasantries and salutations one might expect. But then by the third such conversation, the voice kept saying things like, 'Yes, that's nice,' and 'Oh, really?' over and over again. My wife was a conversationalist of great intelligence and wit, but this thing seemed like..."

"Electrical Ouija board," said Crowley.

"That was my impression as well," said Sadie.

"How do you know each other?" asked Tesla.

"Aleister has been a customer in the shop a few times during previous trips to New York. He has certain talents I assume you have witnessed. As for me, I have similar interests, and so I am able to advise him on just a few trifles."

"She's brilliant," Crowley whispered to Tesla.

"Now," said Sadie, "I will forgive you for not visiting until now because I can see you've been busy and that it has to do with this newfangled thingamajig. The less I know, the better. What I did perceive, as I saw you dream, is that there is something you need to remember but cannot."

"Yes," said Crowley. "It's the entire key to—"

She held up her hand. "I don't want to know. You've never encountered this kind of problem before, as far as I can tell, and it's a rare one generally. But the solution is obvious. You need to access the Akashic Records."

"The what?" asked Tesla.

"Seriously?" asked Crowley. "I've never bothered with that. Seems overrated. The people who write about those records strike me as Ouija board peddlers."

She crossed her arms and gave him a stern look. "You're truly gifted, Aleister. With your abilities, you might never have needed to access the records. But sometimes your overconfidence creates these little blind spots. Trust me. It will help."

"You can get me to them?"

"Not me, no. But I can guide you to someone who can."

"Someone who lives in the city?"

"No. He lives in Kentucky."

"That fellow? Cayce? The healer? He has access to the Akashic Records?"

"Yes. That is, he has the most direct access of anyone in current space-time. And traipsing about the astral plane searching for someone else to help would take too long. I've managed to get in touch. He's expecting you."

"Sadie, there's no time to go to Kentucky and come back here again physically, and I don't think I'm in any condition—"

"To make the trip astrally? I know, you seem a bit worn-out. But I can help you with that. Give you a boost."

"What are the Akashic Records?" asked Tesla.

"An astral records repository of all events," said Crowley.

"All events?"

"Supposedly. It is reputed to be an aspect of reality in which every occurrence in the universe, past, present, and future, is recorded. A kind of universal filing cabinet. If it works the way it's supposed to, I can find out what happened during the teleportation time gap. I've been dreaming about it, but when I wake up, I remember almost nothing."

"Except being at a strange train station? I perceived that much," said Sadie.

"Yes," he said. "All right, Sadie. I'm ready if you are."

21

rowley lay on a chaise lounge. Sadie sat on a chair next to him, Tesla in an easy chair facing them.

"All right, dear, you know what to do." She stroked his head gently. "I'll be right here. Do be careful." She kissed his forehead.

"I'll be fine." He smiled and closed his eyes.

Crowley relaxed and focused, inducing the requisite physical sleep state combined with staying mentally awake. He felt the familiar floating sensation, the separation from the physical, and was in the astral state, hovering above Sadie, Tesla, and his physical body. Soon he was rushing away, the gray blur enveloping him as he traveled toward another location in physical space-time. Energy for the trip was contributed by Sadie, but it was still something of a struggle.

Crowley had never met Edgar Cayce but knew him by reputation. By focusing intently upon his desire to meet Cayce—

He had arrived. He was standing in a green, sunlit yard behind a white house. A large willow tree stood nearby, its branches swaying in the breeze. White lawn furniture stood near the tree. A voice behind him said, "Welcome."

Crowley turned to see a pleasant-faced young man about his own age, dressed in a summer suit. He, too, was in the astral state. "Mr. Cayce?"

"Mr. Crowley. Welcome to Hopkinsville, Kentucky," he said in a soft Southern drawl.

"Thank you."

"I wish there were more time to chat. Your career is of interest to me. But Sadie has told me there is no time to stand on ceremony, so"—he indicated the lawn chairs—"shall we have a seat and get down to business?"

They sat. "I need to access the Akashic Records."

"I know."

"Sadie says you can help me get to them."

"I can," he said.

"All right then. How do I do it?"

"I need certain assurances from you first."

"Assurances?"

"Mr. Crowley, I almost said no when Sadie asked me to help you. I relented when it became clear to me that not to help you would result in something unspeakable. This is the lesser of two evils."

"I'm not quite following you."

"You need to access the records. And this need has to do with Thomas Edison's new invention, his so-called spirit phone."

"Yes. There is an intention to release into this world—"

"Things neither of us want released. Yes, I know. And you accessing the Akashic Records is the only hope of stopping this."

"Then why not just help me—"

"I will. Patience, Mr. Crowley. I will state this as concisely as I can. It is vital that you know it. We in this business all have our specialties. Mine consists of the diagnosis of illness, and of Akashic Records access. I consult the archives as little as I need to. It's better not to know too much concerning certain matters, and there are some records which even I am unable to get to. When I read of the spirit phone, I was concerned. I went to the archives to see what happened, or would happen, or might happen, as it were. I found a problem."

"A problem?"

"For the period after this month, the archives regarding earth have been narrowed."

"Narrowed?"

"Normally each record for a given event, large or small, has infinite versions, as there are infinite possibilities. Infinite realities, some might term it. The result of what we call free will. This is different. The possibilities are limited and stark. Either the monsters you call the Ferox succeed in entering our physical world, or they don't."

"Right. So I would assume we want to make sure they don't, so I need to access the records. What is the problem here?"

"The problem, Mr. Crowley, is that one of these outcomes—the one in which you succeed—is divided into two further possibilities, and only two. In one of them, you gain a personality analogous to a Ferox, and a more than ten-fold increase in your powers. With this comes the opportunity to start the entire process again, to become that which you have defeated."

"And the other?"

"You lose your powers. Not all of them. But there will be a significant decrease."

"You mean I become non-magickal? Or nearly so?"

"I'm sorry. It's a side-effect of the process. The least bad outcome. And I am afraid your friend, the inventor Mr. Tesla, will also suffer certain reversals in fortune. But then the infinitude of possibilities goes back to normal."

"So the assurance you seek is that I choose this second outcome. But how will I know what to do in order to choose it?"

"You will know when the time comes. Do I have your word, Aleister Crowley?"

"Yes."

"Very well. Let's begin."

22

"This feels a bit ridiculous," said Crowley.

He lay, in astral form, on Cayce's lawn. Cayce sat cross-legged on the ground with his hands on Crowley's head.

"That's understandable. But I assure you, it's true. You have a second astral body. Just as Sadie is helping you from your physical body in New York, I will help you separate from the first astral body to the second. The process is similar. Now kindly close your astral eyes, sir, and concentrate." Cayce grinned.

Crowley did as Cayce asked. He experienced the familiar separation. But then, as he looked down at the "first" astral bodies of himself and Cayce, he felt somehow undefined in form. Hovering near a window of the house to see his reflection, he realized with a start that he appeared to be nothing more than a glowing ball of energy. He heard Cayce's voice say, "Get on with it. You're wasting time."

Focus: Akashic Records. Instantly, he was there.

He struggles to escape the despair and horror, the unspeakable grip. Then the deep male voice fills his consciousness. "You vain little fool. You thought this was all about you."

He snaps back into the astral-yet-physical state. For a second, he feels he is floating. He turns his head to see the wall of rock moving upward in a rapid blur.

The thought comes, instantaneous: Teleportation—base camp! *His surroundings disappear.*

Then he is standing in a new place. He is confused because it is not his base camp. It is not even Tibet. He then forgets that he had ever been in Tibet, or was climbing a mountain, or had a base camp. He knows only this place.

Never has he been in a place so brightly lit. It is a big place. A train station. It doesn't seem like a train station, yet he knows that it is one. He doesn't know how he knows this. He is puzzled, yet he doesn't care. He is supposed to be here. He checks the voucher in his hand, then looks at the sign on the wall. Yes, this is where he needs to be.

There are people walking around him, dressed in strange clothing: Men in close-fitting, plain-looking suits with gaudy neckties and no hats. Women dressed like the men, some with trousers, some with skirts only coming down to the knee. People of both sexes and all ages in short trousers and brightly colored undershirts with odd words or symbols on them. Many of the people are obese, or at least plump. Even the children. He feels it is strange. Yet he feels it is normal. The feeling that it is normal slowly grows stronger.

He looks down at himself, wonders for a moment why he is dressed like a nineteenth-century mountaineer, then forgets about it.

He looks up. There are electric lights on the ceiling, bright squares. The light is stark and white. There is a large board showing departures. The words and numbers themselves are lights. He looks around. It is all so bright, so plain, so functional. He decides that it is an ugly place.

Now he remembers. He needs to get on a train to Washington, D.C. He needs to change trains here. What is this place? Pennsylvania? No, this is New York. Pennsylvania Station. Penn Station. God, what a troublesome situation.

He is traveling from Fort Edward, a small town Upstate, to D.C. He paid for his ticket, or rather he paid for two tickets but received only one. The station employee at Fort Edward told him he needed to present a voucher at Penn Station to get his ticket from there to D.C. So he has to wait in line.

He is annoyed, frustrated. Why wasn't he able to just buy a ticket from his starting point to his destination? It's 2012, for God's sake!

It's 2012? Really? Something about this seems…never mind.

He gets in line. After half an hour, he is third from the front. His train will be leaving soon. "Excuse me!" he says. "I have to catch my train! I need to get my ticket!"

"I'm sorry, sir, you'll have to wait your turn," says the ticket seller.

To hell with this, he thinks. He gets out of line and walks to the exit door, goes out, and is instantly back in line again. He has no perception that this is the second time, nor that he had ever attempted to leave the station.

After half an hour, he is the third person in line. His train will be leaving soon.
"Excuse me!" he says. "I have to catch my train! It's leaving soon!"

"I'm sorry, sir, you'll have to wait your turn," says the ticket seller.

To hell with this, he thinks. He gets out of line and walks to the exit door, goes out, and is instantly back in line again. He has no perception that this is the third time, nor that he had ever attempted to leave the station.

After half an hour, he is the third person in line. His train will be leaving soon.
"Excuse me!" he says. "I have to catch my goddamned train!"

And so it goes.

Each time he is in line is, in his perception, the first and only time. And each time, he feels a greater and inexplicable need to express insulting and irrationally obscene language.

♦ ♦ ♦

"Excuse me! I have to catch my goddamned train, you imbecile!"

♦ ♦ ♦

"Excuse me! Were you born stupid or do you make a concerted effort at it? I need a fucking ticket!"

"Sir, you need to watch your language!"

"Fine! I'm leaving!"

♦ ♦ ♦

"My train is leaving soon! I need a ticket! I hereby declare that if I do not receive it now, this serves as irrefutable proof that all employees of this railway station are moronic shitheads!"

A security guard approaches him. "Sir, you need to—"

"Wait! Who here has fornicated within the past twenty-four hours? A show of hands, please? For those who don't know, fornication is an elegant word for 'fuck.'"

"Sir, I will call the police."

"Fine, I'm leaving. Hornswoggler ratbag."

♦ ♦ ♦

"I will defecate on the counter and rub your goddamned face into it, you incompetent, lazy swine!" he shouts just before punching the security guard in the face.

♦ ♦ ♦

"Bomb! There is a bomb in this station!"

♦ ♦ ♦

He perceives it as the first time in line, like every other time. He has another strange urge he cannot control. When he is third in line, and he sees that his train will be leaving in a few minutes, he starts to sing.

"'I am the monarch of the sea,
The ruler of the Queen's Navee,
Whose praise Great Britain loudly chants.'"

He turns to the woman standing behind him. She is middle-aged and slightly overweight. Her eyes are wide with surprise.

"Come on, you daft cow!" he says. "Sing the line!"

"Huh?"

"I am Sir Joseph and you are my Cousin Hebe! 'And we are his sisters, and his cousins, and his aunts!' Honestly, woman!"

"Sir, you need to calm down," says the security guard who has come to the line.

"Calm down? Calm down! I am the First Lord of the Admiralty! You dare tell me to calm down! Fine, let's try it this way:

"'I am the bugger of the sea!
Sodomite of the Queen's Navee!
And these are my shipmates who will take it up the arse!'
Sing it, you useless wankers!"

♦ ♦ ♦

SIR JOSEPH: *"I am the monarch of the sea,*
The ruler of the Queen's Navee,
Whose praise Great Britain loudly chants."

COUSIN HEBE: *"And we are his sisters, and his cousins, and his aunts!"*

The other passengers look at Crowley and the woman in surprise.

♦ ♦ ♦

SIR JOSEPH: *"I am the monarch of the sea,*
The ruler of the Queen's Navee,
Whose praise Great Britain loudly chants."

COUSIN HEBE: *"And we are his sisters, and his cousins, and his aunts!"*
RELATIVES: *"And we are his sisters, and his cousins, and his aunts!"*

The other passengers look at Crowley and the woman and the other people in surprise.

◆ ◆ ◆

Every person in this area of Pennsylvania Station, numbering perhaps two hundred in all, sings Gilbert and Sullivan's "I Am the Monarch of the Sea," featuring Aleister Crowley as Sir Joseph Porter. When it is complete, Crowley looks at the woman who has sung the role of Cousin Hebe.

"Now I remember. I was falling. How did I teleport here?"

"You have not completed the teleportation. The entity which attacked us in Tibet placed us here in mid-teleport, at which point you were vulnerable. When it could not destroy us, its secondary plan was to keep us here for eternity."

"'Us?' What is this place?"

"An aspect of the astral plane where physical and astral elements can coexist. It is a simulation of a place on earth after your time period. This served to confuse and distract you."

"Yes. I was in-physical but in the astral state of consciousness, and teleporting. Which means you are all—"

"Elements of your astral consciousness, yes. The entity fragmented us and made us appear as separate physical individuals. We could not inform you directly, but we were able to elicit the antisocial behavior necessary to break the cycle we were confined in."

Crowley sees that the passengers are all beginning to merge with one another. He says to the woman, "Thank you. Thank...me. Us. Right." Looking around, he says, "Come on, everybody. Chop-chop." He claps his hands. "We need to get out of here and finish teleporting so I don't become a red smear on the Himalayan landscape."

She cups her hands, and a small white ball of light appears between them. "Here," she says. "Take this rote."

"What? What's a rote?" He touches it. It is absorbed into his body. His eyes open wide. "Oh my."

"Yes. This information is vital. Listen carefully. You will not consciously recall any of this, including the rote, after completing the teleportation. It is an effect of the entity's attack. But you must eventually remember. Chocolate will help you."

"Chocolate?"

"Yes. Eat chocolate. And some dried fruit."

Suddenly the taste of chocolate is on his tongue. He starts in surprise.

"Oh! Right. I see. Fine. Chocolate."

"There is one element of the rote you still will not remember until the moment you need it. This is necessary."

"Who decided that?"

"You did."

For a moment, or so it seems, his surroundings fade into nothingness.

◆ ◆ ◆

Then everything returns into sharp focus.

"I did? Never mind. I'll take your word for it. Now let's finish teleporting to the base camp."

"Forget the base camp," she says. "You need to go to Nikola Tesla."

"Tesla? The inventor? Why? He lives in New York. I can't teleport there."

"Yes, you can. Focus your will." The last of the passengers have merged into one another, then into her. She merges with Crowley, who once again realizes the astral state of consciousness.

His surroundings wink out. He feels a sudden and painful impact.

He is conscious, and in-physical, and in the physical world. Lying on a hardwood floor. At least that's what it feels like, but he can neither move nor open his eyes.

He hears footsteps, then the voice of a man speaking English with a heavy Eastern European accent. "Sir! What is the meaning of this? What are you doing in my home? How did you get in here?" There is a moment of silence, then footsteps again.

Suddenly Crowley begins to shake violently. An aftereffect, he thinks vaguely. Now able to open his eyes, he sees the man. It is Nikola Tesla. Why am I here? Never mind that now. Tesla picks up the telephone from the sofa side table, but before he can call for help, Crowley manages to croak out, "Wait."

Turning from the phone, Tesla looks down.

"Please don't," Crowley says. "I'm all right. Aftereffects."

"Of what? Opium?"

"Teleportation. Could I possibly lie on your sofa?"

◆ ◆ ◆

Crowley was back on the lawn with Cayce, back in his first astral body. He stood up.

"Well?" asked Cayce.

"I got what I went for," said Crowley. "Thank you."

"You should be able to access the records in future attempts without assistance. But be aware: not all knowledge is always accessible. Confine your searches to true necessity, and keep them as narrowly defined as possible."

"I understand."

"I wish I could do more, but I'm afraid this exhausts the extent of my usefulness in this. Please remember your pledge, Mr. Crowley."

"I will. My thanks again, Mr. Cayce." He focused upon remerging with his physical body and began speeding through the grayness. Soon he was once more looking up at Sadie's smiling face.

"Welcome back, darling," she said.

23

They sat around Sadie's table, sharing a bottle of Merlot.

"So," said Tesla, "accessing these records involves directly reliving an experience."

"At least if it's one's own experience," said Crowley, puffing on his pipe. "I had imagined the astral equivalent of pulling a document from a drawer, but it was much more exciting than that." He drained his glass and Sadie refilled it. "But the strangest thing was this item the fragment of my astral consciousness called a rote."

"Yes. The energy ball of information you mentioned. What did it tell you?"

"Wait," said Sadie. "The fewer people who know what you've learned, the better. Did you tell Edgar?"

"No. He didn't ask."

"I thought not. This way there's less for the enemy to get out of us, should it come to that. I think you boys had better discuss this elsewhere."

So they spoke of other things—the newsboys' strike, the Klondike gold rush, the Belgian and British Antarctic expeditions—until they had finished the wine. As parting gifts, Sadie gave Tesla an anthology of Obradović's poems, and to Crowley a novel titled *Daring Desmond, the Elevated Railroad Detective*. "To get your mind off work," she said to him.

She walked them to the door and gave them both a kiss on the cheek goodbye, and it occurred to Tesla that though they had not mentioned an enemy, Sadie realized there was one.

"She's quite perceptive," said Tesla after she had closed the door.

"Oh, yes. Much more than she lets on. And she keeps busy." It was getting toward dusk as they walked along the street.

"So," said Tesla. "The rote?"

Crowley explained as well as he could. Through the terror he had experienced in the attack in Tibet had also come perceptions the rote enabled him to recall: The tattoo Stern had shown them was indeed the symbol used among the Ferox's human followers. The Essential Element was in fact carborundum, though it was, chemically speaking, a compound. Also, to make a spirit phone accessible by a Ferox...

"The carborundum proportion needs to be one half, not one eighth," said Tesla. "The remaining half being equal proportions of the Seven Planetary Metals."

"Right," said Crowley. "That was your analysis from the sample we took at Edison's lab, I assume. The ones with one-eighth carborundum are of the Ouija board variety. But there's something else. In your analysis of the horn sample, did you find any sulfur?"

"Sulfur? No. Why?"

"According to what I learned, sulfur is the Secret Element, the final item needed to summon a Ferox. You'll recall it is reputedly an easily obtainable substance."

"There was no sulfur in the sample," said Tesla. "I'm positive."

"Yet that is what the rote told me. Perhaps the amount was too minute. We'll have to give it further thought."

"All right. But what about adjusting the metallurgic content of the spirit phone as a means of contacting 'ordinary' spirits? Someone's dead grandfather, for example."

"Nearly impossible, at least according to the rote," said Crowley. "No ratio of the Essential Composite elements would be effective, nor with anything added to the mix. My own laborious access to the spirit phone at Columbia notwithstanding."

"So, the easy availability of carborundum and electricity has resulted in this crisis," said Tesla. "But how do we solve it?"

"With the most important thing I learned from the rote: the same thing that has opened this window for the Ferox will also close it—if we can delay or impede 'deluxe' spirit phone production somehow."

"What do you mean?"

"Artificially generated electricity. Telegraphy, phone communication, the transmission of power. It's increasing almost daily, and somehow it creates a kind of astral fog, a barrier around the earth which impedes the Ferox's access to physical space-time. Once it reaches a certain level, earth will be forever closed off to them. The same thing now enabling them to come here will soon bar them. That's why they're in such a hurry. They want to get in before that happens, and they want to get in physically. It seems they have until December, then all bets are off."

"But the instruments being marketed can't be used to contact them," said Tesla. "It makes no sense. Who, if anyone, is making spirit phones meant for summoning the Ferox?"

"I don't know, but someone must be. There is also the question of how they plan to become physical beings. I couldn't get anything on that. My best guess is that the deluxe spirit phones are to play a role and are secretly being disseminated somehow. We have to assume that more exist than just the one we found in Edison's lab."

They walked for a while in silence.

"Well, we have a fighting chance," said Tesla. "We've learned a great deal."

"Yes. Perhaps most interestingly, we've learned that railway stations in the future will be ugly, full of obese people, and grossly inefficient. At least in New York."

"How are the chocolate cravings?" asked Tesla.

"Gone," said Crowley. "I feel like a steak. And an ale. Not a bloody lager."

"All right. Let's get you a steak and some ale."

24

At Tesla's suggestion, they went to Delmonico's Restaurant, a New York favorite. Upon seeing the menu, a delighted Crowley decided upon loin of lamb with mint sauce instead of the sirloin. Tesla chose the glazed ham with Madeira sauce and decided to follow Crowley's example in having ale with his dinner.

"Quite a nice establishment," said Crowley, cutting into his lamb with a smile. "This is actually my first time to visit. On previous trips, I've always been running about too much to sit down for a proper meal. That cottage pie in the saloon was all right, though. So, what was in Edison's notebook? What about the spirit phone plans?"

"The plans don't tell us anything we don't already know. The seven metals, combined in equal proportions along with carborundum, shaped into a cone, placed next to an electromagnet and a three-volt battery." Tesla took a sip of ale. "And no mention of sulfur."

"But the model in Edison's laboratory was composed of half carborundum, not one-eighth."

"Yes, but as you've said, it seems Edison doesn't know that. Now I think I know why. The horn for the Model SP-1 prototype wasn't made by Edison, or anyone under his employ. It'll all be clear as I explain." Tesla began to relate what he had learned from the notebook in Edison's laboratory.

In November 1898, after more than a decade of speculation and planning, Edison had begun secretly experimenting with an earlier, very different version of the spirit phone, one which he now seemed to consider obsolete, though it never got beyond the prototype stage: an instrument for the electrical detection of sound outside the normal range of human hearing.

It was, in a sense, a form of radio telegraphy, the wireless transmission of the human voice which was now only in a speculative, experimental stage. It was an area Tesla had also been working on, but for speaking with living people, not ghosts, and within the normal range of human hearing. Edison's device seemed to have been a rudimentary radiophone designed to detect, amplify, and adjust for human ears extremely low-amplitude, low-frequency sounds. This, Edison was convinced, would be the most likely way to perceive spirit voices. And he apparently believed he had accomplished contact.

In an entry dated December 17th, Edison recounted attaining communication with an apparent male spirit calling itself Andreas. Whoever he was, he reportedly spoke perfectly good English, but with an unplaceable, nonnative accent.

The notes Edison kept on his original spirit phone included his motive for inventing it. As was well-known, his first wife Mary had died in 1884. The cause of death was unclear, but there had long been rumors of an overdose of morphine. Though Edison was now remarried, he had been devastated, and never truly recovered from Mary's passing. He was determined to find a way to contact her.

Andreas claimed that Edison's radiophone spirit communicator was sensitive enough to contact, with great difficulty, only a small number of especially evolved entities of the astral plane, among which Andreas counted himself. He said that in order to contact his dead wife, or the spirit of most any human who had released the mortal coil, Edison would need to build a completely different device, principally composed of a metallic alloy cone and a weak electromagnet.

Edison's initial reaction was incredulity. He simply couldn't believe such a thing could work as Andreas described. But eventually he was persuaded. "Partly," Tesla said, "because this Andreas told him there was another inventor secretly attempting to devise a spirit phone. Me."

"You?" asked Crowley. "Well, were you?"

"No. But since Edison sees me as his chief rival, such a belief must have given him an extra incentive."

The problem, however, was that even Andreas himself was unsure about the exact proportions of the seven metals to comprise the horn. More crucially, he knew an additional substance was needed, but didn't know what it was.

At first, Andreas encouraged Edison to do what he did best: tinker until he found a solution. But the going was slow. Edison had tried dozens of materials: platinum, aluminum, titanium, nickel, zinc, and so on. He had assumed it must be a metal. Then, on the evening of Friday, February 10th, a servant came into Edison's study, telling him there was a man at the door. The man had said his name was Ambrose Temple, that he had urgent business with Mr. Edison, and that he needed to speak with him personally. He had also urged the servant to tell Edison that he bore an important message from "our mutual friend Andreas."

Edison described him as well over six feet tall, in his early sixties, with a full beard and dressed in a very fine suit and top hat. He seemed to be a man of means, though he was vague about his exact occupation.

Upon entering Edison's study and greeting him, he said, "The missing item is not a metal. It is something rather different, though it may be combined with metal, and is now in great abundance." He pulled a slip of paper from his vest pocket and handed it to Edison, saying, "This is all the information you need to complete the spirit phone." He also insisted upon manufacturing the prototype horn himself, but would then leave further production to Edison.

"Then isn't Edison effectively stealing the spirit phone composition from this Temple person?" asked Crowley.

"Not exactly. According to the diary, he gave Edison the information freely and encouraged him to make the patent application in his own name only. Whoever Temple is, he has made no attempt at gaining any public credit for the spirit phone. To be charitable, we could call them collaborators."

"This Temple could be the Ferox's primary human agent," said Crowley.

"Perhaps," said Tesla. "But there is more. After the Columbia demonstration, you speculated that the spirit phones had not been sufficiently tested. In fact, they were not tested at all, unless you count Edison's use of the prototype, which is not truly the same device. He gave strict orders that no one involved in spirit phone production was to attempt to use one, and arranged for no testing sessions. Unheard of, but especially out of character for Edison. Andreas had convinced him that too many different users of one model would diminish its effectiveness, and that no testing was necessary."

"Whether that's true, it's convenient for concealing the true nature of the Ouija board model. Meanwhile, Edison has a deluxe model to keep him under Ferox influence. These bastards are playing him like a violin. Then what happened?"

"The notes end there. And no mention of sulfur. But what could be the purpose of having these defective models on sale?"

"I've no idea. But judging by today's paper, the cat's halfway out of the bag. We have our work cut out for us, Mr. Tesla. I find New York more exciting by the hour."

"As do I. And I've lived here for fifteen years." Tesla sipped his ale. "This is nice. I used to drink beer quite a bit as a student. But I suppose I'll go back to wine after this."

"Wine is good. Benjamin Franklin said it serves as proof that God loves us."

Tesla smiled with a bitter air. "A bit more proof of that would now be welcome."

"Don't despair. As you've said, we still have a fighting chance."

"Yes, well, we should talk to Stern to see if he's learned anything new."

"Yes," said Crowley, yawning. "But first I'm looking forward to a good night's sleep."

25

Three years earlier

So this is what disillusionment really feels like, she thinks, her eyes fixed upon the massive butte dominating the landscape beyond the chain-link fence. Yet the word seems inadequate, as words sometimes are, however one struggles to fit them to experience or imagination.

This isn't what she expected. None of it. She wanted to change the world for the better. Fair wages, strong unions, voting rights for all regardless of sex or race, an end to the evils of child labor. Instead, she is living in a compound in the middle of a wilderness.

Their leader, the Administrator, is charismatic and persuasive. He counsels patience, insisting that certain preparations are essential before any lasting change can be made. At first, she agreed. But not anymore. The more she understood what was happening, the more she rebelled in her heart. It is all against nature, a cure worse than the disease. Her deepest instincts tell her nothing good can come of this. Does no one else see it? Or are they all, like her, too afraid to speak out?

She turns, somehow sensing his approach. The Administrator. Mr. Temple.

He is walking toward her from the compound's Administrative Center, with nods of greeting between himself and the few people outside at this hour. Besuited and top-hatted as usual, he carries a clipboard with a document attached.

She briefly fingers the fabric of her dark-gray coveralls, reminded that Temple is the only member of their community who does not wear the uniform, who does not have a number. Like hers, 00287, embroidered above the left breast pocket.

It was strange at first to wear what she had always thought of as men's clothing, and what with all the pockets, which women's outfits usually don't have. She finds them convenient. Perhaps it is the one good thing about her situation.

"Good afternoon, Martha," he says as he reaches her, handing over the clipboard.

"Good afternoon, Mr. Temple." *She looks at the attached paper. It is a list of the subjects she will teach the newest boys come fall. Penmanship, grammar, arithmetic. Though if she has her way, she will not actually teach them. She takes a pencil from her pocket, then initials and dates the line at the bottom.*

"Thank you for taking the trouble to bring it to me," *she says, handing it back to him.*

"It's no trouble. I felt like a walk. And besides, this gives us an opportunity to speak privately."

She tenses. "Privately? About what, sir?"

"About your intention to escape the compound with two others of our company."

Her mind goes blank for a moment, then she recovers. "Sir? I'm not quite sure what you mean."

"Relax, Martha. You're not in any trouble, provided you cooperate. Let's not dance around it. I know you plan to leave, and with whom. I will allow it, on two conditions."

She abandons pretense, seeing no alternative. "Which are?"

"One: The other two must not know they are being allowed to escape. They must be convinced they are committing a betrayal. Two: At an unspecified date in the future, you must agree to come back. Alone. Assuming I can locate you. Who knows? Perhaps you can evade me."

In for a penny, in for a pound. "I agree," *she says.*

"Very well. Just after three o'clock in the morning, there will be a gap below the fence at the northwest corner of the compound. You'll find two rucksacks containing supplies and ordinary clothing for the three of you. And some petty cash. I'll ensure your departure is not impeded. If they ask, you can simply tell them you were secretly helped by another member of our group, which is true."

"Why are you doing this?" *she asks.*

"It's an experiment. Please be observant about how they adapt to the outside. We'll need detailed information upon your return."

For a long moment, there are no words between them, their eyes locked upon one another. She struggles to contain her thoughts, then senses she is free to speak without punishment.

"These men and boys. Must they exist only to be your creatures, to be used as tools? To live or die at your whim? It is inhuman. Better that they had never been."

Temple's laugh is cheerful rather than mocking. "Martha, you're sounding like the heroine of a melodrama. But I can understand your motives, believe it or not. It's natural to feel sorry for them. But that is only because you lack the proper insight. And you've grown attached to those two in particular. The meaning and purpose of their existence is to fulfill a specific function for the greater good of humanity. Sentimentality has no place in it."

"I see."

He smiles. "No, you don't. But as long as you obey my instructions, no matter. Make no mistake: If you do not, I will know. Until we meet again, Martha."

He turns away and walks back toward the Administrative Center.

26

September 1st, 1899

Tesla, Crowley, Stern, and Donnelly sat around the table in Tesla's laboratory. It was just after ten o'clock in the morning. Stern had telephoned to request that they meet to discuss some substantial new information related to the case. He was also curious to know what Tesla and Crowley had learned.

Stern got right down to business. "Mr. Tesla, perhaps you and Mr. Crowley would like to convey your own information first?"

Crowley and Tesla related all the events since their trip to West Orange and what they had learned thereby, most crucially that the same technology which would allow the Ferox to enter this world would also close it off to them forever, unless they could attain permanent physical entry to Earth before the end of the year. And still unresolved lay the question of how they could possibly achieve this, and that of sulfur as a spirit phone component.

Stern then explained his own findings. "As I suspected, information on Howell is a dead end. We may never know his true identity. However, I also checked the fingerprint records of Marcus Reinecker against those of the bank robber who, shortly before he died, was questioned by Coroner Fitzpatrick. That was in 1896. You will recall that Dr. Fitzpatrick was positive they were both the same man."

"And?" asked Crowley.

"Both sets of prints are an exact match."

Tesla and Crowley exchanged a glance. "But even if they were twins—" began Tesla.

"The chances are virtually nil that they would have identical fingerprints. And yet…" He produced a file from his valise, pulled out two sheets of paper, and slid them across the table. They were identification photos and fingerprint images of the two men. Stern pulled a magnifying glass from his inside pocket and handed it to Tesla.

Tesla examined both sets of prints carefully. "Remarkable," he said, handing the glass to Crowley, who also looked. "There is no chance of a mistake?"

"None."

Crowley asked, "Could they both be the same person, who survived his gunshot wounds three years ago, then allowed the authorities to believe he was dead?"

"Dr. Fitzpatrick is positive he saw the culprit die," said Stern. "He was buried in Potter's Field."

"Resurrection of the dead," said Tesla. "I'm not willing to discount any possibility, but…"

"I don't suppose Reinecker has sat up to chat with the morgue staff?" asked Crowley.

"No," said Stern. "What is your…professional opinion, Mr. Crowley?"

"To reanimate a corpse is, strictly speaking, possible. But then it's sort of not dead but not precisely alive either. I saw it once, in Barbados. It was rather unpleasant. The decomposition doesn't quite stop. But this Reinecker fellow was apparently exchanging hellos in his neighborhood without smelling bad or dropping body parts all over the place. If he's the resurrected bank robber, this is magick beyond anything I've heard of."

"Is it beyond the realm of extreme possibility that our enemy has the power to resurrect the dead in the complete sense of the term?" asked Stern.

"Well, no. But if we're considering that, would identical twins with identical fingerprints be out of the question?"

"No," Stern replied. "We must consider both possibilities. Also, you'll recall I took blood samples from the two bodies at the morgue. I have at my disposal equipment to conduct chemical analyses of my own. Which reminds me." He pulled two small vials of red liquid from an inside pocket. Each had a small label attached. "Here are the samples you requested, Mr. Tesla. I hope they're sufficient."

Tesla briefly examined them. "These are enough. Thank you, Inspector. I may be able to do some different, additional analyses." He pocketed the vials.

"And so, what did you find?" asked Crowley.

"In Howell's blood, nothing out of the ordinary. In Reinecker's, something strange. It's blood, so it naturally contains iron. It also contains traces of gold, silver, mercury, tin, copper, and lead," said Stern. "The Seven Planetary Metals."

"Let me guess," said Crowley. "You also found traces of carborundum?"

"Yes," answered Stern.

"Did you find any sulfur?"

"Sulfur is not a metal, so was not detectable by my test. But it exists naturally in the blood, so I assume it was there."

"He was poisoned? With the same materials used to make the spirit phone?" asked Tesla.

"Apparently so," said Stern. "Even a small dose of the mercury alone would prove especially fatal. There were the chemical traces found on the boat, but no sign of a liquid solution the victim had drunk or been forced to drink."

"Injection?" asked Crowley. "Ultrafine grains of the horn composite in saline?"

"I went back to the morgue yesterday morning to carefully examine every inch of Mr. Reinecker's external anatomy with the help of Dr. Fitzpatrick. There was no sign of any injection mark, though it is not impossible that he was stabbed at the point of injection. Still, Dr. Fitzpatrick is positive the cause of death was blood loss, not blood poisoning."

"So we have a man who may have been raised from the dead," said Donnelly. "And with the apparent ability to survive metal poisoning long enough to be stabbed to death."

"Rather defeats the purpose," said Crowley.

They were interrupted by the shrill ring of the telephone mounted on the wall near the laboratory door. Tesla got up to answer it.

"Laboratory of Nikola Tesla. Tesla speaking." He glanced at Stern and said, "Yes, Doctor. One moment, please."

Covering the mouthpiece, Tesla said, "Inspector, it's Doctor Fitzpatrick calling from the Coroner's Office." Stern got up and took the receiver from Tesla.

"Stern here. Yes, hello, Ed. What?" There was a pause as Stern listened, his expression grave. "All right. Yes, we'll keep it mum. You have my guarantee. Thank you for the information. Goodbye."

Stern hung up and addressed his companions. "Dr. Fitzpatrick has informed me that Marcus Reinecker's body is missing from the morgue."

"Missing? How?" asked Tesla.

"Unknown. His clothing, kept in a box near the body, is also missing."

"Body snatching for anatomical research purposes?" asked Crowley. "It happens."

"These days, rarely. But even then, why take the clothes?" said Stern. He crossed his arms and pondered the two matching sets of fingerprints on the table. "Could he be walking around alive again? Imagine an enemy who can bring their dead soldiers back to life as many times as they wish. If these Ferox or their human agents can actually do this, we need to know. Whoever the mystery bank robber was, I'm afraid there's only one way to positively confirm whether or not he is dead."

"Well," said Crowley, "what's one more felony between friends? Tesla's got some good flashlights we can use."

"Oh my," said Tesla. "Seriously?"

27

September 2nd, 1899

The swells in their steady rhythm lifted and lowered the motorboat, piloted by Donnelly toward the four men's destination. The wind carried the mingled odors of salt spray and petroleum. Electric and gaslights along the Bronx shoreline, reflected upon the surface of Long Island Sound, stood as rivals to the stars and the crescent moon above.

Tesla shone a flashlight on his watch. It was just before two in the morning. To keep himself calm, he asked Donnelly about the details of the boat's design and equipment. Sixteen by four feet, carvel planking, one-cycle four-stroke gasoline engine. One extra can of gasoline. Two oars. Four life jackets. The focus upon data made him as relaxed as it was possible to be under the circumstances. As the island got closer, Tesla noted numerous small white objects protruding like uniform teeth. These, he realized, were grave markers.

For thirty years, Hart Island had served as the potter's field of New York City, the final resting place of convicted criminals whose remains no kin had claimed. There also lay the indigent, the homeless, or the unidentified.

Donnelly killed the engine, deftly steering the boat so that it came alongside the jetty. Crowley jumped onto the shore, was thrown the lines by Stern, and had them tied to the cleats in short order.

Crowley looked around as the other three men disembarked. All were dressed in dark clothing and wore gloves. "You were right, Walter. It is indeed uninhabited."

"The island is inhabited, just not here on the southern tip. We shouldn't be interrupted." Stern turned to face all three men. "Gentlemen, with no exhumation order—as we can assume no judge would believe our story—we are about to violate several New York City laws, particularly those against the desecration of graves. I am willing to do this alone. Anyone who remains here will have some degree of plausible deniability should we be discovered."

"Disclaimer noted, Walter. Let's go," said Crowley.

Stern pulled two shovels from the boat and handed one to Crowley. Tesla and Donnelly produced flashlights. Donnelly carried a large black rucksack.

They walked inland, their lights piercing the night as they went past the grave markers. "These are largely mass graves, dug as trenches," said Stern, "but unknowns are buried individually on the chance they may be identified in the future. And here we are."

They had come nearly to the outer edge of the cemetery. Stern stood before a gravestone, its inscription illuminated by the flashlight beams.

1896-372

DOB UNK—JUNE 14 1896

"I assume," said Tesla, "this is the 372nd individual interred here in 1896, whose date of birth is unknown, and who died on the 14th of June in that year."

"That is correct," said Stern, confirming the information on a document held under Donnelly's light. He folded it up, placed it in his vest pocket, and said, "Shall we proceed?" Donnelly gazed at the grave and crossed himself.

More than two men digging at a time would have gotten in each other's way. Tesla and Donnelly went first, working by the beams of the flashlights held by the other two. They cut easily into the soft topsoil, then dug harder to penetrate roots and stones. Tesla felt a macabre sense of nostalgia, as he had spent a period as a ditchdigger in his youth after resigning from Edison's company in disgust. *No matter what I do, Edison's got me digging ditches,* he thought. At the onset of middle age, it was a little harder than he remembered.

After they had gotten about three feet down, Crowley and Stern took over. "Ah, fresh air and exercise! A cure for all ills," said Crowley as he began to dig. He had insisted upon doing so despite his recent fatigue, and managed to hold his own.

Before long, there was a thud as Stern's shovel impacted hard matter. It was the pine coffin. They dug around it until their feet were nearly level with the coffin's bottom.

Wiping the sweat from his brow, Stern said, "Donnelly, the bag, please." Donnelly handed the rucksack down to Crowley, who pulled from it two crowbars and handed one to Stern. With a creak, then the cracking and splintering of wood, they pried open the coffin.

Within were the skeletal remains of a man, dark hair sparsely clinging to parts of the skull, the rest having fallen to the coffin's bottom. He was dressed in a light-gray threadbare suit, two ragged holes in the front ringed by dark, dried stains: the remains of the self-inflicted gunshot wounds.

Crowley took from the rucksack a drawstring pouch and a leather tool case. Removing a pair of scissors from the case, Stern cut several portions of the blood-stained cloth from the remains and placed them in the pouch. He then cut a lock of hair from the skull. With a small pair of tongs, he removed all three joints of the right index finger bone. After all the samples were in the pouch, Crowley closed it and placed it inside the rucksack.

One last thing remained. Crowley removed a larger pouch from the rucksack and held it open. Stern removed the skull and placed it in the pouch.

"Your souvenir of scenic Hart Island," said Crowley in a hawker-like American accent. He pulled the string closed and placed the pouch in the rucksack, then began to replace the coffin's lid.

"Wait," said Stern.

"What's the matter?" asked Crowley.

"A hunch," he replied, and began to search the now headless skeleton's pockets.

"They would've already done that after he died," said Donnelly as Stern felt around the clothing. He paused at the left breast pocket, took off his gloves, and felt again.

"There's something here," he said.

He pulled out a pocket knife, opened it, and cut into the lining of the jacket. Putting his fingers inside, he extracted a small square of paper. Tesla shined his light upon it from above.

It was a portrait photograph of a pale, dark-haired boy about twelve years of age. The photo was not colorized and had a featureless background. Its subject wore a checkered suit jacket, a dark necktie, and the unsmiling, somber expression common in portraits both painted and photographic.

"A striking resemblance to Mr. Reinecker," said Crowley.

"And the mystery bank robber," said Stern. An examination of the rest of the remains turned up nothing.

"Why do I get the feeling we were meant to find this?" said Crowley. "It feels like we're being strung along."

"Perhaps," said Stern. "But at this point all we can do is follow the string."

They covered the grave and began walking back to the boat. It was just after 4:00 a.m. "We're officially grave robbers," said Crowley. "The things one must do to get ahead."

28

I t was nearly 4:30 in the afternoon. Tesla and Stern sat at the table in Tesla's laboratory, tired. Stern drank coffee taken from the percolator in the laboratory's kitchen. Tesla sipped a glass of tepid water. A folder sat on the table between them. Barely sleeping since their return from Hart Island, they had worked intensively to analyze the samples of bone, hair, and blood taken from the grave, as well as perform special work on the skull. Tesla had given his two assistants the week off with pay, explaining only that there were urgent personal matters requiring his attention.

Donnelly had gone out to investigate the identity of the boy in the picture found in the dead man's jacket. Crowley, who had spent most of the past twenty-four hours meditating in a back room of the laboratory, came out to greet Tesla and Stern.

"Aha! I sensed you were finished with your scientific inquiries. Where's Donnelly? Ah, speak of the devil!" Donnelly walked in from the doorway, scowling at Crowley's choice of idiom. They helped themselves to coffee from the kitchen.

"Well, gentlemen," said Tesla, "we have much to discuss. You seem awfully excited, Crowley. Please go ahead."

Crowley and Donnelly sat down at the table with their coffee. "Well," began Crowley, "I suppose we've all been wondering why we haven't seen more of this apparent cult of the *ferox phasma*, and why we haven't been attacked. Other than the one time at the Waldorf-Astoria restaurant."

"The girl in West Orange said it was because the Ferox think we're not worth bothering about, that we've already lost," said Tesla.

"Yes, that's part of it. But there's more. I tried an Akashic Records search again. It was harder without help this time, and my magick is fading, though I've managed to arrest the decline for now." His expression darkened for an instant. Then he resumed speaking. "I could only get a partial perception, and tried for too much information at once. But this is what I learned: Howell the suicidal chef, Reinecker, and the blonde in West Orange comprise the entirety of the Ferox's human agents at large, except for perhaps one or two."

"Agents at large," said Stern. "Do you mean there are others in reserve?"

"Sort of. That's what I couldn't quite get. They have a large number of people, perhaps a hundred or more, whom they must keep in one location."

"Where?"

"Unknown."

"Why?"

"Unknown. Sorry." He shrugged.

"'In-physical' human agents, then? Not Ferox?" asked Tesla.

"That's the strange thing. Yes, at least half are normal humans. Physically normal, at least. But some of them…the best way I can describe this is that they're human, but not normal."

"Not normal how?"

"There is something physically different about them. I don't know what. But whatever it is, it's very important to the Ferox's plan. So much so that they feel a need to keep them all in one place. They're considered too valuable to risk letting out. So there are less than a handful of arse-tattooed cultists traipsing about."

"That's good to know. Anything else?" asked Stern.

"No. That's all I've got for now. Who's next?"

"Sergeant Donnelly, if you please," said Stern.

"Yes, sir. Well, despite intensive searching, we still cannot match the posterior tattoo found on the two bodies with any tattoo artist in the city. But you'll be pleased to know I've located the boy in the photograph."

"Not just identified him, but located him?" asked Stern.

"Yes. His name is Michael Crane. Age fifteen. He's currently a resident of the New York House of Refuge on Randalls Island."

"The juvenile reformatory?" asked Tesla.

"Yes," said Donnelly. He explained that young Michael had fallen in with the Five Points Gang two years before. Though reportedly not much of a brawler, he was highly useful as a thief until in June he got caught picking a pocket on Thirty-First Street. When it became clear that he had no fixed address, he was placed in the reform school. In court he testified that he had run away from home and could not recall an exact address, nor the names of his parents. There was speculation as to whether he was lying or somehow affected by amnesia. All attempts at finding relatives turned up nothing, and birth records in New York of anyone named Michael Crane referred to different persons.

"We'll pay him a visit. Good work, Donnelly," said Stern. "Did you take down the essentials from his case file?"

"Yes. But there's something odd." He took a sheet of paper from his pocket and placed it on the table. Stern picked it up.

"Petty theft, pickpocketing…'no fingerprints.' Were they taken upon his arrest?"

"They were. The prints are missing," said Donnelly.

"Missing how?" asked Stern.

"Unknown. The Files Section is investigating."

"All right. We can take a set when we go to see him."

"But we still haven't heard from our stalwart laboratory heroes," said Crowley.

"It's been a bit exhausting," said Stern, "but Mr. Tesla and I have managed to fit another piece into our puzzle. Mr. Tesla, if you please."

Tesla went into a doorway behind the table. After a moment, he returned, carrying a tray upon which sat a clay bust of a hairless male head. It bore a strong resemblance to Marcus Reinecker and the mystery bank robber of 1896. He set it down on the table.

"So you did it," said Crowley. "Remarkable."

"Yes," said Tesla. "Utilizing some tools and techniques Inspector Stern was kind enough to contribute, we have reconstructed an approximation of the facial features of the deceased interred on Hart Island."

"It is as yet an inexact science," said Stern, "developed only within the past decade. But we were able to reconstruct the features with reasonable accuracy."

"It now seems safe to assume Reinecker and the bank robber were different men," said Crowley. "Though perhaps twin brothers after all. But what about your other analyses? The blood, hair, and finger bones?"

All eyes were on Tesla. "As I mentioned before our trip to the island, I wished to carry out additional analyses of Reinecker's and Howell's blood. This I have done, along with a comparative analysis of the samples we took from the grave.

"While neither biologist nor physician, I have some fundamental knowledge and maintain contacts within the scientific community. A physician friend in Austria has recently made a remarkable discovery, which he plans to publish next year: Human blood is distinguishable into at least three different types. Each type is characterized by the presence of certain proteins, termed antibodies, produced by the blood cells. They apparently play a role in protecting the body from disease."

"Sounds like a Nobel Prize in the making," said Crowley.

"I should think so. First, I checked Howell's blood. Like Inspector Stern, I found it chemically normal, and type A, as my physician friend would term it. Then, against the sample of Reinecker's blood, I checked three separate portions of the blood remnants taken from the grave to be sure of no mistake. I have found that both blood types are identical."

"So Reinecker and the bank robber could be related, or even twins," said Donnelly.

"So it would seem," said Tesla. "But there is another unexpected factor. Their blood matches none of the three known types. It may even be unique."

"Unique how?" asked Crowley.

"It contains no antibodies. I'll need to tell my friend in Austria about this."

"But if these antibody things protect one from disease, how could either of them have stayed alive?" asked Donnelly.

"There must be other factors at work which keep the immune system functioning. But that is not the real concern here. I also found elements identical to those found by Inspector Stern in Marcus Reinecker's blood. Besides the iron and hemoglobin one would normally find, there were also gold, silver, copper, tin, lead, and mercury. As well as trace amounts of carborundum."

"So his body was also imbued with the Essential Composite," said Crowley. "I don't suppose there were abnormal levels of sulfur."

"I checked. No."

Crossing his arms, Donnelly leaned back in his chair. "Assuming Reinecker had drunk or injected this poison, all he did afterward was get stabbed to death. But the other man was attempting a bank robbery. That's a bit more difficult to do if you've got mercury and lead in your bloodstream."

Stern said, "If he had taken the solution just before entering the bank, it's not impossible. And Fitzpatrick described him as suicidal, or at least fatalistic. But there was no vial, container, or syringe on his person, nor any report of an injection puncture."

"But why bother taking poison?" pondered Donnelly. "He had the gun to shoot himself with. Which he did."

"Perhaps from his perspective he was performing a religious act," said Tesla. "Since the Essential Composite is indispensable to summoning these creatures, their earthly followers may see it as a fitting means of suicide. Mr. Crowley, do you know of any such custom?"

"Taking it into one's body? No. Still, the extant lore is sparse, so who knows?"

"Might there be any practical purpose?" asked Stern.

"The only thing I can think of would be to act as a physical, living conduit to bring in a Ferox, presumably by possession," said Crowley. "In theory it could work. But as you've pointed out, there might be a thirty-minute period at most, then the human host is dead. Also, you need electricity in some form, which Reinecker accessed as lightning, but the bank robber didn't."

"Could possession by a Ferox somehow counteract the fatal effects of the metals?"

"Unknown. But I don't see how. Possession tends to worsen any existing physical health problems of the host, as it is inherently an invasive act."

"In any case," said Stern, "our next step should be to pay a visit to young Michael at the House of Refuge. Mr. Crowley, may I have the honor of your company?"

"The honor is mine, sir."

"Donnelly," said Stern, "see what you can come up with regarding those fingerprint records, and anything else you can dig up on all three of our persons of interest."

"Yes, sir. That's the kind of digging up I prefer."

29

The Administrator sat at the desk in his comfortable oak-paneled office, gazing out the window at the butte, at its most beautiful in the red rays of dusk. He had never tired of this view and was sorry he would soon need to leave it. But small sacrifices were inevitable in accomplishing the greater good.

Despite his previous hopes, occupying two contiguous states was untenable. Still, one would suffice. Getting people to join up was not difficult, but getting people qualified to build, maintain, and run everything was. Once the operation commenced, numbers would be insufficient to staff both compounds, let alone control all the surrounding territory, even with Ferox support. With no time to gather additional numbers, one facility would have to be abandoned, and circumstances dictated it be this one. Crowley and Tesla would thereby be delayed a bit longer and kept at arm's length. For now.

He ate another dried date from the plate on his desk, drained his glass of claret, then turned his attention to work.

He reviewed the items he had signed for placement in his out-basket. Agricultural production data on lettuce, carrots, and spinach. Medical reports, including one case of influenza, one sprained ankle, and the latest health check data on the Q Cohort: again, physically robust but mentally unfocused. They would all need to be liquidated. Maintenance checks done on the wind turbines. Confirming that he had signed all the documents, he placed them in the basket for his secretary to pick up in the morning.

He turned to look at the spirit phone set atop the side table on his right. He would need to use it later this evening. In the meantime, he required the latest information on Crowley, assuming there was any.

Crowley and his friends would find him soon enough, and at just the right moment. He would make sure of it. But it was still too soon. The entire transition would go more smoothly if all four of them were on hand to assist him right away, though it would be hard to convince them at first. They would consider his plan misguided and tyrannical. Doubtless their reasoning was clouded, like countless others, by a naïve belief in natural rights. It was the curse of the modern era. Which was why the time of their encounter needed to be just as the new system commenced, when it was too late to prevent it.

Natural rights. But he had learned long ago the paradoxical truth that rights, by their nature, were not natural.

Deciding his inquiry regarding Crowley could wait a few more minutes, he removed a sheet of paper from a drawer of his desk. It was the unfinished letter his eventual successor must receive. Picking up his fountain pen, he began to write.

But of all the things I have taught you, the most important to remember is the fundamental nature of the rights of man:

There are no rights outside a collective community. The source of all rights is the state. Not God, not nature, nor any other nebulous concept one may cut from whole cloth. Hence what is needed is wise and strong governance, and the absolute power to make just policy.

He put down his pen and reflected, yet again, upon the childhood dawning of this awareness: the cruelest of lessons, born in the depths of misery and grief. Yet it was the memory he treasured most, for it marked his awakening to the path his life—and all lives—must take. He could never forget, and didn't want to.

◆ ◆ ◆

It has been nearly two days since they ate Mr. Dolan. The boy tries to ignore his hunger, and the realization of what he has done to stay alive. He is ten years old today.

He lies on his side under the blankets, staring at the rough-hewn logs of the cabin wall. Beyond it lie the endless depths of snow, a tomb for both the living and the dead. They are trapped.

His brother, who was eight, died a week ago of pneumonia. He, the boy was assured in oblique language, will not be consumed. But the bodies of the other two adults who have died are being saved for later. The freezing weather and the snow outside will preserve them. This is partly to conserve food, for that is what they are now.

But the boy also understands by instinct another reason: to do what they have done—to do that—too soon again would be too much to bear. It is something people aren't supposed to do. But they can't help it. There is nothing else to eat. Nothing. But it will be ensured that no one will eat their kin, and there is always the forlorn hope that rescuers will arrive before they have to start on the next body. (Yes, it is impossible. But better to pretend it is not.)

The adults. It's their fault, he reflects with bitter conviction. Especially the men leading the party, with their overconfidence and their stupid mistakes. Ever since the start of the journey from Missouri to reach the Oregon Territory. A new and better life, his father had said to him. The blessings of freedom, independence, and autonomy—he loved that last word. They were, he declared, what characterized our nation. We go to seek prosperity in our Manifest Destiny. Another term he loved, though he wasn't using it recently.

Not taking enough supplies. Ignoring the established settler route to take a new "shortcut," which turned out to be a nearly impassable, boulder-filled terrain. Getting lost. Running out of food as winter approached. Eating the dogs, then the horses, then boiled oxhide. Then finally the unspeakable act. Each time a bad choice was made, the danger it presented was obvious to the boy, and each time, his warning was met with a sharp rebuke to mind his elders. He has already reached the age at which adults no longer appear omniscient, but this is his absolute proof. He and the other children had no choice but to follow where their parents led them, and this is what it has come to.

If this is autonomy, then autonomy is evil. People, his heart declares with absolute conviction, need something else. Something better. A way to prevent horrors such as this from ever happening. But what? He takes a silent oath that if he lives, he will find it. Or failing that, forge it into existence.

He makes this vow only to himself, for he decided the moment his mother tearfully urged him to consume his steaming bowl of Mr. Dolan that there was no God. Only ignorant people making ignorant decisions which they celebrated as freedom. Like his father.

He is a precocious boy with a wandering mind and a habit of imagining mechanical solutions to every problem he perceives. Having heard of the telegraph, he asked his teacher why they were not connected everywhere instead of in just a few

places on the earth, and why a telegraph could not be used to transmit someone's voice.
Why, he wondered as they began their journey westward, wasn't there a railroad con-
necting the eastern to the western part of the country? For that matter, why not com-
bine a steam engine with a hot-air balloon and fly across the country instead of heav-
ing aside boulders and trudging through the snow and the freezing cold and getting
trapped and running out of food and watching your little brother die and becoming
so hungry you have to—

He stops this train of thought and begins to imagine himself piloting a
steam-powered balloon, joyfully soaring high above the earth, in a world where the
hell he is trapped in cannot be real.

◆ ◆ ◆

He put the letter away. He would complete it later.

He pulled another sheet of paper from a drawer and placed it on the desk.
Upon it was drawn a grid with letters.

K	O	S	E	M
O	B	O	D	E
S	O	F	O	S
E	D	O	B	O
M	E	S	O	K

"Elerion," he said. "I seek your aid, and command you to now appear before me."

Elerion appeared as an olive-skinned, black-haired woman of early middle
age. She wore an indigo, high-necked afternoon dress with a matching wide-
brimmed hat.

"You called me, sir?" she asked.

"Yes. Is there any new information regarding young Mr. Crowley and his
associates?"

"Yes. They have located the one you call Q-75. Due to the psychical safe-
guards Mr. Crowley has erected, I can neither materialize near his group nor
comprehend their actions in any great detail. But it is logical to assume they intend to contact the boy."

"It is as I suspected. And then they will come here. Which means we need to make the location transfer within the next twenty-four hours. Let's do it tomorrow afternoon, at one o'clock sharp. I'll summon you a few minutes beforehand."

"Sir, regarding that, I am duty bound to serve you, as it is the natural relation of mage and demon. But while it may be presumptuous, I beg permission to offer counsel."

Temple gave an indulgent smile and said, "Go ahead."

"The location transfer you intend is in effect a mass teleportation, requiring tremendous energy and resources, the loss of which will leave you in a relatively weakened state, if temporarily. To whatever extent Mr. Crowley and his friends are your adversaries, this could be dangerous for you. And I sense it is not only them you need to beware of."

"Doubtless you refer to the *ferox phasma*."

"So the rumor is true. Sir, I must—"

"Elerion." He said it quietly, but with a sharp and commanding undertone. "I appreciate your concern for my welfare, but—"

"It is not simply your own welfare, sir. Reality itself is—"

"While I am not required to explain myself to a familiar, I shall say this: All measures have been taken to ensure that the final Ferox summoning will proceed smoothly, and with the desired result. As for the headquarters transfer, let me worry about any possible weakening effect. Your agreement is not required. Your role is to obey. Is that clear?"

Her large black eyes regarded him for a moment. "Yes, sir," she said, bowing.

"Good. Have you any other news?"

"No, sir."

"All right. I will summon you again just before one o'clock tomorrow. You're dismissed."

She vanished.

It was getting dark. He switched on the electric desk lamp and contemplated the grid sitting atop his desk. This was why he disliked depending on demons for anything. No matter how much they professed to follow protocol, sooner or later they got ideas of their own. Elerion was useful, but too ignorant to properly understand these things. He needed to give the world an ideal society. And for that, he needed the Ferox, and the people he had recruited, and those he had acquired through special means. And, of course, the spirit phones.

Of the four, he thought, recruitment was the easiest thing to accomplish, especially considering all the changes of the past century. Faith in religion is shaken by the scientist: we are not made by God but descended from apes. The masses move from farm to factory, becoming countless weary cogs in a dismal machine. Slavery is abolished at the cost of over half a million dead, yet the Negro is still exploited, tormented, and murdered. Mass democracy of a kind, and now women want the right to vote, some so they can ban liquor. (As if there were for anyone a "right" to vote.) Communists and anarchists vow to tear apart and rebuild society, and shrill reactionaries vow to crush them. With all the upheaval, it is no great difficulty to find people who think utopia is a simple matter of literally bringing their heroes back from the dead.

A few appearances at spiritualist meetings, bohemian watering holes, and dinner parties of eccentric socialites was all it took to eventually form a congregation of like-minded fools. Their resurrected idols, so they believe, will form a council, elect a leader, and decide how best to lead the world into its new and joyful age. It is for them an ersatz religion, replacing the mental anchor cut loose by Darwin, Marx, and the factory system.

Yes, there will be utopia. But not in the way they expect. Not even close. Sadly, being economical with the truth was necessary to gain their trust and thus accomplish what is necessary for the greater good. They might otherwise get their own ideas, and instead they need shepherding. Autonomy is evil, except for those who know best how to employ it.

Temple turned to the spirit phone again. Speaking of being economical with the truth. He didn't look forward to this, but he had to do it. Such a vile creature. He poured another glass of claret. Switching on the electromagnet, he said, "Andreas, we need to talk."

"Hello, Mr. Temple," said the deep, metallically distorted voice.

"Hello. Things are proceeding more or less on schedule, but some of our operators are exhibiting psychosis. One man shot himself in the head after attempting to murder Crowley. He's been replaced, of course." He took a sip of claret.

"An unavoidable side effect, it would seem. I am aware of what happened, and of the girl you sent to New Jersey. Why did you even let them out of the compound?"

"I needed some feet on the ground to collect intelligence, and they seemed perfectly normal when they left. Apparently, it was the interruption of regular spirit phone use which brought upon their instability, like withdrawal from a drug."

"Your concern is understandable. But as long as the transference takes place on schedule, I sense that the operators will maintain enough presence of mind to complete the task. It is now imperative, however, that none of them be separated from the phones for more than twenty-four hours. And as a precaution, I suggest posting armed guards during the contact sessions. Just in case."

"Already arranged. But I'll need to send one more agent out. Unavoidable."

"I see. And another matter. The boy in the reformatory. Is he not a security risk?"

"I'm still observing his adaptations. Even defectives can yield valuable data. I've ensured he'll never remember enough to jeopardize our operations."

"Very well. Now, about the terms of our agreement," said Andreas. "You are positive the entire state shall be ours to frolic in?"

"Absolutely. I will declare it your personal territory immediately upon taking power. And provide you with plenty of game to hunt. But will Colorado really be enough for you?"

"There are only a hundred of us. As long as you can replenish our supply of meat, we've no reason to venture beyond the state line."

"And you will carry out the eliminations as I request them?"

"Immediately. It will be as easy as breathing. And that will be the extent of our involvement in your regime. We have no interest in politics, especially me. I can tell you from experience, to be surrounded by people spouting ideology is tiresome."

"We have an accord, then."

"Yes. But I suggest you eliminate magick boy and his friends. They'll just cause you grief."

"It suits my purposes to keep them alive. I'm convinced they will agree to join me."

"If they don't, once I'm physical, can I have them?" There was a low-pitched metallic giggle, and Temple was vaguely reminded of fingernails scraping across a blackboard.

"All right," he replied.

30

September 5th, 1899

S tern and Crowley, clad in suits and bowlers and carrying valises, stepped off the ferry onto Randalls Island. They walked in the late morning sunlight toward the large and imposing stone edifice, five stories tall and very wide. Three large domes dominated the roof.

"Impressive," said Crowley.

"Yes," said Stern. "They moved here sometime in the fifties, I think."

The New York House of Refuge was the first juvenile reformatory in the United States. It was a place to incarcerate, and in theory reform, criminals not yet of the age of majority. Its first two locations were in Manhattan; it was established in the Bowery in 1824, but was relocated in 1839 to Twenty-Third Street after its destruction in a fire. In 1854, it was again relocated, this time to Randalls Island on the East River.

In 1899, as Walter Stern and Aleister Crowley made their way toward the reformatory in the bright September weather, no bridge existed between Randalls Island and Manhattan Island. The last such bridge, crossing from the Manhattan side at 114th Street, was destroyed in the Norfolk and Long Island Hurricane of 1821. Afterward, the island's proximity yet physical separation from Manhattan eventually inspired its use as a location not just for the House of Refuge, but also the Idiot Asylum, the Inebriate Asylum, the City Insane Asylum, and potter's fields, the latter before Hart Island became the primary resting place for the city's unclaimed and indigent.

They were almost to the main entrance. "So you're quite sure we will not be remembered?" asked Stern.

"Positive. I've set up the effect perfectly. At least we won't be remembered enough for anyone to identify us. It kicks in as soon as we leave."

Walking up the steps into the entrance, they immediately saw a counter with a sign reading *RECEPTION*. The woman sitting behind it smiled at them as they entered.

"May I help you gentlemen?"

"Yes, ma'am, if you please," answered Stern, showing his badge. "I am Inspector Johnson of the New York City Police Department. This is my associate, Dr. Watkins."

"Charmed, madam," said Crowley, smiling. She blushed slightly.

"What is the nature of your visit, sirs?"

Stern took a notepad from his vest pocket and looked at it. "I believe one of your inmates here is a young man by the name of Michael Crane. He was arrested for pickpocketing on Thirty-First Street on…" He flipped a couple of pages. "…yes, on June 10th of this year. We'd like permission to speak with him, if that's possible."

"Just a moment, please." She reached down and pulled a notebook from beneath the counter. After opening it and running her finger down the page, she said, "Yes, we have a child here by that name. Is he in any trouble?"

"Not that I'm aware of," said Stern. "We're not here to investigate Michael as a criminal suspect. However, I believe he may have some information related to an important case currently under investigation. We would be very grateful to get permission from the warden to ask him a few questions."

"Could you wait here a moment, please?" She went from behind the counter to a door across the hall, knocked and opened it, and went in. Soon a pensive-looking man of about fifty came out of the office. The men said good morning and shook hands.

"I'm Albert Muldoon, warden of this facility. I understand you wish to question an inmate named Michael Crane?"

"Yes. I'm Inspector Johnson. My associate, Dr. Watkins, is not a law officer, but is rather acting as a consultant on…"

"Juvenile criminal psychology," said Crowley. "A rather new and exciting field. Still in an experimental stage."

"And this pertains to a criminal case, Inspector?" asked Muldoon.

"Yes, but as I mentioned to your kind receptionist, Michael is not a suspect. We think he may have some important information, however, and hope to be able to speak with him."

"I will need to be present during the questioning."

"Of course. But we ask that all that is spoken during the meeting be kept in the strictest confidence."

"Of course, gentlemen. If you'll follow me, we have a conference room on the third floor. Miss Jameson, please have young Mr. Crane located and escorted there."

"Yes, sir."

The conference room was large and comfortable, with black leather swivel chairs set around a long oak table. Paintings of the previous reformatory wardens graced the walls. Muldoon sat at the head of the table, Stern and Crowley next to each other, facing the door.

"Juvenile criminal psychology does indeed sound interesting, Doctor... I'm sorry."

"Watkins."

"Dr. Watkins. Forgive me. You seem quite young to have a medical degree."

"Well, I suppose I'm a quick study."

"I see."

"What can you tell us about Michael, Mr. Muldoon?" asked Stern.

"Well, he's been here for only three months, but he is in some ways a model inmate. You see, I have quite a headache keeping things under control here. We must do things in a humane and charitable fashion, to guide these children onto a better path. Yet it is difficult, as many are insolent and rebellious, or occasionally violent."

From what Stern had heard, guards in the House of Refuge at times carried out such humane and charitable actions as extended solitary confinement and beatings of inmates. But there were other things to deal with today, so he addressed the matter at hand.

"I see. And Michael?"

"Michael is one of the quiet ones. He seems reflective, distracted even. I think he only fell into crime because he was easily manipulated by his more devious peers. Despite his list of suspected crimes, and the one they actually caught him at, he makes no trouble here. Though he hasn't really made any friends either. He mostly keeps to himself."

"Does Michael have any unusual markings or tattoos on his body?" asked Stern.

"Why, no, none at all. Why?"

Stern handed him the paper with the tattoo's image. "Nothing like this? On any part of his anatomy?"

Muldoon held the paper for a moment, shook his head, and then handed it back to Stern. "No. I've never seen this marking before. Occasionally some of our boys, especially the older ones, might have tattoos. But not Michael. All our charges get a full physical examination upon entering this facility. Tattoos or unusual birthmarks are noted in case identification might be needed later. If Michael had a tattoo like this, I would have known."

"So it goes without saying that he's got nothing tattooed on his backside," said Crowley.

"That is correct," said Muldoon, brows furrowed.

"Has Michael spoken much about his life before coming here? His early childhood?" asked Stern.

"No. He doesn't seem to remember much. It is a point of concern for our doctors, though otherwise Michael seems to have adjusted well, in his way. We expect he'll be able to go out into the world on his own in a few years."

There was a knock on the door. "Come in," answered Muldoon.

The door opened and a young woman put her head in. "Mr. Muldoon, Michael Crane is here."

"Yes, let him in. You can go."

The boy entered slowly, eyes downcast. He was slender, just over five and a half feet tall, with dark-brown hair. He briefly glanced up, scanned the room, and fixed his eyes on Crowley for a moment. Then he looked down again. Crowley and Stern exchanged a glance but did not reveal their amazement. The photograph did not do the resemblance justice; they were looking at a teenage version of Marcus Reinecker and the mystery bank robber.

"Good morning, Michael," said Muldoon.

"Good morning, Mr. Muldoon," said Michael.

"It's all right, Michael. There's no need to be nervous. You're not in any trouble. These two gentlemen would just like to ask you a few questions. Please have a seat."

Michael sat down at the conference table, opposite Crowley and Stern. Muldoon gave the two men an assenting nod.

"Good morning, Michael," said Stern.

"Good morning, sir," he said, looking down at the table.

"I'm Inspector Johnson, and this is Dr. Watkins."

"Good morning, Michael," said Crowley.

"Good morning, sir." For a moment, his eyes met Crowley's. Then he looked down again.

"Thank you for giving us some of your time, Michael," said Crowley. He turned to Muldoon. "Mr. Muldoon, are you all right?"

"What do you mean?" asked Muldoon.

Crowley's arms were crossed. He looked intently into Muldoon's eyes and said, "I think you're quite exhausted." He slapped his left arm three times, made a fist palm-up, then opened his hand palm-down. Muldoon fell asleep, slumped over the table.

Michael looked alarmed. "What did you just do?" he asked.

"It's all right, Michael," said Stern. "Mr. Muldoon is a very busy man, and his job must make him tired. He needs a bit of rest. In fact, I suspect he is sleeping so soundly that we can speak without waking him up."

"That is my professional opinion," said Crowley.

"You did something," said Michael to Crowley. "With your hand. Some kind of gesture."

"Oh, that," said Crowley. "Just a little quirk I have." He twiddled his fingers.

"Never mind that, Michael," said Stern. "Let's get started. What can you tell us about your parents?"

"I don't remember much about them. We lived in Five Points."

"For your entire life? Before coming here?"

Michael looked puzzled, strained. "I think so…I don't know." He looked out the window beyond Stern and Crowley, then down at the table again. "There are a lot of things I just don't remember. And I don't know why. So I don't worry about it."

"What's the earliest thing you can remember?" asked Stern.

"The earliest clear thing or the earliest thing?"

"Both."

"The earliest clear thing is…being with my mother at home. And…she's holding me tight, and crying, saying she's sorry, that she didn't mean for this to happen."

"For what to happen?"

"I don't know. Something that had already happened. I can't remember clearly before that day. My father was already gone by that time, but that wasn't what she was crying about. It was something else."

"Do you know what happened to your father? Whether he's alive?"

"No."

"Go on."

"She said that I needed to leave, that they were coming for her and there was no way she could escape, but for me there was a chance if I went alone."

"They? Who was coming for her?"

"I don't know." He looked at Crowley, then back at Stern. "Why are his eyes closed?"

Crowley opened his eyes and looked at Stern. "This requires another approach." He turned to Michael. "Michael, I think you're quite exhausted." He duplicated the gesture he had used on Muldoon. Michael continued to look at Crowley, wide awake.

Crowley repeated the gesture, again with no effect. Stern and Crowley looked at each other, then at Michael.

"I don't know what you did to Mr. Muldoon, but it doesn't work on me. I could feel a kind of ripple inside me, but that's it."

"Well," said Crowley, "this is a bit awkward."

"Why don't you just tell me what you want?"

"It would take a long time to explain," said Stern, "but there are some very bad people who want to do some very bad things."

"Criminals?"

"Even worse," said Stern.

"We think you may have information you can't remember, but which we need in order to stop them," said Crowley. "I would like to ask permission to look inside your mind."

"You mean like mind reading?"

"Yes."

"All right," said Michael.

Crowley went to the other side of the table and sat down next to the boy. "All right, Michael, please close your eyes, relax, and empty your mind. Try to make it blank." Michael closed his eyes.

"You're trying too hard. Relax. All right, good." Crowley placed one hand on Michael's forehead, the other behind the boy's head, and closed his own eyes.

◆ ◆ ◆

He likes to come outside and look around, though the weather starts to get chilly at this time of year. The compound is large, though not many things have been built. Barracks and a few smaller buildings. The powerhouse. The wind turbines. But these hold no interest for him. He has come to look at the wide and endless expanse beyond the chain-link fence: The sky, the trees, the layers of red sedimentary rock, at their most beautiful in the dusk. And in the distance, one very tall rock, huge like a mountain. Not red, but gray. Igneous rock. It is peculiar, flat on top, like a giant tree stump jutting out of the ground.

"Seventy-five! Time to eat!" calls the voice behind him. He turns around. It is the grinning face of P-67, his older brother. Older by how many years? Seventeen or eighteen, he thinks. His number is clearly visible on the left breast of his gray coveralls, the same as those worn by Q-75. "Come on, you'll catch a cold," he says.

"All right," Q-75 answers, running to join his senior. They enter the mess hall together and join the line with their brothers. There are dozens of them, boys and men, all wearing the numbered gray coveralls. They are of different ages, but their faces are all identical, all the same as Q-75 and his friend.

◆ ◆ ◆

Crowley's eyes opened. He turned to Stern. "You're not going to believe this." Michael sat with his eyes still closed, breathing deeply.

"Tell me later. We need to—Crowley, your nose." Stern pulled out a handkerchief and handed it to him.

"Damn. Thank you," he said, wiping the blood. "This is getting harder. I don't feel so well. But there are a couple of other things to do." Three times he made a small circular flourish with his hand. "Michael, wake up, please." The boy opened his eyes.

"Your nose is bleeding."

"It's nothing. Michael, you did very well. Thank you. May I ask a couple more favors?"

"What?"

"There's a special illness we are concerned you may have. It can be detected by a quick physical examination, but it would require you to disrobe. Completely. Just for a moment."

Quietly and without hesitation, Michael did as asked. His body had no markings or tattoos. After a few seconds, Crowley said, "All right, thank you. Please dress."

"Am I all right?"

"Yes, you're fine. But just to be on the safe side, it would be very helpful if you could give us a small sample of your blood and let us take your fingerprints."

Michael pursed his lips for a moment. "Sure," he said.

31

"Tesla! Blood!" shouted Crowley as he and Stern entered the laboratory. He pulled the vial containing the blood out of his valise.

"I'm in here," came Tesla's voice from a back room.

They walked in to find Tesla sitting at a bench, peering into a microscope. "I can't really find much else of interest in this blood. So, you have a sample from the young man at the reformatory?"

Crowley handed the vial to Tesla, then went to sit down with Stern to scan the newspapers for anything related to the spirit phone. Nearly an hour later, as Crowley was about to nod off in his seat, Tesla appeared. He was holding the vial, now nearly empty.

"Is this the right blood?" he asked.

"What do you mean?" asked Crowley. "We took it from Michael Crane, yes."

Tesla looked at the vial in his hand, then shifted his gaze back to Crowley and Stern. "The blood type is the same as that of the other two samples. But I have to ask you: are you positive you took this blood from a living person?"

"Yes," said Stern. "He was alive. And seemingly quite healthy. Just a little shy."

"And we checked him to make sure," said Crowley. "He has no tattoos anywhere on his body."

"How long were you with him?" asked Tesla.

"About an hour," said Crowley.

"During that time, did he inject or ingest anything?"

"No," said Crowley. "What are you talking about?"

"Is there any possibility that this sample was contaminated in any way from the time you took it until the time you handed it to me?"

"No," said Stern.

"I'll need to do a more detailed analysis to confirm it absolutely, but I can tell you right now that this blood contains the six other metals of the Essential Composite besides iron. And traces of carborundum. The same as in the other two samples."

"He's alive," said Stern. "Walking around with that stuff in his blood."

"Yes," said Tesla. "Which means those men weren't poisoned. Somehow their blood chemistry *included* those elements, as does Michael's. Whether through some form of special intervention or from birth. I'm guessing the latter. I assume no one at the reformatory knows?"

"Blood analyses are uncommon unless someone seems seriously ill," said Stern. "So it's safe to assume so."

"I got no impression of such knowledge from either Muldoon or Michael," said Crowley. "But how could a person be born and stay alive and healthy with such a blood chemistry?"

"That is what we need to find out," said Tesla.

"I don't suppose there are abnormal levels of sulfur in the blood?" asked Crowley.

"Again, I'll need to check more thoroughly, but it seems there are not. In any case, we were able to use the spirit phone in Edison's laboratory without—wait."

"What?"

"Of course. I'm an idiot! Sulfur *is* the Secret Element. Crowley, do you recall what you drank just before we left the saloon in West Orange?"

"Vin Mariani."

"Yes. A tonic essentially consisting of wine and cocaine. And then you ate raisins covered in chocolate, did you not?"

"But what would that—wait."

"Yes," said Tesla. "Sulfur is naturally present in the blood, but the sulfites used to preserve the wine and the raisins temporarily increased the sulfur level in your system. It's also in all that chocolate you were eating. The sulfur required for attaining contact with a Ferox is not meant as part of the device. It is ingested by the summoner."

"Yes," said Crowley. "Which is why your attempt at contacting Faraday's spirit was unsuccessful and mine worked, albeit it wasn't really Faraday."

"Edison is reputedly an avid consumer of Vin Mariani, though one could simply take a sulfur pill. And it is apparently unneeded for the generally marketed model."

"Why would consumption of sulfites aid in attaining contact?" asked Stern.

"I'm the idiot," said Crowley. "I should have figured this out. I surmise that the Ferox can smell the increased sulfur in the contactor's blood."

"Smell it? They're ghosts."

"Not quite 'smell' in the physical sense. But sulfur is especially detectable by certain entities, including human spirits, hence its frequent use in occult and alchemical processes."

"Well," said Stern. "It's turning out to be an enlightening evening. But to return to all three of our persons of interest, there is additional news, but I want to make sure I'm right."

Tesla sat down as Stern pulled a file from his valise and produced the fingerprint records of the two men, and the fingerprints taken that morning from Michael Crane. All three sheets lay on the table side by side.

"Amazing," said Tesla.

"All three sets are identical," said Crowley. "The boy is a physical duplicate of Reinecker and the man buried on Hart Island."

"Who were, it would seem, physical duplicates of each other," said Stern. "You were right, Aleister. We can at least rest assured that the resurrection of corpses is not among the mysteries we face. Could you tell us in detail what you learned in your psychic communion with the young man?"

"Wait until you hear this, Tesla. It's going to knock your socks off."

32

"You're looking haggard, Crowley," said Tesla. "Why don't you rest for a couple of hours first?"

"No, I'm fine, old fellow. Thank you," said Crowley, though he was pale with dark circles under his eyes. "Let's go out for a bite to eat after I tell my story. That'll fix me up. And let's get Donnelly to join us."

"I'll telephone him later," said Stern. "So?"

"That young fellow had a psychic block put on him," began Crowley. "Most of the information I obtained consists of things he doesn't consciously remember. It even partially prevents him from talking about what little he does recall."

"Which would partly explain his rather quiet, preoccupied nature," said Stern. "Though he also seems to have been designed that way, so to speak."

"We must assume he is connected, however unwittingly, with this apparent cult of the Ferox," said Tesla. "We know little about them, but why would they allow him to live a relatively normal life?"

"Unknown," said Crowley. "I also don't know who blocked his conscious memory, or how, but it was bloody hard getting in there. What I picked up wasn't clear or complete, but this is what I learned:

"The boy was born and grew up in some kind of…I don't know what to call it. A facility. A fort. A compound. Perhaps a half dozen long wooden buildings, like army barracks, and a few smaller buildings. All fenced around. And something about the way the fence is designed makes it visually blend in with its surroundings."

"You mean the compound is invisible?" asked Tesla.

"Not quite invisible. Just somehow very hard to see unless you're looking carefully. I guess if you were far away enough, you wouldn't know there was a fence or any buildings there."

"Magick-with-a-*k*?" asked Stern.

"Hard to say," said Crowley. "It was a fragmentary perception. I got no magickal or psychic impression."

Stern nodded. "And you also detected people?"

"Yes. As we've surmised, the boy and the two men were all born as duplicates of one another. All three of them lived in this place, and not only them. I saw dozens of them. They were of three distinct age groups: twelve or thirteen, just under thirty, and about forty."

"All identical except for their ages?"

"Yes," answered Crowley. "They wore some kind of uniform. Gray coveralls. On the left breast was embroidered a letter and a number, by which they would call each other. Michael Crane was called Q-75. He was in the youngest group. He was deeply attached to an older duplicate called P-67, in the middle group. They all referred to each other as brothers, but these two had a special bond.

"They ate meals together in a sort of mess hall, like in the army. Everything was regimented, with scheduled bedtimes and risings, group exercises. And some kind of…indoctrination. Something utopian, with the air of a revival meeting. And basic education: the three Rs plus some natural science classes. The younger ones, that is. The two older groups had already completed the courses. No literature, history, art, nothing like that. But everyone had to attend those indoctrination sessions. The oldest group were the fewest and seemed listless and unfocused. They got fatigued easily."

"How did they acquire food?" asked Tesla.

"The place is pretty big. It has a little farm. Pigs, cows, chickens, fields for growing various grains and vegetables. And I saw a couple of wind turbines and a powerhouse."

"A hidden, self-sufficient community," said Stern.

"Were there any people besides these duplicates?" asked Tesla.

"Yes. Men and women both, not duplicates. They would teach the classes to the children, direct and supervise the agriculture, and so forth. They also wore the gray coveralls, with much longer numbers on the breast. But somehow,

I couldn't get a focus on who was in charge overall. No impression of an administrator or manager."

"Where was it?"

"I had no perception of a geographic location," said Crowley. "But there was a peculiar natural landmark. A very tall rock formation, like a giant stone tree stump, flat at the top. Igneous rock, I think. It was in the distance and looked hundreds of feet high. It would be an enjoyable challenge to climb."

"I think I know where that is," said Stern. "Mr. Tesla, do you have a United States atlas in your library?"

"I do," answered Tesla. "One moment, please." He went into a back room and soon returned with a large, heavy volume titled *Illustrated Atlas of the United States*. He placed it on the table in front of Stern. Checking the index, in under a minute Stern had the page he needed.

"Is this it?" he asked as he turned the book toward Crowley, pointing to an illustration.

"This is it," said Crowley. "'Devils Tower, Wyoming.' I quite like the name."

"I'm surprised that, as a mountaineer, you hadn't heard of it," said Tesla.

"So am I," said Crowley.

"A secret camp of physical duplicates," said Stern. "Remarkable."

"And it's in the West, where the bank robber claimed to be from," said Crowley.

"It seems the bank robber was the man called P-67," said Tesla. "He and Q-75, alias Michael Crane, escaped together, took assumed names, and lived as father and son here in New York. At about eighteen years' age difference, it would be plausible. But Michael mentioned his mother. Was there a woman in the camp who escaped with them?"

"Hard to say. I got a vague impression of the two of them speaking privately about leaving the camp, but no sign of how they did so, nor of who, if anyone, accompanied them. It also seems related to the posterior tattoo."

"How so?" asked Tesla.

"I gathered that getting the tattoo is part of an initiation to make one a full-fledged member of their group. And they decided to get out just before it was Michael's turn."

"That explains why Donnelly couldn't find anyone in New York who had made the tattoo," said Tesla.

"Yes. And yet I sensed a reluctance to leave. It seems that just about everybody likes it there, or at least doesn't hate it, and has no real interest in what lies beyond the fence."

"On another point," said Stern, "here we have an isolated, confined location, a camp of mostly men and teenage boys, and relatively few women."

"I see what you're getting at," said Crowley. "I sensed an almost vestigial sex drive in our young fellow today. And he's fifteen. Indirectly, I have the same impression of all the duplicates."

"Biologically engineered men," said Tesla. "Created to be compliant and unquestioning, with minimal sex drive and no curiosity. With blood chemistry that matches the composition of the Essential Composite."

"It sounds like the ultimate dream of every tyrant in history," said Crowley. "If whoever is managing things on this side of the veil seeks such power, he presumably thinks that creating these men as physical conduits for the Ferox will help him to attain it."

"But if possession by the Ferox is the object, once it is achieved, the complacency will surely disappear," said Stern. "If your description of these beings is accurate, no human could hope to dominate them. Perhaps the object is simply to make the physical hosts as susceptible to possession as possible."

"Or perhaps the human running things here and the Ferox are operating at cross-purposes, each trying to outwit the other," said Crowley. "I know how these things turn out, sparse as the record is. My money's on the Ferox."

"The knowledge and equipment one would need to effect such a thing," said Stern. "It boggles the mind."

"Indeed," said Tesla. "Crowley, were the duplicates all born naturally? I mean, physically born by a woman?"

"I couldn't get any impression on that. Such knowledge was apparently forbidden to them. But if they weren't born by women, how were they born?"

"I have some ideas. But another question is: these men are all duplicates, but duplicates of whom?"

"Yes," said Stern. "We have to assume there is an original. A normal human from whom genetic material was taken to make them." He considered the picture of Devils Tower for a moment. "Gentlemen, Donnelly and I are normally restricted to New York City and its environs. However, we do have a certain latitude in extenuating circumstances. Let us go and investigate this place."

Crowley turned to Tesla. "I've always wanted to go out West and see all those big strapping cowboys. We'd better pack our bags and check the timetable at Grand Central Depot. I'll bet it's at least a couple of days each way."

"Assuming there is space available on such short notice," said Tesla.

"There is no need to take the train," said Stern.

"Then how are we supposed to get there?" asked Crowley. "Fly?"

"Precisely," said Stern. "Sergeant Donnelly and I will serve as pilots."

Crowley and Tesla looked at each other, then back at Stern.

"I beg your pardon?" asked Crowley.

33

Nine days earlier (and yet not)

Time conterminous, place beyond: a state unknown to and thus unrecallable by the mage Aleister Crowley.

It is a large space, seemingly larger than its purpose would warrant, yet it defies and subverts the idea of largeness (or smallness) as understood physically. Any attempt at applying to it the concept of measurable, physical dimensions would, if carried far enough, lead the would-be measurer to insanity.

It is white, and bright, with no obvious source of light. There is an impression of walls rather than the surety that walls are there.

There is a window, however. Or at least a place through which one may see. It is large, transparent, existing yet made of nothing. Beyond it is another infinite yet bounded white space, and within it stands Aleister Crowley, with his scraggly beard and mountaineer's garb. Seemingly addressing no one, he shouts obscenities as he demands a railway ticket. His voice is barely audible through the window.

And on this side of the window, the white realm in which Crowley is not (and which he will never learn of), is a long oak table. Upon it sit various items: test tubes, beakers, pencils, dip pens, two microscopes, stacks of notebooks, an abacus.

At the table sit two demons in laboratory coats who stare into the microscopes, jotting down notes. To the casual observer—were it possible one could be here—they would appear as two nondescript young men. But in this place, where the astral and corporeal mingle, where demons can handle physical objects, to look upon them long enough would result in hints of their true appearance. This, like attempting to physically measure the white space, would prove unpleasant.

Behind the window, Crowley stands alone, though in a sense he is not. He interacts with aspects of himself invisible to nearly anyone else.

"I will defecate on the counter and rub your goddamned face into it, you incompetent, lazy swine!" he shouts, then throws a punch into empty space. One of the demons looks briefly toward the window, then dips his pen into the inkwell and continues writing.

At that moment, next to the table appears their master, Mr. Ambrose Temple. They turn to acknowledge his presence. He is impeccably dressed as usual, in morning dress and top hat.

"Progress?" Temple asks, stroking his beard as he regards Crowley through the window.

"We are nearly done," says one of the lab-coated demons. "We have reconfirmed that in cases of covert rebellion, all P Cohort duplicates are susceptible to a degree of psychic manipulation to engender feelings of shame and guilt, making them open to more conventional means of psychological influence. This is evinced by your experience with P-45."

"I am aware of that. Get to the main point."

"Yes, sir. As determined previously, there are no indications of defects in the physiology of the P Cohort. Both the magickal and engineering procedures were balanced perfectly. The sedition demonstrated by P-45 and P-67 were apparently anomalies resulting from random environmental factors."

"We hypothesize the same in regard to the Q Cohort member Number Seventy-Five," adds the other demon. "Environmental factors on earth, that is. Not here. Our analysis has also reconfirmed that this was the ideal location to manufacture them all."

"Very well," says Temple. "I'll be sending the remainder of the O Cohort here for liquidation. Make the preparations."

"Yes, sir. And the Q Cohort?"

"I'm still observing them. Liquidation pending. No further analysis necessary."

Temple turns to again watch Crowley, who shouts, "Bomb! There is a bomb in this station!"

"Mr. Temple," says the second demon.

"Yes?"

"Sir, I wonder if the constant occupation and use of this plane of existence might cause an undue strain upon the resources required to—"

"*Let me worry about that.*"

"*But, sir*"—he glances at the window—"*even the annex you have added cannot hold the mage.*"

"*I am aware of that. In any case, it wasn't me who added it. Do not attempt to impede his escape. I will summon you within twenty-four hours local time to receive your final report.*"

"*Yes, sir. We shall await your summons,*" says the first demon. The next moment, Temple vanishes.

"*Tesla? The inventor? Why?*" comes Crowley's voice from behind the window. "*He lives in New York. I can't teleport there.*" After a moment, he too vanishes.

The two demons look at each other but say nothing. They turn their attention back to the microscopes.

34

September 6th, 1899

The four men walked through the woodland trail toward the locked gate of the eighteen-foot-tall chain-link fence. It was nearly nightfall, as Stern had insisted that daytime flights were to be avoided if at all possible. Beyond the gate stood an imposing if ordinary-looking brick warehouse, set within a large plot of land.

The sign on the gate read PRIVATE PROPERTY. TRESPASSERS WILL BE PROSECUTED. No houses or other buildings were visible around the property.

"A balloon that can get from here to Wyoming faster than a train would have to be both powered and navigable in some way," said Tesla. "I'm very curious to see this."

"You will soon have your wish, sir," said Stern as they came to the gate. He pulled a key chain out of his pocket and unlocked the face of an unusually large padlock, which opened up like a small door. Within was a combination dial which required seven numbers to open.

Once inside the gate, Stern relocked it. They walked toward the warehouse in the twilight as he selected another key from the chain.

"You know," said Crowley, "perhaps you should find a more isolated location than a clearing in the woods of a Long Island town."

"There are rumors of a more elaborate facility in Nevada, out in the desert, though I've never been there."

"Is this place US government property, then?" asked Crowley.

"Officially, no," said Stern. "Legally, the property is owned by a company in Virginia which exists only in name. That company is in turn the subsidiary of another such company. Eventually, if one could follow the trail of paper, someone somewhere within the government would be found who manages the place as a sort of absentee landlord. Degrees of separation are maintained, and thereby plausible deniability."

"Does anyone besides the two of you come here?" asked Tesla.

"Yes. But I don't know who or how often. Information in this line of work is rather…"

"Compartmentalized?" offered Crowley.

"Yes."

They arrived at the door of the warehouse. It was painted a dark green and made of steel, placed within a much larger pair of sliding doors which took up nearly the entire side of the building. Welded into the smaller door was a lock similar to the one on the gate. Stern opened the lock's outer face, performed the seven-digit combination, and opened the door. It was dark inside, the only visible things vague boxlike outlines.

"Welcome, gentlemen," he said. "Please follow me." He walked in, turned around, and placed his hand on the doorframe to his right. There was a click. The whining sound of a generator starting up pierced the darkness, and in a moment, the interior was flooded with light.

Dozens of incandescent lights hanging from a high ceiling illuminated a large space of unplastered red brick walls. Unmarked crates sat here and there, their sizes ranging from that of a large suitcase to bigger than a train carriage. A musty odor, as of a library of very old books, mingled with the smell of gasoline from the generator sitting in the corner to their left, its cables leading along the wall up to the ceiling. Near the opposite wall was an iron spiral stairwell leading up to a railed loft upon which sat more crates.

"Though we call it a warehouse, it's more like a hangar for the airship," said Stern.

"Looks like a warehouse," said Crowley. "Where's the airship?"

"Patience, Mr. Crowley," said Stern. "You shall see it shortly. Donnelly, let's do the security check."

Donnelly nodded and picked up a crowbar sitting next to the largest crate, which looked about the size of a Pullman railway coach, though perhaps a bit wider. He stuck the crowbar into a cranny of the crate and pulled. Nothing gave. He tried a few more places, without success. "Seems good," he said.

"What seems good?" asked Crowley. "You can't get it open."

"I think that's the intention, Crowley," said Tesla. "This crate is designed to withstand conventional attempts at opening it, and Sergeant Donnelly was testing its strength."

"That is correct," said Stern. "It's not likely anyone could break in here, but it's good to have extra precautions. All right, Donnelly, open her up."

Donnelly pressed the lower right corner of the crate's frame on the side facing them. He then pressed another place along the frame, about a foot above the corner. There was a low hissing sound from the crate. He got up, walked to the lower left corner of the frame, pressed it, and stepped aside.

The hissing became louder. All four sides of the crate opened slowly from the top. Each side was hinged at the bottom, the insides made of a smooth gray metal. "And here it is," said Stern. "The airship. Or rather a large part of it."

"Remarkable," said Tesla. "Aluminum?"

"Yes, mostly," said Stern. "The outer hull, that is."

Before them stood a silver-gray metallic cylinder, nearly as large as the crate that had housed it. Its forward end tapered into a rounded nose with cockpit windows. There were three windows and a door along each side. Flanking the hull were two rotatable propellers, each one fixed to a shaft with engine casing, protruding port and starboard. Atop the hull was a hump topped by a glass dome. Four wheels were mounted on a frame attached to the bottom.

"This thing flies?" asked Crowley.

"Indeed it does," said Stern. "But not in its current state. It requires a bit more assembly."

Soon Stern and Donnelly got to work opening more crates in the same manner as the first one, with various items and tools taken out. In a short while, the balloon was attached, and an hour later was nearly full of the helium being pumped into it from a large wheeled tank. Inflated, it was large and oblong, silver-gray with thin black crisscrossed lines.

"How were you able to get this much helium?" asked Tesla, peering intently at the balloon's stabilizer fins.

"I'm not entirely sure," said Stern. "Despite its rarity and expense, we are amply supplied with it. Hydrogen would be easier to get, but of course it's highly flammable."

"Why isn't it floating now that it's got that gas in it?" asked Crowley as Tesla walked around the airship in fascination, careful not to touch anything but taking in every detail.

Donnelly explained that behind the doors under the ship's fuselage was a compartment with ballast in the form of a couple of crates of rocks. They would simply be released when it was time to lift off. To land, the pilot had to gradually release helium until the ship was heavy enough to descend.

Crowley studied the fuselage, putting his hand on it. "I've heard of these airships, but I've never seen one. The ones you read about from public demonstrations can't make any really sustained flights. But I heard something a few years ago about sightings of very fast, high-flying ships. In at least one case, the occupants claimed to be from Mars."

Stern and Donnelly looked at each other and laughed.

"That was you?" asked Crowley.

"It was in 1896," said Stern. "We had to land just outside Sacramento, California due to engine trouble. Some curious locals came to the ship and we had to say something. My contact in Washington was rather upset at first, but it was later decided that stories of visitors from other planets were a useful form of…" He turned to Donnelly. "What was that word again?"

"Disinformation," said Donnelly, who then checked a pressure gauge on the helium tank. "Balloon's full," he said to Stern, then pulled a lever, cutting off the supply of gas. Stern uncoupled the hose from the balloon.

Stern pulled his watch from his vest. "It's just after seven o'clock in the evening. If the weather is with us, we should arrive in the vicinity of Devils Tower within eight hours, or about 5:00 a.m. local time. I've made some calls to request the assistance of colleagues, who should be there to meet us. Donnelly, are we packed and provisioned?"

"Indeed we are, sir."

"Very well. All aboard, gentlemen. I'll join you once the airship is outside and I've locked up."

Donnelly opened the door on the starboard side of the craft. With a flourish and a smile, he said to Crowley and Tesla, "Your chariot awaits, gentlemen." They climbed through the door.

The interior of the cabin was more comfortable-looking than they had expected. Along each bulkhead, port and starboard, were three easy chairs of mahogany and red velvet with rolled armrests, bolted to the deck and equipped with safety belts. Behind these were a sofa, easy chair, and coffee table, also bolted down. It looked more like a narrow, oddly shaped parlor than the inside of a vehicle, except for the metal overhead with its single round hatch. There was also a lavatory and shower located at the back, along with a weapons locker secured with a combination lock.

Crowley settled into the front starboard-side passenger seat. Tesla, seated opposite him, stared at the cockpit controls.

"Donnelly, this is fascinating," said Tesla. "I have a hundred questions."

"I'm glad you like it. We'll have plenty of time to talk once we're at cruising altitude. In the meantime, please strap in."

He went into the cockpit, sat down in the pilot's seat, and fastened his seat belt. Before him and below the window was a board, also of mahogany, dotted with dials and switches. Before each of the two seats was a control yoke.

After ensuring his passengers had their seat belts fastened, Donnelly turned a switch. The propellers came to life, their hum filling the cabin. Out the cockpit window, they could see the huge warehouse doors slowly dividing until they were completely open.

Donnelly pushed the yoke forward and the airship left the warehouse. He stopped and waited as the doors closed again. Soon Stern came aboard. After a quick glance to ensure Tesla and Crowley were strapped in, he got into the copilot's seat opposite Donnelly and secured his belt.

"All set. Take us up, Donnelly."

"Releasing ballast," said Donnelly as he reached up and pulled down a lever above the window.

The ship began its ascent. The warehouse, barely illuminated by the crescent moon, slowly began to recede. Climbing to about a hundred feet, the silver-gray vessel turned 180 degrees and flew west, accelerating as it rose into the night.

35

Through the windows they saw the infinite field of stars, the darkness below broken by lights from the towns of eastern Long Island. Before long the vast glow of Manhattan came into view, countless gas, arc, and incandescent lamps shimmering like a nebula fixed upon the ground. Then once again they flew above darkness.

"Status, Donnelly?" asked Stern.

"Altitude 6,550 feet, speed 175 knots. She's purring like a lion cub. Weather ahead looks calm at the moment."

"Very well. I'll relieve you at"—he looked at his watch—"zero four hundred hours Greenwich time. Let me know if you need to use the facilities." He turned to Crowley and Tesla. "Shall we have dinner, gentlemen?"

As it was to be a brief journey, and the airship had no cooking facilities, their food supply consisted of hardtack and beef jerky. The ship was well-supplied with potable water and also had a coffee percolator. "I miss Delmonico's," was Crowley's only comment.

"I am disturbed," said Tesla to Crowley, "about the nature of young Michael's life in the compound which you saw in his memories. People with alphanumeric designations instead of names. Everyone wearing the same uniform. What does it mean?"

"A highly regimented society, it would seem," said Crowley. "Someone's idea of utopia. But it's not consistent with what we know of the Ferox. They're disciplined, in their way. Highly focused upon attaining their desires. Yet paradoxically, the least disciplined beings in existence. They would care nothing for utopian reforms, nor even tyrannical ones. They simply want to indulge their cruel appetites."

"Well," said Stern, "perhaps our journey will provide us with some answers in that regard."

They continued to eat in silence. After they had finished, Stern said, "Anyone for a game of billiards?"

"Billiards?" asked Tesla and Crowley together.

"Yes. Though having heard of your skill at the game, Mr. Tesla, I feel a slight trepidation."

"Billiards on an airship," said Crowley. "This I've got to see."

"If we can play, of course I'm quite willing, as well as curious," said Tesla.

"Wish I could join you," said Donnelly, adjusting some of the controls as he munched on a piece of hardtack. "Though Inspector Stern always beats me."

"He's being modest," said Stern. "All right, just a moment, please." He got up from his seat and went to the port forward side of the cabin, just behind the cockpit. There a part of the bulkhead protruded and had double doors, forming a locker extending from deck to overhead. He opened it. Within was a billiards table, its green felt top facing them, secured to the bulkhead by leather straps. Stern began to unfasten the straps and said, "Might I request your assistance, Mr. Tesla?"

The table was surprisingly light, and Stern explained that it was made mostly of plywood. As Stern and Tesla held it on both ends, Crowley pulled down the four folding legs. "Amazing," he said, smiling as the men set it down. There was just enough room for them to walk around the table and take shots.

"There seems no danger of a cue breaking a window during a shot," said Crowley.

"Yes," said Stern. "But not just because of the adequate space." Stern explained that the windows were resistant to much more force than that of a mi-saimed pool cue. As for the billiard table, its plywood construction made it less durable than a conventional table, but served well enough for airship use.

"Did you request this from your secretive federal masters?" asked Crowley.

"No, actually," answered Stern. "I was told it's an experimental initiative to see how feasible recreation is while airborne. There's talk of someday having permanent airborne observation posts, and even ways of traveling into space. Personally, I think they're getting ahead of themselves." He turned back to the locker, pulled out a burlap sack of balls, and emptied it onto the table.

"There's no way any kind of serviceable billiard tabletop is made of plywood. What's under the cover?" asked Crowley.

"Some kind of new stuff," said Stern. "Synthesized from petroleum, I'm told." He pulled a triangle from the locker, then paused and asked, "Shall we make it cutthroat, gentlemen?"

"That sounds fine," said Crowley. Tesla nodded.

Stern put the triangle back, and he and Crowley began to separate the balls into three sets. Noting the look on Tesla's face, Stern said with a smile, "I will try to get you details of its manufacture, Mr. Tesla. I beg you, no investigative tearing of the tabletop cover."

"Of course," said Tesla.

The balls were separated into three groups: one though five, six through ten, and eleven through fifteen. A quick game of rock-paper-scissors gave Crowley the first shot, Stern the second, and Tesla the third.

"Seven," said Crowley, who then took his shot, sinking the eight ball. Shaking his head, he bowed with a small flourish to Stern.

"Eleven," said Stern, and sank the fifteen ball. "Hmm," he said as he pondered his erroneous shot.

"Three," said Tesla, and sank the three ball into the corner pocket.

They played at a fast pace, with Tesla winning two games out of four, and Crowley and Stern one each. By the time they had put away the table, they had been in flight for nearly two hours. Other than a quick restroom trip between games while Stern took over the controls, Donnelly insisted he didn't need a break and said that Stern should sleep for a couple of hours before his turn in the cockpit.

"I suppose you're right, Donnelly," said Stern. "Shall we retire, then, gentlemen? Just a moment, please." He opened the sliding door of a chest welded into the starboard bulkhead and pulled out three hammocks, all of which were soon hooked onto rings protruding from the cabin's overhead. They then took turns washing and brushing their teeth in the bathroom, which was narrow but serviceable.

"Wake me up if there's anything amiss, Donnelly," Stern said as he climbed into the hammock and put his hat over his eyes.

"Aye, aye, sir," Donnelly replied. The hum of the engines lulled the three men to sleep.

36

Tesla dreams.

He is flying. Not in an aircraft, but by himself, arms stretched out behind him. The sky is a brilliant blue, with scattered white cumulous clouds above him. He wonders if this is astral travel. He decides to attempt a change in direction toward one of the clouds. Instantly, he flies straight upward. The cloud appears larger and larger as he approaches it from below until he finds himself in a heavy wet mist. He comes out the other side soaked. Astral travel would not involve getting wet, *he thinks.* This must be a lucid dream. *He turns his attention to the earth below.*

Below in the distance are green plains and forests, and the houses and churches of more than a dozen hamlets. Though he has never seen it from the air, not even in a photograph, he instantly realizes he is flying over his home town of Smiljan. With a surge of joy, he decides to fly down and see it. As his descent begins, he hears a voice say, "Niko."

He freezes, finding he is able to stand still in midair. He turns to look.

Before him, also standing in midair, is a tall black-bearded man in a black cassock and cylindrical hat, the kalimavkion. *It is the garb of an Eastern Orthodox priest. His arms are crossed, his expression stern.*

Tesla stares. All he can say is, "Father."

"'*Perhaps I may get well if you let me study engineering,*'" *the man replies.* "And I allowed that. I allowed it because you were ill with cholera, and I was afraid to see another son die. And you recovered. So instead of a priest, as I had hoped, you became an engineer. Or should I say, a gambler?"

"I quit gambling," *says Tesla.* I want to wake up, *he thinks.*

"I'm not letting you wake up. So? You didn't quit soon enough to be with me as I lay dying." *His features take on an angrier cast.* "You were out placing bets instead."

Tesla stares and says nothing.

The features of the tall man soften, become downcast. "Your elder brother Dane. He would never have gambled. He would have been at his father's deathbed. Why was he thrown from the horse that killed him?"

"Stop," says Tesla.

"I'll say it, then, because you don't have the courage. It was because you frightened the horse." His features harden again. "Was that on purpose, Niko?"

"It wasn't!"

"Are you sure? You were jealous of him, weren't you? You knew he was more gifted than you."

"I was seven! I didn't mean it! I was skipping in front of the horse!"

"And then later you escaped conscription instead of going into the army like a man. Dane would never have done that, had he lived."

"You told me to! You ordered me to head for the hills!"

"You should have refused. Coward. Coward with your little electric toys. Why do you think you have a right to return to our village?"

Tesla looks at the village far below, then to the man in the cassock. "You are not my father," he says.

The man laughs, and in an instant, the distance between them closes. Tesla is face-to-face with Owen Howell, former employee of the Waldorf-Astoria, the bloody bullet hole in the side of his head.

"Time to clip your wings, buddy boy."

The powerful hands grip his arms hard, painfully, and he is held over Howell's head. He sees the ground far below. Then he is flung down like a rag doll. There is a helpless acceleration as the houses and churches of Smiljan come ever closer to meet him.

Closer. Closer. The church bells begin to ring. A strange ringing: cadence rapid, tone shrill and insistent. Then an instant of confusion as he is still in the air, yet feels an impact.

◆ ◆ ◆

Tesla opened his eyes and wondered why everything was black. The unignorable sound of a claxon rang in his ears. Then he realized his face was pressed downward against a cabin window, and it was still night. It took another second to realize that the direction of the window should not be down.

"Emergency!" came Donnelly's shout over the claxon. "Stabilization is lost! We're losing altitude!"

37

"Shit!" exclaimed Crowley as he and Stern disentangled themselves from one another. Both men, like Tesla, had been thrown into the starboard bulkhead, which was now in effect almost the deck: the airship was listing to starboard at a sharp angle, and the vessel's steady, gradual descent could be felt in the pit of one's stomach.

Donnelly was in the cockpit, sitting atop the left side of the copilot's seat, having released his seat belt to remain upright. His head tilted right as he read controls, moved levers, pushed buttons, and moved the yoke in his attempts to correct the ship's attitude.

Stern crawled over to the cockpit and turned off the claxon. "What happened?"

"I don't know! I was just about to wake you for the second shift when we suddenly listed starboard and started going down."

"What's the helium level?"

"I don't know. Look. The dials are all frozen." It was true; every dial on the control panel, including altitude, speed, helium level, and fuel, pointed to the extreme right: sixteen thousand feet, three hundred knots, sixty-five pounds per square inch, full level of fuel.

"Engines?"

"They're running. You can hear them. But there's no way to check their status from here. We have engines, electricity, cabin pressure. That's it."

"We must be listing at forty degrees at least," said Stern. "How the hell is this happening?"

"Those dials have been magnetized," said Tesla. "Something on or near the ship is doing it."

"There's been no indication of any other aircraft," said Donnelly.

"What was our last altitude before this happened?" asked Stern.

"Twelve thousand five hundred feet. Position forty-four by ninety-five," answered Donnelly. "We're over southern Minnesota."

"That helps. No mountains to speak of."

"There's another problem. As soon as we began listing, I checked on the parachutes. They're gone."

"What?"

"I'm positive I saw them before we took off. Now they're gone."

"They've been teleported away by someone," said Crowley. "This is powerful magick."

"All right," said Stern. "I'm going to check the balloon. If there's an obvious puncture on this side, we might be able to patch it in time."

Stern pulled a pair of gloves from a pocket and put them on. Making his way to the now starboard overhead hatch, he turned its round handle counterclockwise and opened it outward.

Stern reached in and flipped a switch, revealing a cylindrical compartment lit by electric lights placed at intervals along its length. He went in. It was meant to be climbed up, and ladder rungs extended along what was now the bottom, making it awkward to crawl through. Reaching the end, he came to another round hatch. He turned the handle about two inches counterclockwise.

No rush of air, indicating no change in air pressure. The window beyond was intact. Stern turned the handle all the way and pushed the hatch open. Beyond, he could see the faint outline of a circular bulkhead, and above it, blackness. Within was the space housing the airship's dome of clear glass. He entered.

Mounted on a hook was a large handheld lamp with a cable leading into the bulkhead. It resembled an oversized lollipop. Though powerful, it was prone to burnout if used for more than thirty minutes. With a silent prayer that it would function under present circumstances, Stern picked it up and switched it on.

It worked. Visibility was affected by reflection from the glass, but not severely. Ignoring the worry he could see in his own reflection, he shone the beam onto every inch of the balloon he could. It looked taut. He then checked the apparatus linking the balloon and fuselage, the propellers and engines, and the cabin's upper hull. Around and above him were the stars: beautiful, cold, indifferent. Below was blackness. He went back, closing the hatches behind him.

"No holes visible," he said. "The balloon is taut. Nothing appears damaged. A pinhole puncture wouldn't make us fall at the rate this feels like. But what is making us fall?"

"There were no foreign objects visible?" asked Crowley.

"No."

"Let's check the hold. Tesla said the controls are stuck because they're magnetized. I feel there's something on board that shouldn't be here."

"All right."

Stern slid open a panel in the deck, revealing a hatch. Opening it, he reached inside and flipped a switch, and the hold beyond was flooded with light. Reaching in further, he released a telescoping ladder into the hold.

"Let's go," said Stern to Crowley and Tesla. "Donnelly, just…do whatever you can."

"Yeah," said Donnelly.

Stern climbed down first. Hanging off the end of the ladder, it was a short drop onto the corner where the deck and the starboard aft bulkhead met.

"You were right, Aleister," said Stern as he moved aside to let Tesla drop down.

"Amazing," said Tesla as Crowley climbed down after him.

A large mass of dark gray, irregularly shaped rock lay before them, taking up nearly the entire starboard forward quarter of the hold.

"This was teleported in," said Crowley. "I assume by whoever took our parachutes. Mr. Tesla, I will yield to your more expert judgment, but I believe this is magnetite."

"Yes," said Tesla. "But…does anyone else feel like their watch is being pulled forward?"

"Yes," said Crowley.

"Me too," said Stern. "But I don't believe magnetite is supposed to have this strong an effect."

"It's not," said Tesla.

"That ore's been magickally enhanced," said Crowley. "I didn't think anyone could do this."

"I assume that means you can't teleport it out of here," said Tesla.

"Not a chance."

"Let's get back into the cabin," said Stern. "We can try and get rid of it by opening the outer hold doors."

"I don't think that's going to work," said Tesla. "That ore is magnetically sealed to the hull."

"We have to try. Come on." They climbed back into the cabin.

"Is it just me or does it feel like our descent is gradually getting faster?" asked Crowley.

"I'm afraid you're not imagining it, Mr. Crowley," said Stern. "Donnelly, please tell me you can still operate the outer hold doors remotely."

"I wish I could. All remote controls are inoperable along with just about everything else. So there's something in there?"

"A mother lode of magnetite."

"How the hell—"

"Teleportation, apparently. But we've got to get rid of it. All right, stay at the controls. I'll harness myself into the hold and open the doors manually. Can you estimate how much time we have?"

Donnelly held up a legal pad. "I've done some calculations based on guesswork, but there's not even a visual fix on the ground to gauge from."

"Your best guess."

"The helium's providing drag, but we're still accelerating. I estimate nine minutes till we hit the ground, at a velocity of fifty-five feet per second. Just enough to kill us on impact."

"Just enough. I'll bet that's on purpose," said Crowley.

"All right," said Stern. "Keep trying the controls anyway, but don't break any handles. We need everything working once that stuff's off the ship." Removing a safety harness from a compartment in the cockpit, Stern began putting it on.

Fastening the last strap of the harness, he then removed from a drawer in the cockpit two headsets with long coiled cords. Handing one to Donnelly, he hooked the other onto his harness. Donnelly put on his headset and inserted the end of the cable into an opening near the bottom of the control panel. He adjusted its mouthpiece.

Tesla was leafing through the airship's general manual, titled *Airship Specifications: Construction, Maintenance, and Equipment.* The legend *TOP SECRET* was printed at the top of the cover. Crowley was looking out the window at the blackness beyond. "What are those things?" Tesla asked Stern.

"Sound-powered telephones," said Stern. "No external power source required."

"Never heard of them," said Tesla.

Climbing into the ballast hold hatch, Stern paused and said to Tesla and Crowley, "Any ideas?"

"Yes," said Tesla. "But we need the outer doors open first."

"Working on it," said Crowley, face downcast.

"Please do. I'll keep you posted." Stern's head disappeared into the hole and the hatch closed.

"What's the matter?" Tesla asked Crowley. "You look like a schoolboy who just failed an exam. We need to focus on fixing this problem."

"I was arrogant, Tesla," said Crowley. "Insisting I was the most powerful mage on earth. Obviously, I'm not. I should have anticipated something like this."

Tesla set the manual against the armrest of a seat. "For God's sake, man, forget that. Think! I know how to get that ore off the ship, but I'm also convinced something magickal is going to get in my way. You said we needed to combine our skills to fight these things." He grasped Crowley by the shoulders. "Let's do this, Mr. Crowley."

Releasing his grasp, he again picked up the manual, checked one more page, and placed it back on the seat. He went to the back of the cabin, unlatched and opened a drawer which had been built into the starboard bulkhead, and pulled out a wooden tool kit. Opening it, he began to check its contents.

As Tesla looked through the tools, picking each one up to examine it briefly, he asked, "Do you recall how, on the day we first met, you dealt with what you knew would be my panic at experiencing astral projection?" He replaced a pair of pliers, pulled out a screwdriver, studied it for a moment, and looked at Crowley. "If you weren't here and you wanted to prevent Stern from opening those doors manually, how would you do it?" He put back the screwdriver and closed the tool kit.

Crowley's eyes lit up. "Yes. That's it. Tesla, you're a genius!"

Tesla shrugged. "I know. You'd better get a harness on. But can you counteract such a thing?"

"Yes," said Crowley. "But I'll need to call for help. Sergeant Donnelly, could you possibly hand me a harness?" Donnelly complied, then went back to vainly nudging buttons and levers.

"Help?" asked Tesla. Then he understood. "Ah, right. Have at it." He picked up the tool kit and made his way toward the cockpit. "Sergeant Donnelly, I'll need to open that panel located beneath the copilot's controls."

"All right. Can I help?"

"Yes. If you could please hand me tools as I ask for them." He handed the tool kit to Donnelly, took out a screwdriver, and began to unscrew the panel.

Stern's voice came through Donnelly's headphones. "Donnelly, send Crowley down here."

"He's putting a harness on as we speak," replied Donnelly. Releasing the mouthpiece button, he said, "Mr. Crowley, your presence is requested in the ballast hold."

"I'll be right down," said Crowley.

"Seven minutes, twenty seconds remaining," said Donnelly into the mouthpiece.

"Acknowledged," replied Stern.

Crowley opened the hatch, climbed down, and closed it after him.

"Invisible barrier, I assume?" asked Crowley.

"Yes," said Stern. He spoke into the mouthpiece. "Donnelly, there's some kind of invisible barrier around the magnetite and the manual door release. It's covering the forward half of the starboard bulkhead. We'll see what Mr. Crowley can do about it. I'll keep you informed."

"Acknowledged," replied Donnelly.

The two men stood on the port side of the ballast hold, grasping rungs in the bulkhead to keep their footing. The mass of magnetite still sat at the other end of the inclined deck. "The manual release lever is over there," said Stern. He pointed toward the middle of the starboard bulkhead, next to the magnetite. Attached to the bulkhead was a boxlike protrusion about a foot square with a small knob on it. Above the knob was stenciled the legend *MANUAL DOOR OPERA-TION*. "But I can't get to it." He motioned for Crowley to follow, and they made their way gingerly down the deck-cum-bulkhead.

They got to the starboard side, nearly to the bulkhead, and Crowley felt a familiar pressure as he was prevented from going any farther. His body was gently pushed back as if by a thousand tightly coiled springs. He made his way toward the magnetite and tried to touch it, with the same result. "These barriers can last at least half an hour, even with no reinforcement," said Crowley. "Generally, one can be removed sooner only by he who has erected it."

"Yes, but if we can't get this stuff off the ship in a few minutes, we're done for. It's beyond anything I'm equipped to deal with. Is there anything you can do?"

"Yes, I believe so."

"Good. I'll stand by at the manual door control."

Crowley climbed back to the ladder and hooked his harness to one of the rungs. Stern, his harness currently not attachable to anything on the starboard side, lay facedown against the barrier, just before the lever compartment. The long cable of his phone set was plugged in on the port side.

From his pocket, Crowley produced a pencil. Bending down upon one knee, on the deck he drew a grid, then wrote within its outer squares:

M	E	T	A	L	O
E					L
T					A
A					T
L					E
O	L	A	T	E	M

Crowley intoned, "Ashtaroth! I seek your aid, and command you to now appear before me!"

The next moment, what appeared to be a young man stood a few feet from Crowley. Or rather he was levitating in a standing position. Of short stature, he wore a black sack suit and a bowler. His pinkish complexion and freckles were framed by black hair and a handlebar mustache.

"I come as commanded," he said, his tone of formality mingled with a trace of resentment.

"Much appreciated," said Crowley. "There is a large amount of unwanted stuff behind you. Iron ore. Magnetite. I need it removed from this ship. It is protected by a magickal barrier. Kindly get rid of it for us."

"I see from what you have inscribed that you seek aid regarding metals," he replied. "And I am required to obey your commands, if able, but it is beyond

my power to remove this substance. It is made impervious to demonic manipulation by those entities you know as the *ferox phasma*, who call themselves the
One Hundred."

"The One Hundred?" asked Crowley. "What—never mind. Can you remove the barrier?"

"I can, sir."

"A demon in a suit and bowler?" asked Stern.

Ashtaroth turned 180 degrees in midair and regarded Stern. He smiled
with a mischievous cast to his features and asked, "Would you like to see my
true form?"

"No, he wouldn't," said Crowley. "Ashtaroth, is removing the barrier all you
can do to aid us? I command you to answer truthfully."

The demon turned back to Crowley. "It is," he said. "I also remind my master, with all due respect, that I may be commanded to perform only one task between one sunrise and the next."

"Can any other demon under my authority remove the ore? I command
you to answer truthfully."

"No."

"Very well. Remove the barrier and be gone."

"As you wish," he replied.

At the same moment Ashtaroth vanished, Stern fell against the starboard
bulkhead. "Ouch! Damn. All right, hang on." He hooked his harness into one of
the now accessible bulkhead rungs, then said into the phones, "Barrier removed!
I'm about to open the doors!"

"Acknowledged," replied Donnelly. "Time remaining: three minutes, elev-
en seconds. Estimated altitude: eight hundred feet."

Stern opened the case which housed the lever. "Hold on! Stay against the
bulkhead!" he said to Crowley. Both men rechecked their harnesses and clung as
securely as possible to the bulkhead rungs. Stern pulled the lever down.

Slowly, the two halves of the ballast hold deck began to open outward, revealing a line of blackness between them. A rush of cold, howling air filled the
hold. Within half a minute, where there had been a deck there was now a rectangular black void. The ship still listed, with the magnetite still adhered to the
starboard door.

"Doors open!" Stern shouted into the phone. "Magnetite still attached!"

"Are you both harnessed and attached to a bulkhead rung?" asked Donnelly.

"Yes!" answered Stern.

"Both harnesses are in good condition, I trust?"

"I believe so! Why?"

"Good. Hold on!"

Stern's grip on the rung was broken as he felt himself pushed away from the bulkhead. He fell, and a split second later felt the jarring, abrupt jerk of his harness strap. He found himself hanging outside the airship, the blackness below him. Crowley was dangling opposite. The magnetite was gone. The ship began to correct its list.

"Are you all right?" came Donnelly's voice.

"We're dangling like marionettes."

"Stand by. We have control back. Are you hanging higher than the edge of the ballast hold doors?"

"Yes."

"Good. I'm closing the doors. Descent has been arrested. Currently at 521 feet, heading two-seven-zero. I'll keep us at five knots till you're back inside."

"Roger that," said Stern.

Within a minute, Stern and Crowley were standing in the now magnetite-free hold, its doors securely closed. "Well, that was exciting, though a bit cold," said Crowley. "I assume Tesla magnetized the entire ship with the same polarity as the magnetite, thereby repelling it. He's quite a clever fellow."

"Yes, he is," said Stern. "Let's hope the rest of our journey is boring."

38

September 7th, 1899

A head was Devils Tower, its majesty now illuminated by the first rays of dawn from the eastern horizon.

Stern was at the controls, guiding the ship down as he gradually released helium. Donnelly had insisted on remaining in the copilot's seat for the rest of the flight as a precaution. Stern had persuaded him to get some sleep, if only in the cockpit, promising to wake him if necessary.

No settlements were in evidence. The closest town was about a hundred miles away and had less than three hundred people. A single unpaved road, leading west, was the only sign of human influence.

"Those colleagues you mentioned are nowhere in sight, Stern," said Crowley.

"So it seems. I had a feeling this might happen."

Stern brought the ship down to a smooth, vertical landing as Crowley indicated the approximate location he could recall from his probe into Michael Crane's memories.

Stern and Donnelly armed themselves with revolvers. Tesla declined the offer of a weapon. Crowley was a good shot but sensed that firearms would provide no advantage here. He accepted one just in case.

Stepping out of the airship and into the morning light, they took stock of their surroundings.

"There were supposed to be fifty other agents here," said Donnelly. "Where the hell are they?"

"I requested fifty agents when I called," said Stern. "But the reply was vague. 'We will act upon your information.' Then he hung up. I didn't recognize the voice."

"I don't like this," said Donnelly. "At least Jimmy should have been here by now."

"Who?" asked Tesla.

"Our counterpart here in Wyoming," said Stern. "And South Dakota as well."

"He's supposed to be here to resupply us with helium and fuel," said Donnelly. "Must have been delayed somehow."

"Him I was able to call directly," said Stern. "He'll be along."

"It's over this way," said Crowley, leading the party in the opposite direction of Devils Tower.

"I see no sign of any camp or structure," said Stern. "If this place really is here, it's well hidden indeed."

It was rocky in places, yet abundant in greenery, the air sweet with the scent of the ponderosa pines spread about the landscape. Low mountains and reddish sedimentary rock stood in the distance. Soon, ahead of them was the translucent shimmering of a wide rectangular outline. They stopped.

"There it is," said Crowley. "It's hidden by...I don't know what. And I can feel the presence of magick. But not there." He indicated the outline before them.

"Then where?" asked Donnelly.

"I don't know. There's something I can't quite latch on to."

"Mr. Tesla," asked Stern, "could this be done through some form of engineering?"

"By the manipulation of light spectra perhaps," said Tesla. "Remarkable."

They resumed walking toward the outline. As they got closer, it took form: a high, gated chain-link fence surrounding a vast area. Clustered near the gate were about a dozen gray-painted wooden buildings, a low water tower, and two wind turbines. There were no signs or postings in evidence. No one could be seen within. The gate was not locked.

"This is the place," said Crowley. "But no one is here."

"Can we be sure of that?" asked Donnelly.

"Reasonably sure," said Crowley. "When necessary, I can sense the presence of living people, if not their exact number. The only minds I detect are we four."

"Still, let's not take any chances," said Stern as he and Donnelly drew their revolvers. Stern pushed open the gate, and they entered the compound. The fence again faded into near invisibility as they went farther inside.

Several of the structures were long one-story buildings, apparently barracks. They went inside the nearest one. There were twin rows of metal bunks and lockers, but no mattresses. They walked along the length of the barracks. All the lockers were empty. At the far end was a separate room with toilets and showers.

"Mr. Tesla," said Crowley after a few minutes. "May I ask how many bunks you count?"

"Exactly one hundred," said Tesla.

"As do I," said Crowley.

"And the demon you summoned on the airship referred to the *ferox phasma* as the One Hundred," said Stern.

"Assuming one hundred duplicates to act as vessels," said Tesla, "this may have been where they slept."

Crowley started suddenly.

"What's the matter?" asked Stern.

"Please continue searching. There is something outside the compound I must attend to."

"What?" asked Donnelly.

"I'm not sure," said Crowley. He turned and ran out of the barracks.

"Crowley!" called Donnelly. "Where are you going?"

"Perhaps someone should go with him," said Tesla.

"I'll go," said Donnelly. He chased after Crowley.

Donnelly saw that Crowley was already out of the gate, running toward Devils Tower. He ran out of the compound in pursuit.

As soon as he went through the gate, Crowley was gone. He stopped, looked around, but saw no sign of him.

"The hell with it," Donnelly said, and began to run toward Devils Tower.

After a minute, he stopped. Something was wrong.

"It's not getting any closer. What the hell?" He looked right and left again.

"Crowley!" he called, then continued running.

◆ ◆ ◆

Stern and Tesla continued searching the compound. The several barracks were bare of all possible accoutrements, and random dusting indicated even the absence of fingerprints. They entered another, smaller structure which seemed like an administrative center. There were desks, chairs, and cabinets, but no books or documents. A nearby mess hall had tables, chairs, and kitchen equipment, but there was no sign anything had ever been cooked there. An apparent warehouse was empty of wares. There were incandescent light sockets everywhere, but no light bulbs. An area obviously meant for agriculture had pigpens, chicken coops, and arable land, but neither animals nor crops. Finally, they arrived at the powerhouse, from which came a faint hum as they approached the door. Like all the other buildings, it was unlocked.

They entered, and the source of the sound was before them: a red-painted metallic apparatus of two rectangular units, one larger than the other, connected by a thick insulated cable. A large switchboard stood against the wall behind it.

"A diesel engine coupled to a dynamo," said Tesla. "Quite advanced. See the enclosed switchgear behind it?"

"Yes. State-of-the-art, I'd say." Both men knew that older dynamos included a great deal of exposed metalwork, including the switches used to operate them, requiring operators to wear thick leather gloves as protection from electrical shock.

"Nothing truly out of the ordinary," said Tesla. "Except this thing is much quieter than any dynamo has a right to be. An impressive piece of engineering."

"And yet it doesn't seem to be powering anything," said Stern. "Why leave it running?"

Tesla stepped behind the engine-dynamo coupling to stand between it and the switchboard. Looking down, he said, "It is powering something. Have a look."

Connected to the dynamo by a smaller cable was a green metallic box about one foot square, its sides assembled with screws. It was surrounded by a haze which distorted and obscured it.

"What's this?" asked Stern. "The effect is like what we saw at the compound fence."

"Yes," said Tesla. "Let's see what happens when we deactivate it." He turned to the switchboard.

"Are you sure that's a good idea?" asked Stern. But before he could finish speaking, Tesla had pulled down the main switch.

The hum of the dynamo grew fainter and lower in pitch, then was gone. A moment later, smoke and sparks began rising from the green box. This was followed by a muffled sound, as of a small, contained explosion. The sparks ceased.

"Let's have a look outside," said Tesla.

They stepped out the door. The fence and gate were now plain to see in the distance.

"That's what kept the compound concealed," said Stern.

"Yes. I think it somehow manipulated the visible light spectrum. But how it could do so from inside an enclosed space, I can't imagine." They went back inside.

"This device was designed to destroy itself when switched off," said Tesla. "I would like to have examined it." Taking a small tool case from an inside pocket of his jacket, he extracted a screwdriver to open one side. The interior was a blackened, charred mass.

"It seems safe to conclude that this compound has been abandoned," said Stern. "Assuming Crowley's access to young Michael's memories yielded accurate results."

"Yes. And I share Crowley's suspicion that we were intentionally lured here," said Tesla. "But why? And where did everyone go?"

"It might have something to do with whatever Crowley ran out of here for."

"Yes. Speaking of whom, we should find him and Donnelly."

"Agreed. There seems nothing more we can learn here." Stern then did a double take, looking in the corner of the room, left of the door.

He went to the corner and crouched to pick up a small object.

"A matchbox," said Tesla.

"Yes," said Stern as he stood up. He shook the box, opened it, and looked inside.

"Empty," he said, handing it to Tesla, who read the legend on its face.

JACOB'S TAVERN
346 BLEECKER STREET

"'Jacob's Tavern.' A New York City address. Greenwich Village."

"Yes. And a place I'm familiar with, by reputation. It's a bit unconventional."

"You mean bohemian?"

"To say the least. Spiritualists, theosophists, and others of a mystical bent frequent the place. And of course, there are anarchists, poets, painters, and so forth. I believe young Mr. Crowley has patronized it."

"I see. But I could have sworn there was nothing on the floor when we came in."

"So could I. Someone continues to drop us a trail of crumbs."

They left the powerhouse, and as they approached the gate, they could see Donnelly outside the compound, looking at Devils Tower. At the top of the butte was a small, distant figure waving its arms, jumping up and down.

"It's Crowley," said Stern.

"He's naked," said Tesla.

"What the hell?"

◆ ◆ ◆

Exiting the compound, Crowley paused, looked around, and closed his eyes, focusing to locate the magickal disturbance he had detected. "Oh my," he said, opening his eyes and looking toward Devils Tower.

"So you found it," said a voice behind him. He turned around.

Before Crowley stood a tall, smiling, gray-bearded man in a morning coat and top hat. Or rather the appearance of one. He was a flat image in monochrome, like a moving picture, faintly shimmering. Crowley could see through him.

"Oh yes, I can see you're surprised by this." The man opened his arms, looking down at himself, then back at Crowley. "It's quite possible to make the astral form visible to someone in-physical. How could the most powerful mage on earth not know how to do this?"

"Who are you?"

"I think you have other concerns at the moment. Not that it matters much. I simply came to gloat at the impending demise of you and your friends."

"What's up there?"

"Fire of Agni. Even with your airship, you can't get airborne in time to reach it. Your helium supplier has suffered a slight delay, I'm afraid."

"Shit," said Crowley. He turned around and ran toward Devils Tower.

There was an explosion of clear liquid from the ground in front of him, covering nearly his entire body. Crowley felt the instantaneous takeover of his astral consciousness, forming an energy barrier over his exposed skin as the acid reached him.

It was too fast for the barrier to cover his entire body, but his hands and head were shielded as the acid began to eat away at his clothes, which he quickly tore off. The revolver fell to the ground, a misshapen, half-melted mass.

"You're pretty fast," said the man, now standing between Crowley and Devils Tower. "I'm afraid I'm out of tricks for now. But you're still not getting up there in time. Your powers are lessening, aren't they? Unfortunate. I also have your friend over there occupied." His gaze went beyond Crowley, toward the nearly invisible compound. Crowley turned around. Donnelly was running in a circle around the fence, oblivious to Crowley and the other man.

Donnelly stopped. "Crowley!" he called, looking toward the western horizon, perpendicular to the gate and Devils Tower. He began to run again, circling the fence clockwise.

"Just a little illusionist's trick. You could call out to him, but of course he wouldn't hear you. Enjoy your journey to the other side." He vanished.

The remains of Crowley's clothes were tatters of hissing rags upon the ground. His shoes and socks had been spared the acid. Clad in nothing but those, he resumed his run toward the butte.

How the hell am I going to do this? thought Crowley, ignoring his fatigue. The Fire of Agni was a massive incendiary explosion contained within a commonplace object. It could be neutralized only by the physical touch and concentration of a mage. He had to get to the top of an eight-hundred-foot butte within what he assumed were minutes or even seconds.

Soon he was at the base of Devils Tower. He began to catch his breath in large gulps.

"There was supposed to be a stake ladder here!" he said aloud. He had read of the ladder in the atlas in Tesla's laboratory. It must have been removed by the man in the top hat, but there was no time to worry about that now. He looked up, then closed his eyes and concentrated.

Try as he might, he could not teleport.

But there was one thing he could do. He picked up a rock and rapidly inscribed a grid into the dirt.

T	A	S	M	A
A	G	E	I	M
S	E	V	E	S
M	I	E	G	A
A	M	S	A	T

"Ashtaroth! I seek your aid, and command you to now appear before me!"

"You're naked, sir," said Ashtaroth as soon as he appeared.

"Never mind that. I need you to get me up there." Crowley pointed upward. "Levitate me to the top of this butte!"

"It is difficult," replied Ashtaroth. He removed his bowler and ran a hand through his dark hair.

"Why?"

"There is magick here which inhibits my ability to levitate persons or objects. I cannot determine its source. I can levitate you part of the way up, but not to the top. And I cannot carry you, as I am not a physical being."

Crowley looked up, then back at Ashtaroth. "Can you get me up there a little at a time? As much as you can."

"Yes. With intervals of perhaps one minute."

"All right. Do it! Go!"

Crowley rose straight up, the wall of the butte rushing downward before him. After about ten seconds, he was levitated forward, and found footholds and handholds in the rock face.

"I must temporarily let go," said Ashtaroth, who was floating next to him.

"Go ahead," said Crowley. He felt the hold of the levitation leave him. Looking down, he estimated that he was about fifty feet up.

For an instant, he reflected that his recent waves of fatigue would make this more difficult and dangerous. He then quashed the thought and focused his will.

Crowley began climbing, carefully checking for handholds while scaling as fast as possible. He was soon covered with sweat. With no gloves, it was painful, and his hands began to suffer small scrapes from the strength of his grip. Ashtaroth, levitating to match the pace of Crowley's climb, remained at his side.

"I imagine," said Ashtaroth, "that you are the first individual to climb this butte both naked and without the use of conventional equipment. It is surely a first in the annals of mountaineering."

Crowley paused for breath, scowled at Ashtaroth, and continued climbing.

"Be careful of your nether parts," said Ashtaroth.

"I know!" said Crowley, panting. "It's the foremost thing on my mind."

"I can levitate you again."

"Please do."

"May I inquire," asked Ashtaroth as they ascended together, "as to what is on the top of this butte which so urgently requires your attention?"

"Fire of Agni," said Crowley. "It's a kind of magickal firebomb with a radius of at least three miles."

"I am familiar with it. It requires the physical touch of a mage in the process of neutralization. I detect an object of a magickal nature above but cannot positively identify it."

"Same here," said Crowley. "He must have disguised it somehow." They stopped, and Crowley once again began scaling the rock face. His hands bled. He ignored the pain.

"You could in theory command me to carry it away to a safe distance," said Ashtaroth. "However, I am unable to carry most physical objects, especially of a magickal nature. This includes any object used as a vessel for the Fire of Agni."

"I know." The sweat and blood on Crowley's palms were causing them to slip. He had to slow down a little.

The alternation between levitation and climbing continued, and after about seven minutes, Crowley pulled himself to the top.

Ashtaroth stood in midair over a large rock about twice the size of a bowling ball. "It is here," he said. "This rock."

Crowley sensed it as well. Drenched in sweat, bleeding from his palms and dozens of scrapes all over his body, he scrambled to the rock and lay his hands upon it, focusing in his mind: *Neutralize Fire of Agni!*

At that moment, the shimmering monochrome man in the top hat appeared.

"Hello again," he said. "I lied about the Fire of Agni. The rock is a harmless beacon. I just wanted to help you get a little fresh air and exercise. Enjoy the view." He vanished.

The rock was stained red as Crowley's hands came away from it. He looked down at his bloody palms, then toward the horizon, and said, "You dirty son of a bitch."

Though the view was indeed spectacular.

◆ ◆ ◆

Stern and Tesla walked over to where Donnelly stood catching his breath. He said, "I was running toward the Tower but somehow couldn't reach it. Crowley was nowhere in sight. Then suddenly he's up there buck naked. What the hell is going on?"

Just then a large covered wagon came over the rise of the unpaved road, pulled by four horses. The driver was a man of about seventy, with a white beard, an old-looking brown suit, and a matching Stetson "Boss of the Plains" hat.

"Jimmy!" shouted Stern, waving.

"He is the perfect image of an elderly cowboy," said Tesla.

"Well, he is one," said Stern. "Among other things."

Jimmy waved his hat, put it back on, and brought his team to a halt about a dozen yards from the other three men. He walked up to them and shook hands with Stern.

"Hey, Walt. Nice to see you again."

"It's good to see you too."

"I thought there'd be a lot more of us here."

"So did I."

"By the way, do you know why there's a naked fella jumping up and down up there?"

"Well, he's the bohemian type," said Stern.

"It's a long story," said Donnelly.

"Isn't it always?" said Jimmy as he shook Donnelly's hand. "Good to see you again, Patrick."

"And you," said Donnelly. "I was a little worried when we didn't see you on our arrival."

"Yeah, sorry about that. Got delayed. Darnedest thing. Horses wouldn't budge. None of them. Not in this direction, that is. It was like somebody'd cast a magic spell or something."

"Well, as a matter of fact…" said Stern.

"Oh. Again. Well, the older I get, the stranger this world seems, Walter." He looked behind Stern. "This is the place you mentioned, I assume. A kind of hidden compound?"

"Yes," answered Stern. "Though hidden no longer. We've given it a once-over. If you could examine it in more detail over the next couple of days and send me a report, I'd truly appreciate it."

"Happy to oblige," said Jimmy. "The powers that be don't like us sharing information, but to blazes with that, says I. Though I feel a bit chagrined at not having found it myself."

"You have too wide an area to cover," said Stern. "And we were lucky enough to stumble upon a special source of information."

Jimmy nodded and turned to Tesla. "Forgive my rudeness, sir. Jimmy Dower," he said as they shook hands.

"Nikola Tesla."

"I thought I recognized you. I've read some of your articles on alternating current in *Electrical World*. Highly impressive."

"You're too kind." Crowley was still waving his arms in the distance.

"Not at all," said Jimmy. He glanced at the airship, then said to Stern, "She's looking good. Got you here with no problems?"

"We did have some…rather serious technical issues en route, but they were repaired thanks to Mr. Tesla and our naked jumping man."

"Well, speaking of that, I'd better get your ballast and helium taken care of. And the fuel." He looked at Crowley again, took off his hat, and scratched his head. "There's supposed to be a stake ladder, but looks like somebody removed it. How'd he get up there?"

"Magick, probably," said Donnelly. Crowley sat down and crossed his arms.

"Of course." He put his hat back on and said, "Could I ask you to give me a hand, Patrick?" He walked up to the wagon and uncovered it, revealing a large helium tank and hose, and numerous large canisters of gasoline.

"Where's the ballast?" asked Donnelly.

"Right here." Jimmy slapped the wagon. "Since I'm here, I can tether you to the wagon and unhook when you're ready to take off."

"It's heavy enough?"

"Yup."

Within thirty minutes, the airship was floating a few feet off the ground, tethered to Jimmy's wagon.

As they shook hands, Jimmy said, "Sorry I won't get to meet your birthday-suited friend. Please give him my regards."

"We will," said Stern. "Thank you, Jimmy. Let's keep in touch."

They got on board and buckled in. From the cockpit window, Stern gave the signal for takeoff. Jimmy unhooked the tether and the airship began its ascent.

Rotating the propellers, Stern steered toward the butte. Once they were directly over it, he rotated them again to direct the airship down, opposing the helium's lift. They could remain this way for as long as twenty minutes before it began to stress the engines.

They were about two feet over the top when Donnelly opened the door. Crowley came aboard, naked, dirty, bloodied, and covered in sweat.

"Our helium supplier sends his regards," said Donnelly, shutting the door.

"Thank you. Damn that bugger of a demon Ashtaroth! He decided to pull out the rule book and insisted I couldn't compel him to levitate me back down once I had commanded him to bring me up only."

"Why did you need to come up here?" asked Tesla. "What happened to your clothes?"

"All in good time, Tesla," said Crowley. "I need a shower first, though I slightly dread it." He held up a scraped, bloody palm.

"My, you do look a mess," said Stern, looking back from the pilot's seat. "Yes, better wash up and get some bandages on you. I shall waive the seat belt rule for takeoff in this case. But from what little I know of such summonings, I think Ashtaroth was technically in the right."

"Yes, technically," said Crowley. "But he only asserts the rules when it suits him. Pedantic little wanker." He walked into the ship's head and closed the door. Soon the sound of the shower could be heard, punctuated by small cries of "Ow!"

Stern brought the airship up and turned east. Out the window, below in the distance, Jimmy stood next to the wagon, waving his hat in farewell.

A short while later, Crowley was clean, dry, bandaged, and dressed in a spare set of utility coveralls. After consuming a large quantity of water, hardtack, and jerky, he spent most of the return flight deeply asleep.

39

September 8th, 1899

This time Crowley chose the sirloin of beef with mashed carrots. He ate with an expression of absolute ecstasy. "Ah, back to Delmonico's and civilization," he said, taking another long pull of his ale with his bandaged hand. Tesla had chosen the baked Spanish mackerel and a bottle of Chardonnay.

"It's good to see you in better spirits," said Tesla.

"How could I not be? Goodbye to hardtack and jerky." They clinked their glasses. "And, for as long as possible, to snotty little demon familiars."

"Well, he was indispensable in saving us from the magnetite, even if your climb to the top of Devils Tower proved moot."

"Yes, yes, he has his useful moments, I suppose. In any case, it would seem our journey to the Wild West has brought us more questions than answers."

Tesla laughed. "Wild it was indeed. You took an impressively unconventional approach to mountaineering."

"It wasn't so funny at the time," said Crowley. "I thought we were about to be incinerated."

"Well, joking aside, it was truly an impressive ascent. And we've got at least one answer, I'd say. From your description, it would seem the mystery mage you encountered is none other than Ambrose Temple, the man Edison described in his journal. But if he views us as his enemies, why didn't he actually attempt to kill us?"

"Indeed. From what I saw, I'm certain he could have used the Fire of Agni had he wanted to. Instead, he played an elaborate practical joke on us."

"He confounded Donnelly so that he couldn't see you, planted a sort of magickal decoy at the top of Devils Tower, and…made his astral form physically visible, you say?"

"Yes. He appeared and vanished, seemingly at will. And I could see through him. It was not a physical form."

Tesla took another sip of Chardonnay. "Unless he lied about it being his astral form. There might be a way of producing such an effect with technology."

"Technology? It was magick that distracted Donnelly and lured me up Devils Tower. I could feel it."

"Yes. But when you saw the man in the top hat, did you also sense the presence of an astral form?"

"No. I assumed he was preventing my detection of it somehow, but…"

"Go on," said Tesla.

"Why would he bother doing that if he was going to appear anyway?"

"Yes. And you said he appeared flat, with occasional distortion. There are theories, mine included, on ways by which such an image could be transmitted through a process not unlike radio telegraphy. What you saw sounds amazing, but not necessarily arcane."

"So even if Donnelly's confusion and my being lured to the top of the butte were done by psychical ability…"

"The appearance of the man was somehow achieved electrically," said Tesla. "Along with the concealment of the compound."

"So we are dealing with an adversary skilled in both technology and magick. It must have been he who teleported the magnetite into the airship. Ashtaroth believed its magnetic enhancement was done by the Ferox, but it was more likely with their assistance. They cannot directly affect the physical universe by themselves. Usually."

Tesla drained his glass. "Thank you," he said as Crowley refilled it. "He's toying with us. He didn't kill us because it somehow suits his purposes."

"Or perhaps he actually couldn't kill us," said Crowley.

"What do you mean? A moment ago, you said he could have."

"I meant he had the magickal ability to do so. Perhaps the technological ability as well. But if he is in league with the Ferox…"

"He's acting on their orders? Then why would they want us alive any longer than it's possible to eliminate us? Besides, wasn't the attack in Tibet meant to kill you? To destroy you physically and psychically, as you put it?"

"True," said Crowley. "I'm just thrashing about for a way to make sense of all this. Perhaps their goals are at cross-purposes somehow. Then there is the question of how and why the compound was deserted. And now this." He produced the matchbox from his pocket.

"Are you still up to going there tonight?" asked Tesla. "You've had a tiring time of it."

"I wouldn't miss it. I'll telephone our two stalwart officers of the law."

40

Crowley, Tesla, Stern, and Donnelly walked up to the basement entrance. The sign above read *JACOB'S TAVERN*.

"All types in this place," said Crowley as he led them down the stairs. "If it hasn't changed since the last time I was here." The stairway, dimly lit by incandescent lamps along the walls, turned right before leading them to the tavern's door. They went inside.

The center was dominated by a bar forming a triangle with the wall behind it, but most patrons sat drinking at tables set along the walls: men in shirtsleeves and vests, ladies in bangles and feathers. One woman was telling a man's fortune with tarot cards. A young man sat absorbed in a large beer and a copy of *Das Kapital*.

Crowley said, "Jacob Whitaker, you scoundrel!" to the man behind the bar. He was about sixty, with a white beard and close-cropped hair.

"Crowley!" he answered with a broad grin as they shook hands over the counter. Crowley introduced his companions, and soon each man had a pint of dark ale before him. Jacob then drew one for himself, saying, "Free beer. Best part of the job."

"Welcome to the only basement tavern on Bleecker Street that actually has a liquor license," he said in a toast.

"Jacob apparently never tires of saying that," said Crowley. He had earlier explained that while basement bars in Manhattan tended to be both unlicensed and unsavory, Jacob prided himself on running a respectable establishment.

"You're English?" asked Stern.

"Yes. From Bristol. I used to be a navigator on passenger ships on the run between here and Liverpool. By the time I retired, I'd made a lot of friends in

New York and decided to open this place." He glanced toward the door. "Ah, there he is, finally." He added in a lower voice, "New fellow. Think I'll need to give him the sack. Always late. Surly attitude." He turned toward the door. "Davy! You're almost half an hour late!"

A gaunt, pale young man in a flatcap and threadbare suit stood in the doorway, a canvas rucksack slung over his shoulder. He swung the rucksack in front of him, opened it, and pulled out a revolver, pointing it at Crowley.

"You! You been makin' time with my girl, you low-down English weasel!"

"Davy! What the hell are you doing?" shouted Jacob. Customers began exiting the tavern.

"Why am I always the one having guns pointed at me?" said Crowley.

"This is not a good idea, Davy," said Stern. "Why don't you put down the gun? Then we can talk about whatever is troubling you."

"Shut up, copper! Yeah, I can smell you bastards a mile away. Don't do nothin' stupid." When the last customer had left, he closed the door and locked it.

Tesla leaned over to Crowley and whispered, "Did you...?"

"No! This is a pretext. He kills us, kills himself. Tracks covered. Jacob is left alive as a witness, and Davy gets written off as a madman. Case closed. Isn't that right, Davy?"

"You made time with my girl!"

"I wouldn't try auditioning for the theater anytime soon."

Davy leveled the gun at Crowley's head. He smiled as his trigger finger wavered forward and back.

"Stopping me from pulling the trigger? I heard you could do that. But not forever. You look kinda tired already."

Stern and Donnelly pulled out their own pistols. "Thank you," they both said to Crowley.

"Well," said Stern. "It seems we have the advantage. I would very much prefer to take you alive, Davy."

"I bet you would," he answered.

"Stern," whispered Crowley. "I'm about to lose my hold." Blood trickled from one nostril. "I don't think he's going to surrender. I'll deflect his shot."

Davy's arm swung upward and to his right, his shot hitting the ceiling. He lowered his arm to shoot again. Stern and Donnelly fired first, and Davy crumpled to the floor.

Donnelly went forward and kicked the pistol from Davy's now limp grip, still keeping aim. Stern moved the rucksack aside. One of the bullets had gone through it, and the sound of broken glass was heard from within. Davy bled from wounds in his chest and abdomen. Stern crouched down next to him.

"I don't think you're going to make it, Davy," said Stern. "Is there anything you'd like to say?"

"They got it set up. You can't stop it."

"Where, Davy? Where do they have it set up?"

"It's the garden." His eyes glazed over. "The garden." His breathing stopped, eyes still open. Stern closed them and stood up.

"Christ almighty," said Jacob.

"I don't like this," said Crowley. "He was told to say that by that top-hatted bastard. I'd bet on it."

"We'll make sure the body gets removed in short order," said Stern to Jacob. He moved to pick up the rucksack, which then began to move. The sound of breaking glass came again.

"Now what?" said Jacob.

A bulge repeatedly appeared at different places in the rucksack. Stern and Donnelly backed away in alarm.

"Oh my," said Crowley. "I think I know what that is." He pulled a drawstring pouch from inside his jacket and opened it.

"What?" asked Jacob.

In the space of a few seconds, a knife blade poked out from the rucksack, then in again, then out again, opening several holes. Next, human fingers appeared, close together, stretching outward, tearing a larger hole as the palm opened, fingers splayed.

Jacob blanched and whispered, "God in heaven." The disembodied hand crawled from the rucksack.

On its fingers, it scuttled across the floor like a lightning-fast crab, bleeding from several small cuts. Reaching the door, it leapt at the doorknob, turned the knob of the locked door, and fell.

"We have to catch it!" said Crowley. He gestured with his right hand, then staggered. "I can't immobilize it."

He ran to the door and brought the pouch, open end down, toward the floor. The hand dodged it, jumping like a bullfrog onto the counter to scramble along its triangular length, knocking over abandoned glasses to leave a trail of beer and blood drops. It stopped at the far end of the bar and began to move about in a circle, as if unsure of what to do, fingernails clicking on the wood surface.

Tesla opened his valise and pulled out a device: a wooden handle with a switch and two metal prongs extending from one end. "Crowley!" said Tesla. "Can you immobilize it just for one second? When I tell you?"

"I'll try." He turned to Jacob. "Shot of whiskey, please?" Jacob, not taking his eyes off the hand, reached under the counter and brought out a bottle of bourbon. He uncorked it and handed it to Crowley, who took a long swig.

"All right," he said to Tesla. "Just give me the word."

Tesla took the pouch from Crowley and handed it to Donnelly. "Can you stay here and distract it, please?" he whispered.

Donnelly held up the pouch. "Hey, Mr. Hand," he said. "Look here. Nice, comfortable bag for you." The hand seemed to react, standing still with its fingers toward Donnelly, then slowly backing away.

In the meantime, Tesla was slowly making his way around the bar, inching toward the hand. He got to a position about two feet away and stood still.

"Now, Crowley!" he said.

Crowley raised both hands in front of him, fingers outstretched. The hand began to shake, as if restrained by invisible straps.

Tesla touched the prongs of his device to the hand and flipped the switch. There was a crackling sound. The hand trembled, enveloped by sparks like miniature lightning bolts. After a few seconds, Tesla switched it off.

"That should do it," he said.

Crowley put down his hands and staggered into a chair. He pulled out a handkerchief and wiped the blood which trickled from his nose. The hand lay inert on the counter.

"Jacob, have you any empty jars?" asked Tesla. Jacob stared at the hand, mouth agape, seeming not to have heard the question.

"Jacob?" asked Stern, putting a hand on Jacob's shoulder.

"What? Yes, yes. A jar. Right away." He reached under the counter, pulled out an empty mason jar, and handed it to Stern. "Just get that thing out of my place, please. Drinks are on the house. Crikey."

Stern took the pouch from Donnelly and walked to the other end of the counter to join Tesla. Placing the hand inside, he closed and tied the drawstring, then placed the pouch inside the jar and tightly closed the lid.

"I suppose we should assume it needs air. Jacob, might I borrow an ice pick?" Jacob complied, and Stern opened a single hole in the lid.

"That should do for now," said Stern. "I wonder if it's still alive. If that is the proper term."

"I believe so," said Tesla. "It seems rather resilient. But I'm glad the shock was effective."

"This is quite a device," said Stern, picking it up from where Tesla had laid it on the counter.

"My idea of a means for police to pacify culprits without lethal force," said Tesla. "But in its current form it can deliver only one shock before requiring a recharge."

"Then it's a good thing it worked the first time." He turned to Jacob. "I'm sorry for the disturbance in your establishment, sir. I suppose you would like an explanation?"

"Actually, no," said Jacob, pouring himself a shot of whiskey. "I get some pretty unusual clientele here, and I've seen some pretty strange stuff, but this takes the cake." He drank his shot, then poured himself another one. "If you can have the cadaver and…" He indicated the mason jar. "…*that* removed from the place, that's good enough. Some things are probably better not knowing."

"Well, there is one good thing about all this, Jacob," said Crowley, grinning. "At least you won't have to give Davy there the sack."

41

September 9th, 1899

T hough Davy had not specified precisely which garden he meant, the most obvious possibility had to be checked. Crowley, however, was physically and magickally spent after the events at the tavern, so carrying out their task psychically was for now out of the question.

After returning to Tesla's laboratory to confine the hand and access some special equipment, they managed to hail two hansom cabs from Houston Street, as only three passengers at most could fit into one cab. Tesla took with him the same suitcase he had carried in West Orange, and at just after midnight they arrived at Twenty-Sixth Street and Madison Avenue. Disembarking, they walked across the street toward Madison Square Garden.

There it stood, illuminated by the electric streetlights: large, beautiful, ornate yet unostentatious. To simply call it a building might seem almost a veiled insult. Opened to great fanfare in 1890 to replace the original structure of the same name, it was constructed of stone in the Renaissance Revival style and took up the entire block, quietly dominating its surroundings. Atop a minaret-like tower far above stood the famous statue of Diana, ancient Greek goddess of the moon. This place was said to be the largest event venue yet created. They were here to meet the architect.

They stood at the corner, waiting. "Where is he?" asked Stern.

"He will be here," said Tesla.

"Niko!" came a deep voice from the shadows, and out walked a burly, fair-skinned man about Stern's age and nearly as tall. His bright red hair was matched by an equally red handlebar mustache.

"Stanny," said Tesla as they shook hands. "Thank you so much for meeting us on such short notice."

"Not at all," he said with a grin. "I love the intrigue of it all."

"Gentlemen," said Tesla, "it is my honor to introduce to you Mr. Stanford White, architect extraordinaire, whose work includes this very venue."

After brief but polite introductions, White led them through large double doors into the plush and spacious lobby. It was dark, and Crowley and Donnelly produced flashlights.

"Your cooperation and confidentiality are deeply appreciated, Mr. White," said Stern.

"Happy to oblige, Inspector. It's fortunate I happen to keep a private apartment upstairs and was there when Mr. Tesla telephoned. I have free run of the place at all hours."

"I've heard you sometimes hold rather exciting parties up there," said Crowley. Though married, White had a reputation as an eccentric, hedonistic playboy whose parties included bevies of attractive young women.

"I do indeed, sir." His eyes lingered on Crowley for a moment. "Perhaps you'd like to join me sometime."

White then turned to Tesla. "All of you are invited, of course. Speaking of which, Niko, we've missed you at the Players. Mark Twain's been itching to visit your lab again."

"When the current tasks before us are completed, I hope," said Tesla, declining to add that as much as he valued White's friendship, the reputedly libertine nature of his parties wouldn't suit him.

"That sounds like fun," said Crowley, promising to contact White as soon as he had some spare time. *I knew those two would hit it off,* thought Tesla as White conducted them into the birdcage-like elevator at the far end of the lobby.

White closed the door and pushed up the lever. "Going up," he said. Each darkened floor of the building passed briefly into vision through the metal grating as they ascended.

White pulled the lever back down as they reached the top floor. He led the way through a red-carpeted, oak-paneled hallway to a door at the end. Unlocking it, he said, "Welcome, gentlemen, to my home away from home."

They entered a vestibule, then a parlor as luxurious as any they had seen. The window commanded a fine view of the city. Urging the men to be seated, White went to a liquor cabinet in the corner and poured himself a brandy. The other four men declined his offer of a drink as Tesla opened the suitcase and began arranging some items within.

"Do you really have a red velvet swing up here?" asked Crowley. "I read about it in the *World*." No one needed to mention that White reputedly let his many female visitors take a ride on it.

White walked to a door across from the sofa and opened it, switching on the electric light of the room within. Near the far wall was a red velvet-covered bench suspended from the ceiling by ropes, also covered in red velvet. Smiling, he switched off the light and closed the door.

Tesla had completed his assembly of the parts extracted from the suitcase and now held an odd-looking device: a short wooden pole with two concentric metal loops at one end and a boxlike panel and leather fastening straps at the other. A wire connecting the two ends ran the length of the pole. On the panel were a power switch and two indicator dials, one green, one red. Tesla strapped the device to himself.

"So what does this do?" asked White, taking a sip of his drink.

"It detects metal," said Tesla. "I have calibrated it to indicate when it is near any object with the metallurgical properties we are seeking."

"The metallurgical properties of what?"

"A spirit phone."

"Seriously?" asked White. "What—never mind. You need to keep things secret. I understand. I'm not surprised the government would get you involved in some kind of cloak-and-dagger stuff."

"You haven't bought one?" asked Crowley.

"A spirit phone? Never." He drained his glass and refilled it. "A fellow I know with a connection to Edison offered to put me on the preorder list, the first hundred customers. I said no. Even if the thing works the way it's supposed to, I have enough to deal with from living people."

"We are not sure what precisely we are looking for," said Tesla, "except that it most likely includes a spirit phone."

"I see," answered White. "I won't ask how you apparently know all the metals the thing is composed of."

"Thank you, sir," said Donnelly, who then turned to Tesla and said, "There's lots of metal in here, all over the place. Can this thing really distinguish a spirit phone from everything else?"

"It won't be easy, but it should," said Tesla. "The spirit phone horn contains silicon carbide, which I believe is ferro-magnetized by mixture with iron, which is also ferromagnetic. This device emits an electromagnetic wave at a very low frequency. Exposure to it causes anything metallic to emit its own magnetic wave, which shifts out of phase with the original wave. The phase shift will be slower with ferrous materials, but faster with the nonferrous metals comprising the rest of the horn's composition. If I can detect both a fast and a slow phase shift simultaneously, it will indicate the proximity of a spirit phone."

"Or any one of many other items and structures herein?" said White. "Still, it sounds much more advanced than any metal detection device I've read about. All right, we might as well get started. Just let me get one more drink to fortify myself." Tesla switched on the metal detector.

From top to bottom through the length and breadth of the architectural marvel of New York walked the five men: the rooftop garden, the several bars and restaurants, and various rooms and offices (keys to all of which White had, requesting reciprocal confidentiality on this point). Twice they encountered roving security guards, each of whom eyed Tesla's device curiously but said only good evening as he passed. White told them that he and his friends were testing a new invention called the combination pedometer-stethoscope.

They arrived at the concert hall, dark and cavernous, silent but for their footfalls. They were getting tired.

"This whole place is truly an impressive work, sir," said Stern.

"Yes, if I do say so myself," said White. "I love it. I hope to die here." Donnelly crossed himself.

Tesla zigzagged through every row of seats, finally standing before the stage. "I've got something," he said. The green and red dials were both at the extreme right.

There began a low-pitched hum, barely audible.

"I believe it is in the orchestra pit."

"Yes, it is," came a faint and tinny voice from the darkness below. High-pitched, male. The sound of calm, implicit brutality.

White froze. Face a mixture of terror and inquiry, he turned to Tesla.

"It is nothing that can harm us," Tesla said, wishing that were truly so.

The voice began repeating in a singsong chant, "You will all die soon, and horribly. You will die soon, and horribly. You will—" It stopped as Tesla switched off the detector.

"The electromagnetic wave must have activated it," he said.

They descended into the orchestra pit.

At first, seats and music stands were all they could see. After a few seconds, Donnelly said, "There." His light was focused upon a black, mounded shape against the wall at the stage end of the pit. It looked too small to be a spirit phone.

It was a black silk cloth, like the one Edison had used in his demonstration at Columbia College. Donnelly pulled it off. Beneath was a spirit phone horn, set upon its side. Next to it was an envelope.

White exhaled a long sigh, regaining his composure. He picked up the envelope and handed it to Stern, saying, "I believe it's for you, Inspector." Stern opened it. Within was a typewritten note.

Gentlemen,

I am afraid you have arrived at the wrong garden!

However, as a token of my goodwill, I have extended a helping hand. The most southerly point of arrival is best.

I look forward to meeting you all in person.

Yours sincerely,
A.T.

"I won't ask who A.T. is," said White. "Nor will I ask what is meant by a helping hand, arrivals from the south, or anything else. In fact, I think it's better I never find out."

"Thank you for your understanding," said Stern.

42

"Reports of depression, insanity, and suicide among spirit phone users. Senators issue resolution demanding an investigation. Still no comment from Edison Manufacturing.' It's not looking good." Crowley took a long pull on his pipe and blew out a few smoke rings. He was seated at the laboratory table, reading the *New York World*. The front-page titles included *Mysterious Airship Sighting over Wyoming* and *Tons of Magnetite Fall on Minnesota Farm—Local Authorities Baffled*. "I wonder if this is part of the One Hundred's plan or just a side effect."

Tesla sat in a chair, arms crossed, regarding the hand. It was scrambling about inside the large glass case he had placed it in after examining it. Its wounds were healed.

"I analyzed Davy's blood," said Tesla. "It was normal."

"I'd assumed as much," said Crowley. "One of their normal human helpers. Normal as in non-duplicate. I wonder what his vision of utopia was?"

"No idea."

"How the blazes could those cuts heal so fast?" asked Crowley.

"Unknown," said Tesla. "Presumably, it is some property of the Essential Composite blood chemistry." Tesla had confirmed the nature of the blood, along with a fingerprint identification confirming that it was indeed the right hand of Marcus Reinecker.

"So we have the killer of Reinecker in custody," said Crowley. "But putting a hand on trial for murder seems to lack legal precedent, especially if it's the victim's own. I guess it would have to be judged a suicide of sorts."

"If you'll indulge me, let's review what we previously discussed regarding this point. What would prompt the hand to kill the person it was formerly attached to?"

"I suspect it was a consequence inherent to the separation process, which was done to test whether the Ferox's—or the One Hundred's—physical entry into this realm would have the desired effect. You'll recall their desire to inflict misery and death with no karmic consequences to themselves. Just as the newly liberated spirit—liberated from the Ferox's perspective—wishes to inflict such harm, the hand wished to do so to its body: the same desire in microcosm. The hand is analogous to a Ferox, and Reinecker is analogous to all people—all souls—other than the Ferox. But it was not the typical Ferox summoning. There must have been someone assisting, presumably our friend in the top hat."

"So you're saying that Reinecker's consciousness is now inhabiting that hand?"

"Yes. Or at least a remnant of it. A Ferox wouldn't want to get stuck in a hand. Though one was apparently summoned to help the process along somehow."

"And you still can't get access to its mind, assuming it has one?"

"No. It's like trying to mind-read a potato. Yet we must assume that the 'A.T.' who wrote the note was Ambrose Temple, and that this is the 'helping hand' referred to."

"Well, then. Shall we proceed?"

Crowley picked up a legal pad and pencil from the table. He and Tesla walked over to the glass case. The hand stopped moving, seemingly aware of their presence.

"Mister…Hand," said Crowley. "Or Mr. Reinecker. Mr. Reinecker's hand. I don't know whether you can hear or understand me, but I am about to provide you with a pencil and paper. If you can write, please tell me the location of those who wish to bring the *ferox phasma*, also called the One Hundred, to earth."

The case was covered by a board, upon which rested a heavy toolbox. Tesla lifted the board an inch, allowing Crowley to slip the pencil and notepad inside.

The hand went to the legal pad and felt the pages, running the sheets between its fingers. Finding and gripping the pencil, it began to write.

KILL ME

"Oh, God," said Tesla. The hand continued writing.

KILL ME KILL ME KILL ME
KILL ME KILL ME KILL ME
KILL ME KILL ME KILL ME

"I would be happy to oblige," said Crowley, "if I knew how. It either can't understand us or cannot reason enough to communicate any information."

Tesla covered the case with a cloth and sat down, looking shaken. The sound of the scribbling, now muffled, continued.

"I've examined it as thoroughly as I can," said Tesla. "I am at a loss as to how it can be alive, or at least animated somehow. Nor can I discern how it apparently has some form of sensory perception beyond touch. There of course appears to be no central nervous system—that is, no brain—with which to register sensation."

"Yet it can write."

"Yes. And its blood chemistry is composed of the Seven Planetary Metals plus carborundum, as the hand is Reinecker's."

"But to stay alive, how does it gain nutrition?"

"I have no idea. Magick-with-a-*k*?"

"Hmm. So what did you actually discover?"

"In my analysis, I attempted to learn the secret of its healing properties. In this I failed. But I did discover this: the amount of oxygen in the blood is much lower than normal, though not enough to be lethal. You're a mountaineer. In your experience, what does that indicate?"

"Being at an especially high altitude. But we're practically at sea level here."

"My theory is that however this thing breathes, assuming it does, exposure to a high-altitude environment results in more oxygen deprivation and a slower recovery upon returning to lower climes than a full human body."

"But how do we know it was ever at a high altitude? Maybe for this thing, lower oxygen content is a normal condition. Besides, even if it is hypersensitive to elevation, would any nearby mountain ranges be high enough for such an effect? The Catskills?"

"I don't think it spent any time in the Catskills. At least I have no evidence of such. But I found something else."

"Yes?" The scribbling sound from the case stopped.

"There were traces of soil under its fingernails, upon which I performed a chemical analysis. It contains minute traces of igneous, sedimentary, and volcanic rock."

"Meaning?"

"It is not soil from New York. The soil here is rich in particles of sedimentary rock, particularly limestone and shale, but not volcanic or igneous rock. I infer that we seek a high-altitude location with geologic features reflected in the soil I detected. You will also recall that Temple's note said we were in the wrong 'garden,' whatever garden he meant."

Without another word, they walked into Tesla's study, located at the back of the laboratory. It was a small room, lined with oak bookcases and a small desk set before a window. From one of the bookshelves, Tesla removed the United States atlas.

Placing it on the desk, Tesla opened it. Soon he had the page he was seeking.

Garden of the Gods

Garden of the Gods is a wilderness area located in central Colorado, at coordinates 38° 52′ North 104° 53′ West. It is noted for its interesting geological features, which include large deposits of igneous, sedimentary, and volcanic rock. Its numerous formations of pink and red sandstone are particularly admired for their distinctiveness and beauty.

"I believe this is the place," said Tesla. "He wants us to arrive from the south."

Just then Stern and Donnelly walked into the laboratory. "Any news, gentlemen?" asked Stern. Tesla brought them up to date.

"Well, that is interesting," said Stern. "It seems, gentlemen, we are flying again."

"I'd like to bring some items along from the laboratory, just in case," said Tesla.

"Certainly."

"I don't like this," said Crowley. "It's almost too easy, as if we were meant to find these clues. The chap in the top hat is luring us in."

"Perhaps," said Tesla. "But what other choice do we have but to go?"

"All right. But this time I'm bringing food. And before we go, there's someone I need to speak with."

43

Thomas Edison sat at his desk. The laboratory and its offices were closed, and the sun had just set. He switched on the desk lamp. Though convinced he was alone in the building, in an attempt to maintain his composure, he forced himself to appear calm, belying the terrible turmoil within.

But even this effort could not hide the toll the past two weeks had taken. Persistent insomnia and lack of appetite had left him thinner, and pale, with dark circles under his eyes. He was unshaven, his hair unkempt.

Taking the spirit phone from his desk drawer and activating it, he immediately said, "Andreas, we need to talk. You said there would be small, temporary problems with users of the spirit phone, but it's getting worse. A total product recall may be necessary. I can't delay issuing a public statement much longer."

There was no reply but the low hum and the faint blue glow.

He tried again. "People are going insane. Killing themselves. The government's getting involved. I can't get ahold of Temple. What the hell is going on? Andreas!"

"Thomas," came the voice, with its tinny, distorted quality, yet sweetly familiar.

"Mary," replied Edison, at first speechless beyond saying her name. He had always had to speak with Andreas first. This was new.

"Darling," she replied.

"Where is Andreas?"

"I think he's busy with something. But that gives us more time to speak to each other." Their conversations had in part been about her life in the spirit realm, which she described as a kind of paradise where one's deepest desires were made manifest. It was, Edison had decided, not so different from the claims of many spiritualists and mediums during the popularity of séances which had gripped the Western world the past few decades. But at the moment there were more urgent matters.

"Yes, but…there is a problem with this device. The spirit phone. Some of its users are having mental disturbances. There have been some deaths. I need to speak with Andreas."

"Is it really that important, darling?"

"Yes. Is that not obvious?"

"I see. Well, in that case, first let me show you a little trick I can do."

"What? What are you talking about?"

There came a deep and mournful impact in the pit of Edison's being as the reply came out of the spirit phone: the first word was in Mary's voice, the second that of Andreas, then each word alternating between them.

"Here's my trick," came the female-then-male-then-female voice. "I'm really good at doing impressions."

"No."

"Yes," replied the voice, this time only that of Andreas. "It was never Mary. It was always me."

"No! Where is she? Where are you keeping her?"

"I'm not keeping her anywhere, you stupid faggot. Though rumor has it she's getting it in both ends from Samuel Morse and Michael Faraday. We call that a spit roast where I come from."

"You son of a bitch!"

Laughter, filled with the stench of spiteful mirth, emanated from the spirit phone. When finally it stopped, Andreas said, "Your impotent rage is so sweet to taste, you pompous shithead. I wish I could stick around to enjoy more of it, but I have an important appointment. Fuck off and goodbye." The venomous laughter came again, even louder, then faded away.

For a few seconds, through the abyss of grief and despair, Edison considered calling for Mary, the real Mary. But he knew it was hopeless. Whatever this thing was, it couldn't do that. Somehow he had always known this, but had tricked himself into ignoring his suspicions. He still couldn't understand what Andreas—whatever he really was—wanted, but it was nothing, at this point, that he could prevent.

Elbows on the desk, head in his hands, he said, "You damn fool. You damn fool." He took the key chain from his pocket. Reaching down, he unlocked a drawer, removed from it a small revolver, and placed the barrel against the side of his head.

"I'm coming, Mary," he said, and pulled the trigger.

44

"So tell me again, how are you going to do it?"

"Do what?"

"Run the world. Even with the enforcement we can provide, it seems a bit…overambitious."

Even through the metallic distortion of the spirit phone, the voice of Andreas carried its tone of mocking skepticism to Ambrose Temple, who sat at his desk in an office identical to the one he had occupied in Wyoming.

Temple was silent for a moment. He turned away from the spirit phone to take in the moonlit view out the window, the mountainous landscape covered by its blanket of stars. Beautiful beyond anything the human hand could create. Even so, he felt once more the regret that he would never again see Devils Tower, nor enjoy the freedom to travel the world. To accomplish his aims, he would have to stay here permanently.

He turned back to the spirit phone. "As I've said before, I have no such expectation. I will at first appoint de facto monarchs in America and a few other nations, and give general standing orders. I'll keep Colorado as my impregnable enclave, and thus have the time and leisure to consider subsequent steps—"

"'—to reform human society,'" came the tinny, mocking voice.

"Yes," said Temple, betraying not a trace of the irritation he felt. "It will be an incremental process, not to be completed in my lifetime. Which is why I require an heir."

A hearty metal-tinged laugh, and the blue aura grew larger. "In other words, you're making this up as you go along. And it all amounts to the same thing: megalomania posing as altruism. That's all political power ever is. You really think you're different than the governments you aim to displace, posthumously or otherwise?"

"Yes."

"Then have it your way, sir, as long as we get to hunt our delectable squealing meat. As for your so-called heir, he'll never agree to it. You should have killed him and found someone else."

"There is no one else. And as regards his agreement, I can be very persuasive." He pulled his watch from his vest pocket and opened it. It was nearly midnight. "In any case, we have important work tomorrow. I suggest you prepare to position yourself for the final stage."

"Yes, I suppose you're right."

"Are you sure you've all had enough contact with the operators to make the transition complete?"

"Absolutely. I very much look forward to meeting you in person, Mr. Temple."

"As do I, sir. Good evening."

"Good evening."

He switched off the device, and the blue aura faded away.

45

Edison stared at the pistol in his hand, incredulity crashing against the rush of adrenaline. Fighting off the urge to vomit, hands trembling, he opened the gun's chamber. It was empty. He had always kept it loaded.

"Looking for these?" came a voice from the doorway.

He looked up to see a pale young man in a dark-gray suit and homburg. In his open palm he held six bullets.

"An understandable but unwise attempt," said the stranger as he pocketed the bullets. "Suicide only intensifies the dilemmas which motivate one to seek it." There was a tinge of fatigue in his voice.

Edison stood up. "How did you get in here?"

"Well, it wasn't so easy. But I suggest activating your alarm system at knock-off, not when the last man leaves the building."

"Who the hell are you?"

"I'm Aleister Crowley. It's an honor, sir, but we've no time to stand on ceremony."

"What do you want?"

"Information. What can you tell me about Ambrose Temple?"

Though Edison was confused and shaken, and had little idea what this was about, he decided to trust this strange young man who had just saved his life. But in recounting the story of how he had met Temple, and all their meetings up to that point, he was unable to provide any new information to Crowley.

"If you'll allow me, sir," said Crowley, walking up to the desk. "For want of a better term, I'm a mind reader. Might I ask you to sit down again and close your eyes?"

What the hell? thought Edison as Crowley's hands gently grasped the front and back of his head. After a minute, the hands were removed.

"I was hoping to find a chink in his armor, but there's nothing beyond what I already know. Well, it's not your fault."

"It seems so obvious now. Temple and Andreas have been lying to me. But why?"

"I don't have time to go into details, but there are a couple of things you should know. The spirit phone you've been using is the only type that allows contact with Andreas and spirits like him. It's composed of half silicon carbide, not one-eighth like the ones you've been selling, which are basically just supernatural parlor trick machines."

"Those dirty bastards. Somehow, I knew. I knew it was never Mary I was speaking to, but I didn't want to know. Look, young fellow. Crowley, was it? I don't understand everything that's going on, but I'd say Temple and Andreas have some kind of unsavory intentions."

"Yes, you could say that."

"And it looks to me like you plan to find them and stop them."

"Yes."

"Take me with you." Edison's eyes blazed, and some of the color had returned to his face. "I've a score to settle."

"I thought you'd say that," said Crowley, crossing his arms. "But your recent ordeal has left you weakened, physically and psychically. You're in no condition to accompany us."

"Us? Who—"

"Mr. Edison, I would say that you are quite exhausted." Crowley slapped his arm three times in rapid succession, extended a fist palm-up, then opened his hand palm-down. Edison slumped forward onto the desk, unconscious.

Crowley was about to leave, but hesitated. Impelled by an instinct he could not account for, he placed his hands upon Edison's head again and closed his eyes, delving even deeper into both his own consciousness and that of the inventor. Searching the infinity of inner space, he found what he sought: a place to connect. Forging a link between their minds, he then detached from it, confident it could be reestablished if needed.

"Can't hurt. Might come in handy, I suppose," whispered Crowley. "Get some rest, Mr. Edison. You'll start to feel better after you wake up." He turned around and walked out the office door.

46

September 10th, 1899

The eight-hour flight had been uneventful but for some slight turbulence over Kansas, and Stern brought the ship in for a landing just as dawn was breaking over the mountains. He had chosen a spot about half a mile south of the southernmost point of Garden of the Gods. They were reasonably sure no one had seen them, but at this point secrecy was less important than haste. Stern and Donnelly had been unable to make arrangements for ballast, fuel, and helium replenishment.

They exited the airship, each man carrying a large rucksack. "There's human activity going on," said Crowley. He pointed north. "That way."

"How many people?" asked Stern.

"Hard to say. At least a hundred or so."

"All right. Please make the call."

Crowley produced a paper upon which was written a grid:

B	E	R	O	M	I	N
E						
R						
O						
M						
I						
N						

Holding it in front of him, he said, "Ashtaroth, I seek your aid, and command you to appear before me now!"

Ashtaroth appeared. "I come as bidden," he said with a tip of his bowler.

"Yes. Please proceed as we discussed yesterday."

"I understand. But first, please allow me the presumption to remind my master that I am limited to one task per day and can do nothing beyond this until sunrise tomorrow at the earliest."

"Yes, yes, I know. But don't you even care if these things invade earth?"

Ashtaroth paused to consider the question for a moment. "It would have little or no effect upon my realm. I am bound to your service, but am otherwise a disinterested party."

"Fine. Proceed."

Ashtaroth raised his hands, eyes closed. After a few seconds, he opened his eyes and put his arms down. "It is done," he said.

Stern, Donnelly, and Tesla looked at their hands, then at each other. "We're still visible," said Stern.

"Only to yourselves and each other," said Ashtaroth. "I suggest looking in a mirror to quell any doubts."

Stern took a hand mirror from his rucksack and held it up. "My God," he said. There was no reflection but the sky behind him.

"Your clothing and any items you carry up to a certain size, including your rucksacks, will also be invisible," said Ashtaroth, "but only so long as you carry them. The effect will last approximately three hours but may vary considerably for each individual. I suggest taking no more than two hours to complete your task." At that, he vanished.

"We're invisible, but we can still be heard," said Crowley. "Silence is still necessary if we need to get through guards."

"All right," said Stern. "Remember the plan. Let's go."

They began to walk north, single file. Stern took the lead, followed by Donnelly, Crowley, and Tesla. It was beautiful country, a large open area with red rock formations sharing space with evergreens, and majestic mountains rising in the distance. At the highest among them, Pikes Peak, Tesla had conducted an experiment three years before to demonstrate the audibility of sonic vibrations through four miles of stratified rock using the melody of the song "Ben Bolt" played on an Autoharp. It seemed like a hundred lifetimes ago, and Tesla wondered when—or if—he could return to his usual experiments.

After a while, Stern halted and briefly consulted a map and compass. "This is it," he said. "We are in the Garden of the Gods."

"But no sign of a compound or settlement," said Tesla.

"Let's keep moving."

Within a minute, they discerned a large, shimmering rectangular outline.

"This is the place, I believe," whispered Stern.

Crowley nodded.

"What can you detect?"

"I'm tapped out, Walter," he answered. "I can only tell you there are people in there. I'm sorry."

Stern gently clapped him on the back. "Don't worry." He then addressed all three of his companions. "What we will almost certainly need to do will be difficult, but we must do it. Do not hesitate."

"Fine," Crowley whispered back. "I won't hesitate. But can you explain to me again why we can't simply convey our evidence to the government so they can send in the army or something?"

"I have recent indications that several key persons within the government are in league with our enemy. If so, they could use the army or other forces to arrest us on the pretext that we are criminals or terrorists, and issue orders not to go anywhere near this site."

"It seems worth the risk to me," said Crowley. He sighed. "All right. We're here. Let's do this."

They began walking again and were soon at the gate of a compound essentially identical to the one in Wyoming. No people were visible.

"No guards," said Crowley in a low voice. "The gate is unlocked. Luring us in."

"Let's go," said Stern. They walked into the compound.

As soon as they were inside, Crowley pointed to the nearest barracks. From one of its windows, they could see a faint blue glow, and heard a low, monotonous hum. Walking in silence, they came to the window and peered inside.

Within, lying on one hundred bunks, were one hundred men who all looked exactly the same. All exactly like Marcus Reinecker. They appeared to be sleeping. Each man had a brown leather strap around his head. From each strap led a wire attached at the other end to the horn of a spirit phone which sat atop a small table at the foot of each bunk.

In front of each spirit phone was a stool upon which sat a man or a woman, each of whom wore a headset resembling those of the sound-powered phones on the airship. These too were attached by a wire to each of the spirit phones. They spoke with animation, earnest faces bathed in the blue light invading every part of the barracks as the hundred metallic cones hummed their low-pitched chorus.

Standing at regular intervals, armed with carbines, were guards. Their purpose was not so much to protect the operation from outside interference—their leader had assured them there would be none—as to have a precaution against the small but real risk of an operator suddenly becoming violent. A few had become ever more erratic with each contact session, but this was to be the last.

Everyone—the men in the bunks, the spirit phone operators, the guards—wore gray coveralls with letters and numbers on the left breast. On the far wall of the barracks was painted the symbol:

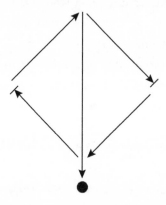

"Presumably they have all taken their sulfur pills," said Tesla.

"Crowley," said Stern. "We should be close enough. We need confirmation if you can get it."

Crowley closed his eyes and bowed his head. After half a minute, he opened his eyes again and nodded. "They're calling them," he said. "But..."

"What?"

"This has got to be the core group, but even they don't know what they're doing. They think they're calling up the spirits of people they regard as wise, as saviors of humanity. With those Reinecker copies as their vessels. *Permanent* vessels. It's something beyond simple possession. I couldn't get everything, but…it's a crazy, contradictory mixture. Abraham Lincoln, Karl Marx, Plato, Confucius. One man thinks he's calling up Jesus Christ."

"But they are actually calling up the One Hundred, are they not?" asked Stern.

"Yes," answered Crowley.

"Then we must proceed according to plan," said Stern. "Go."

They fanned out, each man arriving at a different corner of the barracks. From each rucksack, a bundle of twenty-five sticks of dynamite, fuses twined together, was taken and placed against the corner. A small bundle of copper wire was wrapped around the fuses, with a small antenna attached to the wire.

Having set the dynamite, they ran out the gate and stood on the other side of the fence. Tesla produced a small wooden box with a single red metallic button and a telescoping antenna. He pulled the antenna out to its full length.

"Shall I do it?" asked Stern.

"No," said Tesla. "I'll do it. God forgive me." He pressed the button.

Nothing happened.

He pressed the button again. And again.

"I don't understand. It's…"

"Plan B," said Stern. "We light the fuses. Let's go."

"I'm afraid I can't let you do that, gentlemen," said a voice behind them. They turned and saw the flat, flickering monochrome image of a tall bearded man in a suit and top hat.

"It's him," said Crowley. "The man in Wyoming."

"Indeed! And now I'm the man in Colorado. Except this time I am physically here, though not in this particular spot. Mr. Tesla, the dynamite will not detonate no matter how many times you press the button. As for lighting the fuses, kindly have a look inside the compound."

Turning to look, they saw guards from inside the barracks gathering up the dynamite and taking it inside.

"I've ordered them to ignore you, unless of course you decide to go in with guns blazing. I promise you would be outnumbered and outgunned."

Tesla turned back to the flickering image. "How did you disable the detonator?"

"By transmitting a signal to interfere with its function."

"What kind of signal? Sent from where?"

"That's my little secret." He grinned. "I don't suppose you have a plan C?"

"How can you see us?" asked Crowley.

"There are ways, Mr. Crowley. Look in your mirror."

Stern and Crowley pulled out their mirrors and saw their own reflections. They were once again visible.

"You are not the only one who can summon demon familiars, Mr. Crowley. Do you recognize this?" The flat image of the man produced the flat image of a large sheet of paper. Upon it was written a grid:

M	A	C	A	N	E	H
A	R	O	L	U	S	E
D	I	R	U	C	U	N
A	L	U	H	U	L	A
S	E	R	U	R	O	C
U	N	E	L	I	R	A
L	U	S	A	D	A	M

Crowley stared at the grid and said nothing.

"What is it, Crowley?" asked Tesla.

"Yes, go on, Crowley," said the man in the top hat with a mocking grin. "Tell them."

"It is an incantation," said Crowley, "to hinder a mage from operating."

"That's right," said the man. "And why didn't you consider this a possibility?"

"Because I believed no mage on earth was powerful enough to affect me with this spell."

"And you were wrong. The price of arrogance is steep, Mr. Crowley. But I must admit, a lesser mage would have been completely incapacitated, or nearly so. Your ability to resist the spell was greater than I had anticipated. Perhaps you could have even broken it, had you realized what was happening."

"Why are you doing this?" asked Stern.

"All in good time, Inspector. I find this way of conversing so impersonal. Let us speak in person, at a place where you gentlemen will be less able to attempt mischief. Please meet me by your airship." The image vanished.

47

They arrived at the airship, and there was the man in the flesh, in top hat and morning dress.

"How nice to see you all in person," he said. "Before we begin our chat, I warn you that any attempt at violence will have unpleasant consequences." He smiled.

"We'd best listen to what he has to say," said Crowley.

"Very sensible of you. It is not my desire to harm any of you. Now, I shall attempt to explain things to your satisfaction, with the caveat that there will be elements I elect not to reveal."

"Mr. Ambrose Temple," said Tesla. "The actual inventor of the spirit phone."

"An honor, Mr. Tesla. As for the spirit phone, one might say it was a collaborative effort, though I'm happy for Edison to take the credit. You see, he's a sentimental man. You know his motive for attempting to develop such a device."

"You gave him the information on the metallurgic properties of the horn."

"Once I had obtained it."

"And the engineering of human duplicates. How did you do it?"

"First things first, Mr. Tesla. You are aware, of course, that time as we understand it has no particular meaning in the astral realm. What we term past, present, and future exist…" He paused to consider.

"Conterminously," offered Crowley.

"Conterminously. Thank you, Mr. Crowley. The entity which attacked you in Tibet is the leader of the Ferox, the same entity who identified himself to Edison as 'Andreas.' It was he who discovered a way to expand their psychic capabilities, paradoxically devolving in spiritual enlightenment. He then encountered a limit to the process. He could go no further, nor regain access to earth to indulge in his destructive appetites. His two choices: begin the arduous journey of rescinding his refusal to evolve, of getting educated, so to speak, or remain where he was. Neither option appealed to him, and I had been searching for an entity with his qualifications. Once I had established contact, I proposed a deal, leaving certain points unspoken."

"What qualifications?" asked Tesla.

"In his earthly life, Andreas was, or rather will be, a telephone engineer."

"Will be?" asked Crowley. "Oh."

"Yes. He will also be responsible for the deaths of over fifty people, mostly young women, beginning about eighty years from now and ending in his eventual capture, trial, and execution. Though now that the transfer process has begun, he will instead be here, as a permanent physical incarnation of a Ferox."

"Violent psychopathy. Technical expertise," said Tesla.

"Yes. Precisely what I needed. I knew Edison had been tinkering with ultrasensitive radio telegraphy to build a spirit communicator, as was I. In rare cases, one may attain sporadic contact, as I did with Andreas. Once he had accepted my proposal, I had him contact Edison. After that, it was just a matter of Andreas giving Edison instructions on how to make the device more reliable for communication, at least with him, until I could learn how to build the current model."

"And Edison never contacted Mary," said Tesla.

"He believed he had, but it was actually Andreas, as I'm sure you know. I wanted to spare Edison the knowledge, but Andreas has a bit of a cruel streak. To ensure Edison never realized that 50 percent carborundum was needed for the effect I actually want, and what that effect is, I insisted on making the prototype for him to use. Thus, he remained in contact with Andreas, whose influence was sufficient to prevent him from noticing the discrepancy. He knows now, but no matter."

"You exploited the man's grief to deceive him," said Tesla.

"Regrettably. I needed the lesser model on the market, with maximum public confidence. At first. And for that, I needed Edison's fame and prestige."

"Why did you need the other type on the market?"

"You know what's happening out there." He swept his arm toward the horizon. "People are yearning to contact their dearly departed with the spirit phone. At first, it seems they do. But only at first. Instead, they get the astral equivalent of a clever parrot, repeating phrases back at them, spouting nonsense, all in what they remember as a loved one's voice. The gap between expectation and result is destroying faith in both the technological and the spiritual. It is a world in despair. I will step in to fill that void."

"So you're simply seeking power," said Crowley. "You're going to end up like the others who have attempted this. The Ferox will kill you. Or worse."

"I seek no power for its own sake. That will be clear soon enough."

"How were you able to do all this?" asked Crowley.

"I am a man of means. Those means have been acquired more or less covertly, my true identity shrouded. In decades spent developing my knowledge, my goal has been to bring the Ferox into this world, physically and permanently. Haste was necessary. As you have learned, man's unrelenting increase in electrical generation has created a barrier, a kind of fog the Ferox have difficulty penetrating. The transition must occur within the year or all is lost."

"How did you learn the composition of the Essential Composite?" asked Crowley.

"After a lifetime spent searching the world's libraries and archives, I was in despair. Then I found what I needed in, of all places, the Columbia College Library! I had searched there previously, finding nothing. I still don't know who deposited it."

"Deposited what?"

"A fragment of a manuscript, describing the precise composition, placed within the pages of an unrelated volume. It's in English, most likely from the early 1600s."

"John Dee?" asked Crowley.

"Yes. The handwriting is almost certainly Dee's."

"John Dee?" asked Donnelly.

"An occultist," said Stern. "Reputedly very powerful."

"When was this?" asked Crowley.

"My birthday! The afternoon of February 9th. I could not have asked for a better present. And now the only devices capable of contacting the Ferox are here, except the one in Edison's possession."

"And thus you believe you can take over the world?" asked Tesla.

"I have no such ambition. Societal changes will be incremental, completed long after I am gone. It is not I that will take over the world, but a system."

"What system?" asked Tesla. "What are you talking about?"

"You have seen it today. The uniforms, the alphanumeric designations, the regimentation—this shall be the new order. At least the bare bones of it. Man's technology of destruction increases apace: repeating rifles, machine guns, dynamite. Soon the means to completely destroy ourselves will be realized. Yet man is also malleable, perfectible, and I will do the shaping. Autonomy results in the self-destructive mob. This mob must be molded into a happy, complacent herd. People must be told what to wear, what to eat, what to say, what to think. That is the path to happiness. The duplicates are a means to that end."

"How did you create them?" asked Tesla.

"It was as much a process of magick as of science. I would like to show you where and how I made them. How I manipulated their growth and aging at will. Join me, and together we will use such knowledge to give the world a just and lasting peace.

"And you, Mr. Crowley. Become my apprentice, my heir. I have bested you, but at your age, I couldn't do what you can. Under my tutelage, you will surpass and replace me. We will forge a new age of peace and prosperity."

"By calling forth creatures who will cause untold misery and death."

"Patience, Mr. Crowley. They will be powerless to cause any harm beyond what is necessary."

"Who was the original of the duplicates?" asked Stern.

"That will remain my secret. Now, you must be wondering about Reinecker—or rather P-45. He was an escapee, as were Q-75 and P-67. That is, they believed they were. I let them go, along with one of our members who'd had a change of heart—Michael's stepmother, so to speak. She is with us again, undergoing reeducation."

"Why did you let them go?"

"I needed to see whether exposure to the pathogens of a major city would result in problems. It worked out fine. Except Q-75—the one now called Michael—is part of a mentally flawed cohort. They lack concentration. They'll have to be liquidated."

Stern's features hardened. "You're going to murder a hundred children?"

"Murder? You lack perspective, Mr. Stern. Leaving defectives alive could have unpredictable consequences. It is potentially an act of murder *not* to liquidate them. Consider the greater good."

"There were cohorts A through O, then?" asked Crowley. "All 'liquidated?'"

"Yes. Most recently the O Cohort. They were prone to various ailments. In any case, P-45, alias Reinecker, got out as a child, right after getting the tattoo. I helped arrange his adoption by the German couple. I wanted to learn how a duplicate would adapt to a more conventional family unit, then withstand the shock of its sudden demise. He was quite resourceful. Much more so than P-67, who was a disappointment, frankly."

"You mean to say you killed Reinecker's stepparents?" asked Donnelly.

"As I said, he was resourceful, and I needed to learn how resourceful. Certain poisons are undetectable even under autopsy. He and P-67 were the only delinquents in their cohort, so I made two new ones. It was troublesome, as I had to accelerate their growth to match the rest."

"Murder. For the greater good," said Tesla.

"Sadly, yes. You think I care nothing for the suffering of innocents, yet I know more of it than you can imagine. But I digress. P-45 returned to us in contrition, begging to rejoin the group. I agreed, on condition that he participate in the yacht experiment. I needed to confirm that the desired result was possible. It was a unique variant of a Ferox summoning, modified to produce the effect you have witnessed. Andreas sort of pushed Forty-five's soul into the hand. He found it quite humorous."

"The yacht was yours?" asked Stern.

"Yes. It was quite a special process, requiring the use of the lightning rod. And I withheld certain facts about the expected outcome to ensure Forty-five's cooperation."

"Why did you leave the traces of Essential Composite on the yacht?"

"The same reason I arranged for Reinecker's corpse to disappear, caused mischief on your airship, teleported the matchbox to you in Colorado, and had Davy reveal this location. To test your abilities while leading you all here. I even facilitated Andreas's attack on you in Tibet, Mr. Crowley. Your response was impressive."

"Who are all the non-duplicate cultists?" asked Crowley.

"Cultists?" Temple laughed. "I suppose you could call them that. They act as spirit phone operators to summon the Ferox, and will be functionaries in the new government. They're mostly from the fringes of respectable society. Easily manipulated, eccentric fools. Each believes he is bringing to earth a famous personage who will inaugurate utopia. They're in for a keen disappointment, I'm afraid."

"How are you getting away with all this?" asked Stern.

"How?" replied Temple. "Have you not wondered, Inspector, why your requested fifty agents did not appear in Wyoming?"

"You son of a bitch."

"Now, watch your language. I have allies in government and industry. Just enough to thwart interference. To be duly rewarded once things get underway."

"What about that symbol? The tattoos and the wall of the barracks?" asked Crowley.

"Oh, that. Just a little something I thought up. My followers believe it symbolizes a cessation of a societal cycle of ascendancy and corruption, and the establishment of a perfect civilization. Which is true. Just not in the form they expect."

"Nor will it be what you expect," said Crowley. "Stop this, before it's too late."

"You underestimate me, Mr. Crowley. The Ferox will cooperate with me because they have no choice. There is a special feature to my duplicates, to be activated once the transition is complete." He pulled his watch from his vest pocket and opened it. "It shouldn't be long now."

"Special feature?"

"Yes. Built into their physiology. Any attempt by a Ferox to leave the compound, or attack me in any manner, will result in violent nausea, a crippling migraine, and unconsciousness for approximately one hour. That was another reason for the experiment with Reinecker's hand. Once the transition was complete, I provoked it into violence against me, which it couldn't accomplish."

"You intend on keeping them prisoner? Sooner or later, they will escape."

"No, they won't. I've accounted for every possibility."

"By the way," said Tesla, "at least one spirit you intend to summon is—or was—female. Might she not object to inhabiting a male body?"

"Ah yes, Katie Bender. You've met her. She went to you by accident because one of our operators believes he's summoning Michael Faraday, who is actually her. Twenty-seven of the Ferox are female, in that they were female in physical life. None care about the sex of the vessel. They believe they will be able to transfigure at will."

In an instant, Donnelly pulled out his pistol, aimed it at Temple, and cried out in pain as he dropped it. The pistol glowed red on the ground. Donnelly held his hand up to see a burn in the palm.

"I remind you of my warning, Mr. Donnelly. You and Mr. Stern are potentially useful, but not indispensable."

"Even if you can keep these things under control, what good will they be to you here?" asked Tesla. "How can you use them to establish this world state you speak of?"

"In learning how to make them physical, I confirmed a side effect of the process. They will be able to kill *remotely*. With a sufficient exercise of mental will upon an individual—for approximately six consecutive hours—death by cerebral hemorrhage will result.

"Do you see? The Ferox can neither escape nor oppose me. They want nothing more than to inflict suffering and death, and will be completely dependent upon me to satisfy that desire. They'll have to stay here, where I'll bring them the occasional victim. In return, they will remotely kill any statesman who dares refuse my orders."

"What are you going to establish?" asked Stern. "A monarchy? A communist state?"

"Monarchy? Communism? Capitalism? Something else? I don't know yet, and it doesn't matter. Those are merely details. The totality of control over human behavior is what is important. After a few generations, no one will be aware there had ever been any other system."

"Try to understand," said Crowley. "This is insanity. Do you realize what they will do once they break free? What it will take to stop them, even assuming that's possible?"

"You disappoint me, Mr. Crowley. You doubt my plan and refuse to see the value of this opportunity. Your skills would be of so much use. Will you not join me?"

"No," said Crowley.

"No," said Tesla.

Temple held up an arm, fingers outstretched, toward Stern and Donnelly. They fell to the ground, limbs stretched out in four directions as if pulled by invisible hands. They began to moan, faces twisted in pain.

"You are forcing me to do this," said Temple.

48

In the barracks of the compound sat the one hundred operators, intent upon their task: the honor of bringing into the world the one who would save it. The other ninety-nine spirits, each operator was convinced, were of secondary value at best.

The guards, expecting no interference but with weapons at the ready, kept careful watch as the hundred voices kept calling the hundred famous names. This was the final contact session, but it was taking longer than usual. The assumption was that, upon the entry of each spirit into its vessel, there would be a physical transformation into what the personage had looked like during his or her previous time on earth.

The vessels lay on their bunks, eyes closed, semiconscious from the sedative given to them a half hour before. Each one's consciousness would be absorbed and subsumed by the incoming spirit, becoming a mere subconscious appendage. They faced this fate with serenity, convinced of its rightness and necessity. The Administrator, their creator, had assured them of this, and that was enough.

The girl who had served Crowley and Tesla in the saloon in West Orange was there, calling upon Queen Dido of Carthage. She found it ludicrous that the man to her right, a self-described "reactionary monarchist" of late middle age, was trying to contact King Arthur, who was obviously mythological. This man, for his part, thought it strange that the young man on his right considered himself a Marxist yet was trying to summon Jesus Christ, who, he insisted, was the world's first communist.

But none of the operators thought of these things at the moment. The Administrator had announced that everything was ready, the prerequisite number of contact sessions had been reached (how this was determined, they did not know), and it was now time to call forth their designated sage.

A bookish, pensive young man, convinced that Julius Caesar was the personage to lead the world into its new and flawless age, spoke with urgency into his mouthpiece. "Caesar, hello? Are you there? Are you there? Gaius Julius Caesar, I wish to speak with you. Can you hear me?"

"Yes, thank you, Jonathan. I can hear you," came the answer. It was friendly, deep, a voice of fatherly confidence. "The fog is suddenly thicker. It was more difficult than usual to find you."

"Well, this is the last time you'll need to," said Jonathan, smiling.

"Yes, but we must wait for the others to arrive."

"Yes. Caesar, you said that I hear you in English because of…" He searched for the term. "…transference of nonverbal communication to the listener's language, or something like that. Does that mean, once you're physical, you'll only be able to speak Latin?"

"I am confident I will be able to speak your language, Jonathan. The knowledge of the vessel shall provide it for me."

"I see. Oh, wait. I almost forgot." At his feet was a small stand with a banner upon it: their society's emblem, the same as that emblazoned upon the wall. He placed it on the table next to the spirit phone to indicate he had attained contact with his sage, then continued his conversation with Caesar.

Several more banners were placed upon tables, and soon all one hundred were displayed. One of the guards eyed them as he walked a circle around the bunks with military precision. Upon returning to his post, the guard next to him repeated this procedure.

"I count one hundred," said the first guard.

"I count one hundred," said the second guard.

The first guard walked to a button set into the wall behind them and pressed it. A claxon, like a very loud telephone bell, sounded for a few seconds and stopped.

"Caesar, it's time!" said Jonathan. "Please enter your vessel!"

"Yes. Wait, please. It is…somewhat difficult."

"You can do it! The world is depending on you!" Ninety-nine other encouraging voices blended with Jonathan's.

The blue light of the spirit phones began to fade and at the same time appeared around the semiconscious duplicates. They opened their eyes. Their bodies went into convulsions, then vibrated at a speed that seemed impossible. Then came a hundred screams, agony on each face, the blue glow of bodies brighter as that of the spirit phones ceased.

"What's happening? What's gone wrong?" said Jonathan as he stood up and pulled off his headphones. The other operators had done the same.

The glow of bodies became fainter, the vibrations slower, until both stopped. All the vessels lay inert, eyes closed. Operators and guards exchanged anxious glances. No one spoke.

Soon eyes began opening, hands feeling heads, arms, legs, torsos. Slowly, the men in the bunks began to stand up.

A cheer went up among the operators. The guards shook hands with one another.

Jonathan saw standing before him the vessel he was convinced now housed the spirit of Gaius Julius Caesar. "Welcome, Caesar," he said. "Welcome to the nineteenth century."

The presumed Caesar stretched his limbs, then looked at Jonathan sidewise with a grin that made the young man back away. Why, Jonathan wondered, had the vessel not physically transformed into Caesar?

Turning from Jonathan, the man cupped his groin and shouted, "Seems like it works properly!" He raised his arms upward and thrust his pelvis forward, letting out a whoop, which was echoed by the other vessels.

The bedrock of Jonathan's convictions, everything he knew to be true, was under assault by a battering ram of the unexpected: a sense of unknown danger where he had assumed no danger could exist.

"Caesar?" asked Jonathan. No other words would come.

The man walked over to Jonathan, put his hands on his shoulders, and smiled.

"I hate to tell you this, man," he said. "But I ain't Caesar. And I'm tired of hearing the sound of your voice."

Jonathan's eyes bulged as the hands crushed his windpipe in a split instant, the face of his killer contorted in ecstatic rage.

49

Stern and Donnelly lay on the ground, spread-eagled, limbs slowly stretching, faces masks of agony. Temple stood with his arms crossed, facing Crowley and Tesla. "I need your talents, gentlemen," he said to them. "It would be an added benefit to have the skills and experience of Misters Stern and Donnelly. But they are not absolutely essential."

"Stop!" shouted Tesla. "Do you think you can win our loyalty through coercion?"

"No. But once you see there is no option but to join me, you will do so. At first, no doubt, through some notion that you can mitigate the severity of my justice, initiate what you see as reforms to the regime. I doubt you can succeed. But perhaps you can prove me wrong. Agree to join me and I will release them."

"All right!" said Crowley. "We will join you! Release them."

Tesla turned to Crowley. "Crowley—"

"Tesla, trust me. Please." To Temple he said, "I swear loyalty to the regime you are about to inaugurate, in perpetuity." He then turned to Tesla and nodded.

Tesla hesitated, then looked once more at the pain-racked faces of his companions. He looked at Temple. "I, too, swear loyalty and service to the regime."

"Very well," said Temple. He looked down at Stern and Donnelly for a moment, and their limbs went slack, their expressions of agony lessening. Tesla and Crowley went over to check on them.

"You'll find no serious injuries. It was just rather painful for them," said Temple. "You see, I'm not an unreasonable man. Once the Ferox transition is complete, we can discuss your duties in detail. For now, Mr. Tesla, I appoint you my Minister of Science and Technology. Once the new government is officially in place, I'd like you to get to work on the free energy project for which you have been continually denied resources by those shortsighted robber barons. You'll have all the funding you need."

"Thank you," said Tesla with no trace of gratitude. He helped Donnelly to his feet as Stern leaned upon Crowley, grimacing.

"Buck up, my good man. You'll feel better once you get to work with no one impeding you. We'll also need to develop new forms of technology for surveillance, as well as weaponry, public transit, and so on. We'll speak about it later. Mr. Crowley, I appoint you my chief lieutenant, Executive Officer of the New Order. Also, I wish you to learn as much as you can about the technological side of things from Mr. Tesla. Someone will need to take over the helm after I am gone."

"I am honored," said Crowley with a slight bow.

"Misters Stern and Donnelly I place in charge of internal state security, a term which will eventually refer to the entire planet."

At that moment, a faint but shrill scream came from the direction of the compound, followed by the sound of several gunshots.

"They've arrived," said Crowley.

Temple looked momentarily puzzled. "Apparently so. I should have detected their arrival. They are perhaps trying to impede my perception in order to pull some trick on me." Another scream, then another. The gunshots multiplied.

"It sounds like the spirit phone operators are under attack," said Crowley.

"I anticipated this possibility. But assuming the One Hundred have all arrived, the operators are now quite expendable. I have other rank-and-file members waiting in the wings. Come on." He walked toward the compound at a leisurely pace, and the other four men followed.

Temple spoke calmly over the din of screams and gunshots, as if on an afternoon stroll. "By the way, while my unique operation on the yacht required lightning, the ancients could normally contact *ferox phasma* without it, provided they had an Essential Composite vessel. A jar containing vinegar, with an iron rod housed in copper, served as an electrical cell. Their real problem was gathering enough carborundum."

"Interesting," said Crowley. "I suppose we underestimate our forebears."

"Indeed. Anyway, because of the fog, I was racing the clock, as I also needed to do additional tests and analyses on all the duplicates before I could be absolutely sure they were suitable. A poorly functional entry of the One Hundred would likely be worse than none at all."

"I see," said Crowley. "But I have detected no such fog in my own astral travels."

"It is a fog only from the One Hundred's perspective. No other entity perceives it. It is apparently an effect of their devolution, the astral world's equivalent of an immune system response. Moreover, while time is conterminous in the astral realm, the Ferox can't necessarily predict what's going to happen here on earth. Thus, successfully coming here is not a foregone conclusion for them, and they've been pestering me to get on with the process.

"Anyway, besides reconfirming the suitability of the vessels, each of the One Hundred needed repeated contact sessions to become increasingly familiar with a particular operator's personality. That's why I was a little surprised Katie Bender went to you by accident. I suppose she was a bit too enthusiastic."

The compound came into sight, and they stopped about fifty yards from the entrance. The gunshots and screams had stopped. Two guards had driven a four-wheeled gun carriage near the gate. From the barracks, its windows spattered with blood, came the One Hundred, one by one, all in identical guise. Soon all stood outside, some still wiping blood from their hands onto their gray coveralls. They looked cheerful, with the air of revelers on their way to a party.

One stepped forward and turned to face the others. Then, head upturned, arms raised, fists clenched, he released a roar: a sound of fury, of ecstasy, of joyous cruelty. The others joined in, a hundred screams as from the depths of Hell. Silent again, they faced the gate.

"Stay back!" cried the guard at the machine gun. "If you come forward, I'll fire."

The Ferox in front looked at the guard and grinned. "Oh, really? You'll fire?" He looked back at his companions and said, "He'll fire." They laughed.

He turned to the guards again. "All right. Go ahead. Fire." He began to walk toward the gun carriage.

The rapid fire of the machine gun burst rang out, and the Ferox began to jerk violently as he was riddled with bullets. After about ten seconds, the firing ceased. He was still standing, and the blood pouring from his wounds began to staunch. Though clearly in pain, he smiled and said, "That tickles."

The firing recommenced in a wider arc, and dozens of Ferox were hit. From the rear, a blur of gray shot into the air, landed in the gun carriage, and swirled around for a moment, the gray joined by patches of red. The movement stopped, and a Ferox stood in the gun carriage with bloodstained coveralls. He sat down for a moment, catching his breath. The bodies of the two guards sat slumped in the carriage, their heads torn off and lying on the ground. "And that's what happens when you fire," he said.

The Ferox stood up and turned to face the gate. "Mr. Temple!" he shouted. "It's me. Andreas. Formerly known as Julius Caesar by a now dead dipshit. Thank you for freeing us. But I'm afraid there's been a change of plan. We're not staying here, and you're not using us as your tools."

"Welcome back to earth," said Temple. "Though I'm afraid you will find leaving the compound rather difficult."

"Oh, really?" he asked, stepping off the gun carriage, still slightly out of breath. "Just as you thought I would find it difficult to know your true intentions? Or to get my hands on you and rip you apart? Time to feel pain, you arrogant motherfucker." With an expression of unbridled rage, he walked out of the gate and straight toward Temple.

The next moment, the five men were standing by the airship. "What the hell happened?" asked Stern.

"Teleportation," said Crowley. "Of all five of us. I didn't think that was possible. Thank you, Mr. Temple, though I'm afraid you have only bought us a respite."

"Impossible," said Temple. "They cannot be able to do this. It is simply not possible!" Turning to Stern, he asked, "Can you get us out with the airship?"

Stern punched Temple full in the face, and he went down.

"You son of a bitch. Now you want my help? After bringing about the end of the world and putting me and Donnelly on the torture rack to boot?"

"I wanted your help from the beginning," said Temple, wiping blood from his nose with a handkerchief as he got up. "I don't know what's gone wrong, but if we can buy some time, we might be able to fix it. Hurry, we must go! Get us airborne!"

"We can't," said Donnelly. "We needed to get here quickly and had no time to arrange for helium or fuel for the return trip."

"And let me guess," said Crowley to Temple. "You can't teleport us any farther. Not even yourself."

Temple closed his eyes for a moment, then opened them. "No," he said. "They're blocking it somehow. They aren't supposed to be able to do this! Not from within the vessel bodies!"

"Underestimation of one's enemy," said Crowley. "For that is what you have made them. The price of arrogance is steep indeed. By the way, however this turns out, I don't think keeping those things both alive and under your control is an option. Thus Mr. Tesla and I are hereby absolved of our oath to serve in your new order."

"There seem to be limits to their abilities, however small," said Tesla. "Andreas was out of breath after killing those two guards."

"That will be of little consequence," said Crowley. "They are, in their own fashion, limited, but there are a hundred of them and five of us. Still, they will likely come here at their leisure, to toy with us. It's in their nature."

"I have an idea," said Tesla. He ran into the airship, then soon came out with an armful of tools and components. "Donnelly! Give me a hand here!" he shouted, dropping the items on the ground and opening up the starboard engine.

As they worked, Crowley said to Temple, "Tattoos on the arse? Seriously?"

"It appealed to their sense of exclusivity," said Temple.

"So do you have one?" he asked. Temple gave an irritated look but said nothing.

Soon there were two posts inserted into the ground, port forward and port aft of the airship. Each was wrapped tightly with copper wire and topped by a metallic sphere. They were connected by wires to the airship's electrical generator.

"I think I see what you're doing, Tesla," said Temple, "but even if that prevents them from getting through—which I seriously doubt—they can just walk around it, or leap over it like Andreas did when he killed the guards."

"Yes," replied Tesla. "That's why I need the assistance of you and Crowley. I'll need you to remove the inhibition spell you have placed upon him."

Temple pulled out the grid he had folded up in his vest and tore it in half.

Crowley's eyes lit up. "That's much better." He turned to Temple and, in a grudging tone, said, "Thank you." Temple bowed his head slightly.

Quickly, Tesla explained what was required.

"Will you need to call upon familiars?" asked Tesla.

"Any task directly performable by the mage should not be trusted to a familiar," said Crowley.

"Agreed," said Temple.

"Have you sufficient weaponry on board?" Tesla asked Stern.

"Sufficient for a while, but not indefinitely," said Stern. "We will also need a contingency plan."

After a few more minutes of hurried discussion, they were all in position: Tesla in the cockpit, Stern about ten yards from the port side of the airship with a machine gun set on a swivel, Donnelly at the starboard side identically armed, Crowley and Temple by the nose of the fuselage.

"This is only going to work so long as the fuel holds out," said Donnelly. "We're now at about 15 percent full."

"We'll improvise," said Crowley.

Then came a voice from beyond the trees. "Temple! Oh, Temple! We're coming to get you!"

Soon the Ferox were in sight, approaching the airship.

"They've all maintained the same form," said Crowley. "All duplicates."

"Presumably, they're trying to conserve energy for purposes of destroying us," said Temple.

"There's a cheery thought." Crowley couldn't pick out Andreas from among them, then decided it didn't matter.

Tesla turned over the engines, bringing the generator to life. The propellers turned, unable to lift the ship with the balloon's insufficient helium.

From one copper-wrapped pole to the other, a stream of lightning appeared, crackling with energy. Crowley concentrated, hands stretched out toward the lightning. He then moved his arms up, then down at his sides. As he did so, the lightning expanded upward and outward, forming a dome of energy around the airship, the view beyond obscured but still visible.

Temple then held up his hands, chest-high, palms facing each other about a hand's width apart. Soon the shield of lightning increased in intensity, crackling and pulsating with a green aura.

A Ferox stepped to the shield, touched it, and drew his hand back in pain. He and several others walked around it. A rock thrown by one of them was vaporized as it touched the field of energy.

"You can't get in, I'm afraid," said Crowley, raising his voice over the noise of the engines. "I don't suppose you'd be so kind as to go away?"

One put his face as near the shield as he dared and said, "The more you make us wait, the more painful it's going to be for you. But go ahead, little rabbits. You can't do this forever. We can just wait, because we're physically immortal. And guess what? There are more of us than just a hundred. So many more. After we rip you bastards apart, we're going to bring down the fog. Tear down the electrical grid and leave just enough juice to power the spirit phones. Build more bodies like these and bring more of us in. And more, and more. We're the hunters. You're the prey. Do you know how liberating it is to be able to do anything you want? Anything, to anybody, with no punishment? With no consequences?" He looked back at his companions. "You know, maybe we shouldn't kill them. We could keep them alive for a few years and—" He broke into paroxysms of laughter.

One of them shouted, "Fuck waiting! This thing can't hurt us!" He ran into the shield directly opposite Stern.

He was stopped in his tracks, then slowly pushed his way through, the energy stretching over him like gossamer webbing. He pushed through to the other side. His hair was gone, his skin half-charred, half-melted. He staggered, fell, got up, and walked toward Stern, who opened fire.

Stern had loaded the machine guns with special bullets of a new type and of limited quantity. Upon entering the creature's torso, they burst in dozens of small explosions. He inched forward, pushing against the wall of firepower. Stern aimed at the head, blowing off part of the cranium. Brain matter and skull fragments fizzled as they hit the electrical shield behind. Yet somehow he was alive and conscious as he kneeled and, with a dazed, enraged expression, stared at Stern.

"Kill…you…" he said.

Stern pulled a small round object from beneath the machine gun swivel, walked to the Ferox, and shoved it hard into its mouth. "I don't think so," he said.

"Explosion!" Stern shouted. Pulling the pin from the grenade, he dived away from the Ferox, whose head blew apart in a small but powerful incendiary blast. The body slumped forward and lay inert on the ground.

"What was that about no consequences?" shouted Stern as he remanned the machine gun.

242 • Arthur Shattuck O'Keefe

"It seems they can be killed," said Temple.

"Or maybe not," said Crowley. "I'm willing to bet that even with that much damage, it can regenerate, if slowly. To actually kill them, you might have to take them apart at the atomic level."

Donnelly said, "Even if that one's really dead, we don't have enough bullets or grenades to kill the other ninety-nine. We need to conserve ammunition." He and Stern began taking single shots to the head, causing the creatures to stagger. However, they remained standing. All of them stood outside the shield, surrounding it, waiting silently.

"Fuel is at less than 10 percent!" shouted Tesla from the cockpit.

"We need to turn this shield into an offensive weapon," said Crowley. "But even our combined abilities cannot both maintain it and use it as such."

"Yes," said Temple. "We need demonic assistance after all, I'm afraid."

"Agreed," said Crowley.

"Can you take over both aspects of the shield for a few minutes?"

"Yes."

Crowley and Temple faced one another, palms out, fingers pointed upward. The process and concentration of augmenting the intensity of the shield transferred from Temple to Crowley.

Temple immediately pulled out a notepad and pencil from an inside pocket of his jacket. At almost superhuman speed, he sketched a grid.

H	A	M	A	G
A	B	A	L	A
M	A	H	A	M
A	L	A	B	A
G	A	M	A	H

"Elerion, I seek your aid, and command you to come before me now!"

No one appeared.

"Elerion, I seek your aid, and command you to come before me *now*!"

Still nothing.

"I think someone's interfering," said Crowley. The Ferox were grinning behind the shield.

"Apparently so," said Temple. "Mr. Stern! Mr. Donnelly! Please get the undivided attention of our guests for a moment!"

Stern and Donnelly began firing at full automatic. Dozens of Ferox staggered, fell, got up again, then fell again in the hail of bullets.

"Elerion! I—oh, good, you're here."

Elerion stood before him, clad once again in an indigo dress. Upon seeing her, Stern and Donnelly went back to single shots.

"Hey, demon bitch!" called a Ferox, thrusting his pelvis forward and back. "Come on out here and we'll give you some servicing!"

She turned to him and said, "I am not a corporeal being." She then lifted her hand palm-inward and made a fist. With a snap, the Ferox's head twisted to one side and remained so as he staggered and fell, his companions laughing at his plight.

"Hey, that was pretty good," said Donnelly as the Ferox snapped his head back into place and got up. "Could you do more of that, please?"

"It would do you little good," she replied. She turned to Temple. "You called, sir?" Her tone was one of barely constrained anger.

"Yes. The electrical energy shield that is now protecting us. I need you to harness it as an offensive weapon to incinerate the creatures surrounding us. Get to it."

"I will not," she replied. "I must leave you to the fate you have created."

"What?" asked Temple with an expression of incredulity.

"Excuse me," said Crowley. "Elerion, was it? I'm sorry to interrupt, as you are not my demon familiar. However, as I'm sure you're aware, the familiar is supposed to do what the mage commands. And we're in a bit of a pinch here. So if you could please do what Mr. Temple said, I would consider it a great personal favor."

She regarded Crowley as he spoke, but said nothing. She turned again to Temple.

"Fuel is at 5 percent!" shouted Tesla.

"Your actions have fundamentally altered conditions within the astral realm and beyond," she said.

"Beyond? What—"

"It is beyond your comprehension. Yes, even yours. But know this: the creatures you have made physical and set loose upon this earth will not only inflict untold suffering and death, but will cause the destruction of everything here. In the demon realm, we see it as a completed thing. You have changed the rules with your meddling. I am no longer subject to your will."

"Ashtaroth said he didn't care about all this," said Crowley.

"Ashtaroth is a fool," said Elerion. To Temple she said, "Look," and pointed at the Ferox Stern had dispatched. It was still inert, but had slowly begun to heal. "There is a natural order to things. In your desire to control human nature, you have destroyed it."

"Then help me change it back!" said Temple. "Please."

"This way will avail nothing," said Elerion.

She walked to Crowley and looked into his eyes.

"Remember," she said.

Crowley's eyes went wide. Elerion disappeared. Crowley began to shield his consciousness from external detection as strongly as possible. This required removing his concentration from the electrical field.

"Crowley! What the hell are you doing?" shouted Temple, lifting his hands to focus upon taking over the shield.

"Two percent!" shouted Tesla.

"Elerion! Come back!" shouted Temple. "Please! I'm sorry! I was wrong! Damn you, Crowley, help me keep this thing up!"

"Plan Omega!" shouted Crowley.

Temple looked horrified. "What? No! No! Belay that!"

"Plan Omega!"

Stern and Donnelly began firing on full automatic in a wide arc, intermittently throwing grenades. The scores of Ferox fell, got up, fell again.

Crowley entered the airship and climbed into the cockpit.

"Lock all the doors and cut the engines," he said to Tesla.

"Are you sure?"

"Yes."

Tesla reached over, activated the master lock, and turned off the engines. The electrical field outside began to diminish.

"Tesla, no!" shouted Temple. "Turn it back on!"

Donnelly's machine gun stopped firing, Stern's followed a few seconds later with a last click of the now-useless trigger. They were out of bullets and out of grenades.

The field disappeared. Ferox who had been shielded from gunfire by those in front stepped over and around their wounded comrades.

"Well, look what we've got here," said one. "Let's just take our time and decide which one to take apart first." He laughed.

"It has been an honor, Mr. Stern," said Donnelly.

"The honor is mine, Mr. Donnelly," replied Stern.

They had agreed to keep five final bullets in reserve, but for the moment still had pistol shots to spare. Pulling out two revolvers each, they walked toward the Ferox, firing.

In the cockpit, Crowley said, "You have it set on a timer, correct?"

"Yes, ten seconds, as we agreed."

Temple began pounding on the door of the airship. "Let me in!" he screamed over the sound of gunfire. "You dirty cowards!"

"I have an idea," Crowley said to Tesla. "It may not work, but it's all we've got."

Temple's shouting gave way to a scream of agony. "Whatever it is, let's do it," said Tesla.

"As soon as you activate the timer," said Crowley, "I need you to close your eyes and clear your mind of everything except one thing: me. Focus upon staying with me. It's going to be a very bumpy ride. Ready?" Temple's screams continued unabated.

"Yes."

"Do it."

Tesla reached under the cockpit control panel and flipped a switch. He closed his eyes. As the seconds ticked by, he felt Crowley's hands upon his head. *Stay with me,* said Crowley's voice in his mind.

Five seconds later, the airship was consumed in a fiery blast.

50

I t was astral travel. That much Tesla realized. Before closing his eyes, he had guessed as much, for an instant wondering what possible good it could do. Ensure a less unpleasant death, perhaps, and an easier transition to whatever awaited them in the afterlife. In the next instant, he reminded himself that Crowley had said to clear his mind and focus upon staying with him, so he did.

More than lifting out of the physical, as on the day Crowley had astrally escorted him to Tenderloin, the sensation was one of being abruptly torn out. It was, he would later reflect, unavoidable under the circumstances. Two other things were different. It was indeed, as Crowley had said, bumpy. The same grayish blur and sensation of rushing movement were there, but this time it was like running a motorboat in choppy waters against a gale-force wind that was solid rather than gaseous.

Suddenly, in the midst of this, Tesla felt a sensation of intense, burning agony. Every fiber of his being felt on fire. It seemed to go on forever, yet somehow he could not scream, and at the same time he felt himself starting to slow down and drift.

No! came Crowley's presence. *I feel it too. Stay with me! It will pass. Stay with me.* His voice was coaxing, soothing.

After an unknowable interval, the pain slowly faded, and the sense of choppy seas and solid wind was gone. The journey now felt more like the one made to Tenderloin, but not entirely. There was no true sense of a direction followed, yet Tesla felt as if he were somehow traveling in an incorrect manner. No, not quite incorrect. Unnatural. His thoughts were not in terms of human language, but it was the closest approximation.

Then he began to feel anxious, as if he had to be somewhere but the place he had to be was gone. This feeling intensified, as he was headed toward a different place, against his will, than the one he needed to go to. And yet…it was strange: it was the place he needed to go to, and yet it was not. A rising tide of panic threatened to consume him.

Tesla opened his eyes. He was in the physical, in a bed. Moonlight filled the room. *Teleportation? How?* Then he recalled the demon Temple had summoned. Elerion. Perhaps she had assisted Crowley somehow. But Temple's teleportation of them from the compound had seemed instantaneous.

These thoughts were immediately overwhelmed by a surge of emotion: panic, despair, confusion, fear. He had no clear memory of anything. He was Nikola Tesla. He was in a bed. What else did he know? What else did he remember? Nothing and everything, a horrible chaotic jumble of memories he could neither order nor comprehend. He could not understand where he was, why he was there, or anything that had happened before the moment he opened his eyes. He began to cry hysterically. After a moment, the weeping changed to maniacal laughter, then weeping and laughter at the same time. He was vaguely aware of a voice, someone else crying and laughing.

He tried to get out of the bed. His body felt sluggish, painful yet numb, resisting every attempt at movement. He began having convulsions. After a minute, they subsided, and he forced himself to move. Something, some deep part of his mind that was still somehow under control, compelled him to fall onto the floor and crawl to the closet located opposite the foot of the bed. Still laughing, still crying, he got to the door, reached up, and turned the knob. He pulled the door open.

On the floor, in the right back corner beneath the many suits and coats hanging within, lay a large, brown leather suitcase. Crawling into the closet, he dragged it out and opened it. Nearly the entire space within was filled by a box with a switch, two dials, and a headband connected by wires to the box.

With shaking hands, he put the headband on and set the dials: 225 volts, 0.7 amperes. He flipped the switch.

His body began to convulse slightly as the electricity passed through his brain. After a few seconds, he switched it off. He could hear the voice from the other room crying more softly now. He reset the dials: 240 volts, 0.8 amperes. Power on.

Again his body convulsed, more strongly this time. He turned off the switch and held up his hand. The shaking had abated. He looked around and realized he was in his apartment. Crowley...who was Crowley? The name stuck in his mind.

One last shock should do it. He increased the voltage to 250 and flipped the switch. He let the electricity course through himself for ten seconds, then turned it off.

He still felt awful, and disoriented, but now more in control of himself. Slowly, memory returned, still confused and chaotic. He remembered who Crowley was and realized it was he who was crying in the next room. He took off the headband and walked into the parlor carrying the electroshock device.

Crowley lay on the floor next to the sofa. He was crying, laughing, and babbling incoherently.

"Sadie...First Lord of the Admiralty...Thank you, Mr. Cayce...Essential Composite...Ashtaroth, you dirty bugger...Stay with me, Tesla...Tesla! Lager is fine, yes!"

Tesla placed the device on the floor and knelt down to place the band on Crowley's head. It was only then he noticed that in order to attach the band, he would have to pull down the fur-lined hood of his coat. He realized that Crowley was dressed in mountaineering garb and needed a shave, and that he himself was wearing pajamas.

"Oh my God," said Tesla as he began to administer the shock treatment.

51

August 27th, 1899

They sat in the parlor, drinking copious amounts of water. Dehydration was apparently a side effect of the process, as was hunger. They ate sandwiches Crowley had made from the contents of Tesla's kitchen.

"Temporary transfers of consciousness across time are rare but not unknown," said Crowley. "They're considered inadvisable."

"I can't imagine why."

"I've made this a permanent consciousness transfer, which is not supposed to happen. I've never heard of anyone doing it, actually, as even the temporary ones involve a low survival rate. It will eventually have disturbing effects upon our personalities, and will cause largely negative outcomes in our lives, but there was no choice. It will have a much stronger effect on me than you, as I was the one implementing it."

"But now what? Attempt to stop them again from this point in time?"

"No. Not from this point. Even with what we now know, Temple knows we're aware of the situation and will adapt his tactics to whatever we do. The only way to be sure is to stop it earlier in time and conceal our actions from him as effectively as possible."

"Then why didn't you bring us back earlier?"

"To make the jump together, we could only go back as far as the moment we first met. Here."

"Then what do we do?"

"There needs to be one more temporal transfer. Temporary. By you, solo. With my assistance, here. We have to make it as brief as possible. My abilities are fading again, but not as badly. The interference Temple placed on my powers is in effect, but not on the future aspect of my consciousness that has come back here."

"Then why not just break Temple's spell?"

"Even Temple's perception ability has its limits, but he would immediately detect any attempt at breaking his inhibition spell, and attack us soon thereafter. He needs to believe we don't presently know about him. Besides, it would take time, and the farther we get temporally from where I need to send you, the less chance of success. We have to do it under present conditions."

"Couldn't we just seek him out and explain what's going to happen?"

"No, Tesla. You remember the way he talked. Even if he believed us, he'd just keep to his world state plan and make adjustments to prevent the physical Ferox from getting loose. Which of course will fail, and we're back where we started."

"Yes. And he seems to have enough influence in high places to prevent any intervention by official authorities. Or at least to slow it down." He sighed. "This is beyond belief. I have memories from today until two weeks from now all mixed together with my memories from before this."

"It will get worse before it gets better, I'm afraid. We've altered things in quite a fundamental way."

"What gave you this idea?"

"Elerion, the demon Temple summoned. Or rather she reminded me that I had thought of it. It was a part of the eternal train station scene the Ferox had trapped me in. The one part I couldn't remember, even while doing the Akashic Records check."

◆ ◆ ◆

"Chocolate?"

"Yes. Eat chocolate. And some dried fruit."

Suddenly the taste of chocolate is on his tongue. He starts in surprise.

"Oh! Right. I see. Fine. Chocolate."

"There is one element of the rote you still will not remember until you actually need it. This is necessary."

"Who decided that?"

"You did."

For a moment, or so it seems, his surroundings fade into nothingness.

◆ ◆ ◆

But not quite. He and the slightly overweight woman are still there.

"I'm the best element of your astral consciousness for this task," she says. "Just follow my lead. Lirion, I seek your aid, and command you to appear before me now!"

"You can't do that without a—" Crowley stops speaking as Lirion appears.

"I come as summoned," says Lirion. She gives the impression of being confused yet trying not to show it. "What is this place?"

"How did you do that without a grid?" Crowley asks the woman.

"Those rules don't apply here," she says to Crowley. Turning to Lirion, she says, "At some point, it will prove necessary to perform a permanent temporal transfer of consciousness into the past. We must not remember this necessity consciously, even at the astral level. I will see to that. We need to be reminded at the moment it is required. To minimize the chances of detection or interference, this must be done by a demon who is not our familiar. Task another demon with this. Do not tell us who."

"It is not within my power to command another demon on behalf of a mage to whom it is not bound."

"Then can you request it? You know what is at stake here."

"I will do what I can," says Lirion, and disappears.

"We'll have to settle for that," the woman says.

◆ ◆ ◆

Then everything returns into sharp focus.

"I did? Never mind. I'll take your word for it. Now let's finish teleporting to the base camp."

"Forget the base camp," she says. "You need to go to Nikola Tesla."

◆ ◆ ◆

"We have one chance at this. If it doesn't work, then what we saw in Colorado will surely happen, and the game is up. You'll need to go back alone, with my help here. It can only be a temporary jump. Temple's desire to make us his lieutenants should allow us to proceed unmolested as long as he doesn't detect what we're doing. You need to destroy the prototype, and the plans and notes."

"I'll need to confirm whether there are others in existence. It might take a few days."

"All right. As I said, the farther away in space-time we get from when the prototype was made, the harder it's going to be until it proves impossible. But we also need to rest. Twenty-four hours. Let's get some sleep. After we wake up, I'll need to give you a bit of training." With that, he lay on the sofa and almost immediately began snoring.

52

As Crowley sleeps, his mind awakens in a way not unlike a lucid dream. He feels the familiar sensation of separation from the physical. It is not a rare thing for him during sleep, yet this time it feels different. He realizes that someone, or something, is causing him to astrally project and to travel in a direction—if that is the word—he is completely unfamiliar with. Temple? The Ferox? Alarmed, he tries to arrest his progress and to perceive who or what is causing this. It has no effect. The usual rushing grayness becomes a kaleidoscopic chaos of countless colors and shapes, spinning around him as he accelerates with ever-increasing, ever-impossible speed, his astral form tumbling end over end. He considers separating his second astral body from his first, as Cayce taught him, but decides it would be too dangerous a risk. He surrenders himself to this state and waits to see what happens.

He now stands in a room. It is a large and dark space, filled with oak: desks, chairs, tables, wainscoted walls, cases filled with hundreds of books. On one small table sit seven red candles, the room's only source of light. On another sits a large ball of crystal, next to which is a black cloth. Behind the table is a window. It is pitch-black outside.

"You have come," says a voice behind him. He turns around.

There stands a tall, thin, elderly man with a long gray beard and a prominent nose. He is dressed in a skullcap and robe, both black, with a white ruffled collar. His dark-brown, piercing eyes regard Crowley.

"John Dee," says Crowley.

"Yes."

"You are in your physical body."

"Yes."

"And you can see me."

"Yes. I have called you."

"What year is it?"

"Sixteen hundred and eight. And in case you might be interested, it is All Hallows' Eve, and we are in my home in Mortlake, Surrey. In England."

"Why have you called me?"

"I am burdened with a laborious decision. I am now in my eightieth year and have not long to live. You see before you the last living soul with the knowledge to summon the ferox phasma. *I wish it to die with me, so that none may again bring them to earth. Yet as of late, I have intimations that I should write and leave a record of the summoning process. How could such a thing be possible, I wondered. My meditations have led me to you."*

"I am—"

"No," says Dee. *"We have little time, and there is a better way. It is by you called..."* He pauses to find the word. *"...the rote. Make me one."*

"I can't..."

"You can. Trust your will." Dee puts his right hand, palm downward, over Crowley's head.

"Ah!" says Crowley. *"That's it!"*

"Yes," says Dee. *"That is it. If you please, good sir."*

Crowley holds his hands cupped before him. Soon, a small ball of white light appears between them.

Dee places his hand over the rote, which is absorbed into his palm. His eyes widen slightly. *"I see,"* he says. *"I do not envy you. Very well. I will write it and make the needed arrangements. It will pass through many hands through many years until it arrives at the place where your friend may find it."*

"Why not just not write it? Then nobody will know how to call them."

"No. I see now that if I do not write it, someone will know how to call them. You. If I leave no instructions, you will learn to summon them regardless, for you are clever to a fault. And you will be the one who brings them to earth, with none to stop you. So I will write it. You must also forgo aid from the state, as such would bring naught but disaster. It is the only way. I am sorry." Dee walks to the table upon which sits the crystal ball.

"A word of counsel, young sir. As the power weakens, by whatever cause, this"—he places his hand upon the crystal ball—*"may in small degree augment it."* Remov-

ing his hand, he says, "You may go." He picks up the black cloth and drapes it over the ball.

Instantly, Crowley is back within the chaos of colors and impossible speed, spinning end over end. He focuses upon reengaging with his physical body. The colors become duller, his movement feels slower, and the spinning of his astral form gradually slows and then stops. The familiar gray blur returns. He once more enters the physical.

◆ ◆ ◆

Crowley awoke and sat up on the sofa.

The realization struck him. *Dee. It was he who wrote the memorandum ordering that I get no help.*

He lay down again. *Oh, well. What the hell,* he thought as sleep once again overcame him.

53

August 28th, 1899

It was just after six o'clock in the evening, and outside the window, the red brick skyline of Manhattan was bathed in the copper glow of dusk. Crowley had managed that morning to drag himself out of bed long enough to go to a nearby curio shop and purchase a small crystal ball. When Tesla asked what it was for, Crowley replied that he was acting on the advice of a fellow mage and would explain later.

Tesla now lay on his bed. Crowley sat in an armchair next to him, the crystal ball on the bedside stand.

"Good," said Crowley. "I'm satisfied you can initiate and maintain the hermetic element of self at will. You're a quick study. Perhaps we can make a mage of you."

"I'll keep my psychic training within the bounds of this mission, I think."

Crowley smiled. "Fine," he said. "I won't lie to you, Tesla. Even under the best of conditions, this kind of trip frazzles the nerves and disorients the psyche, as we've both seen first-hand. To do another one in quick succession will considerably compound the effects. Are you sure you had the electric shock device in your closet in February?"

"Positive," replied Tesla. "I've kept it here, in the closet, since the fire that destroyed my previous laboratory in 1895. It helped me get over the depression, which was considerable. Though there are doctors who consider it dangerous."

"And you're sure you were at home alone during our target day and time? That reduces the chances of complications upon entry."

"Yes. I tend to remember things well. And I wrote it down in my journal."

"Good. Now let's review places and tasks."

"Here, the college library, my laboratory, Edison's laboratory. Find and destroy all information on the spirit phone's metallurgy, along with the plans and notes. Complete the prototype, confirm no other spirit phones exist, then destroy the prototype."

"Yes. And keep to those locations only. Your movements must be as geographically narrow as possible or I might lose track of you."

"You've mentioned that five times already. I promise, no trips to the Riviera."

They could not go back together. Tesla did not have anywhere near the psychic training required for an independent transfer, and joint assisted transfers could go no farther back in time than when the two individuals first met. Crowley could go back alone, but he would not be able to perform the technical tasks Tesla was going to undertake. In any case, at the time Tesla was going back to, Crowley was in England.

"This is going to take at least three days," said Tesla. "You said earlier that the passage of time here and in the past will be synchronized, and that your constant presence is needed here. How are you going to eat or sleep or use the toilet?"

"I'm not. I'll be fine. I've set up sufficient barriers to prevent Temple from perceiving our activities. They should hold long enough for us to proceed unmolested, but the risk of detection increases as time passes. Just make sure you get into the library before he does. I can just about get you back to the night before. We'll have to hope he wasn't lying about the date or time."

"All right. I'm ready if you are."

"Let's do it, then. Close your eyes and relax."

Tesla closed his eyes. The next moment, he felt Crowley's hand upon his head, and at once came the relaxed, pleasantly heavy state: body asleep, mind awake. He was then vaguely aware that the hand had been removed.

He heard Crowley in his mind. *I have induced the astral state, and soon you will begin the trip back. I will guide you from here. Once you are in-physical there, my ability to contact you may be sporadic, but I can maintain a more or less constant awareness of your whereabouts. I'll stay with you here physically for the entire time until you return. Any questions?*

No. I'm ready.

Right, then. Off you go.

It was far more difficult than the astral travel to Tenderloin had been, but easier than the trip back from Colorado in September. The perception of an unnatural direction, or orientation, was there, but less so. The feeling of going against the force of a solid rather than gaseous wind was also less intense. There was no perception of time in the usual sense, but somehow everything felt slower, more methodical and precise.

There was also no sensation of burning pain as there had been in the other time-jump. Somehow, he and Crowley hadn't spoken of it, and it occurred to Tesla only then that it must have been the result of their physical bodies being in the explosion. But the explosion would presumably have killed them instantly, and he wondered why the feeling had seemed to last so long.

Best not to think about it, came Crowley's voice, so he didn't. He perceived the grayish haze rushing by, and waited. Then suddenly, everything came to a halt.

The Administration Determined to Crush Aguinaldo's Forces With All Possible Speed

Washington, Feb. 7—The Journal's forecast of the administration's pro-gramme in the Philippines was verified to-day at the Cabinet meeting, where it was decided that the war should be pushed, even if Aguinaldo were driven into the sea.

Tesla sat in the easy chair in his parlor, holding the February 8th, 1899 edition of the *New York Journal and Advertiser.*

He dropped the paper onto the floor and began to shake, his mind a chaotic jumble of mixed and contradictory memories vying for space, for validation as reality. He began to breathe rapidly, panic threatening to overwhelm him as tears streamed down his face.

Steady, Tesla. I'm with you. Crowley's voice came clearly into his mind. *I can't perceive your situation precisely. Have you arrived?*

Tesla stared at the grandfather clock. 6:20. It was dark outside.

Tesla! Are you at home?

Yes, answered Tesla in his mind. "Yes," he said aloud.

All right. Pick up the paper and read the date aloud. We have to be sure.

With trembling hands, he reached down, picked up the newspaper, and looked at the date on the front page.

"February 8th, 1899."

Good. Now check the calendar.

He looked at the calendar on the wall. "February 1899," he said, and began to giggle.

Tesla! I need you to hang on a little longer. If somehow we've been misdirected, it could be disastrous. Make the call. Last thing. Please.

He reached over, picked up the phone on the side table, and contacted the front desk.

"Front desk. How may I help you?"

"This is Mr. Tesla, in room 1333," he said, managing to keep his voice under control. "Please tell me today's date."

"The date, sir?"

"Yes, the date. What is today's date?"

"It's the 8th of February, sir."

"The year?"

"Sir?"

"What year is it?!"

"It's…1899, Mr. Tesla."

"Thank you." He hung up and began to laugh and cry at the same time, shaking uncontrollably.

"It's February 8th, 1899! I'm here, yet I'm not. I remember today, yet I don't. I have a young Englishman talking in my head." He began to laugh in a high-pitched voice.

Tesla! Go to the closet!

"Go to the closet!" he shrieked in imitation of Crowley's accent, then laughed, then began to cry in great, heaving sobs. After a minute, he stopped crying and sat down on the floor.

"What good is anything, really?" he said. "Why are we doing this? Maybe we all deserve what the monsters want to do to us."

Go to the closet. Now.

"Perhaps the window would be better."

Damn it, Tesla. Go to the bloody closet!

Tesla sighed. "Damn, you're annoying." He pulled himself up and shuffled to the closet in his bedroom. He opened the door, pulled out the suitcase, and proceeded to self-administer the shock therapy.

About half an hour later, after having consumed a considerable amount of food and water, Tesla sat in his kitchen. A bottle of bourbon and a shot glass sat on the table. He poured himself a shot and drank it down.

I have the vague perception you're drinking. Please do so in moderation.

"I am," he replied. He could answer in his mind, but decided to vocalize instead, at least in private. "Second and last shot." He poured and drank it, then replaced the cap on the bottle and looked at the clock on the wall. It was only a little after 7:00 p.m., but Tesla was exhausted. "I'm going to bed," he said.

That's probably best. You have an early day tomorrow. Get into the library as soon as it opens.

"I will."

And set your alarm clock, just in case.

"I will."

I'll break off communication for now, but I should be able to keep general track of you most of the time. If you need anything, shout.

"I will." He walked into his bedroom and set his alarm clock for 5:00 a.m.

Good night. Sleep tight.

"Good night," he said. Getting into bed still fully clothed, he was soon asleep.

54

T esla was in the Columbia College Library as soon as it opened at 9:00 a.m., having waited outside for a short while with a small number of other early patrons. Some were students of the college, though as the library was open to the public, there were a few middle-aged and elderly persons as well. It was a cold morning with an increasingly heavy snowfall, and everyone was grateful for the limited shelter from the elements offered by the portico of the neoclassical structure.

He immediately walked to the circulation desk, identified himself, and requested permission to access the Rare Book and Manuscript Collection. About five minutes later, he was in the collection room. There were few other patrons at this hour, and he had the room almost to himself.

You're there, I perceive. Crowley's voice again.

I am, answered Tesla in his mind.

All right. She should arrive fairly soon. Browse the books and try not to look conspicuous.

Tesla sat at a table and began perusing an eighteenth-century French translation of Caesar's account of the Roman Civil War. A few minutes later, a female voice whispered, "Mr. Tesla."

He turned around and there was Lirion, dressed for the winter in a dark-green full-skirted dress with matching hat and cape.

"Lirion," whispered Tesla. "You came."

"Yes," she answered. "It was wise of Mr. Crowley to summon and instruct me prior to initiating your journey. But I must say, it was difficult to get here."

"Thank you for taking the trouble."

"Please follow me," she said.

They walked along the shelves, straight into the recesses of the collection. Crowley had explained that since Temple was not at this point aware of any specific text containing the needed information on the Essential Composite—the author, for example, or a title—he was unable to command any demon, however powerful, to seek it out. What Lirion now sought was only a fragment, with no known title. Temple had said nothing about the volume in which he had found the fragment, so physically searching for it might take weeks, which they didn't have. But with knowledge of its general location—the Columbia College Library—and its authorship by the Elizabethan court astrologer John Dee, Lirion had enough information to locate it, assuming it was here.

Lirion stopped. They were in a section devoted to original editions of seventeenth-century English literature. "It is here," said Lirion, indicating a dark-brown volume which Tesla then took from the shelf. No title was visible on its spine, but upon opening it, he saw that the title page, yellow-brown with age, was still intact. It read:

THE
WORKES
OF
Beniamin Ionson

Imprinted at London by
Wm. Stansby
An. D. 1616

"Ben Jonson," said Tesla. "The first folio from 1616."

"The name seems familiar," said Lirion.

"He was an English playwright. A friend of Shakespeare's. I think I know where in this book the fragment is."

Tesla opened to the table of contents, then after a moment, turned to a place near the end of the book. Within lay a fragment of yellowed paper, torn at the edges, which had been placed between the pages. The title page of the play read:

THE
ALCHEMIST.
A COMEDY,

First Acted in the Year 1610,
By the King's Majesty's Servants,
With The Allowance of
the Master of Revels,
The Author Ben. Jonson

"It seems appropriate somehow," said Tesla. Returning the book to its place, he unfolded the fragment and read. Parts were missing or completely illegible.

-- of the Essentiall Composite, the proportions of which are of utmoste concern to he who would summon one of the Ferox Phasma, or ------ being in ------ One Hundred. Regarding the size of the vessel by which ---------- must be no lesse than seven inches, & its Depth no lesse than three inches, and thus the amount of the Metalls must be such that a vessel of no less than this size --------- Other than these requirements, the size & ------ at the will of the Operator. Included within its composition are the Seven Planetary Metalls, all to be combined in equall proportions. In addition, in an amounte equall to the Seven Planetary Metalls in total, shall be combined the Essentiall Element. Should the proportions be otherwise, the spirites summoned will be not -------- but those of low knowledge and no wisdom, taken to the pretence of -------- As to the Essentiall Element, it is not a metall but a substance exceedingly rare ------ like diamonde, though most usually of grain or dust which may be combined in the casting ------, and may best ------ within and among stones which, in rare cases, fall from the skye, or in the depressions, in divers parts of the worlde, left by such stones. Yet even in the case one may obtain it, the ------ exceedingly small, most usually of the consistency of dust ------ sufficient quantities ------ exceedingly difficulte ------ As to ------ the Secret Element, it is simply sulfur, to be consumed by the Operator just before the Summoning of ------ amount needed is small, and ---- by drinking wine which has been preserved using sulfur --

"Can you confirm its authenticity?" asked Tesla.

"Yes," said Lirion. "It is Dee's writing. Almost any demon would recognize it."

"This basically conforms to what we already know," said Tesla. "And to what, at this point in time, Temple doesn't know."

"And you have memorized it?" asked Lirion.

"Of course," said Tesla.

The fragment began to burn in Tesla's hand. There was no sensation of heat, and the fire produced neither smoke nor ash. In a moment, it was gone, leaving no trace. *Happy Birthday, Temple,* he thought as the last of the flame vanished.

"Locating the fragment, authenticating it, and destroying it," said Tesla. "You have performed three tasks for Mr. Crowley on the basis of a single summoning."

"I agreed to stretch the rules somewhat. These are special circumstances."

"Thank you."

"You're welcome." And with that, she vanished.

55

Tesla walked into his laboratory and locked the door. He had given his assistants the rest of the week off, telling them he was going to perform some delicate experiments and leaving strict instructions not to be disturbed. He took off his coat and jacket, removed his collar and tie, and rolled up his shirtsleeves.

He was walking toward the lab's deep sink when he was gripped by a sudden wave of fear and displacement. He froze as the memory came unbidden, both real and nonexistent. He was sitting at home, in the easy chair of his parlor, reading the January 14th issue of *Electrical World*. It was an article about wireless telegraphy.

Helplessness and confusion consumed him, fueled by a paradox he understood yet in the depths of his psyche could not accept. *I remember. It was February 9th. But today is February 9th. I was at home, at the Waldorf-Astoria. I am at home, at the Waldorf-Astoria. I am in my laboratory on East Houston Street. I am at home, at the Waldorf-Astoria. Reading. Wireless telegraphy.*

◆ ◆ ◆

It will be seen from the patents hereinafter cited that the present subject is not new. It has occupied the attention of inventors for at least fifty years; and, indeed, if we include signaling by flashlight or by sound, it will be found that for thousands of years man has been endeavoring to communicate to distant points without the intervention of artificial connecting media. It would, however, go beyond the limits of this article to mention—

Tesla!

◆ ◆ ◆

At Crowley's shout, Tesla snapped back into the present reality. In front of him was the far wall of the laboratory.

Are you all right?

"Yes. Thank you."

Please do your best to keep yourself together. If I detect another lapse, I'll give you a shout if I can. As we have discussed, the enemy's perception is somewhat disabled by the "fog," but they still might be able to detect us and alert Temple. The danger increases the closer we get to our goal. We need to start keeping contact to a minimum. I'll bring you back once I get the word from you, or when at most ninety-six hours have elapsed.

"All right. Thank you, Crowley."

Tesla, there's one other thing.

"Yes?"

I think I can manage things all right, but if by any chance I'm unable to recall you, you'll return here spontaneously.

"When?"

Hard to say for sure. In a week, perhaps. Without my guidance, it's possible you'll overshoot the date and bounce forward and back a bit before settling into your proper space-time.

"You didn't mention this before. It sounds unpleasant."

It just occurred to me. Sorry.

"Please try to make sure it doesn't happen."

It probably won't. But I wanted to let you know, just in case. Good luck.

He went to the deep sink, drew a bucket of water, and walked to the far end of the laboratory, coming to a corner in which sat a small forge. He set the bucket down.

From its inception, the idea of having a forge had been more for a hobby than a major element of research. As a specialist in electricity and electrical phenomena, Tesla had mostly been content to leave metallurgy and the construction of metal components to others. Yet he had long had a personal interest in metals and their chemical properties, so he had constructed the forge. But due to the press of other business, it had lain virtually unused. Until now.

It was made of brick, its cylindrical crucible sitting on a grate within a recess built into the middle. An overhead vent with an electric fan was installed to funnel smoke into the building's ventilation system. A large pair of tongs hung from a hook on its left side. On the right was a hose leading to a pressurized tank of propane gas. This was the feature of the forge which made Tesla's assistants nervous. He remembered how they had gently reminded him of the 1895 lab fire and urged extreme caution.

"Let's be careful, then," he said, looking at the fire extinguishers installed nearby.

Tesla had always been able to commit to perfect memory, if he so chose, the geometry of any object he encountered. With flawless clarity, he saw in his mind the dimensions of the spirit phone cone, and got to work.

Opposite the forge, behind Tesla, was a tall cabinet and a table upon which sat yesterday's *New York World*. He opened the newspaper and laid it on the floor. From beneath the table, he dragged out a wooden box, knelt down, and removed its top. Within lay two bags, one containing fine sand, the other pulverized clay. The box was lined with black rubber. He opened each bag and emptied it into the box. He then poured in about half the water from the bucket and stirred the contents of the box with his hand until it was of a uniformly moist but stiff consistency, then repeated the process with a little more water.

He began scooping out part of the sand mixture from the box, depositing it on the newspaper. After a minute, he began carefully shaping within the box a depression, a hole about twelve inches wide but tapered the deeper it went: a cone-shaped hollow. He had memorized the needed dimensions perfectly, and while he was sure of his precision, he wanted to leave nothing to chance. He got up and went to the tool cabinet, returning with a ruler, a pair of scissors, a pencil, and a sheet of paper.

Measuring and marking on the sheet, he cut off a three-inch-square piece, then placed it at the bottom of the cone-shaped hollow in the mixture. It fit perfectly any way he turned it. The bottom was precisely three inches in diameter. He removed the paper, placed it on the table, and knelt before the sand mixture on the newspaper.

Within a few minutes, he had carefully shaped a solid cone from the mixture. Though convinced it was unnecessary, he confirmed its dimensions with the ruler and found them to be exact.

He needed to let the molds dry and bond, and was beginning to feel out of sorts again, so he went to the cot and lay down. It was ten minutes before eleven. He set his alarm clock for noon and closed his eyes.

The noon alarm woke him with a start. He got up and checked on the molds. They looked good. He pulled a key from his pocket, went to the cabinet, and unlocked it. Within were shelves occupied by dozens of sealed jars. He removed eight jars and placed them on the table. Each one was labeled:

Gold - Au
Silver - Ag
Iron - Fe
Mercury - Hg
Tin - Sn
Copper - Cu
Lead - Pb
Silicon Carbide - SiC

Tesla regarded the jars, arms crossed. "Time to play alchemist," he said.

Using a beaker and scale, he measured out equal proportions of the metals into a single jar. First the gold, silver, and iron filings. Then the mercury, quivering in its liquid consistency. The tin, copper, and lead. Then finally the black grains of carborundum, or silicon carbide, equal in proportion to all the metallic elements combined. Tesla then poured the jar's contents into the forge's crucible.

He pulled on a pair of long asbestos gloves and switched on the overhead fan. He opened the valve of the propane tank and flipped a switch at the side of the forge. There was a blast of heat as fire filled the space beneath the crucible. He stepped back, waited, and soon began to sweat. Within half an hour, the contents of the crucible were a white-hot molten mass.

He slid the box containing the hollowed-out sand mixture across the floor, placing it next to the forge. Removing the tongs from their hook, he used them to grasp the crucible and tip it over, emptying its molten contents into the sand mold. Its cone-shaped hollow was now about half-full of the liquid metal.

Replacing the crucible and the tongs, he turned off the propane but left the fan running, and took off the gloves. He went to the cabinet and removed four large nails from a drawer. Then, kneeling at the solid cone mold lying on the newspaper, he firmly inserted all four nails at the wide end of the mold, halfway in, equidistant from one another.

Picking up the cone mold, he placed it narrow end first into the cone-shaped hollow. The last few inches of the mold protruded, propped up by the nails. The liquid metal came up almost to the edge of the hollow.

He went to get a glass of water. Staying on fire watch would be necessary while the metal cooled and hardened.

He didn't dare leave the laboratory. That evening, he dragged the cot to the forge area. Making extra sure all the windows and doors were locked, he fell into a heavy sleep at 7:00 p.m. He awoke at about 5:00 the next morning and wanted breakfast.

Later that day, he broke the sand mold and removed from its remnants the only usable spirit phone horn in the world. He put it in a suitcase and carried it home.

56

February 11th, 1899

It was cold. The sky was clear, with countless stars and the faintest sliver of a crescent moon. Nikola Tesla strode with purpose through West Orange, carrying his black suitcase, his boots crunching upon the previous day's snowfall.

He was immaculately dressed and groomed: greatcoat and homburg, black hair perfectly coiffed, mustache neatly trimmed. Strange, perhaps, that in such a crisis he should be so concerned with his appearance. But if worse came to worst and all was lost, he thought, why not go down looking his best?

As he walked, the saloon he and Crowley had visited—or would visit—appeared across the street on his right. He stopped and turned to face it. Two stories, brightly lit within, warm and inviting in the glow of the streetlamps. Music from the saloon's piano drifted through the closed windows, and he began trying to identify its title to distract himself from the slight urge he felt, even now, to go inside and lay his money on the betting table.

He remembered the name of the piano piece: "Mississippi Rag" by William Krell. There was a surge of men's laughter, spontaneous and uninhibited in the way only liquor can induce. He thought of his father, and guilt more than any sense of urgency prompted him to continue on his journey.

"Sir," came a voice from behind Tesla. He stopped and turned around.

Before him was Ashtaroth, his attire again a symphony in black, this time a long fur coat and a Russian *ushanka* upon his head instead of a bowler. In a manner both servile and irritated, he said, "I have been instructed to inform you that you may now proceed unhindered to your intended destination."

Before Tesla could reply, the demon bowed stiffly and vanished. At that moment, the streetlights went dark. He produced a flashlight from his coat and continued walking.

Ashtaroth's involvement was needed. Whereas Lirion's specialty was information, his was effects upon matter and, to a lesser extent, people. To disable anything electrical that might impede him, Tesla could have proceeded identically as in the August break-in. But these circumstances demanded speed, with minimal time spent using equipment. There were also locks that required opening. As Crowley could do little to affect matter from across time, he had cajoled Ashtaroth into aiding them. Tesla knew this multiform task was, like Lirion's action at the library, against the rules of mage-demon relations. Ashtaroth had been persuaded through an unspecified but clear threat from Crowley.

He remembered the summoning in his apartment, and Crowley's stated determination to deliver Ashtaroth—if he refused—to some kind of terrifying fate which both of them precisely understood but did not describe in Tesla's presence. When Ashtaroth said that Crowley would be obliged to share this horrible but undefined circumstance, and that it would be unending, Crowley replied, "Then I shall. Either do exactly as I command or I *will* carry it out." Tesla could tell it was no bluff, and saw in Crowley a quiet ferocity—a cruelty even—which frightened him. He didn't want to know what Crowley would have done, and never asked.

As Tesla walked, a wind appeared, bitter and icy, and the night turned darker. He looked up to see rapidly growing cloud cover, and within a minute was walking against an Arctic-level blizzard which bit into him with razor sharpness. He was sure there had been no snow on this night but was soon enveloped in the storm, all sense of location lost. He pocketed the now useless flashlight.

Tesla! Crowley's voice spoke again in his mind.

I thought it was dangerous for us to talk.

We have to risk it. I assume you can't see much of anything at the moment. You know the way to Edison's lab, but you can't psychically navigate a blinding snowstorm by yourself. Let me do the driving while I give you the latest news.

Tesla felt his motion prompted as if by a beacon magnetically pulling him in the proper directions. He was barely conscious of the occasional pauses and turns.

I'll be brief. They've found an opening in the fog and are altering the weather patterns.

They can do that?

Apparently. But only for a limited time. From what I can gather, it's a tremendous strain on them, requiring a more or less collective effort. With nothing but the prototype in existence and no one presently using it, it seems this is all they can do, other than try to dissuade you. Which they will.

What about Temple?

They either can't contact him or for some reason have decided not to. All right, we've arrived.

Crowley guided him to the front gate. It was unlocked. The guardhouse was invisible in the blizzard, though Ashtaroth had promised both guards would be asleep.

How are you holding up? asked Tesla.

There was a pause. *I'm holding up. I think you can manage the rest of the way. Good luck.* With that, Crowley's psychic presence vanished.

Even if this is all they can do, it's bad enough, thought Tesla. Still blinded by the wind and snow, he walked until his hand came upon the door, which to his relief was also unlocked. He entered and closed it behind him.

Tesla stood inside the laboratory complex of Thomas Edison, brushing snow from his clothes, grateful for the surge of relative warmth within. Removing a small metal case from his coat pocket, he took out two sulfur pills and let them dissolve on his tongue.

He pulled out the flashlight and swept the beam around the room, illuminating the large, high-ceilinged space filled with technology.

Tesla couldn't avoid a sense of nostalgia, recalling again the time Edison had let him use this place to conduct experiments after the destruction of his laboratory. Though they were rivals, Edison of all people could understand his ordeal.

He walked upstairs, to the second floor, and came to the door of Edison's private office. The door was ajar. He opened it and entered.

He walked to Edison's desk and stepped behind it. Reaching down to open the bottom left drawer, he found it unlocked.

And there it was once again. The prototype in its pinewood box. At this point in time, Tesla was the only person to have seen it except for Edison. With it were the plans, at this point incomplete, and the notebook labeled *Spirit Phone Model SP-1*.

He took the box out of the drawer, placed it on the desk, and opened its top. It was the same as before except for one missing item.

Tesla placed the suitcase on the floor, opened it, and removed the horn. He placed it into the box, narrow end down, securing it into the opening in the base. He switched on the spirit phone's electromagnet. From the box came the low-pitched metallic hum. The blue aura began to surround it.

Tesla now had at his disposal the world's only functioning spirit phone—as far as he knew. This was the point he needed to confirm. He recalled his question to Crowley, asked before departing. "I thought this was supposed to be impossible. Are you certain I can contact *him* and not a Ferox? The spirit of a person who is also physically living at the time I make contact? Existing on the spiritual plane, yet in the future?"

"Yes," Crowley had answered. "I said it was *almost* impossible, but it can be done, as I have established a psychic link with him. I can arrange for him to access the phone. It will be similar to what I did at Columbia. As you've seen, past, present, and future are all conterminous on the astral plane. He's there. Ask only what is necessary, and be as brief as possible. Maintain the hermetic element of self. You will almost certainly need it."

Tesla stared at the box with its faint blue aura. Then he closed his eyes, mentally focusing on the personality of his desired contact, and vocalized his intent.

"Thomas Alva Edison, I wish to speak with you."

The low hum continued. There was no response.

"Thomas Alva Edison, I wish to speak with you," he repeated. Minutes passed in small eternities.

"Tesla." The voice from the horn was faint and tinny, but unmistakably Edison's.

Tesla's eyes snapped open. "Answer quickly," he said. "What did I say when you denied me the bonus you had promised? Quote me!"

"I never actually promised it."

"There's no time for debate. Quote me!"

"'You low-down cheating blackguard. After all I have done for you, you deny me what you yourself promised, and what I have undeniably earned by my efforts.'" Crowley had insisted that it was highly unlikely anyone but Edison himself would be able to produce the quote on the spur of the moment. And as things stood, highly unlikely was the best they could hope for. This was as close to confirmation of Edison's identity as Tesla could get.

"All right," Tesla said. He had to take a calculated risk and assume this was not one of the Ferox in disguise.

"Tesla. I'm sorry. I'm so sorry."

"Forget that. You had no way of knowing. No one did."

"You did."

"I got lucky. Never mind. I need to ask you several important questions. In my current location, it is now February 11th, 1899." He pulled out his watch and shined the light on it. "11:52 p.m. I am in your laboratory, in your office. But my questions shall refer to the period of your entire physical life span. Answer concisely, and to the best of your knowledge. Are there any other spirit phones in existence besides this one, anywhere on earth?"

"No."

"Your plans and notes were in the drawer. Are there any others, in any form, anywhere?"

"No."

"At present, besides yourself and Ambrose Temple, I and Crowley know about the spirit phone. Does anyone else, anywhere?"

"No."

"Are you sure?"

"Yes."

"Does anyone besides me know about the correct horn composition? How to make it work?"

"No. As far as I know."

"Niko." It was a new voice. Deep, male, and seductive.

"Tesla, don't—" Edison's voice was cut off.

"There, that's better. Let's chat, shall we?"

"You're too late," said Tesla.

Laughter, deep and mirthful. "You are so clever. You and that hedonistic boy. We didn't anticipate this."

"Apparently not."

"So once again you have proven your worth, your genius. And now do you want to stop us? Think of the possibilities. You could rule this world that will otherwise come to show you so much ingratitude. You offer them free energy to make their pitiful lives easier. They will spurn it and forsake you. Deny you your due. Just like Edison did. And those moneygrubbing robber barons who refuse you funding because they can't see beyond next month's profit margin. But we, Niko, we can give you what you deserve. What you have earned."

Resentment, bitterness, anger. The deep, burning desire for revenge. All these and more welled up within Nikola Tesla. He was drawn to the voice, to its praise. To its deep, unrelenting seduction. His body trembled as his rage was joined by a slowly surging ecstasy.

"We got off on the wrong foot, I think. Now we can start fresh, with you in charge instead of Temple. Keep the spirit phone. Patent it. Perfect revenge against Edison for cheating you out of that bonus. And do you know what will happen to you otherwise? Poverty. Obscurity. Others getting the credit for your achievements. And with what's going to happen to Crowley, well." He laughed. "Disposing of him will be an act of mercy. I suppose you've developed an attachment to the vain little fool, so I promise a quick death for him."

"Yes," said Tesla. "That sounds…reasonable."

"Of course it's reasonable. And your father. You've always wanted to know if he forgave you. It's terrible not knowing, isn't it? Perhaps you would like to contact him. It can be arranged. We want only the best for you, Niko. And you want us."

Another part of Tesla, the part Crowley had briefly trained him to keep sealed and separate, spied a sledgehammer in the corner of the room as the voice kept repeating, "Niko. You want us."

He could feel it trying to break through: probing, retreating, probing again at the portion of consciousness made inviolate. Tesla felt a small piece of the psychic armor removed, as if by two strong and nimble hands, and he realized there was very little time left. His body moved slowly, a sensation as of walking underwater. He got to the corner and wrapped both hands around the handle of the sledgehammer.

"Stop! What are you doing?" Tesla, yet not Tesla, screamed at the hermetic part of himself the Ferox could not influence. Dragging the hammer after him, he slowly made his way back to the spirit phone.

"No!" screamed Tesla. Down came the sledgehammer, smashing the box, silencing the voice. The blue aura flashed briefly, then was extinguished.

Happy birthday, Edison, thought Tesla as he sank to the floor, back against the wall, body convulsed by shudders.

57

February 12th, 1899

The blizzard had passed, and the first rays of dawn shone through the laboratory windows as Tesla walked through the door, exhausted. He had crammed the shattered remnants of the spirit phone into the suitcase along with the plans and notebook, and in the lessening blizzard, made his way to the still open saloon in West Orange. Public transportation was immobilized, but in the wee hours, the snowfall having abated, a local man had offered Tesla a ride on horseback into Manhattan. He had tried to refuse, but the man was insistent, saying that he was headed into town anyway to see his sister. It was a long ride, and Tesla felt sorry for the horse.

He walked with the suitcase to the forge. Placing it on the table, he unlocked the nearby cabinet and took out a number of jars labeled:

Gold - Au

Silver - Ag

Iron - Fe

Mercury - Hg

Tin - Sn

Copper - Cu

Lead - Pb

Silicon Carbide - SiC

He began pouring the contents into the forge's crucible in various, random proportions. When he was finished, he pulled out more jars:

Platinum - Pt
Aluminum - Al
Bismuth - Bi
Gallium - Ga
Zinc - Zn
Strontium - Sr
Cesium - Cs
Calcium - Ca
Sodium - Na
Lithium - Li

He poured random proportions of these elements into the crucible as well, and fired up the forge. When it was all melted together, he threw in the notebook, the plans, and the remains of the spirit phone, watching them burn and dissolve in the liquid inferno.

Shutting down the forge, he let the mixture cool and solidify in the crucible, then placed it, crucible and all, into a wooden crate which he nailed shut. With a grease pencil, he marked a large X on the top of the crate.

There were three safes in the laboratory. He opened the largest one and emptied it of all its contents—plans, notes, sensitive financial documents. He placed the crate inside the safe and locked it.

"Crowley."

Tesla? It's been a little difficult to find you. Is it done?

"It's done. It's destroyed."

Everything?

"Everything."

All right. You're in the lab, I perceive. Please go lie on the cot and I'll bring you back.

He lay down and closed his eyes, and this time the direction felt correct.

58

August 31st, 1899

Tesla's eyes opened to the sight of his bedroom ceiling. He was in his bed, back in the physical, and he knew that it was August 31st. He was convulsed by a wave of shudders, and cried out in a weak voice. But it was not as bad as the first or second such journey. In the space of an instant, he experienced a strange realization.

In his consciousness lay two sets of memories, two realities.

One was the time from February till August, leading up to the moment he first met Crowley, and the announcement of the spirit phone, leading to the subsequent horrors they would both face.

Merged with and parallel to this first set of memories was a second set, the time from February till August, during which he had lived and worked in a completely different way: experiments, socializing, reading, theorizing, and countless other things. With this came a future with no horrors to confront, no monsters to fight.

Slowly, this second set of memories grew stronger, covering and obscuring the first. And yet mingled with these, causing the vestige of distress and confusion, were the future memories that would not come to pass: the airship journeys, the confrontation with Temple and the Ferox. And yet it was all real; otherwise, the astral time journeys would never have—

"Tesla," came a weak voice. He turned, and there was Crowley, pale and haggard, the crystal ball cradled in his lap.

"Paradox is par for the course. Try not to think about it. It'll just drive you mad."

"Crowley."

"Welcome back." He smiled. "Did Edison's friend Andreas offer you a deal?"

"Yes."

"Me too. He found me, but it was all he could do. Thank you for saying no."

"And you, too. There's just one thing. I can't remember…"

"The spirit phone's mineral composition? And how to build one? No, neither can I. And that is on purpose."

"How?"

"The simplest way to explain it is that while you were on your trip back to February, I arranged for the destruction of all Akashic Records referencing the stuff. The Essential…something."

"Essential…" Tesla paused, thinking. "The Essential Composite."

"Yes, that. See? We can barely remember the name. Good thing."

"But how could any of those records be destroyed?"

"I'm not sure myself. It took a kind of special permission, and I can't even remember that much very clearly. I've altered the fabric of reality itself in a very fundamental way, and I will have to pay a price for it. I don't yet understand how or why, but there it is. Anyway, even if Temple figures out what's happened, he can't get the information out of us. We don't have it."

"No one on earth can make the spirit phone."

"That's right. No one. Though we won't know for certain until the end of the year. In the meantime, we've done everything that can be done."

"What about Stern and Donnelly?" asked Tesla. "Will they remember about Colorado and…?"

"Their deaths which shall not come to pass? They'll likely have some fragmented memories, vague nightmares, which may have already begun. But nothing like what you and I will have to put up with. We're about to become stranger than we already are." He wore a weary grin.

"Right. We should pay them a visit. Explain things."

"Yes." He placed the crystal ball on the nightstand and slowly stood up. "But for the moment, if you'll excuse me, I think I need to get some sleep."

Tesla moved over. "Forget the guest room. Lay down here."

Crowley collapsed onto the bed and instantly fell asleep.

Tesla looked at the young, pale, exhausted face inches from his own. Then after a moment, he too drifted off to sleep.

◆ ◆ ◆

The Administrator stands in the fading light of dusk, his back to the gate of the compound. He views his beloved butte through falling snow and the steam of his breath. Pulling the grid from his pocket, he summons Elerion.

"You called, sir?" she asks, the question producing no steam.

At first, he is silent, expressionless, looking into her black eyes.

Then he speaks. "Yes. It's all over, Elerion. Though I hardly need to tell you that. Everything has changed, and I cannot change it back."

"Do you wish to punish me?"

He looks again toward the butte. "No. What would be the point? I'm not the vengeful type. Besides, I suppose I was wrong, if only on points of procedure. And yet, if I cannot shape this world into what it should be, what it must be, I do not wish to remain."

"I see. Have you any final instructions?"

"Yes. But first, let me tell you a story. One that I have never told anyone."

"I am listening."

"In my youth, I made a friend. Perhaps one of the few true friends I have ever had. He was a drifter, a drinker. But he was also a biologist. Self-taught. Brilliant. We met at a mining camp in Colorado."

"A biologist. He helped you with your plan to create the duplicates?"

"More than just helped. The idea had come to me of making duplicates as vessels for the Ferox. Of forging them with blood chemistry to match the Essential Composite. But he was the one who showed me how it could actually be done."

"What happened to him?"

"There were elements I elected not to reveal to him. We were, as far as he knew, attempting to devise a way to replace lost limbs, degenerated organs. We joked that he might need to grow a new liver. Though he had his drinking under control by that time."

"Then he learned of your actual plan."

"Yes. He became suspicious, then found a journal in which I detailed my intentions. He threatened to go to the authorities. I suppose that at the very least I might have been forced to escape being confined to a lunatic asylum."

"*You killed him.*"

"*Yes. The old-fashioned way. I shot him in the head with my derringer. We were living together in a neighborhood where hearing occasional gunshots was not wondered at. But I kept the body.*"

"*To use its genetic material to make the duplicates.*"

"*Yes. He was the original. I compelled him to help me after all. It was quite the irony. But I miss him so. It is both comfort and pain to see his face in every member of every cohort I have created.*"

He looks down for a long moment, then back at Elerion.

"*It all has to go into the astral-physical space, the white realm where the duplicates were made. Compounds, equipment, duplicates. Everything. For immediate liquidation.*"

"*And the ordinary human members?*"

He shrugs. "*Let them live. Even if they tell the story of our attempt, who will believe them? And even if they do, so what?*"

"*I understand.*"

"*Ensure I am never found. After all I have ordered is accomplished, you and all other familiars are released from my service. You may go.*"

Bowing, she departs.

He places the paper back in his pocket, and from another, he removes a derringer.

"*You win, Mr. Crowley,*" *he says, placing the barrel beneath his chin.* "*Enjoy the world you have made.*"

He pulls the trigger. The report, strong and sharp, causes birds to scatter skyward as his body falls limp to the ground.

Slowly, the corpse and the compound behind it fade into nothingness.

59

December 31st, 1899

I t was less than five minutes before midnight as Tesla and Crowley stood in the main foyer of the Waldorf-Astoria in their white ties and tailcoats, flutes of champagne at the ready. Men in tailcoats and women in colorful evening gowns stole glances at the clock over the mantelpiece as they spoke.

Then came the chant: "Five, four, three, two, one! Happy New Year!" With a cheer, glasses were clinked and drained. Revelers broke into a rendition of "Auld Lang Syne."

Crowley looked around, then briefly pulled back a curtain to look behind it. "It's 1900. No monsters. I suppose we're safe."

Tesla smiled. "It's good to be able to joke about it."

"Yes. By the way, thank you again for the long period of hospitality."

"It was my privilege."

After a brief recovery, Crowley had returned to England in September, then arrived back in New York on Christmas Day—both ways by ship rather than teleportation—and checked into his own room at the Waldorf-Astoria. Intervening events had been a series of questions without answers, with no sign of Ambrose Temple nor of the duplicates. Attempts to contact Michael Crane at the New York House of Refuge resulted in the report that he had apparently run away, and that the competent authorities were on the case. The compounds in Wyoming and Colorado, as far as they could tell, had simply disappeared.

"I wonder if Temple somehow 'liquidated' them all," said Tesla.

"It's unlikely we'll ever know. Though perhaps we may eventually see strange stories in the press of mysterious people with inexplicable blood chemistry. By the way, did I mention I've bought a house in Scotland?"

"Yes. Thirty-four acres by a lake. It sounds beautiful."

Crowley looked into his empty glass, then looked at Tesla. "I'd love to invite you to visit. But I perceive that our remaining in association would only magnify the negative effects of this. I mean, of the price we'll pay for having saved the world. So I've decided to head out next week. I haven't decided where yet."

"I see. I suppose it cannot be helped. But I will miss you, Mr. Crowley."

"I'll miss you, Mr. Tesla. It has been an education."

Tesla laughed. "Coming from you, that is the supreme compliment."

"I suppose if we had met under normal circumstances, we'd have hated each other."

"Perhaps." Tesla drained the last of his champagne. "Please don't forget your promise. The one final check of the spirit phone remains."

"Superfluous, but all right, I promise." He smiled and said, "You're such a worrier."

"Thank you for indulging me. What are you going to do? When you got back here you said something about having joined an order of mages."

"Yes. Even with my abilities reduced, I still intend to explore the arcane and expand my knowledge. To that end, I plan to travel and do some more mountaineering this year."

"That sounds like a worthy plan."

"And yourself?"

"I'll keep inventing."

"That, too, sounds like a worthy plan."

They stood in silence for a few minutes, watching the revelers. Then Crowley spoke.

"Do you think Edison has kept to his idea for a spirit phone?"

"Knowing him, he hasn't given up on it completely. It must have been a shock to find it was missing. Everything he'd been working on."

"Yes, well. It couldn't be helped." A waiter came and refilled their glasses.

60

January 8th, 1943

A s to its true purpose, the nineteenth-floor office in Manhattan did not officially exist. Its four occupants—two men and two women—were to all appearances engaged in operating a small public relations firm. They were in fact collecting, analyzing, assessing, recording, and reporting information of interest to persons unknown—unknown only in the sense of their individual identities. Like the men and women of this office, they were in the employ of the federal government, and the data which concerned them primarily related to the war which America had entered—officially—some thirteen months before.

The two young women sat at desks in the front office. They were dressed fashionably in colorful A-line dresses with knee-length skirts and puffed shoulders, their dark, shoulder-length hair styled in pompadours. Though employed as secretaries, their knowledge, skills, and duties went far beyond the clerical. Today, however, was a slow day.

On their desks sat typewriters, but there was nothing to type nor to file. One of the women was reading *The New York Times*. Her coworker was deeply engaged in a book of crossword puzzles.

"Jenny, what's a nine-letter word for 'good?'"

"Copacetic. Betty, did you see this?" She held up her paper. "Nikola Tesla died."

"Tesla? The inventor?"

"Yeah. Yesterday. I mean, his body was found yesterday."

"Found? You mean like there was foul play?"

"No, nothing like that. He was living at the New Yorker. One of the maids found him dead in his room. It says here his health had been bad for the past couple of years. I guess it was a heart attack or something. He was eighty-six."

"Oh."

"There were all kinds of inventions he talked about. Death rays. Remote-controlled airplanes. Stuff like that."

"Someone's going to be looking through all his papers and equipment. I'd bet on it. Just in case there might be something useful for the war effort."

"Yeah," said a smartly dressed young man emerging from the back office. "And there's the rumor that he and Mr. Stern were acquainted. But that sort of thing is out of our purview. Word is the FBI's got control over all of Tesla's stuff."

"I would like to have seen what a death ray looked like," said Betty, and went back to her crossword.

Just then the phone on Jenny's desk rang. Answering it, she said, "Good morning. Stern Promotions. May I help you?" She listened, then said, "Yes. Yes, sir. I'll inform them right away. We'll be standing by." She hung up.

"Ted," she said to the man, "we're getting a package delivery this morning."

"Of what?"

"He didn't say. We're to await instructions."

Ten minutes later, two men arrived, dressed in identical blue coveralls and caps. One pushed a hand truck upon which sat a square package wrapped in brown paper and cellophane, tied crosswise with twine. The other carried a clipboard, attached to which was a sealed envelope and an invoice. Ted had them bring the package into the back office, signed the invoice, and accepted the envelope, upon which nothing was written.

There it sat on the floor among the several filing cabinets and two desks, which occupied much of the room's space. Out the window could be seen the art deco vista of Manhattan, frosted by the thin coating of yesterday's snow.

Another besuited young man had been sitting at one of the desks going over a folder. He now stood up and asked, "What's this?"

"Special delivery, Stan," said Ted. Jenny and Betty soon joined them.

Though it was known to all that the delivery men were not in fact delivery men in the ordinary sense, Ted waited until they had left before opening the envelope. From within it, he removed a sheet of paper, which he unfolded and began to read aloud.

"The item delivered together with this memorandum was found among the effects of the late Nikola Tesla."

"What?" exclaimed Stan.

"Wait. *Your office is tasked with keeping said item in temporary custody. Regarding the—*"

"What the hell?" said Stan. "We're not supposed to deal with stuff like this."

"Does the memo say we're not allowed to open it?" asked Jenny.

Ted scanned the paper. "No, but—"

She immediately untied the twine and tore off the wrapping, revealing a wooden crate, its lid marked in grease pencil with a large *X*. Along its edge were more than a dozen splintered holes where nails had been removed. Jenny lifted the lid off.

"What's this?" asked Stan.

Within the crate was what appeared to be a thick ceramic bucket with an open spout and no handle. It was filled almost to the brim with a solid, grayish matter which gave off a dull metallic sheen.

"What the hell?" said Ted.

"Not a death ray," said Betty in a tone of mild disappointment.

"It's a crucible," said Jenny.

"A what?" asked Ted and Stan together.

"A crucible. My grandfather used to work in a steel mill in Pennsylvania before he retired. I visited a few times after hours. It's a kind of cup where you melt metal before pouring it into the mold."

"OK. Except this metal wasn't poured out," said Stan.

"Get this," said Ted, tapping the memo. *"Regarding the circumstances of the item's discovery, it was found nailed into the crate in which it is delivered to you. The crate in turn had been deposited in a locked safe in the laboratory of Mr. Tesla."*

Stan took a step back. "Shit! So this is—"

"No evidence has been found of hazardous radioactivity or contagions."

"Oh. Good."

"You are hereby instructed to hold the item for safekeeping and await further instructions."

"Safekeeping?" said Stan. "Why us? And why the hell would someone melt down a bunch of metal, nail it up in a crate, and then lock it in a safe? The guy was a lunatic."

"Is there anything in the memo about what kind of metal this is?" asked Jenny.

Ted shook his head. "Nothing," he said.

There was a knock at the inner office door, followed by a voice saying, "Excuse me."

There stood a man of about seventy, dressed in a black greatcoat and homburg, sporting a gray goatee. He placed his homburg on the hat rack by the door, revealing a clean-shaven head. "Please forgive my interruption," he said in an accent unmistakably British. In his left hand was a walking stick with a ball of crystal set at the top.

"And who might you be, sir?" asked Ted.

He set both hands on top of the walking stick. "My name is Yessar-Smik. I realize it is an unusual name. I'm not originally from these parts."

"And what can I do for you?"

"I've come to inspect the item just delivered." He indicated the crate.

The four ostensible employees of Stern Promotions were aware of the appearance and identity, assumed or otherwise, of every person who might appear in their office on a basis of official authority. This smartly dressed man was completely unknown to them. Ted replaced the lid of the crate.

"Sir, I'm afraid I don't recognize you as—"

"Zed-zed-three-one-two-seven."

"I beg your pardon?"

"Zed-zed-three-one-two-seven. I recommend you get on the phone to Mr. Walter Stern and tell him I'm here and that I said 'Zed-zed-three-one-two-seven.'"

Betty had hurriedly scribbled the alphanumeric expression on a notepad, torn off the page, and handed it to Ted.

"Mr. Stern is retired," said Ted to the man.

"Yes, but he still lives in New York. Quite close to this office, in fact. I promise you, he'll be very interested to know I'm here."

This was confusing. They were people used to following a certain protocol in everything they did, and this situation was outside their experience or expectations. Ted hesitated, then decided to do as this strange old man demanded. Picking up the receiver of the telephone on his desk, he began to dial.

After a moment, he spoke into the phone. "Good morning. This is Ted Jakes calling from Stern Promotions. May I speak with Mr. Stern, please? Yes, it's important. Yes, thank you." He held the phone, glancing skeptically at the elderly visitor.

"Hello, Mr. Stern? Yes. Yes, we're all fine, thank you, sir. Uh, sir, there is a gentleman here who—yes? You know?" He paused to listen. "Yessar-Smik." Laughter could faintly be heard from the phone. "Yes, I have it written down here. Yes, that's it. I see. Yes, it has been delivered. Will do, sir. Thank you." He hung up.

"Mr. Crowley?"

"Yes," he said. "I hope you'll forgive me. 'Yessar-Smik' is a private joke between myself and Mr. Stern. I couldn't resist."

"I see." Ted pulled a chair from its place against the wall, placed it next to the crate, and removed the lid.

"Thank you," said Crowley, seating himself. He looked down at the solidified mass of silver gray. Cradling the walking stick in the crook of his left arm, he wrapped his left hand around the crystal ball at its top. Bending forward, he placed his right hand upon the metal and closed his eyes. The others exchanged puzzled glances.

After about half a minute, he opened his eyes. "Well, that should do it," he said. "Nothing of interest here. Not anymore. You can do as you like with it. It might make a nice conversation piece."

"What is it?" asked Jenny.

"That, my dear, is something I am not at liberty to divulge."

At that, they sat down and passed the time speaking of trivialities such as winters in New York versus London and how the rationing systems were proceeding on each side of the pond.

Finally, Ted said, "Mr. Stern said you'd been involved in certain important and sensitive matters during the last century. From what he told me, they were lucky to have someone as good as you."

"Good?" asked Crowley. He paused for a moment, reflecting. "I suppose I was effective, in my way. But good? Over much of my life, professional or otherwise, I have been arrogant, abrasive, obstinate, unreasonable, at times even cruel. I don't know if 'good' would describe me. Though perhaps the closest I ever came to it was the time I spent with the man who melted this down." He tapped the metal twice with his stick.

"You give yourself not nearly enough credit, Mr. Crowley," came a voice from the outer office. In walked a tall white-haired man with an equally white mustache. He appeared to be nearing ninety, yet carried himself with a confident, athletic bearing.

Crowley stood up and shook his hand. "Walter. It's been too long."

"A pleasure to see you again, young Aleister." He hung his fedora on the hat rack, then indicated the crate. "And?"

"It's a useless lump of metal, as it has always been since it got melted down. I knew it was superfluous to come here and check on it, but he made me promise I would do so right after he died. You know how nervous he could be about these things. As if locking the damned thing in a safe would have made any difference."

Stern laughed. "True, but it's better to be safe. Shall we go make a toast to the old boy's memory?"

Crowley glanced at the clock on the wall. "It's eleven o'clock in the morning, Walter."

Stern shrugged, smiling.

Crowley laughed, then turned to the four young people. "You may keep or dispose of this as you will. Thank you for your hospitality. We two old men are going to go and reminisce."

"Thank you, everyone," said Stern. "You're all doing a fine job."

"Sir, really," said Ted, "what should we do with this thing?"

"Just keep it here. I'll send someone to pick it up later."

"Thank you for checking it," Stern said to Crowley as they exited the building onto Madison Avenue.

"Well, just as you say, it's better to be safe. There are few such things I can do anymore, but that's one of them."

"Yes. You've kicked the cocaine habit? And the laudanum?"

"Years ago. And the heroin too."

"That's good. Though since we last met, the press seems to have dubbed you the wickedest man in the world."

"Hmm. That's old news. It would be so chic to be wicked. The truth is, I'm just a bit of a bastard sometimes. Though you fellows kept me on my best behavior back in the day."

They stood for a moment regarding the canyon of skyscrapers and its bustle of humanity: the long, curvaceous automobiles and the countless pedestrians covered by fedoras, homburgs, pillboxes, berets, all walking briskly toward whatever business awaited them.

"All this still exists because of us," said Crowley, lifting his gaze toward the rooftops. "For better or for worse."

He turned back to Stern and said, "So what are you going to do with it?"

"Keep it as a memento. If they'll let me."

"God almighty, Walter. A memento of *that*? Well, to each his own. How's Donnelly?"

"Fine, last I heard. He's retired to San Diego. Fed up with the winters here. So, Delmonico's?"

"Why not?"

They walked, reminiscing.

Author's Note

I've long had an interest in tales of the paranormal. One day–it was August 15th, 2009–I had been reading, or rather rereading, a chapter on Thomas Edison in the book *Phantom Encounters* (1988), a volume of the Mysteries of the Unknown series published by Time-Life Books. Titled "The Quest for Ghostly Voices," it describes Edison's reputed attempt to invent a device to communicate with the dead. Though Edison publicly stated this intention, including in an interview with B.C. Forbes in 1920, there are no known extant notes, plans, or equipment suggesting an "Edison spirit phone," nor even an attempt at building one.

And then it hit me: what if Edison had really built a spirit phone, and what if it worked? That could be a novel, I thought.

I immediately decided that Aleister Crowley and Nikola Tesla should be involved, and made them protagonists, with Edison as a supporting character. Thus began three solid weeks of furiously writing into legal pads while exploring possible plotlines and characters, followed by a decade of intermittent research and writing until the book was finally complete.

When I conceived of *The Spirit Phone* on that summer day, I assumed no one had ever published a fictional work with such a premise. But in fact, the late J.N. Williamson's *Horror House* (1981) is, as far as I now know, the earliest novel featuring a version of Edison's rumored invention. I learned about it through correspondence in 2020 with Williamson's friend, horror author Mort Castle. The only other novel I know of with an Edison spirit phone is *Spellbound* by Larry Correia (2011). Williamson's novel incudes the classic element of the haunted house, while Correia presents the reader with an alternate 1930s in which magic is commonplace and the spirit phone is a big-budget project with massive electricity requirements.

As for my own book, I was initially stuck on how to carry through with the story, a key point being my initial assumption that the spirit phone should be a single unique device, kept secret from the public. How could I mesh that with the conflict between protagonists and antagonists? Then I decided that if Edison believed he had succeeded in building a properly functioning device of this kind, it wouldn't be kept a secret. He'd market it. So I made Edison's spirit phone a portable consumer product complete with an advertising campaign.

The latter 19th century—or rather a certain version of it—in which *The Spirit Phone* takes place was characterized by advancements in technology unprecedented in history. If you think about it, the gap between the Pony Express and the telegraph is infinitely greater than the gap between the telegraph and the smartphone. Today we take for granted the notion that technology will advance, for good or ill. That's why there is a modern genre of science fiction. But for people who could travel and communicate only as fast as a horse or a sailing ship, telegraphs, telephones, and steam locomotives must have seemed like magic.

And yet, perhaps some began to feel that "magic" was missing from their lives. With scientific breakthroughs removing some of the world's mysteries, the spiritualist movement swept the Western world, a trend no doubt encouraged by increasingly secular legal systems which no longer demanded imprisonment, exile, or death for people with "incorrect" spiritual convictions.

It was only a matter of time before the idea of blending the metaphysical with the technological or scientific came to the fore. Aleister Crowley expressed this with the motto, "The aim of religion, the method of science" in describing his explorations of the occult. The words appeared on the cover of the first edition of *The Equinox*, a journal he founded in 1909. Edison's notion of using technology to contact the dead is perhaps the logical extension of such a concept.

Speaking of Crowley, as one might expect in a novel, I've taken some liberties with history. The real Aleister Crowley visited New York for the first time in July 1900, but in *The Spirit Phone* he arrives in August 1899 (in a highly unusual manner), and not for the first time. The Crowley of this novel is also a lover of ale, inspired in part by the real Crowley being heir to a brewing fortune, though I think he was actually more of a wine drinker. The fictional Crowley's involvement in espionage also occurs earlier in his life than the real Crowley, who claimed he had acted as an agent for British Intelligence during World War I. And of course, the fantastical magic (or magick) employed is different from the ceremonial magic practiced by the Crowley of history. Crowley's membership in the Hermetic Order of the Golden Dawn is hinted at, but not explicitly mentioned.

The other main character is Nikola Tesla, a man who looms so large in modern popular culture that a friend suggested I consider replacing him with a different inventor. (It has been said that Tesla is forgotten by history, but a quick Internet search shows that even if that were the case, it is no longer.) In *The Spirit Phone*, I've included mention or depiction of inventions the real Tesla is credited with, such as his alternating current system, as well as technology which suited the purposes of the story but which to my knowledge the real Tesla didn't invent, such as an improved flashlight and a metal detector. The story of the $5,000 bonus Edison promised Tesla and then reneged on is a famous element of Tesla mythology, and I have used it in *The Spirit Phone* while leaving it an open question. (In Tesla's own biography, he states that it was the manager of Edison's machine works, not Edison himself, who had promised the bonus.)

In writing this book, the most important things about the real Crowley and Tesla which I drew upon were those personality traits I consider well-established historically. Crowley was rakish, charming, adventurous, and hedonistic even as he was disciplined and focused when necessary. Tesla was germophobic and obsessive in certain aspects of his behavior, perhaps even neurotic, yet with a suave demeanor and sophistication that made him many friends. Both men were visionary in their outlooks, and both loved a good table. Crowley was an occultist with a deep regard for science, and Tesla was a scientist and inventor with a keen interest in life's mysteries. They had so many differences, and just enough in common, that I see them as the ultimate speculative fiction odd couple. It's unfortunate they never met in real life, so I had to make it happen here, with some embellishments.

As evening fell on the day I conceived of this book, I went to sleep tired from writing. I had a dream. I was in a bookstore, excited about a new novel I'd heard of called *The Spirit Phone*. I wanted to get a copy, but couldn't find one anywhere. Then I heard a voice say, "The book isn't written yet. If you want to read it, you'll have to write it." Then I woke up and wrote it. I hope you like it.

Arthur Shattuck O'Keefe
May 13th, 2022

Acknowledgments

To those who have lent support in one form or another during the journey from conception to publication of *The Spirit Phone*, I would like to express my gratitude.

I am grateful for encouragement in the early stages of development from Timothy Lashley, Peter Sidell, Tony Bruin, and Marshall O'Keeffe.

A big thank you to all who viewed one or more versions of the completed manuscript and provided suggestions and/or encouragement: Patrick Parr, Matthew Allen, Megha Wadhwa, Ben Stubbings, Dax Thomas, Andrew Jones, David Cozy, Michael Snyder, Marshall O'Keeffe, James Bates, Samuel Gildart, and Matthew Perkins. Even the advice I chose not to follow was important because it compelled me to consider my decisions more carefully.

For valuable advice and suggestions over the past several years on how to properly craft prose, I'd like to thank Atsuko Kashiwagi and David Cozy.

Without the support and professionalism of the team at BHC Press, this book would not have seen the light of day. A huge thank you to Vernon and Joni Firestone for agreeing to publish *The Spirit Phone*, and to Joni for her continuous guidance and updates. I also thank both Joni and my editor, Jamie Rich, for their outstanding commitment to the art and craft of getting a manuscript into proper shape, as well as Hannah Moseley for expert proofreading and Vernon Firestone for a fantastic cover design.

I would like to thank my friend Patrick Parr, an author whose example, advice, and encouragement were valuable beyond words during my efforts to complete the first draft.

For infinite patience and understanding as I spent countless hours writing and revising the manuscript, and for endless encouragement, I thank my partner, Shiho Nishinouchi.

About the Author

Arthur Shattuck O'Keefe was born in New York and lives in Kanagawa, Japan. His short fiction has appeared in *The Stray Branch*, *Ragazine*, *Manawaker Studio's Flash Fiction Podcast*, and *Flash Fiction Magazine*. He has written articles for *PopMatters*, *The Japan Times*, *Japan Today*, *Kyoto Journal*, and *Metropolis*. He is an associate professor of English at Showa Women's University in Tokyo. *The Spirit Phone* is his debut novel.

Lightning Source UK Ltd.
Milton Keynes UK
UKHW012113151122
412269UK00017B/137/J